FAMILY TIES

FAMILY TIES

A NOVEL BY

SYRELL ROGOVIN LEAHY

G. P. PUTNAM'S SONS / NEW YORK

To All My Cousins

The author wishes to thank Yale University Press for permission to use the poem
"Why There Are Children" by Leslie Ullman, from the book *Natural Histories* by
Leslie Ullman, copyright © 1979 by Leslie Ullman and Yale University Press. The
poem originally appeared in *The New Yorker* magazine.

Library of Congress Cataloging in Publication Data

Leahy, Syrell Rogovin.
Family ties.

I. Title.
PS3562.E23F3   1982   813'.54   82-9835
ISBN 0-399-12741-0   AACR2

Printed in the United States of America

Why There Are Children

The woman inside every woman
lights the candles.
This is the woman sons look for

when they leave their wives.
Daughters become wives
thinking they travel backwards

to the dresser covered with lace,
the hairpins still scattered there
and the cameo earrings.

The same gnarled tree
darkens the bedroom window.
The hair coiled in a locket

conceals the hands of men and children.
When a woman shivers on the porch
perhaps at dusk, it is the other

wanting a shawl. When a woman
in her middle years rises
and dresses for work, the other

reaches for the cameos
remembering a great love
and herself on the brink of it.

—Leslie Ullman

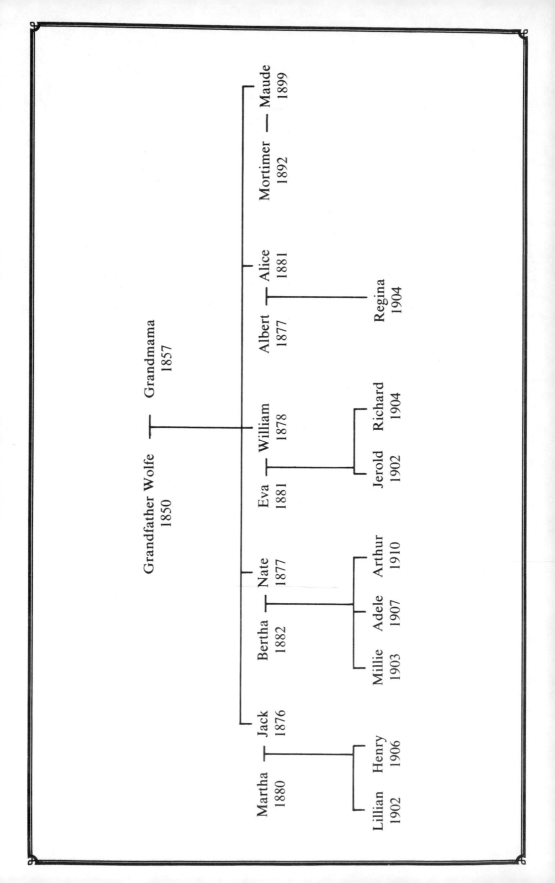

PART I
JUNE 2, 1917

1

The dress she would wear was blue, sewn by the same dressmaker who had made her mother's, and her underclothes were white, bought in the same fine store on Fifth Avenue where her mother had bought hers. Today the dresses hung in separate closets in the summerhouse, covered with muslin, waiting for tomorrow, waiting to be worn at Aunt Maude's wedding.

"Ready, Regina?" her mother called from the kitchen.

"I just have to put my shoes on," she called back, pulling the muslin with careful fingers to look once more at the blue beneath, her favorite color for the most wonderful day of her life. Tomorrow she would wear it and she would be truly happy, the way only people in novels were happy. She closed the closet door and pulled her shoes on quickly. It was not a morning to keep her mother waiting.

"Oh, there you are." Mother looked her up and down, shaking a dish towel and hanging it over the side of the cupboard. "Very nice. You look almost like a high-school girl already. How long is it now, three months?"

Regina nodded. Her parents still took every opportunity to mention her accomplishment, her acceptance to Hunter High School. Grandmama thought she might be the first granddaughter to go to college—but Grandmama didn't say it when the other granddaughters were there to hear.

"Let's go," Mother said now. "Let's see how the preparations are coming."

They left the house, turned right, and walked up the little slope toward the tops of the two brick chimneys just barely visible over the little hill. Gradually the rest of Grandmama's house emerged, the hustle and bustle within spilling out of its doors and windows, the excitement of the wedding almost tangible in the breeze this bright June morning.

A good distance beyond the great house that Grandfather had built in 1880 with only two rooms was Uncle Willy's and Aunt Eva's small summerhouse. Regina scanned the distance for a sign of their two sons, Richard who was her age and very nearly her best friend, and Jerold who was two years older and who sometimes made funny things happen to her heart just by smiling or saying something nice.

9

"I can't see Richard or Jody," she said to her mother.

Mother stopped and peered into the distance, the wind whipping the skirt of her cotton dress just above her ankles. Then she laughed. "You have wonderful eyes, Regina. I can hardly make out the house!"

Walking downhill, Regina glanced off to the left, where Uncle Nate's all-year-round house had been built close to the road with a little stand out front where Aunt Bertha or the cousins could sell fresh produce during the summer months. A few geese congregated like gossiping mothers behind the house, but there were no real people about. Uncle Nate would be somewhere out in the fields working as hard as he could to make up for tomorrow, when almost nothing would get done on the farm beyond what was absolutely necessary.

Regina ran the last short distance to the house, bursting in ahead of her mother. The house was hardly recognizable. Furniture had been moved away downstairs, where the ceremony would take place. People she had never seen before seemed to be everywhere, cleaning, polishing, banging kitchen utensils. Grandmama, her feet scarcely touching the polished wood floors, flew into the room, stopped, and smiled broadly at her granddaughter.

"You've come," she announced. "Just in time. I expect Jackie any minute now. Where is your mamá?"

"Right behind me. Where's Aunt Maude?"

"Wait. I get her." And flying again, she went up the stairs.

It was only a few minutes before Aunt Maude, still flushed with sleep, came down, her nightgown trailing on the stairs as tomorrow her wedding dress would.

"Regina!" she half-shouted, "it's tomorrow. It's only one day away. Look at the weather. We'll have our sunshine and blue sky and Momma has nothing to worry about." She took Regina's hands and began dancing around the empty floor, her gown billowing, her dark hair flying, her breath suddenly coming in short intakes.

"Maude!" It was Mother, speaking sharply from the entry, sounding almost angry, as though Aunt Maude were a small child and not her own grown sister. "Stop that nonsense. You'll strain yourself."

Maude leaned against the fireplace to catch her breath. Then she laughed her wonderful throaty laugh, hugged Regina to her, and whirled her once in a complete circle so that Regina's feet barely grazed the floor. Laughing, they held each other a moment for support.

"Really, Maude."

"There's nothing *wrong*," Aunt Maude said in a husky whisper.

Freed, Regina looked over at her mother. The usually placid face was lined with concern or irritation. Mother rarely raised her voice at her own daughter, and here she was angry at her sister who tomorrow would be Uncle Mortimer's wife.

At that moment they all heard the sound of the Pierce-Arrow just outside the house, then its door slamming, and then Uncle Jack and Aunt Martha entered through the front door with their children, Uncle Mortimer only a few steps behind, his hat in his hand.

There was much noise of hellos and kisses, and then, above it, Grandmama's voice sharply: "Maude, upstairs, quick-quick," and Maude, throwing a kiss to Uncle Mortimer, hurried up the stairs, smiling, holding her nightgown before her.

Aunt Martha, who always looked poorly after a trip, looked exceptionally pale as she stood with her right hand across her heart, nodding faintly at the greetings and scarcely smiling. Grandmama, after hugs and kisses, put her arm around poor Aunt Martha and led her to the stairs, murmuring solicitously as they went, while Lillian, Aunt Martha's fifteen-year-old daughter, stood watching, her face anxious, her eyes riveted on her retreating mother.

The attention seemed to produce an immediate palliative effect on Aunt Martha, who paused at the foot of the stairs and asked Grandmama quite softly, "Is she well?"

"Quite well," Grandmama answered, guiding her daughter-in-law purposefully up the stairs. "We are all well, and in a little while you'll be fine too."

Regina turned away. With Grandmama close by, Aunt Martha would surely recover.

"Regina," Uncle Mortimer said with some surprise. "You were lost in the crowd. How are you?"

"I'm fine. Can I see the car?"

"Right this way. Lillian? Want to look it over?"

Lillian looked from him to the empty staircase and back again. "No, thank you. I think I'll go upstairs."

"Henry?"

Lillian's eleven-year-old brother looked perplexed. His father had disappeared, and he was plainly torn between his desire to inspect more closely the car he had just arrived in and his concern for the whereabouts of his immediate family. "Later," he said, and succumbing to the fear Aunt Martha seemed almost by her very existence to instill in the members of her family, he followed them up the stairs.

Regina didn't mind. She had ridden in the Pierce-Arrow last evening for the first time and wanted to see it up close in daylight, with or without her cousins. The sleek black touring car was Grandfather's pride and joy, bought early in the spring when the wedding plans were starting to be made for Aunt Maude, but Grandfather could not drive and had no intention of learning. The car was an object of beauty, to be looked upon by its owner with pride and to be driven by his sons and sons-in-law. Grandfather was almost sixty-seven. Forty years before, he had crossed an ocean with his young wife to start a new life and a family. He had long ago accomplished what he had set out to do as a young man; now, in his old age, he would not learn to drive.

Outside, Uncle Mortimer reached into the luggage section and drew out a large cloth.

"I can help you clean it," Regina volunteered.

"All right. Why don't you polish the lamps?" He handed her a cloth of her own and bent to clean the spokes on a rear wheel.

"Are you nervous, Uncle Mortimer?" Regina asked, rubbing the soft cloth over the splattered glass.

"About getting married?" He looked up at her with a smile. He was a very handsome man with strong, regular features and a glorious smile. "Not in the least." The smile disappeared. "Did Maude tell you she was nervous?"

"Oh, no. She was dancing in circles when she came downstairs."

"That's good. That's just what I want to hear."

"Will you stay at the farm this summer, after you get back from your honeymoon?"

"Weekends," he said, standing up and stretching his long body out of the cramped position he had been assuming. "We'll probably come out on Friday nights."

"Couldn't Aunt Maude stay here and you come out on Friday nights the way Poppa does?"

"I don't think so," Uncle Mortimer said, looking very serious. "I can't let Aunt Maude out of my sight."

"Oh, *Morty,*" Aunt Maude's voice came from somewhere above them.

They looked up to see her leaning out of an upstairs window, still in her nightgown.

"What kinds of stories are you telling my poor niece?"

Uncle Mortimer threw her a kiss. "True stories," he called up to her. "Get dressed and come down. I miss you."

Two hands suddenly appeared on Aunt Maude's bare shoulders, and with a look of surprise she was pulled inside and the window decisively shut.

Regina laughed. "That's Grandmama."

"It is indeed," Uncle Mortimer agreed. "What a woman."

Poppa was the last member of the family to arrive, having decided to work this Saturday morning at his printing business, Friedmann Brothers, Printers and Engravers, not far from where they lived in Brooklyn, since he would surely come in late on Monday. His arrival gave Regina that special feeling that now the family was complete. Each of the houses on Grandfather's farm had a whole family in it, and Grandfather's "mansion" had two.

In the evening, after a light supper, they dressed for the big party Grandmama was giving for the family and some friends. Everyone would be there except Uncle Nate's youngest child, Arthur, who was only seven and would sleep on Grandmama's bed (if Aunt Bertha was lucky).

When she was all dressed, Mother brushed her hair for her, turning the brush to form long soft ringlets.

"There," she said proudly, standing back to admire her work, "isn't that nice?"

"Prettiest girl I know," Poppa agreed.

"I wish I were tall like Aunt Maude."

"Maybe you will be," Mother said.

"But when? I'm almost thirteen now."

"Later," Poppa said. "There's time. There's time for everything."

Poppa took a lantern with him so they could light their way home, and they were on their way. As they came to the top of the hill, the lights of the great house beamed from every window, lighting their way. From the other direction, Uncle Willy was arriving with his family, Aunt Eva holding her long skirt carefully, Richard and Jerold walking stiffly in their dress-up clothes. All four of them waved as Regina's family approached, and the seven of them entered the big house in a group.

Lillian had already come downstairs with Uncle Jack, and Grandmama seemed to be everywhere you turned. She looked magnificent, strong color in her face, her hair still wonderfully dark and full. She was a bosomy woman but she had maintained a fine waist, which Grandfather often pointed to proudly, sometimes to Grandmama's embarrassment. While Grandfather spoke with a strong and distinctly German accent, Grandmama's speech was more faintly accented and she claimed with a wink that she was French, a lady from Paris.

All around the room, uncles and aunts were sipping wine from Grandmama's great punch bowl. Even Lillian had a cup in her hand, but Lillian was the oldest of the cousins and Mother said she was entitled to certain privileges because of it.

Suddenly someone's arm was around Regina's shoulder.

"Come, my darling," Grandmama said grandly, "something to drink." She spoke to the uniformed maid at the punch bowl, and a glass was filled. "Here you are, Regina," Grandmama said, handing her the glass with a flourish.

"Momma!" Regina's mother said with obvious shock. "She's a child. She's only twelve years old. She's much too young to drink wine."

"Not at all, Alice. I gave some to Lillian, and Jackie didn't say a word, did you, Jackie?"

Uncle Jack raised his eyebrows and shook his head. "I'll never make a liar out of you, Momma," he said.

"You see?" Grandmama smiled triumphantly. "And if Lillian can have it, Regina can too. Have a taste, darling, and tell me how you like it."

The punch was refreshing, but it stung slightly. "I think it's good," Regina said hesitantly.

"There, she thinks it's good, Alice. She has good taste, your daughter. She'll grow up to be something special."

Poppa laughed. He had long ago given up arguing with his mother-in-law, largely, he told the women in his family, because he had grown tired of losing.

"She'll be a beautiful bride one day," Grandmama said, looking at Regina with glistening eyes. "All my little girls will be brides. All of them."

Regina slipped away. She had lost sight of Richard and Jerold after their arrival and she wanted to find them, wanted to talk to them after the long winter when they saw each other infrequently. Today was the second of June and only the third or fourth weekend they had all been out to the farm together. She spotted Richard and waved. She and Richard played games together, like chess, which Uncle Willy had taught them one rainy weekend two summers earlier, and now that they were older, they talked more, sharing small intimacies like their fears of high school. Richard would enter Stuyvesant in September, which his brother had been attending for two years. It was his brother, Jerold, that Regina wanted most to talk about—but never did. Now fifteen, taller than Richard but still boyishly lean and on his

13

way to being unbearably handsome, Jerold was frequently tantalizingly nearby but did not often join them to make a threesome.

Carrying her cup carefully, she greeted the aunts and uncles, the great-aunts and great-uncles, brothers and sisters of her grandparents who had traveled up for the party and would spend the night several miles away at the nearest hotel. But mostly she kept her eyes alert for Jerold. Turning toward the doors to the back garden, she saw Aunt Maude and Uncle Mortimer strolling through the crowd on the last night before their marriage.

Aunt Maude was wearing a long white gown that seemed to ripple as she moved. Her shoulders were partly bared, and her height, her long neck and full bosom, like Grandmama's, made her seem stately and regal. Tonight she was a princess who tomorrow would be a queen. As she moved about the room, she scarcely stopped smiling. Close beside her was Uncle Mortimer. Aunt Maude turned frequently toward him to speak a few words, to touch his fingers. What were their secrets? What were all the private, beautiful things they had to say to each other? As Regina watched, they passed quite close to her and she heard Uncle Mortimer say, "Maude, darling."

Thrilled by the words and the sound of her future uncle's voice as he spoke them, Regina watched them step outside just as Jerold, walking beside cousin Lillian, came in from the garden. For a moment her heart failed her. Lillian was talking animatedly, moving her head in a coy manner, while Jerold listened politely. It was the first moment of Regina's life that she was consciously jealous of another person. It was wrong, she knew. Poppa might laugh, but Mother would be angry. Lillian was her cousin and had as much right as anyone else to spend the evening talking to Jerold—but it hurt, hurt in a stabbingly painful way. She looked away, hoping now to find Richard or one of Uncle Nate's girls to talk to, but they were all being shown off to relatives or giggling over something, and she didn't feel like giggling right now. She put her punch cup down on a table, took a small sandwich, and went out into the night by herself.

Something rubbed her leg, and she looked down to see Uncle Nate's Irish setter wagging his long furry tail. She talked to him quietly and shared her sandwich with him. She wanted to sit on the ground under the big shade tree, but that would ruin her dress, so she stood, patting the large dog and looking in the sky for constellations she had read about in school but never seemed able to identify. After a while, the dog grew bored and sauntered away. Regina walked along the back of the house, passing one of the "seams" that Grandfather liked to show people, a point at which he had built a large, relatively recent addition. She ran her fingers over it, feeling the old and then the new, and kept walking toward the end of the house closest to Uncle Willy's house.

Suddenly, from just around the corner, she heard laughter, a tinkle of laughter like a little bell with a slightly sour tone at the end, a bell with a warp in the metal.

"Is that what they told you?" a woman's voice asked with scarcely concealed derision.

There was no response, and the woman continued. "I suppose I shouldn't be surprised. My mother-in-law likes to run things her way and keep her little secrets. Perhaps she thought if you knew the truth . . ." The voice died away, and as it did, Regina recognized it as Aunt Martha's.

Edging nearer the corner of the house, she held her breath. A man's voice, muffled and indistinct, said something, and Aunt Martha laughed again. She had certainly recovered from the indisposition that had sent her to bed earlier in the day. Her voice was firm now and her laugh almost flirtatious.

"Do you really?" she said. "They probably didn't tell you about Herbie either, did they? She tried to keep that from me too when Jack and I were married. They all seem so open and honest when you meet them, but underneath, it's a family that keeps its secrets."

"Why don't you just tell me about Maude?" the man asked quietly, and Regina realized it was Uncle Mortimer talking. "There's a war going on, and I had thought I would be part of it. If I can't leave her—"

"There you are," a voice called from somewhere behind Regina. She turned to see her mother silhouetted in the light from the open doors. "We've been looking everywhere for you."

Reluctantly she retreated to the light and noise of the party.

"Aunt Eva says she hasn't laid eyes on you since we arrived," Mother said, smoothing Regina's hair, "and Richard's been asking for you too."

"Who's Herbie, Momma?"

Her mother's face changed slightly in some way she could not define. "I don't know," Momma said, as if she'd never heard the name before in her life. "No one here tonight is named Herbie."

Regina waited for her to ask why she wanted to know or whom she had heard the name from, but the next thing Momma said was, "Come inside and we'll find Aunt Eva and Uncle Willy," and she followed her mother in to say hello to her favorite uncle and aunt.

It seemed to be a long time afterward—she had talked to everyone by then—that she heard Aunt Maude say, "I think I've lost him." Then she laughed. "Maybe he's run off with someone else. I told Momma she shouldn't invite all the beautiful cousins." Aunt Maude squeezed Lillian's shoulder as if she meant Lillian in particular. "Oh, *there* he is, under Momma's shade tree." She lifted her dress and ran through the dark to the tall figure that seemed almost a part of the tree trunk. As she approached, the figure separated itself from the tree and joined itself in a rush with hers, his dark arm around the white of her dress.

Looking back across the room, Regina saw Aunt Martha talking and smiling with Aunt Bertha and Regina's mother.

"Time to go home," Poppa said. He was standing next to her and holding the swinging lantern.

"Oh, Poppa, it's too early."

"You look half-asleep already. If you fall asleep walking down the aisle tomorrow, I don't know how I'll show my face at the table."

"What about Momma?"

"She'll come back later. Come on, now."

"Albert, we'll walk her." It was Aunt Maude with Uncle Mortimer close beside her. "Morty and I are taking a walk. Stay awhile."

"Well . . ."

"Stay and have some coffee, Albert. Come, Regina."

"Don't forget your shawl, darling," Uncle Mortimer said. "It's getting cold out." He looked chilled himself, as if the weather had changed and caught him unprepared, as if something he had longed for all his life had this moment been taken away from him. He watched her leave with visible regret, as though perhaps he should have gone and she should have waited.

Aunt Maude returned hatless but with a flowered shawl around her shoulders, and after some quick good-nights the three of them walked out into the night.

She awoke to the sound of murmuring in the bedroom next door.

"Oh?"

". . . asked me about Herbie."

"Regina?"

". . . Martha must have . . . should keep her mouth shut."

"Hard to understand . . ."

She drifted off, only to awaken again to new voices, not inside, not in her parents' room, but outside, behind the house, and there was something strange about them, strange and a little frightening. She pushed the blanket aside and crawled to the window at the foot of the bed. Moving the shade, she looked out on a wedge of darkness. Gradually stars appeared, then dark, distant shapes, and then, approaching from the right, the figures of her aunt and uncle, Maude in her shining white dress and Mortimer tall and lean in his dark suit. They were arm in arm, hardly moving, talking to each other in almost whispers.

"It doesn't matter," Regina heard him say.

"But you wanted it," Aunt Maude whispered back. "You told me, Morty. Of course it matters."

"Nothing matters. Nothing except us."

They stopped moving and kissed on the lips, then again, then a third time, turning to face each other, to hold each other in a different and closer way.

"Nothing matters," he whispered again.

The shawl covering Aunt Maude's shoulders slipped down her back, then fell the rest of the distance to the ground.

Regina let go of the shade and quietly sat back in the middle of the bed, moving slowly so the bed would not creak and give her away, even breathing with care so the two people outside would not be disturbed, wondering as she sat in her room, so close to them yet separated by so great a wall, what had happened to Uncle Mortimer, what he had heard, what he now carried with him. The whispering resumed, a different whispering from before, different words at a different pace, her aunt and uncle speaking to each other with almost frantic haste, confiding the great secrets of their lives.

Regina listened breathlessly, entranced. She had never imagined, never dreamed. She had thought the world was school and shopping, cleaning the house, washing and sewing. She had thought that getting married was wearing a long white dress and having a big wedding. But she saw now there was something else, some great secret known to everyone and spoken about by no one. She listened so that she would remember, these words and this way of speaking them. It would happen to her someday and she would recognize it because once before, on a night in June, she had been a witness.

Suddenly it was very quiet again. Regina leaned her ear against the window shade but heard nothing. Cautiously she pulled the shade back and peered through the window. The stars were still there, and the dark shapes, but her uncle and aunt were gone. Pressing her forehead against the glass, she searched the ground for the shawl. It too had disappeared.

From a distance she heard a woman's laugh, then, after a moment, a man's. She pulled her head away from the window and lay down on her back, stretching her legs to relieve the cramp. Then she got under the covers and went to sleep.

Regina stood next to Richard, holding her flowers and feeling strangely nervous. The house no longer looked like a house, and Grandfather walked so stiffly in his black and white clothes, Regina feared he might break. Violins were playing somewhere, but she couldn't see where they were. Only a few moments before, Mr. Rush, Uncle Mortimer's father, had walked by, talking to a guest.

"Imagine, the middle of the night and he's gone from his bed. I don't think he slept an hour all put together. All night out by himself walking."

The other man had said something in Mr. Rush's ear and they had both laughed and gone to their seats.

Now, with all the voices quieted and only the sound of the violins, she could see him way up ahead, Uncle Mortimer, tired and drawn, waiting for his beautiful bride. On cue Mother left the safety of the kitchen, where they all waited, gave her arm to a man, and walked down the aisle. Regina started to count. Then, just at the right moment, a lady standing beside her whispered, "Go," and she started the long, slow walk.

At first everyone seemed to be a stranger, and an unusual fear crept over her, a fear that she might somehow be in the wrong place, among the wrong guests, at the wrong wedding. She clutched the little bouquet that she held at her waist and wondered what she would do when she got to the end of the aisle if no one was there whom she knew. And then she saw Aunt Eva, sitting next to Uncle Willy and smiling encouragingly at her. Regina smiled back, relaxed her grip on the flowers, and as she looked, all the faces became those of her cousins—Lillian sitting next to Henry—and the aunts and uncles, and there was Poppa looking as proud as if she herself were the bride.

She came to the end of the walk and took her place next to her mother, who nodded toward the aisle. Richard was halfway down, balancing the ring on a pillow covered with Grandmama's lace and trying to hold back a smile.

Then there was a gasp, and Aunt Maude, her face veiled in white, started down the aisle on Grandfather's arm. Uncle Mortimer seemed to lurch forward as he saw her, and for a moment it appeared that he would not wait for her to arrive but might go to meet her, to take her away from Grandfather before their walk was over, but he stood tensely, his eyes never leaving her, until she reached the canopy, and then he went to claim his prize.

17

Grandfather stopped, and throwing his arms around her in an enormous hug, gave her up forever.

The ceremony took only a few minutes, and Regina watched transfixed, the bridal bouquet in her arms. Mother lifted Aunt Maude's veil and placed it over her head. Then the rabbi spoke, wine was sipped, a ring given. Aunt Maude and Uncle Mortimer kissed, a long, wonderful kiss, and Regina heard a strange sound, looked beyond Mother, and saw Grandfather, a handkerchief to his face. Grandfather was crying.

Suddenly there was bedlam. The bride and groom, having turned and started up the aisle, were waylaid by the friends, the relatives, the great crowd that had assembled for their wedding day. Happiness was everywhere; the whole world was celebrating. Regina realized with a start that Aunt Maude had forgotten to take back her beautiful bouquet, but really, it was lucky. Now she had two arms free to throw around her friends.

The wedding party dispersed into the crowd as the violins began to play. Regina, trying to make her way outside through swirls of slithery fabric, heard Grandmama say, "Ach, Poppi, it's a happy day," but poor Grandfather looked lost.

The guests spilled out of the house like pools of color, the ladies in their beautiful silks, the men in summer suits, and there, moving among them, the billowing white of Aunt Maude. Regina left the white bouquet at Aunt Maude's table, found Richard, and they ran onto the grass adjacent to the platform with the tables, to watch.

Grandmama came out, her face shining. "I am so happy," Regina heard her say to no one at all. "I am so happy." Then the uncles and aunts came. Cousins were scattered everywhere.

"Regina, I've been looking everywhere for you!" Mother sounded excited, as if something in her were bubbling.

"Where am I sitting, Momma?"

"Over there. The table with the 'two' on it."

"Come on, Richard. I want you to sit next to me."

They found the table and sat in adjacent chairs. There were places for eight around the table, just the number of first cousins on Mother's side of the family. Waitresses in uniforms with little white aprons over their long dark skirts were setting out dishes of fruit at all the tables. Slowly the people on the grass moved toward the canopy and found their places. Uncle Nate's children arrived together, Millie, who was almost fourteen, Adele, who was almost ten, and little Arthur, the youngest of the cousins, who was seven. Millie was a smily, talkative girl with rather a high voice, while her younger sister spoke less often but with a sharper tongue.

Jerold arrived, and Regina's heart did a little flip-flop.

He sat in the empty seat to her left and said, "I looked for you last night. Didn't you come?"

"I was there." She felt suddenly defensive. He had spent the evening with Lillian. Why should he tell her now he had looked for her?

He leaned over and spoke so that no one else could hear. "Why didn't you rescue me?"

She felt herself coloring. "I thought . . ."

"It was awful. She never stopped talking. I hear you're going to Hunter."

18

"Yes." She was beginning to feel wonderful.

"I think you'll like it. I know a girl who goes there. She likes it very much. When are you coming out to stay for the summer?"

"The day that school ends."

"Well." It was Uncle Jack with Aunt Martha and their children. "I see we've got just two places left."

Henry sat down immediately next to Millie and whispered something to her that made her giggle. Lillian, however, stood behind the empty chair, her eyes running around the table.

"But, Momma," she said unhappily, "it's the children's table. I'm not supposed to be sitting at the children's table. I'm the oldest."

"But they're your cousins, dear," Aunt Martha coaxed. "You wouldn't want to sit with people much older than you, would you?"

Lillian looked at little Arthur sitting between his sisters, and then her eyes fell on Regina. "They're babies," she said miserably, her voice wavering, and turned to her father. "Poppa, Grandmama promised. She said because I was the oldest I—"

"Come, Lillian." Uncle Jack put his arm around Lillian's shoulders and led her away, onto the grass, where he talked to her in privacy.

"I like this table," Millie said in her high, birdlike voice. "Don't you, Adele?"

Adele looked as though she weren't quite sure, but her head bobbed in assent.

Lillian and Uncle Jack came back to the table. Aunt Martha, standing behind Henry's chair and whispering to him, looked up anxiously.

"Nothing to worry about," Uncle Jack said.

But Lillian looked very unhappy. She held herself carefully erect, her chin slightly too high, her mouth not at all steady. She sat down, meeting no one's eyes. Instead, she concentrated on the floral arrangement in the center of the table. Some of the flowers were already starting to wilt.

"I like your dress, Lillian," Millie said.

"Thank you," Lillian answered carefully. "It's crepe de chine. I like crepe de chine so much better than taffeta." She tossed a swift glance toward Regina, who felt an instantaneous anger at the slight to her beautiful, rustly blue dress. "Taffeta's really for babies," Lillian finished.

"Keep quiet," Adele ordered. "The rabbi wants to say something."

He spoke very briefly, concluding with a short prayer before eating. As soon as he said "Amen," there was a rush of sound—voices and the clinking of silverware on china.

"You can eat now, Henry," Lillian instructed her brother.

"I don't like it."

"But you haven't tried it."

Henry chewed a grape with great intensity and then spit out what remained. "I don't like it," he stated with finality.

"I like it," little Arthur called from across the table. "I'll eat it."

Plates were passed back and forth while Regina watched, trying to suppress the anger that Lillian always seemed to provoke.

"Ignore her," Jerold said. He spoke carefully so that Lillian, sitting on his left, could not hear him. "She's just feeling sorry for herself that she has to eat with us. You're so much prettier than she is, it probably makes her jealous."

He said it as though it were obvious, and she found, almost to her surprise, that she felt a little sorry for Lillian.

"I thought the wedding was beautiful," Millie announced in her shrill voice.

"Did you see me?" Richard asked. "Did I walk too fast?"

"I saw everybody. I especially saw Uncle Mortimer. I like Uncle Mortimer."

"Some people looked scared when they walked down the aisle," Lillian said. She didn't look at anyone in particular.

"I didn't think so," Jerold said with the air of an expert. "Well, maybe Aunt Maude. Maybe Aunt Maude looked a little scared."

A feeling of relief and gratitude washed over Regina. She turned to Jerold and smiled happily.

"Oh, Brother," Adele said suddenly, "you're making a pig of yourself."

In front of little Arthur were three half-empty dishes of fruit, and his short arms were reaching for a fourth.

"You're going to be as fat as your father," Lillian said.

Arthur seemed unperturbed, but Millie looked crushed. "You're mean, Lillian," she shrilled. "You are a very mean girl."

"Lillian's not so mean," Richard said with the air of a mediator.

"Yes, she is," Regina whispered in Jerold's ear.

Jerold started to laugh, and in a moment, everyone at the table was laughing, including Lillian. The fruit dishes were whisked away and chicken and vegetables raised on the farm were served, together with a white German wine. The cousins started to eat, and Regina sipped the wine tentatively.

"After two glasses you start to glow," Jerold informed her.

Regina blushed and put the glass down.

"You glow without it," her cousin said softly. "That's the best way, you know, to have it come from inside."

Across the table Arthur was well on his way. His glass was already nearly empty.

From the edge of the platform the violins began, and Aunt Maude and Uncle Mortimer began to dance a waltz on the grass. There was some applause and then other couples joined them. Uncle Jack came over and took Lillian as his partner.

"Come on, Richard," Adele said. "Dance with me."

"I can't dance."

"I'll show you." Adele had already stood and was waiting impatiently. Richard looked around for help and, finding none, followed miserably after his cousin.

"Would you like to take a walk?" Jerold asked.

Regina nodded and stood up. They started across the grassy field beyond the canopy, where already splashes of bright color preceded them, friends of Aunt Maude's making their way through the long grasses.

"My father talked to me about college the other night," Jerold said as they walked.

"Will you stay in New York or will he let you go out of town somewhere?"

"Probably out of town," Jerold said. "He wants me to be a lawyer." He spoke without enthusiasm.

"Is that what you want to be?"

"You have to be something, I suppose. Being a lawyer is probably as good as anything else."

It was obvious that he was protecting Uncle Willy. "He wouldn't force you, Jody. Uncle Willy isn't that kind of person."

Jerold pulled a piece of grass and twisted it. "I've been reading about China, about the Great Wall. I'd like to go there and see it. I'd like to go to Japan and see the temples." There was an excitement in his voice that appealed to her. He was talking about things he might not be able to do, but there was none of the whine that Lillian's voice had held when she saw she was doomed to sit at the children's table, none of the reproach.

"I want to go to Paris," Regina said, "if the war ever ends. I'm going to learn French at Hunter. Grandmama's told me all about Paris."

Jerold looked at her as though he had just that moment discovered a kindred spirit. "I'll meet you halfway," he said.

"All right."

He held out his hand. "Constantinople," he said.

She grasped his hand and held it, and for a moment, something wonderful happened. A feeling passed through her, and although she had never experienced it before, it came with the familiarity of something she had long known. It had something to do with the warmth and firmness of Jerold's hand, something to do with its promise.

She let his hand go and dropped her eyes. They had reached the edge of the wood and stood now in its shade. The strange feeling had embarrassed her, and she was afraid to look up at him.

"I won't forget," Jerold said, breaking the silence.

Finally she was able to meet his eyes. "Jody?"

"Yes?"

"I think you'll make a good lawyer."

"Why?"

"Because you strike a good bargain."

Something in his face seemed to open as she spoke, a flicker of understanding shining in his eyes. With a sudden determination, he bent and kissed her on the mouth. A wave of heat passed through her. For a moment her eyes filled as though she were going to cry, and after that she felt utterly weightless, as though the floor of the forest had dropped and left her standing on thin air. Carefully she touched her lips with the tips of her fingers. Hot as her cheeks and shoulders felt, her lips were absolutely cool. She dropped her hand and leaned gently back, feeling his hand against her, a gentle support.

After a minute he said, "Thank you," and for a long time after the wedding, she wondered if it was for the kiss or for what she had said.

2

In the chill of an early November afternoon Regina walked down the long flight of stairs descending from the El, touching ground near the point where Sixth Avenue and Broadway converged noisily at Thirty-fourth Street. A pair of trolleys moving in opposite directions passed each other with a roar, drowning out Aunt Maude's "Hello!" as Regina reached the east side of the street. She shifted the books she carried and exchanged a kiss with her aunt.

"Momma says hello and why don't you and Uncle Mortimer come out some Sunday. There, I've delivered my message and I'm free for the rest of the afternoon."

"Good. Then let's get some ice cream. Your grandmama says I'm too old and it isn't proper for married ladies"—Maude tilted her head slightly upward to indicate the snobbery of the comment—"so you've got to be my excuse."

"I don't mind." Regina smiled. "It's not exactly a difficult favor." She followed her aunt into a nearby coffee shop.

"Well, how's Hunter High School?" Aunt Maude asked as soon as they had ordered. "I had such a good time when I went to high school, being in the city for the first time, living with all of you. And then, of course, I met Morty." Her voice had an echo of nostalgia.

"I love it. I'm finally learning French. If Uncle Mortimer goes to war in France, I'll give him a quick course so he can get around."

"I think he's changed his mind," Aunt Maude said with a small sigh of regret. "He was so keen on enlisting, and then, the night before we were married, he said he didn't think he'd go if they didn't draft him."

"The night before you were married?"

"Mm. Oh, here it comes. Doesn't it look *good?*"

The ice cream was heaped on tall stemmed dishes. Regina started to eat, remembering.

"Anyway," Aunt Maude went on, "I'm glad I don't have that to worry about anymore. Morty's twenty-five now and married and they're not likely to draft him. So ..." She paused dramatically. "We're going to have a baby."

"You *are?*"

Aunt Maude beamed. "Next spring. I haven't told a soul—except Uncle Mortimer. I was saving it for you."

"You must be so excited. What does it feel like?"

"It doesn't feel like anything yet. But Morty is driving me crazy. He wants me to stay home all day and rest. He said I shouldn't come to meet you today because it would be too exhausting." Aunt Maude laughed. "Look at me. Do I look tired?"

"You look happy."

"I am. Gloriously. You know, I'll be just the age my mother was when Jackie was born." She sighed. "Morty just can't get over the surprise. Your grandmama made us promise we wouldn't have children till the war was over. She was afraid if he went away . . ." Maude looked pensive for a moment. "He really wanted to join, and then, suddenly, he just changed his mind."

In her memory Regina heard the sour tinkle of Aunt Martha's laughter. Is that what they told you? the voice around the corner of the house sang. Is that what they told you?

And as if the echo in her own mind had mysteriously been transmitted to her aunt's, Maude leaned forward and said, "Regina, have you ever heard your mother or anyone else in the family talk about someone named Herbie?"

Regina could feel herself pale, feel the flutter of an unknown fear. She said, "Yes," hoarsely and saw Maude's eyes, somber and tense now, grasp her own.

"What did you hear?"

She shrugged, embarrassed. "It was just . . . well . . . I overheard something, a piece of something. It didn't make any sense. I asked Momma later who Herbie was and she said she didn't know anyone named Herbie."

"And that was all?"

"Yes." She scraped the spoon across the top of the ice cream, filling it. "No." She put the spoon down and looked up at Maude. "No, that wasn't all. It's just coming back. Later that night I woke up and heard my mother telling Poppa that I had asked. Who is he, Aunt Maude?"

"I don't know. I don't know any more than you. I've just heard little things over the years—the way you did. I thought he might be . . . Oh, it's all too silly," her aunt said, her mood changing quite unexpectedly. "He's probably some old uncle my father has hidden away in a closet somewhere. Nobody named Herbie can possibly be important enough to let our ice cream melt. Let's finish up and do some shopping. I want to look at a pair of shoes at Bedell's. They've got black kid with that nice little Louis heel I wore with my wedding dress, and they're three dollars and seventy-five cents. Then maybe we'll go across to the Waldorf Astoria and walk down Peacock Alley." She spoke quickly and enthusiastically, as if the previous conversation were forgotten or had never taken place. "Did I tell you Uncle Mortimer and I spent the first few days after we were married at the Waldorf Astoria?" she asked as she gathered her bag and gloves together. "It's simply *elegant.* Ready?"

"Ready." Regina followed her aunt out into the street, and they turned toward the corner of Thirty-fourth. "What are you going to name the baby?"

"Oh"—Maude smiled her sparkling smile— "we'll think of something. There's lots of time. Come. Let's not waste the afternoon."

They walked toward Fifth Avenue, went in and out of stores, crossed the street and looked inside the Waldorf-Astoria, and finally, late in the afternoon, parted to go home in opposite directions.

"A kiss for Alice," Maude said, juggling her packages as two soldiers passed, looking at her appreciatively.

"And for Grandmama."

"Yes. I'll run upstairs and see them after dinner. I'm so glad you came in to see me, Regina. I hope you won't be up all night conjugating French verbs."

"There's just some history to read. And a short piece for English."

"Good. Well, good-bye then." She bent to kiss her niece.

"Good-bye."

"Regina . . ."

Regina stopped. "Yes?"

"If you ever hear anything about . . . about Herbie"—Aunt Maude was suddenly very serious—"you'll tell me, won't you?"

"Of course I will." And she had thought her aunt had set the matter aside.

"Thanks, dear. I really would like to know." Maude smiled again and threw a kiss. " 'Bye, now," she said brightly, and turning, she disappeared into the rush-hour crowd.

Uncle Willy's apartment was large and elegant, full of books with fine bindings and a polished desk that Uncle Willy used when he worked at home in the evening. In a tiny room a maid lived, to help Aunt Eva keep the rooms clean and to prepare the meals.

The apartment had become the meeting place of the family, situated as it was in the East Eighties in Manhattan. Uncle Jack lived in Harlem and Aunt Martha's frequently delicate health could not tolerate a trip to the Friedmanns' in Brooklyn, nor was she able to entertain on what she considered a "large scale." But a few times a year she managed the shorter trip to Uncle Willy's for the sake, she said, of keeping the family together.

It was May and warm and everyone was talking about Aunt Maude. Since the announcement of her pregnancy, telephones had appeared in the homes of all the New York members of the family, although Grandfather refused adamantly to use one. It was a matter of weeks now, or possibly days, and everyone was breathless.

The family ate together and then the cousins left for Richard's room. Lillian seemed in a good mood that afternoon. She talked easily to Regina about high school, comparing notes on Wadley and Hunter High. Once she heard her mother's voice and she flew out of the room, looking distraught, and when she returned only a moment later, she continued down the hall past Richard's bedroom.

Just beyond was Jerold's room. Jerold had slipped out while the girls were talking, and now Lillian was on her way to join him. Watching her pass the open door, Regina felt a stab of pure jealousy. It was absurd. She was just as free as Lillian to walk next door, but she knew, in the circumstances, she couldn't.

"Let's play chess, Richard," she suggested.

Richard got up and opened a drawer. "I think the set is in Jody's room," he said.

Regina looked around unhappily. On the floor, Henry was shooting marbles. "I'll ask him for it," she said, making her way carefully to the door.

Jerold was sitting on his bed, an open book facedown beside him. Lillian stood in the middle of the room, talking.

Regina spoke from the doorway. "Jody, could we borrow—?" But Lillian cut her off.

"Did you have to follow me in here? Can't you tell where you're not wanted? Besides, no one's allowed in here who isn't at least sixteen."

Jerold had gotten to his feet. "You're being unfair, Lillian. Regina has as much right to be here as you do. More, in fact."

Lillian's eyes widened. "Oh, does she? She's just so . . . so smart, aren't you?" She turned and faced Regina. "You're so smart because you go to Hunter. 'I'm learning French. I'm learning algebra.' " She made a grotesque imitation.

"Get out of here, Lillian," Jerold said coldly.

"You can't tell me to get out. I'm a guest in your house."

"Let's take a walk, Regina. Come on, just the two of us."

"And leave me alone, right?" Lillian said with increasing agitation. "You're both so smart, aren't you? Well, I bet I know something you don't know, something about Aunt Maude."

Jerold turned around and looked at her, and Regina, feeling almost faint, held on to the doorjamb.

"She wasn't supposed to have a baby, you know," Lillian said. "Grandmama lied to Uncle Mortimer, but *my* mother knows the truth. Aunt Maude has a bad heart. She had rheumatic fever when she was five, and it left her with a heart murmur. Grandmama never even told her about the heart murmur. My mother thinks it's because Grandmama was afraid no one would marry her if they knew."

Your mother . . . Angry words whirled through Regina's head. She wanted to say what she thought, wanted to hit and scratch and pull all that long hair on Lillian's shoulder. A memory of sour laughter. Is that what they told you? Grandmama cramped in a small apartment upstairs at Aunt Maude's long after they should have returned to the farm. Grandmama scrubbing floors and doing Aunt Maude's wash and making Aunt Maude rest day after day. The swollen ankles and the fatigue. Is that what they told you?

It was impossible to scream what she felt, the terrible anger at Lillian, the overwhelming dismay at Aunt Martha, the disgust at how both of them had used this knowledge to hurt and manipulate.

Helpless, Regina began to cry. From the living room came the sound of laughter and family warmth, and it passed through her mind that maybe it was only a show; maybe they only put up with each other for the sake of appearances; maybe all these relations of blood and marriage were suspect.

There was a light touch on her shoulder. It was Jerold, who had promised to meet her halfway.

"Let's go outside," he said, and holding his arm for support, she followed him out into the spring afternoon.

He waited until the tears were past, until they had turned a corner. "She's just jealous," he said. "She wants attention. She's always taking care of Aunt Martha when she's sick. I think she just wants some special attention for herself. Usually I feel a little sorry for her, but this afternoon I was angry. She had no right to say things like that."

"But they're true, Jody. I heard something the night before the wedding.

26

Then last fall Aunt Maude told me Grandmama didn't want her to have children for a while. It all makes sense now." She turned and looked at his darkening face. "I'm so scared."

He nodded faintly, and then, as though they agreed there was nothing left to say, they turned and went back.

She came home from school on Thursday to find her mother, pale and drawn, sitting at the kitchen table with an ice pack against her forehead.

"What's wrong, Momma?"

"Nothing's wrong. I have a headache, but it's much better than it was." She smiled without looking happy. "Maybe you can cook for us tonight. Poppa would like that."

Regina leaned over and kissed her, and Mother took her hand and squeezed it.

"I'll change my clothes first," Regina said. "I'll be right down." She started to leave the kitchen.

"Regina . . ."

She turned and looked back.

"Aunt Maude went to the hospital very early this morning. Grandmama called after you went to school."

Something caught in Regina's throat. "Is she all right?"

"Of course she's all right. Uncle Mortimer will call from the hospital when there's any news."

With all of Grandfather's complaints, each of his children had a telephone now except for Uncle Nate. Regina went to her room and took off her school clothes. Then, dressed in an old skirt and blouse, she went downstairs and prepared dinner.

She came out of school and saw Jerold on the sidewalk at 108th Street, a handsome sixteen-year-old boy in a sea of girls. One girl stopped and said something to him, and Regina saw him shake his head.

She approached him anxiously, happy for his presence but fearful of his news. She was almost in front of him when he saw her. She looked up at him, afraid to ask. He had grown considerably in the last year. Although he would never be a tall man, he would always be much taller than she.

He walked her away from the school. "Aunt Maude's baby died. Grandmama called this morning just before I left for school."

Her eyes filled. Once in the early spring she had touched Aunt Maude's billowing midsection and felt it move. She walked along beside Jerold because there seemed nothing else to do. He took her to the subway and she handed him her nickel, not telling him that she always took the El home because the subway frightened her, the crowds, the pushing, the underground darkness. Today she was not afraid. He sat beside her, saying something nice from time to time, watching as she pressed the embroidered handkerchief to her eyes. Mother gave her a clean one every day of the week, but they were always too pretty to use. Now there was nothing else.

He changed trains with her and she followed his lead gratefully. She didn't ask him how he had managed to be at Hunter at the end of school or what had made him come. She accepted his presence as one accepts a gift, with gratitude. At the end of this trip would be her mother and her mother's anguish. In Brooklyn he walked her to the door of her house.

"I have to go home now," he said. "I have a lot of homework."

"Thank you, Jody," she said, and opening the door, she realized it was the first thing she had said to him all afternoon.

Poppa always worked on Saturday mornings. Usually, while he was gone, Mother cooked and baked. Today she sat in the kitchen with her sewing once breakfast was finished.

Regina sat in her room by the window doing her French homework. There were sentences to translate from English, and as she finished each one, she whispered it in her best French accent. Mother had wanted her to take German, since so many members of the family knew it, but Grandmama had been pleased with her choice. She was the granddaughter who would visit Paris, who would speak like a Parisian.

Suddenly she heard the front door open and shut. She put the pencil down and listened. She heard her father's voice say, "Alice . . ." That was strange. It was too early for Poppa to be coming home. She opened her bedroom door and listened.

From below there was a low mumble of voices and then a cry, a shriek, a scream of unutterable anguish. She heard her father say something like "jest." What could be funny if her mother was in such pain?

She ran down the stairs calling, "Momma! Momma!," got to the door of the kitchen, and stopped. Mother was sitting in a chair, her sewing half on her lap, her head in both her hands, and she was crying like a little child, screaming as if in pain. Poppa was standing beside her looking lost, as though he had walked into the wrong house and had now forgotten the way out.

"Regina . . ." he said as she appeared in the doorway. "Regina . . ."

She looked from him to Mother and then back again, wanting to ask but afraid, as she had never been before, of hearing the answer.

Poppa patted Mother's back and said, "Come with me, Regina."

Behind them the crying did not subside as they moved into the living room.

"Sit down," Poppa said, and she sat on the plumped cushion of the sofa. "Regina, I'm afraid . . . Aunt Maude . . ." Poppa's voice seemed to stop before he was finished. He took a clean, folded handkerchief from his pocket, lifted his spectacles, and patted each eye. Then he shook his head. "She died, Regina."

"Why, Poppa?"

He shrugged his shoulders, shook his head. "I don't know. They said congestive heart failure. But that's not a reason. It's only what they say."

It was the moment that she understood that they could not help her, that they were as helpless and fallible as she, that much as she wanted their comforting, they craved it themselves. She knew that this time Momma couldn't tell her there was nothing to be afraid of, because there was everything to be afraid of, and they were as powerless to protect her as she was to keep them from harm.

28

But there were things that had to be done, and she had to do them. She got to her feet and walked slowly to the kitchen.

"It's all right, Momma," she said, putting her arm around the heaving shoulders. "I'll take care of you. Everything will be all right."

It was Grandmama's wish that all the grandchildren be present, but Aunt Martha, who had become ill upon hearing the news, was unable to come, and Lillian had been kept at home to look after her. At the funeral they sat in a tight group, the uncles and aunts, the boys in their dark suits and white shirts, the brides of last June listening again to poor Rabbi Kleiner, for whom this seemed a personal loss. When it was over they went to Grandmama's apartment to sit and talk quietly. The uncles had had to help Grandfather walk, but Grandmama had shaken them off. There was a strange man in the living room and Regina wondered who he was. He looked like no one she had ever seen before, and she wondered why he was here.

After a while, Aunt Eva took the cousins into the kitchen and made tea for them, and while they were drinking it, it struck Regina that the stranger in the living room wasn't a stranger after all. It was Uncle Mortimer. She got up from the table and walked back to look. The resemblance was there, but he looked as his own father might have, his face a hundred years old. It was hard to remember him as he had been, driving the Pierce-Arrow with a great flair, walking with Aunt Maude close by his side, murmuring "Maude, darling" the night before their wedding.

When evening came, everyone went home except Regina's mother. She had brought a change of clothes with her and would remain overnight with her parents. Regina kissed her good-bye and went home alone with Poppa to their empty house.

It was the middle of June, almost the end of school, when the call came. Like all the terrible calls that had preceded it, this one went to Poppa at his office and he called Mother at home and she prepared the news for Regina so that it would sound like just another small piece of information.

"Uncle Mortimer has moved out of the apartment," she said when Regina came home from school.

"Where is he?"

"I don't know. Poppa didn't tell me." Mother turned to her cooking.

"Is he all right, Momma?"

"I'm sure he's fine."

"When is he coming back?"

"I don't think he is. He packed his clothes and left a note for Grandmama."

"You mean he's run away?"

"That's silly. Grown-up men don't run away."

"Does Grandmama know where he is?"

"Regina, I think it's time you did your homework."

The next day after school Regina went to visit her grandparents before going home. They had stayed in the city because Grandmama did not want to return to the farm just yet and Grandfather would not leave her alone.

They welcomed her with a show of pleasure that did not disguise the lingering grief. Grandmama in particular had changed. The firmness was gone from her face. Her mouth drooped like an old lady's. Her body sagged as though she had dressed without her corset. She moved without her former agility, but she hastened to make some tea and they sat at the table with a fresh tablecloth and drank from cups carried long ago across an ocean.

"What's happened to Uncle Mortimer?" Regina asked when they were drinking tea."

"Don't ask," Grandfather said.

"He went away," Grandmama countered.

"Does his father know where he is?"

"His father don't know anything." Grandfather poured again and reached for the sugar.

"Maybe he joined the army," Grandmama said. "He went away somewhere to forget. He'll never forget. I'll never forget. If I could join the army and forget, I would go today."

The cake was hard. Grandmama must have baked it days ago. How could so much have been left over to grow stale?

"Poppi," Regina said with a hint of mischievousness, testing something forbidden, "where's the car?" In her mind Uncle Mortimer and the beautiful car were one and the same.

"I'm giving the car away."

"Ach, Poppi, don't talk nonsense. He's not giving anything away."

"I don't need a car. What do I need a car for? Cars are for people with telephones. My little Maude, she wanted a car." He heaved a sigh.

"I think you should keep it, Poppi. It's beautiful and you love it. Jody's sixteen. He could drive it. I could get Poppa to learn to drive. I'll drive in a few years," she promised bravely.

"I don't want that car." It was a final statement. Poppi got up and left the table.

Grandmama pushed the plate of stale cake toward Regina. "So," she said with mock cheer, "how is the French coming? Say something for me in French. Say, 'Next year I am going to Paris.' "

At the end of that week, Uncle Willy drove his parents out to the farm in the Pierce-Arrow. After that day, the car, like Uncle Mortimer, was gone.

PART II

DECEMBER
1921

1

It was not a surprise when the invitation came. Through the early months of 1921 there had been rumors that Lillian had "met" someone. In the summer, during her visit to the farm, she had been fluttery, a different Lillian, spending more time helping in the kitchen than having a good time with her cousins. None of the cousins seemed to have felt affronted. Besides, since Grandmama's stroke a few months after Aunt Maude's death, just before the Armistice, a great deal of help was required in the kitchen.

Now the invitation lay on the foyer table next to the telephone. On New Year's Eve Mr. and Mrs. Jack Wolfe would entertain in honor of their daughter's engagement to Mr. Philip Schindler. Poppa remarked with more hurt than anger that another printer had been selected to do the invitations. Mother assured him that the decision could not have been Jackie's—everyone knew how Aunt Martha was—but Poppa was not placated.

Regina had asked the previous spring and through the fall if she could cut her hair. Her friend Shayna who went to Hunter College with her said she was too old to ask; she was in college now and she must make a decision and carry it out. Poppa said no, and no again. Impatient with the question, he said that the women in his family would not cut their hair and should not ask him anymore.

She looked in the mirror as the engagement party approached, holding the long curls up and back to create the illusion of a short bob. If she didn't do it on her own, there would never come a time when it could be done easily. This party was almost a debut for her. At seventeen she would make her first family appearance as a college student. They would all be there, the aunts, the uncles, the cousins, Richard home from his first semester away. She shivered a little. Surely Jerold would be there too.

The day before New Year's Eve, she took a dollar and left the house. She knew exactly where to go. It was a beauty parlor she passed every day on her way to school. Haircuts were fifty cents and she admired the way the ladies walking out of the shop in the afternoon looked. If she could look like one of them, the fifty cents would be a good price.

She turned the corner where the new Chinese laundry had opened up when Prohibition had closed the saloon whose patrons had caused Momma for years to cross to the other side of the street. Momma did not know that

Richard had taken Regina to a speakeasy the winter before, nor would she ever find out, any more than Aunt Eva would. Down the street a taxi stopped at the curb and Regina saw a young, attractive woman in a fur-trimmed coat get out, light up a cigarette, and blow the smoke conspicuously into the air before continuing on her way. Shocking as the act was, Regina found herself feeling a faint admiration that so young and handsome a woman could be so bold and daring in public. She touched the long curls beneath her scarf and hurried bravely on.

She was more nervous than the first day of high school when Poppa had taken her, more even than that other day four years ago when she had walked down the aisle carrying a small bouquet of flowers. She stuffed the crumpled dollar into her coat pocket and pushed open the door of the beauty parlor.

"I want it cut," she breathed to the woman with spectacles sitting in front of the appointment book. "Can you do it now?"

The woman looked at her book and then down the long narrow shop where chairs were arranged along one wall. "There's an opening now," she said. "Third chair."

She walked down and smiled at the waiting hairdresser. "Can you cut it for me?"

"Oh, yes," the hairdresser said happily. She was very young and had an engaging smile. "Please sit down."

The hairdresser arranged a cloth over her shoulders and looked at her carefully, turning Regina's head from side to side and narrowing her eyes to appraise the face. Then, satisfied, she began to cut.

In front of her on the wall was a mirror, and Regina watched with fascination as the curls fell away from her face and dropped from her shoulders, as the hair took on a new shape, as a face she had never seen before emerged.

The face was beautiful. Grandmama in the old days had told her she was beautiful, but she had said it in a grandmotherly way. Poppa always said she was the prettiest girl he knew, but she was his and that was his way of loving her. But the face that she looked at now was truly beautiful, very round and perfect in every feature. She admired it as though it belonged to someone else, as though the reflection were merely a loan and might be taken away at any moment. Unable to believe what she saw, she covered her mouth with the fingers of both hands, and in the mirror the person staring back at her did the same.

"Do you like it?"

She dropped her hands and lifted her eyes to look at the reflection of the girl holding the scissors. "It's wonderful. I can't believe it's me."

The girl laughed. "I knew you'd like it. You have the perfect face for short hair."

She walked around for a while afterward, the change jingling in her pocket. The December wind touched her neck and chilled her, making her head feel light. She walked past shop windows and watched her reflection march along the street beside her. Twice she bumped into people and apologized. Something about the day made her feel like laughing.

She walked into the house cautiously. "Momma?"

"In the kitchen. I'm baking a cake for dinner. Poppa should be closing early today, and I want . . ." Her mother stopped, the wooden spoon dripping batter as she turned to view her daughter.

34

"Do you like it?" It was a hopeful question, a plea.

Her mother opened her mouth and closed it. The spoon dripped on her apron. Tears came to her mother's eyes.

"It's all right, isn't it, Momma?"

Her mother swallowed and sniffed. "It's beautiful," she said softly. "It's just beautiful."

She waited anxiously for her father to come home, helping Momma in the kitchen. The verdict came soon enough. He walked in the front door a little before six, started to say hello, and saw Regina. His eyes opened wide behind his spectacles. He stared. Then he dropped his paper and his hat and continued through the kitchen. Seconds later his feet were pounding up the stairs.

Mother walked to the foot of the empty stairs and looked up them forlornly. Then she mounted them slowly, wiping her hands on her apron. A moment later the sound of Poppa shouting came down the stairs to the living room.

Regina sat in a chair, holding the fist of one hand in the closed palm of the other. He never shouted. He was a calm, quiet man. She had asked for years for permission to do this, and he had given no hope of ever changing his mind. It was her hair, after all. Why was it so terrible to do this to her own person?

After a while Momma came down, stopping in the kitchen before joining Regina in the living room.

"I know he'll get over it," she said without conviction. "It was too much of a surprise for him, that's all. It was too sudden. It isn't you he's angry at, Regina. He's angry that you're growing up. He's angry that you're so beautiful." Momma sighed. "My cake fell," she said sadly. "When he stomped through the kitchen, it just fell flat as a pancake."

Dinner was painful and largely silent, but the next day, for the engagement party, things were a little better. When they left the house to find a taxi, Poppa squeezed her shoulder and said what a nice dress she was wearing.

The party was in Uncle Jack's new apartment in the East Eighties. Aunt Martha had spent almost a year looking for the right place to live and then had spent additional months choosing the right furnishings. Now, at Lillian's engagement party, Aunt Martha would be able to show off her taste and her accomplishment at the same time.

What struck Regina as they entered the apartment was less the dizzying patterns of rugs, wallpaper, and draperies, the new electric lamps at every turn, or the overfilled look of the living room, but the young man standing close to Lillian. Tall, with dark hair, he could have been a younger brother or cousin of Uncle Mortimer.

Lillian looked up as they entered the living room and hurried toward them. "Regina," she said delightedly, hugging her cousin warmly. "How pretty we look. I'm so glad you came. This is Phil." She looked at her fiancé with pride and affection. "Phil, my cousin Regina. And here are my aunt and uncle, Alice and Albert Friedmann."

It was a new Lillian, a warm, happy, confident Lillian. Regina stood back after the introductions and the giving of gifts, and watched. Was it possible that this Lillian had always existed somewhere below the surface of the one she had known so well? Could it be that this young man named Phil had somehow produced the magic that had liberated the new Lillian from its old shell?

Mother greeted her brother happily. "Where's Momma, Jackie?"

"Don't ask me," Uncle Jack said. "Martha made up the guest list."

Mother stared at him as if she had failed to understand, but there was no answer forthcoming. Looking toward the opening door, he waved and walked away from his sister.

"Martha," Mother said, stopping her sister-in-law, "is my mother coming soon?"

"It was such a terrible decision," Aunt Martha said, oozing compassion. "I didn't want them to feel left out, but it's so hard for Mother Wolfe to get around now, with the cane and all. I thought it would be best if we just didn't invite them."

"I see." It was obvious that Mother didn't see but that she would not challenge the decision. "And Millie? Will she come alone, then?" Millie had been taking care of her grandparents since Grandmama had become incapacitated.

"Alice, dear," Aunt Martha cooed, "we thought it would be best for everyone if Millie stayed home with the old couple."

Regina turned away, not wanting to see her mother's face, wanting less to look at Aunt Martha. The old couple. How dare she think of them that way. Poppi would outlive Aunt Martha with all her headaches and fainting spells. Grandmama without the power of speech was more eloquent than Aunt Martha would be with two tongues and four dictionaries. And poor Millie. Of course Aunt Martha wanted to exclude Millie. What was she besides a little farmgirl, a girl who spent her days and years caring for her grandparents? If Millie were invited, Uncle Nate would surely have to be invited, and what if he came? How would he fit in with all these elegant city people? Perhaps the parents of this handsome Phil would have second thoughts about their son marrying into a family where the grandmother had lost her ability to speak, where an uncle worked a farm, and his daughter was content to keep house for her grandparents.

Almost breathless with anger, Regina pressed through the thickening crowd to find her mother. "I'm leaving," she said. "I don't want to stay here. It's still early enough to visit Grandmama. I can stay there awhile. Maybe Millie would enjoy coming here for an hour or so to celebrate her cousin's engagement."

Her mother looked at her as though she were some unruly stranger she had to contend with. Then she said very sternly, "You will stay here. You will have a wonderful time. You will never tell Millie or your grandparents about this party."

"Momma—"

"And you will not give your uncle Jack the tiniest second of unhappiness."

"Yes, Momma."

Her mother's face softened. "I know how you feel," she said. "It was nice of you to think of Millie."

Someone called, "Alice!" and Mother turned away. Regina presented herself dutifully to her cousin's future in-laws, and then turned to search through the crowd for familiar faces. She heard Uncle Willy's voice and saw them come in, all but Jerold. Richard found her after he had left his coat and gave her a warm hello and turned her around to admire her hair.

"Isn't Jerold coming?" she asked as casually as she could.

"Oh, he had to call for someone. He'll be here soon."

"Call for someone?"

"Some girl. How're you? It's been a long time. Did you hear I got a poem published?"

Some girl. "A poem? Richard, that's wonderful. You told me last summer you were writing, but I didn't know . . ." Some girl.

"It'll be out in March. I'll send you a copy. Say, is there anything like a quiet corner in this place? I have a dozen things to talk to you about. Are you happy with Hunter?"

"Yes, very happy. Richard, is there punch? Could you get me some punch?" Anything to stop the talk. How could he bring a girl to a family party? A boy she knew had invited her out for this evening and she had refused. How could Jerold, Jerold of all people?

"Be right back. There's Jerold now."

She watched him enter with the girl, a girl about his age, hair cut short, little earrings through the tiny holes pierced in her lobes. A pretty, animated girl. Regina watched him take her coat and excuse himself. More than ever now she wanted to leave. It would be lovely to sit with Grandmama and read to her, to sip tea and eat cookies.

"Here it is." It was Richard, balancing two glass cups of punch. "It's good. I sipped one to keep it from spilling." He looked a little embarrassed. "I don't remember which one."

"It's all right, Richard. You're practically my brother."

"Come and say hello to Jerold. You haven't seen him since summer."

"No. I mean, not if he's with someone."

"Oh, come on. You're just his cousin."

He took her free hand and pulled her along. There were hellos and introductions and she smiled and said the polite, expected phrases. Jerold held her hand warmly and asked her something, but she wasn't sure what. The girl was very pretty, very excited to be at the party, obviously delighted to have been escorted by Jerold. From the corner of her eye Regina noticed Phil passing their little group, watching.

"It's very nice to meet you," Regina said finally, having spent enough time that she could excuse herself without being rude. She made her way to Lillian's bedroom, where the coats lay across the bed. The bedroom was friendlier somehow than the rest of the apartment. All of Lillian's old furniture was there, the bed she had slept on since she was little, the dresser Aunt Martha had bought her when she got a little older.

Regina pushed aside some coats and sat on the bed facing the window. Below along the street electric lamps shone, illuminating large snowflakes. She should have invited the young man who had asked her out for the evening. It was only because Jerold was coming that she hadn't, but it was silly. She could see that now. He had gone away to Williams and they had grown apart, not together. Richard had been right. You're just his cousin.

"Regina?"

She turned from the window. Just inside the room was Lillian's fiancé, tall

37

and handsome and as mesmerizing as a treasured memory.

"Oh, hello."

"We're almost cousins now, aren't we?"

"Yes, I suppose so."

He walked around the foot of the bed, and she stood, almost automatically, as if reacting to a hidden signal.

"Are we close enough to kiss?"

"What?" The words seemed not to make any sense.

"I'd like to kiss you," he said smoothly, coming around the end of the bed, "now that we're going to be cousins."

"Please." She knew it had to be a joke, but the fun was missing. He was very close to her now and she had put up her hands to keep him from getting any closer. "Please," she said again.

He took her upturned hands and bent them easily down, taking the last step that would let his body touch hers. She could smell the whiskey he had drunk and it passed through her mind how ironic it was that this was what the family had put it aside for before Prohibition, the celebration of betrothals.

"No!" She turned her face away so that his lips fell on her neck. "Get away. Please." She pushed with ineffectual hands. "Stop."

"Schindler!" The voice rang from across the room and the hands released her instantaneously.

"Jody." It was half a whisper. "Thank goodness."

"Get out, Schindler," Jerold said, leaving the way open for their future cousin to make his exit, and moving toward her as soon as he was on his way. "Are you all right?"

She nodded, the panic ebbing.

"Would you like to go for a walk? I mean outside. We could just go for a walk for a while."

"Yes." She started to look through the coats. Jerold was standing at the foot of the bed. He had not touched her. How different a touch could be, how frightening when it came from the wrong man. Did Lillian know he was the wrong man? "What about the girl you came with?" She looked up, her hand on her coat.

"Lillian asked me to call for her. She's a friend of Lillian's. I'll ask Richard to see her home. I thought you knew." He touched her shoulder very lightly. "Can I help you with your coat?"

Outside it was colder, darker, and windier than she had expected. They held hands through two layers of gloves, walking carefully on slippery sidewalks.

"Richard told me where you went last spring."

"You mean the speakeasy?" She giggled.

"I didn't know you went places with Richard."

"It was a party. He was expected to bring someone. You know how shy Richard is with girls. He's my cousin. Of course I would go somewhere if he asked me."

"Am I your cousin?"

She stopped and the wind and the swirling snow stopped with her. "No." She said it very softly, but in that windless moment she knew he had heard her.

He let go her hand and untied the scarf that protected her head from the cold. "It's beautiful," he said, touching the short ends of her hair, which moved toward him with an electric quality. Then he put his arms around her, pressing his cold cheek against hers, holding her close, very close, so that she could feel the new manness of him, the strength. He kissed her cheek, then moved so that his lips were on hers. She heard him say, "I wish . . ." but whatever else there was, the wind came up again and it was lost.

". . . Somewhere warm," he said.

"Grandmama isn't far from here. Aunt Martha didn't invite them. We could visit with Millie for a while. Jody . . ." She touched his cheek with her gloved hand. "I feel much better now."

He put his arm around her and they walked toward Grandmama's.

"I wanted to ask you about school," he said, and his voice showed a vitality, an excitement, that had not been there before the kiss. "How you like it and that sort of thing."

"I think . . ." Her heart was suddenly pumping violently. "I really wanted to go out of town, you know, like you and Richard, but Poppa said it wasn't right for a girl, at least not the first two years, but I've never liked anything so much. I think sometimes it's what I'd like to do forever, just find a little corner in the library and read and study and keep learning."

"The fairytale princess leading her charmed life," he said, turning the corner as a train rushed by on the Third Avenue El.

"It's charmed already." She raised her voice, and when the train passed it was again as still as a night in winter and they were at the foot of the steps to Grandmama's.

"If I kiss you again"—he was facing her now—"will it break the spell?"

"Never. Never, not in my whole life."

He put the scarf around her head and tied it clumsily, but there was nothing clumsy about the kiss or the rush of heat that followed. They walked up the stairs, leaning on each other for support and laughing.

Inside the apartment a picture of Aunt Maude as a bride smiled happily at them from a shelf. It was the only smiling-bride picture Regina had ever seen. Usually the bridal couple stood stiffly before the hooded camera as though peering into a dismal or uncertain future. Maude had been captured in a moment of unconcealed joy.

They were all up and Poppi took out a bottle of wine when they came in. They had made up a story coming up the stairs about why they were there but they laughed too much telling it and it came out all wrong. Poppi didn't care as long as he had company, and Millie was delighted that they had come to visit, but through the evening Regina had the feeling that Grandmama was watching her—watching them— and there was something in her silent eyes that was not happy.

It was one when they finally left and started back to Uncle Jack's apartment. They had listened to the radio at midnight and heard 1922 enter their lives, the year of Lillian's marriage, a year for love. Regina wrapped the scarf around her neck and tucked it inside her coat and they walked somewhat dizzily through the quiet streets of New Year's morning. Wind blew through her short, shimmering hair.

2

She sat near Shayna on the rock in the sun beside the swimming hole. They had finished school the day before and taken subway, Tubes, and eventually the trolley up Bloomfield Avenue to the top of the hill in Caldwell, where Uncle Nate had picked them up in the Ford. It was because of Shayna that Regina had chosen Hunter College over Barnard. Shayna could not afford Barnard and Regina had wanted to go to college with the friend she had made and become close to during four years of high school. Shayna lived on the Lower East Side with her parents, who spoke the barest English and to whom Shayna spoke only Yiddish. With all her own difficulty in communicating, Grandmama managed to express a small measure of distaste for Shayna's background, a kind of frown and set of the lips that the family knew well, although she was as charming as she was able to the girl herself. It was something Regina had observed before and not quite understood, a clannishness in the Wolfe family that encompassed those of like background and excluded all others with a vehemence that bordered on impertinence.

"Isn't that your cousin?" Shayna asked, looking through the trees at the other side of the pond.

Regina followed her glance, something inside her faltering slightly. Jerold had arrived that morning with his friend from Williams, and she had yet to speak to either of them.

"Who's that with him?" Shayna asked. "It doesn't look like his brother."

"It's Walter Weinberg. From Boston. He's kind of a snob. They go to school together." She had never cared for Walter, but she was pleasant to him out of deference to Jerold.

"Well," Walter said, arriving, "she has cut her hair and emerged from her cocoon a beautiful princess ripe for kissing."

"Hello, Walter." She held out her hand and shook his firmly. "Shayna, this is Walter Weinberg. Walter, my friend Shayna Kardonsky. We go to Hunter together."

"Charmed, I'm sure."

40

Jerold laughed. "Enough. We *know* you, Walter."

"Ah, an oversight. I was overcome by the daring bathing suits on these lovely girls."

Regina felt herself color, and Shayna laughed out loud. Walter bowed gallantly and walked to the edge of the pond. "When I'm sweating in the bank next Monday," he said, "I'll remember this moment with great pleasure."

"How's the water?" Jerold asked, squatting beside Regina, his arm barely grazing hers.

"Cold. Too cold to swim, but we went in anyway. Adele came out a block of ice. I think we should go now." She said it quickly, gathering her things as she finished.

"Why not stay? If it's that cold, we'll be out soon."

"All right." She put the towel back and heard a splash as Walter jumped into the water.

Jerold walked around to the deepest point and dived in, swimming the width of the hole before surfacing. "You were right," he called.

Already his friend, shivering and blue, had climbed out and was frantically wrapping himself in a too-small towel.

Regina laughed. "It's good for you," she said. "My grandfather says cold water makes you live longer."

"Maybe your family," Walter said. "This just took ten years off me."

Feeling daring, she left her place in the sun, walked around to where Jerold had dived, and followed him into the water. She came to the surface and took a deep breath.

Jerold watched her as she swam across the pond, brushing her lightly as she passed. Revived by the swim and the touch, she climbed out of the water. Walter had usurped her sunny spot beside Shayna.

"Let's go, Shayna," she called, picking up her towel. "See you tomorrow." And waving to them, she started for home, her spirits suddenly greatly lifted.

"Walter likes you."

His voice teased a little and she blushed. "Really?"

"He said he'd like to see you again if he comes to New York."

"I couldn't do that." They were carrying a box of vegetables up to the stand where Millie and Adele were working. The farm was still empty of its summer occupants, the Friedmanns and Uncle Willy's family not due to arrive until the weekend before the Fourth. Shayna would start a summer job the following Monday and Walter would return to Boston to work in the family investment company. "Jody?" She set her end of the heavy wooden crate on the ground and he put his end down and rubbed his palms on his dark blue overalls. "Would you tell him for me? That I don't want to go out with him?"

"If you want me to."

"I do want you to."

"All right." He bent and grasped the box. "Ready?"

"Ready."

They lifted together and continued toward the stand.

"Walter's leaving Saturday," Jerold said. "How long is Shayna staying?"

"Till Sunday. She can't ride on Saturday."

"Well, I guess it's just you and me going to market Sunday night."

"When I see your family, I can believe in trees." They were walking back to the Friedmann house after dinner at Grandmama's, and Shayna had spoken.

"All families are trees."

"Mine isn't. It's a lot of little branches that don't hook on to anything."

"But your parents have parents."

"Not anymore. My mother doesn't even remember her mother. Every once in a while someone comes to stay with us till he gets settled, and my mother says, 'This is So-and-so's son or brother,' but So-and-so is just a name. It's nobody I've ever met. It may be someone who died years ago. And here you have a grandfather who says he's going to live to be a hundred."

"He will, too."

"He's quite a character."

They walked up the steps to the porch and Regina opened the door.

"Your cousin's friend is very nice," Shayna said with a measure of uncertainty.

"Oh? Walter?"

"We were talking this afternoon. He said he might take me out when he comes to New York."

"Oh, Shayna, that's wonderful," Regina said with relief and gratitude. "I think he has piles of money. I know he'll show you a good time."

Sunday afternoon they loaded the wagon for market. At eleven at night they climbed on board, Uncle Nate up front with the reins, a lamp swinging beside him, Millie and Adele on one side in the back, Regina and Jerold across from them.

It was a fresh June night and the trip to Newark, over bumpy roads, would take four hours. The stars were never so bright as when seen from this wagon, fragrant with its ripe load. Sometimes Uncle Nate sang a few bars in the quiet night; sometimes he hailed a fellow farmer driving his load to market.

Across the wagon from Regina, Millie and Adele giggled and squabbled and eventually quieted into sleep, while beside her, Jerold took her hand, holding it under the folds of her cotton skirt, holding it as the wagon lulled her to sleep on the road to Newark.

3

Monday was a different day from all the rest. They slept on the way back from market and slept again when they reached the farm. After a swim Regina began to wake up; by dinnertime she had revived completely, body and appetite beyond containment.

Grandmama, using a cane, had done some of the cooking, with Millie close by, and the meal was good and plentiful. Grandmama murmured and nodded at her and moved her hand to indicate there was more, but Regina, hungry as she was, had spent more time talking than eating. Lillian's wedding would be at the Waldorf-Astoria at the end of the summer and there were dresses to be made and a great excitement about the arrangements. Lowering her voice, she told about the haircut she had had in honor of the engagement. Poppi laughed out loud and Grandmama leaned over and patted her cheek.

"It's really beautiful," Millie said with a touch of envy. "I wish I looked like that."

"Cut your hair, Millie, and you'll be beautiful too. I'll go into Caldwell with you one day and—"

"Mm-mm-mm," Grandmama cautioned, the eyes warning severely against interference or complicity.

Regina laughed. "Ouch," she said. "I hurt when I laugh. Uncle Nate really worked me hard today."

"It's too much for girls," Poppi said. "That Arthur got to start working a little harder."

"At least Jerold's here," Regina said. "He's a hard worker."

"And strong," Poppi agreed. "That boy, he's almost as strong as me."

Grandmama slapped him playfully and Regina stood up. "I think I'll start back. Uncle Nate needs me early in the morning." She picked up her plates and carried them to the kitchen.

"I'll do them, Regina," Millie offered. "Go home now."

In her parents' house she lit a lamp and boiled a kettle of water. Tonight she would have liked the luxury of a bath in the city, but there would be no luxuries until September. Instead, there would be pleasures, the pleasure of

43

working hard and cooling off in the pond, the pleasure of long walks and long talks. She took her clothes off and mixed the hot water with cold until it was just perfect, dipped the cloth in, and held it to her neck, her shoulders. It was a good trade, really, luxuries for pleasures.

Clean and relaxed, she put on a nightgown and robe and sat in the living room to read. The light was good but the lamp smoked slightly. She turned the wick down the tiniest bit, watched the smoke evaporate, and, satisfied, settled into the chair. It was only a few minutes later that there was a knock at the door.

"Coming. Who is it?" She jumped up and went to the door, the book still in one hand. "Jody!" She looked up at him. What was he, luxury or pleasure? "Hello," she said shyly, and stood back from the door. "Come in."

He came in, closed the door, and stood looking at her. "Hello," he said, and then, somewhat uncertainly, "We . . . uh . . . didn't have much time to talk last week." He moved his arms purposelessly, as though they had suddenly become an inconvenience. "I mean, with all the company and the market last night."

"I think I better put some clothes on." She backed away from him and he reddened slightly.

"I didn't notice. I mean . . ." His embarrassment caused him further embarrassment. "I'll wait in the living room."

She scampered back to her room and dressed quickly in a blouse and skirt. Leaving her feet bare, she returned to the living room. Jerold was standing near the window. He said, "Hello," when she returned, and smiled. "Did your father forgive you for the haircut?" he asked.

"I'm not sure. We just don't talk about it anymore."

"He'll get over it," Jerold said with casual confidence. "They all do. You look really wonderful, really beautiful. I wanted to say something last week, but with Walter and Shayna and everything else . . ." His voice trailed off. He reached out and touched the soft ends of the bob, his fingers grazing her neck very lightly, and all the lovely moments they had shared through the summers of their childhood seemed to flutter back with his touch, the walks in the woods, the cooling water of the pond, the long, sleepy ride to Newark on Uncle Nate's wagon, the promises.

"Are you going to kiss me, Jody?"

He seemed less surprised hearing the question than she felt having asked it. It had tumbled out impulsively, the words going round and round in her head, the voice coming out of its own volition. The sound of the words startled her, but they seemed to come as a relief to her cousin. For an answer he bent and kissed her. He touched her bare arms, then held them tighter, then slid his hands down her arms so that she could feel the summer roughness of them.

It was all one kiss, one long moment when the feeling floated from its winter home deep inside her to prickle the surface of her skin, a moment when it came to her, suddenly and absolutely, that it was his feeling too, that he knew it as well as she, that he had wondered, even as she had, if it was shared.

The kiss over, he wrapped his arms around her, drawing her close, hold-

44

ing her tightly, as though grateful she had made it all come to pass. He whispered something she could not make out.

"What?" Softly, without moving.

"I said, 'yes.' Yes, I'm going to kiss you. I waited all week to kiss you. Come and sit down." He took her hand and led her to the couch. Across the room from the lamp, it was partly in shadow. They sat and he took her hand.

"It was a good kiss." She looked up at him and grinned.

"You're so beautiful."

"Is that why you kissed me?"

He bent and touched his cheek against hers and whispered in her ear, "No." Then he put his arm around her so that she rested comfortably against him. In the moments since the kiss, he had changed, relaxed, as though the kiss, like a key, had opened a door for him.

"I thought about you in the winter," he said. "After the party at New Year's, I thought about you."

"I thought about you, too. I always do in the winter."

"Always?"

She nodded. The light seemed to change, to flicker, and she glanced at the lamp. It had begun to smoke and she could see through its glass base that the oil was almost gone.

"Leave it," Jerold said. "You're not afraid of the dark, are you?"

"No."

"Richard was. When we were little and we first came out here. He would wake up and we couldn't turn a light on and it frightened him. I used to sit up and talk to him until he fell asleep."

The flame on the spent lamp suddenly went out and the room was country dark, dark with an absoluteness, almost a determination, that one never found in the city with all its distant lights.

"Talk to me until I fall asleep, Jody."

He took a deep breath, almost a sigh.

"Tell me about living away at college. Tell me about Constantinople. I'm still going to meet you there. Do you remember?"

"We remember the same things, don't we?" he said. "It's funny in a way. If it weren't for the winters, we'd be like old friends. Richard says he thinks of you as a little sister." He paused. "I never thought of you that way." He put his arms around her as if to show her the way he thought of her. There was nothing brotherly or cousinly in the way he held her. There was something electric. Then, as if burned by the spark, he let her go. "I can't stay anymore tonight," he said. "I have to go. Let me light a lamp for you and then I'll go."

"Leave it dark," she whispered in his ear. "Then I can watch you from my window."

He disengaged himself abruptly and stood up. "I'm sorry," he said. "Good night."

"Good night, Jody."

The door closed and she felt her way to her room at the other end of the house and looked out the window toward Grandmama's. She heard the crunch of his feet and then saw the shadow of his slim figure walking earnestly up the little hill. At the crest of the hill he stopped, turned, and waved toward her window. She waved back, wondering if he could see her. A moment later he had disappeared down the hill.

But he had left a promise. He would come back.

He was at the swimming hole the next day, but Adele was there chattering about the dress she would wear to the wedding and how Aunt Bertha still could not believe it would be at the Waldorf-Astoria.

"I guess you'll have to cook for yourself Friday night," Adele said suddenly. "Unless my mother invites you, that is."

"Friday?" Regina wrinkled her forehead. "What's Friday?"

"Grandmama's appointment. She sees the doctor the end of every month, and this is the end of June. Millie's going with them, of course. Momma says that's just to keep Poppi from grumbling. He hates going to the city in the summer, but Grandmama won't go without him." Adele stopped to take a breath. "So I guess that leaves you without dinner."

"Regina can cook," Jerold said, as though stating what was perfectly obvious. He had climbed out of the pond a moment before, and now he stood rubbing his face with a towel while water glistened on his body.

"How would you know?" When Adele asked a question, it was more like a challenge.

"She's very competent," Jerold said smoothly. He met Regina's eyes over Adele's dripping hair. "Any perceptive person could see that right off. I thought you were the perceptive one in your family, Adele."

An "Oooh" of frustration issued from Adele, who grabbed her towel and darted away, leaving Jerold and Regina standing with the rock between them.

"Can you?" he asked.

"Can I what?" She was bewildered.

"Cook." He grinned at her.

"Oh." Lately everything he said made her cheeks redden. "I . . . I can't remember anymore." She grinned back. "Any perceptive person would see how confused I am."

She had forgotten to fill the lamp in the living room, and now it was getting too dark to find the oil. She lighted one in her bedroom and sat close to it with her book, but the words drifted away. All day she had thought of nothing but Jerold, Jerold at the door, Jerold telling her she was beautiful, Jerold kissing her, Jerold sitting with her in the dark and talking to her. Except for winters, we'd be old friends. But there were winters, and they weren't old friends. They were two people who touched in a way that old friends did not, who remembered events that were sacred to both of them. They had grown up part of a family, but now, perhaps more importantly, they were part of something else too, something that encompassed only the two of them.

She waited as it grew dark, not knowing if he would come, wanting to see him again, not at the edge of the pond, but here, where they would be alone, where they could enjoy the new intimacy. What if he didn't come? Maybe Aunt Bertha had detained him with questions about college. Maybe Jerold had had a change of heart. He had left so abruptly last night. Maybe he had

had second thoughts about the propriety of their being alone together. Maybe—something tore at what must be her heart—maybe he had changed his mind about her.

It grew darker out, and still he did not come. Would it be like this all summer? she wondered. She would never live through it, seeing him briefly in the afternoon when the others were around and not knowing if he would come to her at night. She closed the book, marking the still-unread page, and drew her knees up on the bed, her back purposely to the window. She would not look for him; she would simply wait.

A knock at the front door brought her feet to the floor. She ran on bare soles, opened the door, and all the anxiousness of the last half-hour dissipated in the sweet night air.

"I'm sorry I'm late," he said, as though he had made a promise and failed to keep it. "Uncle Nate asked me to help move some boxes in the chicken coop, and then I had to wash up. Want to take a walk?"

"I'll get my shoes."

He took her hand when she came back, and they started toward the woods.

"I guess Walter really liked you when he was here," he said. "Especially with the haircut."

"Walter isn't the kind of boy I like. I mean, I'm sure he's a good friend. It's just that I'm attracted to a different kind of man."

"I see."

She wondered if she should have said "man." Poppa and the uncles were men. There seemed a great difference between them and Jerold. They walked on, into the woods. The earth was almost squishy under the trees, and the air was cold. She shivered, and he stopped.

"I should have told you to wear something warmer." He took his lumber jacket off and spread it over her shoulders. "Better?"

"Much better."

"I suppose someone like Richard, who takes you to speakeasies, is more the kind of man you're attracted to."

She stopped and faced him. "You're jealous."

"I'm not. . . . I just thought, what you said a minute ago . . ."

"Jerold Wolfe"—she was laughing—"you're jealous of your brother."

"And Walter," he added.

"And *Walter!*" She clapped her hands together once. "And I thought I was . . ."

"What did you think you were?"

"I was . . . When you didn't come tonight, I missed you."

He kissed her and she put her arms around his neck, feeling the jacket slip as she raised her hands. His tongue played hesitant little games on her lips. A girl at school had told her once, but she had never . . . only once in a while, a kiss goodnight at her door, just a little pressure of someone's lips on hers. If it had been anyone else but Jerold . . . But it wasn't. It was Jerold, her own sweet Jody. She parted her lips slightly and felt his tongue enter tentatively, as though he were waiting to be told, as though he were asking. She opened her mouth, and her whole life changed.

She could feel the instantaneous transformation in him, in his body, in the tempo of his feelings. It was as though she had given him the answer he had wanted, the answer he had waited for. He shivered as though he were cold, but there was a great heat in him, a passion, something she had never seen before in anyone, something she recognized only because it was in her too now, speaking to her in a new voice, telling her things she had never known. Questions she had been afraid to ask were now answered. Connections she had doubted or entirely disbelieved became clear as water and almost as fluent. Being close to him became, suddenly, the most important thing in her life.

He held her against him, tightly, one hand keeping her head just beneath his chin so that his heart beat against her face—she could almost kiss the place if he let her move—while the rest of him pulsed against the rest of her. Trembling, he let her go, bent and picked up the jacket, brushed the leaves off it, and wrapped it around her shoulders. He took her hand and started to walk, stumbling at first.

Still breathless, he began to laugh. "Who said I was jealous?"

She laughed with him, staying close and following his erratic path. Once, through a window, a shawl falling on the grass, and afterward the sound of laughter . . .

She dressed for dinner on Wednesday and climbed over the hill to Grandmama's. The table was set and Poppi was already at his place.

"Come and sit down," he invited genially. "Millie's got a good meal cooked."

"Where's Grandmama?"

"She's in the living room," Millie said. "You want to bring her in?"

Grandmama was sitting in a chair with a magazine. She smiled when she saw Regina, and tried to get up.

"Let me help." Regina held her arms and lifted. "There you go. Where's the cane?"

Grandmama reached for it, gripping Regina's arm tightly. Once she held the cane, she shooed Regina away with her free hand.

"If you don't mind, madam," Regina said, "I'll just stay right next to you."

Grandmama kissed her cheek and stubbornly made her way to the dining room unaided.

Millie had turned into a good cook. She had learned every favorite of her grandmother and mastered it. Poppi joked that they had survived cakes that fell and meat that bled, but the truth was, there was nothing to complain about anymore. They ate exuberantly, entertaining each other with stories, and afterward, Regina helped Millie with the dishes.

"How do you like college, Regina?" Millie asked in her high, girlish voice.

"I love it. Maybe one day you'd like to come and visit me there. You could sit in on my classes if you like."

"Could I? I bet that would be fun. I didn't like high school very much, except for the girls I met, but I bet college is a lot better."

"It is. I'm going to be a student forever. Are you going to look for a job soon?"

"Oh, no. I have enough to do here."

"But you want to meet people, Millie. You want to get married."

Millie shook her head. "I don't think Poppi would like that."

"I'm sure Poppi wants you to get married, Millie. Grandmama does."

Millie shrugged. "Who would take care of them? I couldn't let a stranger do it, could I?"

"Hello."

Regina turned. At the kitchen door stood Jerold. "Oh." She looked down at the platter Millie had just handed her and then back to his face. "Hello. What are you doing here?"

"I came to see my grandparents," he said mischievously. "Hello, Millie."

"Hello, Jerold. They're in the living room. Want anything to eat?"

"No, thanks. Aunt Bertha made enough for a regiment."

When they were finished in the kitchen, the girls joined him in the living room. He was having a brisk conversation with Poppi—when he could get a word in—and Grandmama looked as if she were enjoying it as much as they. Millie brought in a plate of cookies and Jerold took two and then everyone talked and then the sun began to go down.

Regina stood up. "I think I'll go now. Good night, Grandmama."

Jerold got up and took another cookie. "I'll walk you," he said casually. Grandmama's eyes darted from one to the other. Jerold bent over and kissed her; then Regina did the same. They walked out and turned left toward the Friedmann house.

"Why did Grandmama look at us that way?" he asked.

"I'm not sure."

"Because we're young or because we're cousins?"

"I don't know." Aunt Martha's voice: Is that what they told you? "Maybe a little of both."

"I wish she could tell us."

"She will, I think, someday."

They walked on beyond the house, talking about Lillian and Phil, remembering the party on New Year's Eve, wondering if Lillian knew or suspected, deciding apprehensively that she did not. The sun set and there were no more shadows and their conversation dwindled.

He stopped walking suddenly and turned to face her. "I like seeing you at night." He reached out and stroked the side of her breast very lightly.

She inhaled sharply. "Don't do that, Jody."

"I'm sorry." He had dropped his hand.

"I didn't mean . . . I like it when you touch me. I just meant not here." She smiled at him. "It makes my legs wobble."

"You sure?"

"Uh-huh."

He looked at her as though assessing her veracity. "Let's go to your house," he said finally, and they turned and made their way back through the woods.

The house was totally dark. Even the glow from her bedroom was missing tonight. They had passed the house on the way to the woods and had not stopped to light a lamp.

Jerold closed the door and put his arms around her. The kiss was an acknowledgment of their new feeling, an invitation to a deeper intimacy. She

49

felt his body move against her, wanting her, and she feared fleetingly that he would leave. He had left abruptly every night, left at the first flare of what might be called passion. Tonight the time to leave seemed to have coincided with the time of entering the house, and, caught in a paradox, he had chosen to stay. Stumbling in the dark, they picked their way to the living room and lay on the rug. Invited, he touched her breasts. Encouraged, he opened her blouse.

Following his example, she unbuttoned his cotton workshirt and touched his chest, the skin taut on his narrow frame. She moved her fingers lovingly, stopping at the round softness she recognized as a nipple, drawing her hand away as he made a small sound, whispering, "Did I hurt you?" and returning the hand carefully when he whispered "No." Strange that he seemed to know so much more about a woman's body than she did about a man's. Strange what the touch of his hand seemed to do to her; stranger still what the touch of hers seemed to do to him. What a sheltered life she had lived. She had gone to so many parties with so many boys, and she knew nothing about them at all. Clothes and politeness covered the secret of their feelings, the mystery of what those feelings did to them. Perhaps it was better that way. How many men could one bear to know as intimately as she now knew Jerold?

"Regina . . ." It was a whisper. Tonight they would speak only in whispers, tonight, when no one could hear them if they shouted. He moved away from her for a moment, came back, and said, "Regina . . ." again.

She kissed his chest, his shoulder. There seemed such a great heat in the room, maybe in the whole world, as if the oven were on, as if the sun had come out but had forgotten to shine. He took her hand, held it, kissed it.

"Touch me," he said in that eerie whisper. "Please. Please touch me, Regina."

He guided her hand down, away to another place. She experienced the first moment of fear in his presence, his delicious company, and she willed it away. He was the man, of all men in the world, that she could trust. He pressed the back of her hand to him, holding it hard, finding her mouth at the same time and exploring it, as though the kiss were a message or a promise.

He let her hand go, and she turned it, touching carefully with her palm, her fingers, sure of nothing except that he liked it, he would stay there forever if she would stay with him, if she would touch him this way. The surprise was that he didn't. He took her hand away suddenly, holding it hard, so hard she thought it might break, pulling her close, very close, holding the hand, and then letting it go all at once so that the feeling came tingling back as she reached around him. For a moment she thought he might be crying, but he was only lying next to her on the rug, her cousin Jody, her great love, and nothing had changed. It was still night.

He withdrew slowly, moving away, sitting, standing, turning his back to her while he fixed his clothes, saying nothing. He helped her stand and pulled together the open front of the blouse as though it mattered now that it should be set right. Then he said, "I'm sorry," and left.

It was only later, when she took her clothes off, that she began to understand why he had said he was sorry.

50

She awoke Thursday knowing something was wrong, certain she would not see him but unable to explain why. He was not at the pond, and her heart sank, seeing her fears verified.

Instead, Adele was there, catching the last of the afternoon sun.

"Momma says you're to come to dinner tomorrow when Grandmama goes to New York for her doctor's appointment," Adele said, delivering the invitation more in the form of a command.

"No, thank you."

"Why? Don't you like my momma's cooking?"

"I like it very much." She had to look away from her cousin and struggle to keep her voice steady. "Millie's leaving me something, and it'll spoil if I don't eat it."

"Well, if that's the way you feel."

"I'm wearing a suit to the wedding," Arthur announced, climbing out of the pond and shaking water off himself like a puppy. "With long pants. And I'm only twelve."

"Arthur, for heaven's sake, use your towel." Adele leaned back to protect herself from the unwelcome shower.

"You coming to dinner tomorrow, Regina?" Arthur asked amiably.

Regina shook her head. Jerold would be there. He had eaten at Aunt Bertha's every night since they had arrived. She would not force him to see her. She would go to Grandmama's and eat leftovers and be by herself.

She excused herself early after dinner and left her grandparents' house to walk by herself up the hill, down the hill, to the little empty house that waited for her. She lit the lamp in her bedroom and curled up on her bed. Didn't he feel what she felt? How could he stay away when there was such pleasure in their being together, such emptiness in their being apart?

It grew later and later, darker and darker. She promised herself she would not cry and she would not lie to herself. She would not say that she didn't care, that it was all unimportant, that he was only her cousin and it didn't matter. They had touched deeply and sweetly and she felt nothing but tenderness for him and a great hurt inside. At ten-fifteen she blew out the lamp, but it was a long time before she fell asleep, and one of her two promises dissolved in a mess of tears.

She saw them off after breakfast, helping Grandmama into the Ford while Uncle Nate carried out the bags.

"See you Sunday," she called with more gaiety than she felt, turning away as the car started, to avoid the dust.

She swam, but only Adele and Arthur joined her, and Adele sat on her rock, which almost made her cry. How silly, she told herself. It wasn't *her* rock. And it wasn't the rock she wanted anyway. It was Jerold.

She had dinner alone at Grandmama's, finishing the good stew Millie had left in a pot for her in the icebox. She ate slowly, delaying her return to her own empty house. When she was finished, she looked around the kitchen for things to do, but there was little that needed doing. Millie took care of everything. The floor was polished. The shelves were free of dust. She emptied the drip pan under the icebox, then took a dish towel and started to dry the few dishes she had placed on the drainer, rubbing the glossy finish, admiring the pattern Grandmama had chosen as a young girl and been happy with all her life.

"Regina?"

He was standing just inside the kitchen.

She said, "Oh," and then there was nothing else to say and no voice to say it with. Just this feeling that she had for no one else: I want to care for you. I need to be close to you.

"I wanted to apologize," he said, remaining near the doorway.

"Apologize?" She held the dry dish to her heart. "'What do you want to apologize for?"

He looked startled, as if she had failed to hear him. "I'm sorry about Wednesday night. I behaved very badly."

"Oh." She felt the dish pressing against her breast and she put it carefully down on the table. "I thought you behaved badly last night."

"Last night," he echoed. It was clear that he understood her as poorly as she understood him. "I had a lot to do last night. I had to think about what I'm going to do with the rest of the summer."

Something with claws grabbed at her. "What do you mean?"

"If Uncle Nate thinks that Richard can take over my work, I'm going to ask my father if I can work in his office. It'll be good practice, I think," he said with false enthusiasm. "And I'll try to ... I'll try to come out some weekends."

"I don't understand."

"That way"—he stopped and took a deep breath—"that way we won't see as much of each other. We won't be alone together as much."

She felt the tears on her cheeks even before she knew she was crying. She turned away from him and lifted the apron she wore to her face, to blot out the evidence. How many tears this apron must have absorbed. It was Grandmama's, and Regina had seen her lift it in just the same way the summer after Aunt Maude died.

"Please don't cry, Regina." His voice pleaded.

"Are you trying to punish me, Jody?" She turned back to face him. "Or are you trying to punish yourself?"

"I'm trying to keep you from getting hurt."

"You've never hurt me. Except maybe last night." She sniffed involuntarily. "I thought we were ... special."

"We are special. You're very special to me. That's why I'm sorry about Wednesday night, and I promise that it won't ever ... that I won't ..." The promise faded in the growing dusk.

"I'm sure you know what's right."

"I don't." The admission came with stunning quietness.

"Wouldn't it be silly to go back to the city, then? I would miss you so much. I don't want you to be like the boys who take me to parties and are always so polite. I don't want you to act a certain way because it's expected of you or because you think I want you that way. I want you the way you are."

"You make everything harder, and I thought you would make it easier."

"I would if I knew how."

"I want to lie down next to you in the dark," he said, "and I came here tonight to tell you—to promise you—that I wouldn't."

She took the apron off and folded it over the back of a chair. Her heart had begun to pound the way it did when she woke up in the middle of the night hearing a strange sound, but this time there was nothing strange and nothing to fear. She walked around the table and he took her hand and led her up the stairs. On the second floor he opened one door after another, as if willing the ghosts to come out. He left the little room that had been Momma's, the larger room Uncle Jack had shared with Uncle Nate, the room that Uncle Willy had lived in until he went to New York to start high school, the room that Aunt Maude had walked out of a bride, and finally they reached the last room on the floor, the room that was still Grandmama's, the place where the family had started and grown, where children had been born, where they had rested when they were sick, the place where they had gotten well.

He pushed the door open and stood there looking into its darkening interior. Then he went in, holding her hand, and she followed. His first kiss was like the kiss in the woods, like a kiss in the living room after much kissing. He had come tonight to tell her he would not kiss her like this anymore, but the promise of his kiss was more eloquent and more truthful than the promise of his words.

She unbuttoned his shirt and felt his shoulders, full of summer strength. He took the shirt off and sat on the edge of the bed, unbuttoning hers as she stood beside him, taller for the first time than he, and when she leaned over to kiss him from her unaccustomed vantage point, her breasts, loose now, seemed to swing slightly toward him, to reach for him.

"Lie down with me." He pulled his shoes off and worked his way across the bed, which looked freshly made, the sheets crisp and the pillows plumped. Millie thought of everything; everyone's comfort came before her own. Across from the bed, moonlight sifted through sheer curtains, falling like a sprinkling of flour, shaped by Grandmama's shade tree. He held her close so that their bare chests touched, and she wondered why he had chosen to promise her that they would never do this. Somehow there was a mistake in the rules, and it seemed strange that at this late date she was the one who had discovered it.

They lay there for a long time, almost without moving. The moon sprinkles had shifted when he began to move against her slowly, to kiss her very tenderly. The clothes they were still wearing seemed to fall away of themselves. Perhaps they melted in the moondust as she seemed to be melting. It was all very slow, like a clock that had run down, a clock whose hands knew where they were going but might never get there. Or perhaps he was just waiting for the moon to recede another yard, to retreat from where it lapped at their toes.

Finally he moved to obliterate the light, to let his shadow fall on her, and then his body. And when, slowly, shadow and bodies began to come together, it seemed no less than he had promised and more, far more, than she had dreamed.

He held her in the first shimmering moment afterward, a dark beloved shadow on Grandmama's bed, through the window Grandmama's moon all but a memory.

"I love you," he said with amazement, as though he had only that moment discovered it himself.

"I know."

"I didn't . . . I didn't hurt you, did I?"

"No." It would go away. Already she could hardly feel it.

"Regina . . ." He breathed a sigh and she could feel the tension of his joy, the great thrill of his pleasure. "You were the first girl I ever kissed," confirming the other that he would not tell her.

"Talk to me, Jody. Talk to me till I fall asleep, the way you said you talked to Richard when he was little. Tell me everything I don't know."

He made a small sound as though he were thinking and the thoughts were sweet. "I was going to be a journalist," he said, as though the decision not to had been made long ago, "a foreign correspondent. I would live abroad, in the Orient, and send my stories back to the paper by telegraph. I would never marry, but somewhere there might be one very special woman."

She listened, enthralled, as his voice went on, stopping from time to time, laughing at things he alone remembered. It was the first time she realized that his dream was close to the one Richard had, and she wondered if Richard's dream had been born one night when his brother had talked the night-time fear away, if Richard would live the life that Jerold longed for while Jerold did his duty as the older son. But he spoke of the dream with enthusiasm, not regret, and she listened eagerly, captured by the enthusiasm, seeing his images of distant places, and after a while the voice slowed and then stopped and she realized that with his lullaby he had sung himself to sleep.

When she awoke it was Saturday and the family would arrive in a few hours to begin the summer. Jerold stood at the window, wearing his work pants, his chest bare.

"Is it morning?"

He turned from the window. "Yes. Are you all right?"

"I'm fine."

He sat on the edge of the bed. "Are you still happy?"

"Very happy. Are you?"

He nodded. "Now," he said, pushing her hair back from her face, "you see why your father was so angry that you cut your hair."

4

He went to do his morning chores, and she straightened up the room and then wandered aimlessly through the upstairs bedrooms, picking things up, putting them down, thinking and remembering. The sky had turned gray, and as she entered Aunt Maude's room, she saw droplets hit the window.

On the dressing table where Aunt Maude had sat the morning of her wedding was Grandmama's old book of family pictures. Curious, Regina took it and sat in the easy chair, covering her lap and legs with an old quilt to stave off the damp chill of the morning.

She turned the pages slowly, recalling from previous rainy days the earliest images of her grandparents, brown and white and unsmiling, as though to have one's picture taken was as solemn as death, as awesome as war. There was Grandmama with the tiniest of waists, Poppi a young and handsome man in the most elegant of clothes. Some of the early legends were in German, as were the photographers' marks. Many of the pictures carried no explanation, as if they spoke for themselves, their contents once so obvious, so precious, that they could never be forgotten.

She turned a page, and there was Grandmama holding Uncle Jack; then, a page later, Grandmama with Uncle Nate; then Grandmama with Uncle Willy. On the following pages an occasional rectangular gap indicated a picture missing from its place. Instead of the orderliness of the early part of the album, there was a haphazardness after the birth of Mother. You could almost count the number of pictures that had been removed. It seemed a strange thing to do. Was it possible that Aunt Martha or Aunt Bertha had requested a baby picture of her husband or of his family?

Regina turned the pages, noticing the gaps recede as the children grew older. Finally there came the first picture of baby Maude. Even at birth she was beautiful. Poppi looked at her adoringly and Grandmama lost her fight to look serious. Her whole face smiled softly.

The album ended abruptly with Aunt Maude's wedding pictures. Besides the formal ones where the bridal couple and their family posed solemnly, there were numerous informal pictures. Regina found herself but could not remember having been snapped. Still, there she was at the table with her cousins, sitting between Jerold and Richard, all of them laughing. On the next page there was one of her walking with Jerold. How young they looked there. How much Jerold had changed in five years.

She closed the book and worked her way deeper into the chair, drawing the quilt up to her shoulders. Last night she had fallen in love, and this morning the summer was beginning in buckets of rain. Water rendered the windows out of focus, and dampness threw a chill across the room. How strange to look at yourself at twelve and a half when you were almost eighteen. How sad and eerie to see Aunt Maude and Uncle Mortimer on the happiest day of their lives.

She reminded herself there were things that had to be done downstairs, and she folded the quilt and took the album back to the dressing table. An envelope lay there, exactly on the spot that had been occupied by the book. The paper was yellow and parched. She picked it up carefully. A piece of the flap had already broken off in a straight edge. Inside were about a dozen old photographs. She went through them one by one. Grandmama with a baby, and the uncles sitting at her feet. The baby would be Momma. Grandmama with a baby and four children at her feet.

Regina frowned. That was impossible. Nobody had been born after Momma until Aunt Maude came, and Momma was almost eighteen then and Uncle Jack past twenty.

She continued through the pack. In each picture there was someone that didn't belong, a baby, another baby, a little boy about the size of Uncle Willy, a boy the size that Arthur was now, a boy in his teens. She opened the album again and turned to the first page where a picture was missing. It was after Uncle Willy was born. Then another after Momma. She counted the number of blank spaces on that page and the ones that followed and then counted the number of pictures she had found in the envelope. The numbers were the same.

Suddenly there was a noise downstairs of the front door shutting and Aunt Eva's voice called, "Hello? Anyone home?"

Regina slipped the pictures back into the envelope, covered it with the album, and hurried downstairs.

"Well, good morning," Aunt Eva said brightly, removing her hat and setting it on a kitchen chair. "How are you, Regina?"

"Fine." She smiled shyly and turned away from her aunt. "Richard! Hello, we've missed you." She held out her hands, and her cousin took one and gave it a friendly squeeze.

"I didn't mean to bring the rain," he apologized.

"That's all right. It's just good to see you."

"Richard, I think your father needs help," Aunt Eva said gently.

"Come around tonight," he called as he walked toward the door. "We can play chess."

Regina turned back to her aunt, who was watching her oddly. "I didn't expect you so early. You must've been up at dawn."

"That's Willy for you. Once he's packed, he can't spare a minute."

"Can I make you some coffee? I'm having a late breakfast."

"I think a cup of hot coffee would be lovely."

The packages all put away, they sat at the kitchen table and sipped from china cups.

"Aunt Eva . . ." Regina put the cup down carefully. "Did Grandmama have a baby that died?"

"Certainly it's possible," Aunt Eva said evenly. "Women of your grandmother's age often lost one or two children. Many died as babies, especially if they lived in the country and there was no doctor nearby."

"Who's Herbie?" Regina asked, her voice full of apology for asking the question.

Aunt Eva looked down at her lap, as if the answer might be written there in the damp folds of her summer dress. Finally she looked up.

"Perhaps it's good that you asked," she said. "There's so much sorrow in families . . . little ones die . . . and the sorrows become secrets because no one wants to talk about them. Your grandmama had many children. Not all of them lived. Each one that died was a special sorrow. And then, of course, there was Maude." She stopped, and Regina could see that Maude had been as much Aunt Eva's sorrow as everyone else's.

"But Grandmama didn't take Aunt Maude's pictures out of the book."

Aunt Eva looked somewhat startled. "I see," she said. "No, of course she wouldn't take those pictures out. The others—the children in those pictures . . ." She wrung her hands, and her face looked as though she were in pain. "I think what you have to understand . . ."

Regina reached across the table and touched her aunt's hand. "It's all right," she said. "You don't have to tell me. I didn't realize how painful it would be." She stood up. "I better see if Uncle Nate has anything for me to do before Momma arrives. I guess I'll be pretty busy this afternoon." She reached for her cup and saucer.

"Run along, Regina," Aunt Eva said, her voice without its earlier sparkle. "I'll wash the cups."

"Tell Richard I'll be around to play chess tonight."

"Yes." Aunt Eva was still sitting at the small table. "Yes, I'll be sure to tell him."

The next day was Sunday, with everyone working to get ready for market. Vegetables were bagged and loaded on the wagon. Chickens were slaughtered and packed in ice. At night they climbed on board, Richard and Adele, Jerold and Regina. The girls got on first with the help of the boys and Uncle Nate. Richard settled in a spot next to Regina, and when Jerold got on, he sat beside Adele. Adele was starting to think about college but knew she would remain at home. With Millie gone and Arthur still so young, she was needed on the farm. As they rumbled along in the midnight darkness, Adele's solemn voice asked about school and college and Lillian's fiancé whom she had never seen, while Richard talked intermittently about writing and traveling and being away at college. Conversations bounced across the wagon from Adele to Richard and Regina and from side to side where the pairs of cousins sat. Only Jerold and Regina did not speak to each other; but across the space, as vital as a pulse, a bond vibrated between them.

Finally, on Monday, they were alone. They met in the woods, leaving the swimming hole a few minutes apart. He was waiting when she arrived, a blanket he had carried to the pond spread on the ground. It was three days since the night at Grandmama's, and it seemed terribly long, longer when he held her.

"Is here all right?" he asked, whispering, although it was broad daylight.

"Yes."

"I missed loving you."

"Jody . . ." They were both still wet from the pond, still suited for swimming. "What a lovely thing to say."

"I'll never love anyone else."

Was it possible to know? Was it possible at twenty to be so sure?

"Not like this," he said. He slid the shoulder of her suit down. "I couldn't. I wouldn't be able to."

It was light, and she would undress and he would see her. Funny, the little things that frightened one. She turned her back to him and pulled the bathing suit down, stepping out of it carefully. He would be waiting and they would see each other naked. She had seen Richard naked when they were little, but never Jerold, never any man—she turned and faced him—her mother had told her nothing. Which made it lovelier because it was a whole world still unknown and it was all theirs. She would learn from Jerold, always, and from no one else. Like today, when he had come prepared to love her, prepared with a small object she had never seen before, prepared because he cared about her, the way she cared for him. She would never love anyone else either. She knew. And she was not yet eighteen.

Afterward they lay and talked about where they would go when they traveled. The sun moved one crucial inch and beamed through a parting of leaves and warmed them. It would be that kind of summer, the summer of their great love, when leaves would part for the sun, when they would dream everybody's dream and believe in it.

Day after day they left the pond separately and walked off in different directions, meeting at the spot in the woods, lying together on the leafy blanket, making love and talking about love. On other days, when the weather or the intricacies of her body kept them from the delicious activity in the forest, they would walk together, talking, or not talking. There were so many places they could go where members of the family would not see them, and those were the days they talked about the future. In a way, those were the better days, because it was then that they looked off into the years ahead. It was on those days that they made promises.

Once, halfway through the summer, he brought a shovel along to their place in the woods and buried all the little rubber balloons while she laughed and turned away from his mock ritual. He had almost run out of them, he admitted, not having thought very far ahead that morning in Newark when he had slipped away from the market. But she could find no fault with his planning; he had thought much further ahead than she.

She found herself alone with Grandmama at the end of July. Millie was taking her turn at the stand and Regina was spending the afternoon with her grandmother, waking her from her nap, helping her down the stairs, setting the table for afternoon tea and serving.

58

Brewing the tea, Regina talked from the kitchen to Grandmama, who sat in the living room. Coming out with a tray, she was greeted with the old smile, the glint in the alert, knowing eyes.

"I have something to tell you," she said as she poured. "Something to ask you, really." She blushed at her own impudent self-confidence.

"Sit," Grandmama ordered, fluttering her hand in the way she had when she had commanded great numbers of children and grandchildren.

"There's someone I love, Grandmama."

Eyebrows rose, and there was the clatter of the china teacup against the saucer.

"I haven't told anyone," she went on quickly, "not even Momma. And we don't want anyone to know until next winter. Except you."

"What?" Grandmama asked, leaning forward. "What is it?"

"I want to marry Jody," she said softly.

A small moan came from her grandmother, and her shoulders dropped. Her head began to move back and forth very slowly, as if it were part of a clock. "No," she said. "No Jody."

Regina watched her as her throat tightened. It was as if their anguish were equal, as if the news had been as heavy a blow to Grandmama as her refusal had been to Regina.

"Why, Grandmama?"

The head shook again. The hands clung to each other and struck her lap, over and over. "No good," she said finally. "No good."

"But why?"

"Cousins," Grandmama said finally.

"But we're all very healthy, Grandmama. All of us. Even you. What happened to you could happen to anyone."

"No," Grandmama said. "Not . . ." She stopped and looked around helplessly, as though she knew the words were there—she had possessed them once, fluently, liquidly—but they were gone now and her intellect was bursting to express itself, frustrated with the rusty mechanisms of her body. A few words of German escaped her, but they were unintelligible.

"It's all right, Grandmama." Regina pushed back her chair and walked around the little coffee table to sit beside her grandmother, passing the table with the picture of Aunt Maude, forever smiling. "I promise"—she was near tears because she couldn't promise, because it was beyond her to believe in what she was saying—"I promise I'll never do . . . neither of us will ever do anything you think we shouldn't."

And suddenly Grandmama was crying, not just a tear that an apron could wipe away, but the terrible sobs she had hidden from the family four years ago when the world had nearly ended for her. Regina put her arms around her, trying to hold back her own tears because her own beautiful world was starting to fall away at the edges, but what was important now was Grandmama, making Grandmama believe that everything would be all right, that she had nothing to worry about. Her control over the family was firm. All her little brides would make the right marriages. They would seek her permission and abide by her decisions. There was so much life in her, nothing must happen to dampen it, to dilute the spirit.

"Please don't worry," Regina said, reaching for a strength she could only

59

hope was there. "That's why I came to you first. I'll always come to you first, Grandmama. I promise."

But the promise wasn't enough to stop her grandmother's tears.

The next day Regina's parents left for two weeks in the mountains. Poppa was doing well and he had never learned to love farming. Now, in his forties, he wanted to enjoy himself in his own way. Regina accompanied them into the city for a fitting on her dress for the wedding.

Returning alone two days later, she stepped off the trolley at the top of the hill in Caldwell and saw him sitting in Uncle Nate's Ford at the curb, reading the morning paper.

"Jody!" All the way from New York she had worried how to tell him about Grandmama. Now, seeing him, there was nothing to worry about; there was only that feeling, that immense love.

He looked up, dropped the paper on the front seat, and dashed to the trolley, leaving the front door of the Ford wide open. Kissing him, she felt the renewal of everything that was summer.

". . . go for a ride," he was saying, holding the little valise in one hand, the other around her. "Uncle Nate doesn't expect us till later. He said to hang around until you came. God, I'm glad to see you."

"Go where?" She sounded as breathless as she felt. They were together, and together they were invincible.

"Anywhere. Here, I bought some chocolate so we don't starve." He hefted the valise into the backseat and took her around to the door at the curb. "Can you change your shoes?" he called as he went around to the front to crank the motor.

"Uh-huh."

The motor came to life vigorously, as she had only minutes earlier. He got into the car beside her and started to drive. Once outside the town, the roads were largely unpaved and traffic was more equestrian than motor. He pulled off the road and she changed into comfortable shoes. Then, with his arm around her, they walked and ate chocolate from the little bag he had brought along. It gave her a tremendous feeling of independence—a man she loved, a car, a walk in the woods, work waiting somewhere to be done, but not now.

"My father's finally decided to go to Europe next summer." They had wandered up a hill and sat in the sun.

"He's lucky."

"His partner's there now. They couldn't both go together."

"No." She looked at carefully manicured fingers. "How's Grandmama?"

"Fine. Really fine. I had dinner with them last night. She insisted."

"Did Grandmama say anything?"

"Lots." He laughed. "She's improved so much, I can't believe it. We really conversed. Do you know, for the first time I saw that you look like her?"

She lay close to him, wanting to keep the secret from him forever, wanting to dissolve the promise she had made to Grandmama, wanting to forget there had ever been an album of pictures in Aunt Maude's room.

"Jody . . ." She spoke softly, as though a whisper might soften the blow. "I talked to her just before I went into New York. I told her we wanted to get married. She said no."

He didn't say anything for a while. He lay next to her in the summer breeze, her comfort and her great desire. "Did she say why?"

"Because we're cousins."

"That's . . . that's an old wives' tale," he said. "There's nothing wrong with our family. Our parents are all healthy. We certainly are."

"I think she knows something that no one's ever told us, the way she knew something about Aunt Maude and kept it a secret."

He pulled himself up so that he sat with his knees high before him and looked down into the little valley. Then he took her hand. "Are you afraid to marry me?"

"No. I'm afraid not to."

"We'll work everything out," he said. "Everything. I'll talk to my father next winter, maybe even in the fall before I go back to school. Come on." He stood and gave her a hand. "I can't stand talking about winter when we still have so much of the summer left. Will I see you tonight?"

"Of course you will."

"And tomorrow?"

"Yes."

"And the next and the next and the next?"

"You make me feel very good." She brushed off her skirt and they started down the hill, Jerold slightly ahead, his arm taut to keep her from slipping.

"Look how you make me feel." He took her hand and pressed it to the front of his work pants.

"Jody! You're terrible. You're indecent."

"Better to be indecent with you than decent with anyone else." He had begun to sprint down the hill, holding her hand.

"Can I drive the Ford home?" she called after him.

"When did you learn to drive?"

"I didn't. You can show me."

"It's not *that* easy."

"Yes it is. You learned."

They stopped at the bottom, out of breath. "I wish I'd brought one of my balloons along," he said. "I got a hundred."

"A *hundred?*"

"I drove twenty miles this morning so no one would recognize me."

She laughed. "You are terrible."

"They're hidden in my room. If Richard ever finds them . . ."

"Oh, Jody." She was suddenly happy again. He could make her happy. He would always make her happy.

"You going to crank it up too?"

"Crank it up—that's men's work."

"Come on, lady. I don't want any wife of mine waiting at the side of the road for some man to start her car up for her."

"Then you'll let me drive?"

"Sure I'll let you drive."

She took a deep breath and squeezed his hand. "Thanks, Jody."

* * *

Electric wires were strung along the road during the summer, and in August they reached the farm. Aunt Bertha was delighted. For years she had craved electric lights and, more recently, a refrigerator. Now she would have them. Poppi was less enthusiastic.

"Soon I suppose we'll have telephones too. Then no one walks anyplace anymore. They just sit at the telephone and talk all day. Maybe work doesn't get done either."

"We have no one to call out here," Regina assured him. "We don't need phones."

"You know that telephone in New York? Every day it rings. Every single day."

"It's because we all love you, Poppi. No one in the family can live a day without hearing your voice."

He squinted at her. "You're fresh," he said. "Somebody should spank you."

She grinned at him. "Shall I bend over?"

"Not me," Poppi said, aghast. "That's your grandmama's business."

But Grandmama had given up spanking. The tales the uncles told were merely myths now, and none of the cousins really believed them. She was sugar and cream in her old age, spoiling little Arthur, the last of her grandchildren. Not once during the summer did she speak privately again to Regina, but her eyes watched. When Jerold was in the same room, a kind of tense concern radiated from her and they both felt it, as they knew they were meant to. Alone, they talked about it. She told him finally about the album in Aunt Maude's room, but when she went to find it one rainy afternoon, it was gone. She looked briefly in Grandmama's room, her heart almost stopping at the sight of the great bed, the shadows from Grandmama's shade tree lying across it as once the moon had cast its own wonderful shapes.

Early in August Lillian came to visit with her fiancé. He had borrowed a car from a friend, and they arrived with great fanfare, stepping out of the car carefully in their city clothes. Regina saw them, noticing again the resemblance between her soon-to-be cousin and Uncle Mortimer, the tall, dark good looks that she alone knew formed a thin surface over an ugly core. She heard him call his fiancée "Lil" as they walked to the door of the big house, and for reasons she could not articulate, she felt uncomfortable. No one had ever called her anything but "Lillian" since the day she was born.

Regina went inside to see them, but stayed only a few minutes. Phil was polite and friendly, as though nothing had happened, and Regina was happy to forget the New Year's Eve incident. But she found herself momentarily alone with Lillian in the kitchen, and her cousin hissed, "Keep your hands off Phil," and, paling, Regina slipped out the back door, nearly stepping on Grandmama's cheese, which lay wrapped in white cloth, dripping through the planks, leaving a milky puddle for the cat.

In the evening sometimes Regina walked over to Uncle Willy's house and played chess with Richard. On those nights, Jerold sat in a chair behind Richard and read, looking up from time to time to meet her eyes, disappearing before the end of the game and meeting her somewhere in the dark to walk her home, leaving her at her door heavy with the feeling they aroused in each other.

And suddenly it was the last Sunday of August, the last trip to market before leaving for New York and Lillian's wedding.

Jerold contrived to sit next to her in the wagon, leaving Richard stuck beside his critical cousin, forced to listen to Adele's dry, uninteresting comments. Dropping his jacket lightly across their laps, Jerold was able to hold her hand unseen, touch her thigh through her skirt, move his hand slightly, make her feel wonderful in a way she had never dreamed a year or even a season earlier. In two months he had changed into an artful and caring lover, and she had changed too because she knew now that she wanted him forever.

"Regina . . ." he whispered, taking her hand again under the jacket.

She drew close to him so that they could whisper unheard, touch unseen.

"I want to marry you in 1923, after I graduate." He took a breath, as though the declaration had unnerved him. "Is that what you want?"

"Yes."

Across from them, Richard shifted position in his sleep, and Adele, sleeping against him, whined slightly and readjusted herself without waking. When the noises had stopped, Jerold went on, his words still a whisper. "I don't like to talk about it when we're out in the woods."

"I know."

"Nothing's real out there. Sometimes I think even I'm not real."

She had her arms around him now and her head on his shoulder. What was real was this wagon forever heading toward Newark with its cargo of harvest.

"I wanted to tell you here," he said, "because . . ." He kissed her neck as she lay against him, and the wagon and Newark suddenly seemed in danger of becoming as unreal as the forest in which they made love.

"I love you, Jody," she whispered, and his response was as physical as if she had touched one of those tender, sensitive places she had discovered in the months of the summer.

Adele moaned in her sleep and said something unintelligible.

"I'm not going to law school," Jerold said. "I'm going to work as soon as I graduate. I don't see how anyone can object then."

"Where are you going to work?"

"I wrote to Walter. I can probably get a job with his father. It's a pretty large investment company. Walter's going into it too."

"You won't like it, Jody."

He was silent for a long time, and she knew he agreed. Finally he said, "It doesn't matter. I won't like law either. This way I start three years earlier and we can be married. If we're married, I'll like anything better."

"I think you'll like law if you try it."

He waited awhile before responding. "Why?"

"Because it's more interesting than investments—more interesting to you. You like history and biography—law is part of that. I don't think you don't like law. I think you just wish your father wouldn't lay down the law."

He rested his back against the side of the wagon and said nothing. Across from them a sleepy Richard called out, "Leave me alone," and Adele whimpered. A man's voice came flying out of the night, and Uncle Nate returned the greeting.

"It would take three extra years," Jerold said slowly.

"I know. But wouldn't it be worth it if you were happy?"

"Maybe . . ."—he seemed to be figuring it all out as he spoke—"maybe I could start this fall, before I graduate. You don't really need the degree . . ."

"Jody, graduation is only one year away. I'm only eighteen. I don't mind waiting." She did, though. At that moment she minded waiting even until tomorrow. She wanted to turn the wagon back and wake up her parents and say: Momma, Jody and I are getting married. But that was why they were talking on the road to Newark. There was only one way to go on Sunday night, one legitimate direction, and no turning back. And in a few days the summer would be over.

"I'll write to you," he said, leaving the other unanswered, "just before Christmas." He seemed more relaxed now. Even the tension in his arms had dissolved. "I'll tell you the day I'm supposed to come home and the train I'm taking. But I'll really come in the day before on the same train."

She felt a prickle of excitement as she understood.

"Will you meet me at Grand Central?"

"Of course."

"I'll find someplace for us to go. I don't know where yet . . ."

"It doesn't matter."

"You can tell your mother . . ."

"Don't worry about it."

"Will you write? Even if I can't send you answers?"

"I promise."

She rested against him. He would sleep sooner than she, as he had that first night on Grandmama's bed. Maybe it was all real. Maybe getting married would make everything real, the bed in the woods and the walks as well. They were young and modern and they would show Grandmama there was nothing to worry about.

She felt his weight heavily against her, and she shifted to accommodate it. College would come and go, and law school if that was what he would choose eventually. The seasons would change and one by one the cousins would marry, but what would last was this journey, this wagon loaded with its scented harvest, pulled by Uncle Nate's team to the market four hours away. If anything in life was certain, this was. It was something you could always count on.

5

It was the last day of the summer. Tomorrow they would all depart for the city, and Saturday they would meet again at Lillian's wedding.

She carried the last load of corn for the family, leaving a share with Millie at Grandmama's house, and continued on to Aunt Eva's to deliver hers.

"Mm, looks wonderful," Aunt Eva said, holding the kitchen door open. "Come in for a minute, or are you busy? Willy will love this. I hope he gets here in time for dinner tonight."

Regina closed the screen door behind her and sat at the kitchen table. "Uncle Nate says he's never had a better crop. The way it's going at the stand, I wonder if he'll have anything left for market."

"You look hot. Can you drink some iced tea?"

"Yes, please."

Aunt Eva took a pitcher out of the icebox and poured two tall glasses. "At home I have special silver spoons for this," she said, stirring with an ordinary one. "But I'm never at home to use them."

"You have beautiful things," Regina said. "You and Grandmama."

"That's a wonderful house your grandmother lives in. Lots of good feelings in that house."

Regina looked at her across the table.

"Remember the day you made coffee for me at Grandmama's?"

"The day you arrived for the summer. It was raining."

"Do you remember what we talked about that day?"

"Yes." Regina looked at her aunt with a sense of foreboding.

"I think that was the day you asked me about Grandmama's other children," Aunt Eva said.

It was suddenly very quiet. "Yes, I remember."

"I didn't give you a very good answer that day."

"Oh, it . . . it doesn't matter." But she knew it did. She knew suddenly that Aunt Eva had been waiting for her, perhaps all summer, and this was the day she had finally walked into the kitchen.

"It doesn't really do to have secrets in a family. Not everyone keeps them as well as you and I might, and then the ones that don't know feel . . . well, they misunderstand. There's always a reason for making a secret in the first place, but later on, sometimes the reason gets lost.

"After Willy was born, your grandmother had another little boy. You probably saw his picture in the book that day. His name was Herbie and he was a very handsome little boy, but he was born"—she paused—"not quite right. It took a long time for him to learn what most babies learn by the time they're two. And it took years before he spoke. Naturally, he couldn't go to school."

"But then"—Regina held her hands around the cold glass—"my mother knew about him, didn't she? And all the uncles?"

"They grew up with him in the house."

"But when I asked my mother once, she acted as though she'd never heard the name before."

"I know." Aunt Eva picked up a magazine and fanned her face with it. "When Jackie married Martha, Herbie was still living at home with the family. There was quite a hullabaloo when she found out there was someone like Herbie in the family she expected to marry into."

"But why? Accidents happen all the time. Maybe he was just an accident."

"I'm sure that's how Jackie explained it to Martha. Jackie was desperate to marry her." Aunt Eva smiled. "I shouldn't say it quite that way. When I met Willy, I was desperate to marry him too." She looked away, as though she had said something she shouldn't have. "Anyway, your grandparents put Herbie in a special kind of home where he got the attention he needed, and after that, the family kept him a secret. When Nate met Bertha, Herbie was already out of the house."

"But you knew."

"Yes." Aunt Eva went to the icebox and brought back the pitcher of iced tea. Without asking, she refilled both glasses. Her face had lost its usual cheer, and for a slender woman she sat with unusual heaviness. "Willy was always very honest with me," she said. "And I to him," she added quickly. "He told me about Herbie. He said he was the sweetest child in the family. Grandmama never let on how difficult it must have been to raise him. Even with Willy very young when Herbie was born and then your mother coming along, she kept the family strong. Willy made it seem as though Herbie had almost been a blessing. I was so in love with Willy, it didn't make much difference to me. Then I told my parents." She laughed.

"What happened?"

"Oh, my father simply forbade me to marry into the family."

Regina could feel the warmth leave her face. "Because of Herbie?"

"Because there was a chance that one of Willy's children might be born the same way. Because there's always the fear that these things are inherited." She spoke very deliberately.

"But you married him anyway. Did your father change his mind?"

"Not really. I defied him. I was young and rather willful, and I told him I'd never love anyone except Willy." She spoke with a kind of pride. "I was probably wrong, Regina. Probably I would have found someone else to love if I'd tried."

"How can you say that? That's a terrible thing to say." She had expected the opposite. She had expected her aunt to tell her it was true; there would never have been anyone else. How could she even imagine another man besides Uncle Willy?

"It isn't terrible," her aunt said quietly. "It's reasonable. I'm your mother's age, and I can look back now and see it with less"—she stopped, searching for something—"less emotion. Many people marry more than once. People love more than once. The two most terrible days of my life were when my sons were born."

"But your sons are perfect, Aunt Eva," Regina said in a very quiet voice.

"I know they're perfect." She smiled with maternal satisfaction. "But there was always the fear that it was in the family, that it's still there."

"Yes."

"When Maude was born, Herbie was already gone from the house, and no one ever told her. He died when she was five."

"Died?" A chill swept over her.

"Children like that often have other troubles, Regina. His heart wasn't strong. He died when he was about twenty-five. Jerold was two and Richard was just a baby. Maude stayed with me the day the family went to the funeral. I remember when Poppi brought her to the apartment." Aunt Eva pushed her chair away from the table and walked to the window. Regina saw her lift the apron and hold it to her eyes. Whoever was it who thought that aprons were designed to keep dresses clean while cooking?

"I think Maude knew, Aunt Eva."

"I suppose, one way or another. You saw the pictures, didn't you?"

"Yes."

"Then you know . . ."

"Yes." It was the answer to the question she had been afraid to ask, about the little child born after her mother.

"There was another one, when Alice was two or three. He was much worse than Herbie. He only lived a year."

Like a door closing on a lighted room at night, she saw the last rays of hope extinguished. It was dark and it was cold, and Aunt Eva had answered all her questions.

"Willy doesn't know I'm telling you this," Aunt Eva said, turning around. "I only did it because you asked and you'd seen the pictures. Bertha didn't know about Herbie until he died. I've never told the boys." She paused. "I wouldn't want your grandmother to know."

"I won't tell her."

"She has such pride in her family—we all do." Aunt Eva met her eyes. "I wouldn't want her hurt."

"No." She wanted to leave. She wanted to run away, to find Jerold, to have Jerold hold her and hold her and tell her it was all an old wives' tale. There was nothing to worry about. *They were all perfect.* "Thank you, Aunt Eva."

"I hope—"

"I won't tell anyone." She didn't want to know what Aunt Eva hoped. "I have to go now. Uncle Nate . . ." She walked to the door and stopped. "You wouldn't have found anyone like Uncle Willy," she said, her hand on the knob. "And he wouldn't've either. I'm sure of that. Even if you're not, I'm absolutely sure."

She dropped the remaining corn on her mother's front porch and ran. There was nowhere to go, but she ran anyway, into the woods, out of the

67

woods. One day the woods would be gone. Each summer Uncle Nate cleared more trees, increasing his arable land and diminishing what was left of the virgin forest. What did it matter if there were no trees anymore? What did anything matter? There was a poison in the family blood and it ran through all their veins. And what a poison—instead of killing, it destroyed one's children.

She reached the swimming hole and stopped. They were all gone. Swimming was over for the day. She could have her rock, and no one would bother her. Who would want the rock anyway today? Clouds had moved in to obscure the sun. In a few minutes it would probably rain. She sat and waited for it, feeling the storm within evolving at the same time, maturing before the first raindrop, great, uncontrollable sobs, her head on her knees, and then drops as heavy as lead falling on her back. She took her shirt off, and her skirt, then her underclothes, and pulled off her shoes and stockings. The rain was pelting her now, every drop stinging her skin. There was nothing soft about it, nothing gentle. It would clean her skin, but what about the blood? Nothing could clean that.

Standing, she made her way to the deep corner of the pond. The surface of the water was pocked as though pebbles and not raindrops were falling. Any moment now, and her skin would split and the poison blood would leak out and stain the earth. She dived headfirst into the water, hearing thunder in another town or county. Surfacing, she heard it again one town closer, heard her name called, turned her back on all of it, sobbed in the water that was all around her. Heaven and earth were all water.

"Get out of there!" He was standing near the edge, holding her shirt. "It's raining, you idiot."

How dare he shout at her? She was her parents' only child, and if they did not raise their voices, he had no right.

"Regina!"

"No!" She screamed it at him. "No, no!" At the top of her lungs. "I'm never getting out."

"You'll get killed." He dropped the shirt and began to unbutton his own. He looked terrible, as though he had just realized she was not playing a game. "For God's sake, get out of there."

"No. Leave me alone. Go away."

"I'm coming in, then," he called. He had the shirt off and was pulling at his shoes.

"Don't, Jody." There was a flash in the distance, then a terrible roll of thunder. In another minute it would be upon them. She swam toward him as he came down to the water's edge. "Don't, please, you'll get hurt."

He knelt and reached his hand toward her and she took it, standing in the shallow water. It was the first he could see that she was naked. His face paled and he drew her out of the water as he caught her hand. "My God," he said, "what happened? What happened to you?"

He brought her, shivering, up to the rock, sat on it and pulled her down onto his lap, covering her with his shirt, which was almost as wet now as she, holding her, rocking her, asking her please to tell him, please what was wrong, and before the storm was over, he knew why they would never marry.

6

They taxied to the Waldorf-Astoria and sat as a family through the ceremony, Poppa near the aisle. During the time they waited for the music to start, Regina looked around the large crowd filled with unfamiliar faces to find those few she knew and that one she wanted most to see. He was sitting with his brother and parents, and when he saw that they had arrived, he slipped out of the row and came to greet Poppa with a handshake, Mother with a kiss, and Regina with a look meant to calm her dangerously turbulent feelings.

The ceremony was beautiful. If Lillian had had a wish, it must have come true that evening. The flowers, her dress, her handsome fiancé, seemed as perfectly chosen, as tastefully coordinated, as any bride could want. Even her somewhat plain face glowed with a beauty that artificial color could not have created.

They hugged on the reception line, Lillian's face already marked with prints of lipstick. It was a night for kissing, but Regina offered her new cousin, Philip, her hand and he shook it graciously, thanking her for her kind wishes as though she were a distant relative being introduced for the first time.

The crowd gathered outside the room where the dinner would be served. A chair had been brought for Grandmama and she held silent court, with Poppi standing beside her. Regina went to kiss them, and Poppi showed her off.

"This is my next one," he said proudly. "Next year maybe we get another wedding."

She glanced at her grandmother and then quickly away. "I'm still in college, Poppi."

"Later you worry about college. Your grandmama wants some great-grandchildren. Don't you forget that."

"I won't forget."

The doors to the dining room opened and she found her parents and went in with them, following them to the table. Aunt Bertha was already there, admiring the decorations, touching the pink satin tablecloth almost with disbelief.

69

"Jackie certainly does well selling our produce," she said with a touch of what might have been envy. "I wish the farmers made that kind of money."

"They will, Bertha," Uncle Willy said. "The industrial revolution is just beginning in farming. In ten years Nate'll be doing everything by machine, faster and more efficiently, and you'll see the difference in your income. Nineteen-thirty-two. You'll see."

They started to take their places, and Regina pulled out a chair.

"You're not sitting with us, dear," Aunt Bertha said.

"I'm not?"

"No, no." Aunt Bertha looked around the large room, squinting slightly. "You're sitting with your cousins. There they are." She moved her chin in the direction she was looking. "Go and find them. You don't want to sit with us old people." She laughed and took the chair next to Uncle Nate.

She had not even looked for her own table assignment. She had thought that now that she was grown, now that she was almost as old as the bride herself, she would be seated with her parents. She reached the table as Jerold approached from the opposite direction. Their eyes met and he smiled at her reassuringly. She sat, and he sat across from her, behind a centerpiece of flowers. A moment later, he had moved one space so that they could see one another.

Arthur was already at the table, and Adele was standing nearby.

"Where's my sister?" she asked.

"She was with Grandmama," Jerold told her, standing as she spoke. "Here she comes."

Millie came with Richard, who surveyed the arrangement at the table with a troubled look, then took the chair beside Regina.

"Why do you always sit next to her?" Adele asked irritably.

"I don't always," Richard countered.

"Yes you do. Whenever you're with your cousins, you always sit next to Regina. You do at parties. You do when we go to market. You always have secrets together."

Richard, the poet of the family, seemed at a loss for words.

"It's just that we're friends," Regina said, to placate her cousin.

"That's silly," Adele said, sitting in an empty seat beside Jerold. "You're cousins, not friends. And it looks peculiar. People might think you're in love with her, and you can't marry because you're cousins." Pleased with her logic, Adele stared a challenge at Richard.

"I don't want to marry her," Richard said with uncharacteristic anger, and then, as though his loss of temper had signaled the worst of insults, he turned to Regina. "I'm sorry," he said, his face flushed.

"That's all right, Richard." Regina leaned toward him as though she had a secret. "I don't want to marry you either," she whispered.

Richard laughed.

"That's just what I mean," Adele said triumphantly. "That's exactly what I mean."

Millie had sat between Richard and Jerold. To Regina's right there was an empty place, then Arthur, then Adele. As the tables filled, their cousin Henry appeared and sat in the last empty chair.

"Henry," Regina said, "I thought you'd be at the head table."

70

He seemed somewhat embarrassed. "I asked my mother not to. It's too stuffy up there. I thought it would be nicer here."

"This is the best table," Millie assured him. "We're all friends here. Brother." She moved her head so that she could see around the centerpiece. "What are you doing?"

"Nothing." Arthur brought his hands to the tabletop and sat angelically.

A moment later, amid much applause, the bride and groom made their entrance, and then the meal began.

After the first course, there was dancing. Adele looked around the table quickly and fixed her gaze on the bride's brother.

"Dance with me, Henry," she ordered, standing up.

Richard whispered a brief "whew" under his breath and Henry stood obediently, smiling as though the choice had been all his. Pleased, Adele led the way to the dance floor while Jerold prepared to ask Millie for the first dance.

"Will you dance with Millie?" Regina whispered to Richard.

"Let Jerold," he answered irritably.

"He will later."

"I don't know why I always . . ." He stopped and drank some water. "I'm sorry. She just got me sore." He stood and gallantly asked his cousin to dance, and Millie accepted as though it were the invitation she had been waiting for all evening.

"Do you want to dance with me, Arthur?" Regina asked the small boy.

"Huh-*uh*," he said with feeling. "I got something else to do." And before his cousin could repeat the invitation—or offer something worse—he had fled the table.

Jerold was already waiting beside her chair. He escorted her to the dance floor, his hand holding her bare arm.

"I like you in blue," he said, dancing with her.

"Thank you."

"We have to talk, Regina. I can't stand seeing you like this."

"What can we settle by talking, Jody? We have to stop seeing each other."

"I don't know how."

"I don't either."

"We'll think of something. Somehow. I promise."

Later the dinner dissolved into a huge party with much dancing. When it seemed that no one was alert enough to notice anymore, they walked away together and wandered through the public rooms of the hotel. Even at this late hour people came and went, richly dressed and laughing. In a dark corner he kissed her, and she tried to think how she would face the fall and winter without him, how she would face the rest of the years of her life without him.

"Regina . . ." He spoke in the newly confident voice that had developed over the summer, the voice of a man who has taken on the responsibility of loving someone, a man who could make decisons for two people. "We're going to see each other at Christmas the way we planned."

"Yes. All right."

"And when we sit down and talk about it, maybe while I'm home for Christmas, we'll clear everything up."

71

She nodded.

"I can't spend the rest of my life without you."

"I know."

"And I won't. And you won't either."

She smiled.

"That's better. Come, let's take a walk."

Looking reassured, he took her hand and they walked out into Peacock Alley.

Ahead of them a cloud of smoke rose from one of the small brocaded benches against the wall, obscuring the occupant. Jerold dropped her hand and hurried ahead, stopping at the smoke, starting to laugh and waving his hands to clear the air. Approaching, Regina looked down at the bench and burst into laughter. Her cousin Arthur, his shoes not yet touching the floor, sat with his head in the misty smoke, a fat cigar held between his lips.

"Oh Arthur," she said, her eyes tearing from smoke and amusement, "where did you get it?"

The little boy raised a box from beside him and removed the cigar so he could speak. "I saw where Uncle Jack put it," he explained simply. "It's good. Want one, Jerold?" He opened the box and generously offered his cousin a handful.

"Not tonight, thanks," Jerold said, trying to look serious but scarcely stifling the smile that covered his face. "Maybe when I'm a little older."

"Sure," Arthur said, replacing the cigars in the box. "Anytime." He took a puff and coughed. "You too, Regina," he added genially. "I have lots of them."

"Enjoy them, Arthur," Regina said, and waving to the cloud of smoke, the cousins returned to the wedding.

7

Half the country must have been traveling. There were people waiting to take trains and people waiting for people on trains. The immensity of the country and the mobility of its population could be felt that late afternoon in Grand Central Station. The heat inside contrasted with the brisk cold of the street and made her, for a brief moment, feel faint enough to sit on a polished bench in a waiting room. She had walked the mile from Hunter College with Shayna, who had then continued home on the subway. Having plenty of time, they had sauntered down Park Avenue, stopping to look at construction sites, watching for a moment as an old building was razed to make way for one newer and larger and far more substantial, one that would survive the twentieth century. Park Avenue was changing character. One could feel the impending elegance. The black soot of the trains had drifted away when the tracks were sunk beneath the street, and in the spring, grass and flowers would appear in their place.

Now she waited nervously for the train that would bring Jerold to her. The letter had come last week, a pleasant, cousinly letter with greetings for her parents and an almost casual reference to his homecoming. It was the only letter she had gotten since their September farewell and news about him had been sparse as Richard was away too. Still, she had written almost every week, and when the letter had come for her, she had known that he expected her here, this afternoon, for his secret homecoming.

From where she waited, a flight above the level of the trains, she could hear his rush into the station and could feel, at exactly the same moment, the blood rush from her face. She had not seen him for three and a half months, not heard from him except for the letter, not spoken of him to anyone except last week to her mother. For one terrible moment she feared she would not be able to match the face in her head with any of the faces of the passengers making their way up the stairs laden with luggage and packages. The memory face was a summer dream. Today there were winter coats, hats, and gloves. There was all that time between, time he had spent on a distant campus, parties where there must have been girls from neighboring colleges, girls eager to meet handsome young men, anxious to make promises to them.

"Regina!"

From the depths of her own imagined fears, her spirits soared at the sound of his voice. Turning, she saw him, hatted and winter perfect, the white shirt showing crisply at the collar of his coat. He dropped the valise and ran to her, wrapping his arms around her, pressing his face against hers, saying things she could not hear in the noise of all those people around them.

"I missed you." That, at least, was audible. He let her go so he could look at her. "I almost forgot," he said, touching the short ends of her hair, newly trimmed, brushed briefly in the moments before his arrival. "How much time do you have?"

"Till midnight. I told Mother I was going to the theater."

"Good." He kissed her lips quickly and took her hand. "Let's go." He picked up the valise, looked around, and started to walk. Suddenly he stopped and looked at her again. "I should have told you to wear a hat."

"A hat?" She laughed. "I never wear a hat."

"Come on. We'll buy you one."

"Buy me a hat? What do I need a hat for?"

"Shh. Where should we look? Madison Avenue?"

"I suppose so, but . . ." She felt giggly, a mixture of happiness and relief spiced delicately with curiosity and excitement.

They came out a side door somewhere north of Forty-second Street and walked the short block to Madison. On the corner Jerold stopped and looked up and down the street.

"That way, I think." He pointed right, still holding her hand. Then he kissed her cheek. "I love you," he said happily, stepping off the curb. The street was thick with angular black cars pressing in both directions. They made their way between them quickly. "I got all your letters. They were wonderful. I saved them."

"Jody . . ." She smiled at him. "They're not worth saving. They're just letters."

"I saved them anyway. Is it true about Henry, or is that just Aunt Martha's ravings?"

"It's true. He told me when we saw him last month. I think he'll make a good doctor, don't you? He's really very sweet, very kind."

"Here we are." He pulled open the door of a narrow millinery shop and let her go through. "He may spend all his time treating his mother."

Poppa had said the same thing. Aunt Martha's aches and pains had taken only a temporary vacation when Lillian married.

"Good afternoon." The proprietress, tall and thin in a black dress she might have shortened to be more in style, smiled at them and peered through spectacles.

"We'd like a hat," Jerold said, "for my . . . wife."

Regina felt her cheeks heat almost to bursting. She dropped his hand and sat on one of the empty chairs before a mirror. Jerold was walking the length of the tiny shop, looking appraisingly at naked felt forms, passing all those she might have chosen for herself—small, inconspicuous things that would sit unnoticed and unfelt on a head.

74

"This one, I think," he said, stopping before a brown shape with a modest brim. "It'll go well with your coat . . . and your hair," he added. He seemed to be enjoying himself. "And the color of your skin." He bent to whisper in her ear, "If you stop blushing."

She closed her eyes and waited for the hat to be pressed on her head, opened them, and looked at her image.

"It's one of our loveliest models," the woman in black assured her.

The brim made it somewhat difficult to see without raising her chin.

"It's perfect," Jerold said.

"Perhaps a small veil," the woman suggested, reaching for one and holding it artfully against the hat.

"No," Regina said at the same instant that Jerold said "Yes." The woman looked questioningly from one to the other. "No," Regina said softly, and the woman removed the veil.

"Then perhaps a ribbon around the crown?" the woman went on. "A wide one like this, or would you prefer a narrow one? There are several shades to choose from." Spools of grosgrain emerged from a cabinet, wide and narrow, brown, tan, and beige. The woman began unwinding the wide brown. "With a large bow just here," she said, her hands fashioning one as she spoke.

"It's very nice," Regina breathed, watching the hat change.

"Feathers," Jerold said.

The hands dropped. Another cabinet opened and a box appeared, filled with plumage.

"They're beautiful," Regina said.

"Very fine quality," the woman told her, as though imparting a secret she should be grateful to hear. Again the hands went to work. Three brown feathers streaked with orange against the front of the hat. Against the side.

"I like that," Jerold said. He had not taken his eyes off her since the hat was first placed on her head.

"One feather," she told the woman, and watched while the largest of the three was pinned in place on the front of the crown. "Yes." She nodded at her image.

The woman in black smiled for the first time. "You'll be proud to wear it," she said, removing it carefully. "Will you call for it on Saturday? Then you'll have it for Christmas."

"Oh, no," Jerold said. "We need it now. Right this minute."

"I don't know if—"

"We must." He looked very earnest. Regina could never have refused him.

"Let me inquire." The woman took hat, feather, and ribbon and disappeared behind a curtain in the rear.

Regina turned from the mirror to face Jerold. He took both her hands in his and bent to kiss her. Her left hand was still gloved. After he had said "wife," she had thought better of taking it off. His hands were bare and still somewhat cold. His hat lay on an empty table and his hair was slightly ruffled. An intense rush of feeling seemed to flow between them, through their joined hands, through the space separating them. She had had him so completely and so constantly in the summer that the empty months had been a

75

shock the way cold wind was a shock. Now, wherever he intended to take her for dinner, there would be less privacy than they had right here, less chance for intimacy, and being close to it, she would miss it more.

"Well, we've done it for you," the woman said, returning, and Jerold dropped her hands and stood back. "Will you wear it home?"

"Yes," Jerold answered for her, his voice somewhat hoarse, as though the feeling that had aroused her love had diminished his ability to speak. He cleared his throat and reached into his pocket for a billfold.

"I'm sure you'll enjoy it," the woman said, pressing it carefully on Regina's hair.

"Yes. Thank you. It's very lovely."

A moment later they were out in the street.

Oddly subdued, Jerold led her to the curb and dropped his valise. "We'll take a taxi."

"Where are we going?"

"Downtown." He looked at her soberly. "You're so pretty. I hope . . . I haven't seen you for so long . . . Wait here." He stepped off the curb and looked at the traffic coming from the north. A moment later he lifted one arm and a taxi pulled toward the curb. He said something to the driver, then returned to Regina, setting the valise in the front seat and following her into the back.

She got in carefully, dipping her head to protect its unaccustomed treasure. They drove downtown in silence, holding hands. Something had changed Jerold since the hat shop. He started to speak once or twice but never completed a sentence. The taxi was cold and became even colder when the driver opened the window once or twice to signal a turn. Finally they stopped in front of a small old hotel and Jerold got out and helped her out after him. A doorman, rubbing cold hands together, took the valise, and they started for the door.

"Is it all right?" Jerold asked, slowing his stride as the doorman waited impatiently at the entrance.

She nodded.

"You're sure?"

"Yes."

She waited in the lobby, her head just high enough that she could see Jerold's shoulders from beneath the brim of the new hat. She could see him signing something on the counter. Then a large key appeared and there was a call for a bellboy.

He took her arm and led her to the great cage of an elevator. The gate closed and it wheezed its way slowly upward. She had never dreamed . . . It was the first time she had ever been in a hotel—except for Lillian's wedding, of course, but that had been different. The elevator stopped and they stepped out into a dimly lighted hall carpeted in dark colors. The bellboy stopped in front of one of the identical doors that lined the hall and opened it. She followed him in, watching him set the valise down and then turn the handle on the radiator. Steam hissed into the room. There was one window, one double bed, a small bureau with a mirror. She heard Jerold say "Thank you," and then the door closed.

76

He flung his hat on the bed and stood before her, still in his coat. "Is it all right?"

"It's wonderful, Jody. I thought . . . I didn't think we'd be able to be alone."

"I had to . . ." There was a sound almost of desperation in his voice. "It's been so long." He started to unbutton her coat. "Walter fixed it up for me. Sent a money order to pay for the room. I promised I'd do the same for him in Boston someday. If he ever needs it." He took the coat from her and tossed it on the bed, following it with his own. "He doesn't know who I'm here with."

"I don't care."

"Well." He ran his hand down her sleeved arm. "I won't tell him anyway."

He kissed her then, the first real kiss, the first private kiss since the end of the summer. Holding her, he began to open the dozen small fabric-covered buttons down the back of her wool jersey dress. His fingers advanced slowly through the long kiss, and the room warmed. When the dress was open, she slid it down and stepped out of it. She was still wearing the hat. He took it carefully off her head, holding it with two hands, laid it on the dresser, and ran his finger along the edge of the feather with an air of something like triumph. Then he moved the coats in one armful to a chair near the window, got out of his clothes, and took her lovingly to bed.

It was a day like no other. It was the day she grew up and wore a hat. It was the day she lied to her mother about where she was going because she had made up her mind to go where they would not have let her. It was the day she walked into a hotel and went up to a room with a double bed as though she were married, not merely in love. It was a day when the summer with its easy access to love and the winter with its total absence of all but the memory of that love came together on the bed in that room with Jerold, and she understood why he had not merely taken her to dinner and talked to her somewhere, why it had been important to come to this place, to lie on this bed, to do this with the steam hissing into the air. It was the day she knew that whether she married him or not, she belonged to him as surely and eternally as she belonged to her parents.

The room was light because they had never turned off the lights, but outside it was the shortest day of the year, the best day, if any day could be. He stayed very close to her, turning away once to remove the little balloon. When he turned back, she could feel him wet against her thighs. She was almost eighteen and a half and her mother had still not spoken to her of love, although she talked often about marriage. If not for Jerold she would know almost nothing, but she thought that that was good, to learn from the man you loved, from the only man you would ever love.

"I almost forgot," Jerold said. He kissed her shoulder and began to sit up. "I have something for you."

"Stay, Jody."

"I'll be right back."

"Don't go."

He stayed, holding her again, and she felt the pressure against her reassert itself, telling her in still another way that there would be no end to their feeling, that it was infinitely renewable.

"I promise you," he said a few minutes later, "thirty seconds."

He left the bed, reached into the open valise, and pulled out a small pack of papers. "Letters," he said, returning. "I answered all your letters."

"You did?" She accepted them hungrily. "You wrote to me?"

"Whenever I got one from you. And one extra when I had something special to tell you."

"Oh." It came out a sigh, a small wail. She held them without looking at them, then put them carefully on the night table on top of her stockings.

"They're just letters," he said, almost apologetically. "My father writes me letters sometimes, strange letters. They're nothing like my mother's. She writes as though I were dying of loneliness, as though if I don't hear every small piece of family gossip or news, I'll feel like I'm missing something. My father's letters are different. It's as if there were all these things he'd meant to talk to me about over the years and he never got to them and now he's saying it all to me in letters. Every letter is on a different subject, like a lecture, except that they're warmer than lectures."

"What does he write about?"

"All kinds of things. Integrity. Choosing a profession. He wrote a whole long one on the railroad industry." He laughed. "Shall I have dinner sent up?"

"Here? Can we eat in the room?"

"Sure. There's room service. This hotel has a very good kitchen."

"How do you know?"

"My father told me. You didn't think—"

"No. I didn't think anything."

"He sends over for a meal sometimes. His office isn't far from here. Come. I'll give you my robe."

She had a warm bath and a good dinner wearing Jerold's robe. They ate and talked, and it got late.

"I'm going to sit down and talk to my father," he said when they were drinking their coffee. "I'm going to be honest, and I'll ask him to be honest with me. I want him to know how we feel about each other, that we want to marry, but that we're . . . we're concerned about what my mother told you."

She observed him soberly. He would make a wonderful advocate. If she were in court, she could do no better than to have him plead her cause, even if it were lost, even if it were beyond hope. There was something very touching about his optimism.

"Are you nervous?" she asked.

"No." He sounded very certain. "I'm hopeful. I'm hopeful because I can't bear to think of the alternative. I'm one of those lucky people who found the right person without having to take out a hundred girls—the way Walter does. You know, even my father had his problems when he got married. Poppi told him to wait another year, but he wouldn't."

"How do you know?"

Jerold smiled. "He wrote me a letter on how to choose a wife."

* * *

78

She spent the hour between English and history the next morning dozing on a cot in the basement of Hunter College, where the nurse had a small infirmary. On Mondays the beds were full; today she was the only "patient." When she got home, she reread all the letters Jerold had given her—she had stayed up past midnight to read them the first time—and then helped Mother clean some chickens. School was over now until the new year, and in a few days she would hear from Jerold about his talk with Uncle Willy.

When the phone rang Friday and Saturday, she held her breath while Mother answered, waiting for the moment she would be summoned. Finally Saturday afternoon, after a few words that could only have been spoken to a returning college student, her mother called her to the telephone.

"Hurry, hurry, it's your favorite cousin." Mother looked pleased.

"Hello?" Her heart was pounding terribly.

"Regina! It's Richard. How are you?"

"Richard . . . oh . . . hello. I'm fine. When did you get home?"

"Yesterday. I didn't have time to call. How's school?"

"Wonderful. It's fun." The pounding was subsiding. "Richard, it's so good to hear your voice."

"Listen, can we get together? I mean, there's a party tomorrow night, someone I met at school. He said to bring you along. That is, I told him I had this gorgeous cousin—"

"Richard!"

"Well, can you? There'll be lots of interesting people."

"I . . . I'm not sure. You said tomorrow?"

"There's no school the next day."

"Yes, that's true. Let me . . . let me think about it. Uh . . . is Jerold home yet?"

"Yes."

"That's . . . that's nice. How is he?"

"Fine."

"Oh, good." Her nervousness must surely be creeping into her voice. How could she accept Richard today when she was waiting for such an important call from his brother, and how could she turn him down without hurting his feelings? "Why don't you invite him to come along with us? He might enjoy a party too, don't you think?"

There was a short silence. Then: "He can't come."

"Oh? Is something wrong?"

"He's . . . uh . . . he's in trouble with my father."

"What?" She took the telephone off the table, sat down on the floor, and held it on her lap.

"Something's happened. My father's very angry. He won't let Jerold out of the house for the rest of vacation."

"Richard . . ."—her voice was very low, so low it might not carry across the wires to Manhattan—"what happened?"

"I can't talk about it. I can't tell you, Regina."

"Please, Richard. You know how . . . how much I care about both of you."

"It's not something I can tell you." He sounded adamant, adamant and miserable.

"Richard," she said, trying to sound firm, threatening, and perfectly calm all at once, "I have trusted you all my life. I've told you all my secrets. I have saved you from Adele a thousand times. If you don't tell me . . ."

"Just a minute." There was the sound of the clatter of his telephone, then the closing of a door. Then a sigh came across the wire as clear as the sound of her own. "If this goes any further than you . . ."

"It won't."

"Jerold came home from school a day before he said he would. Then he . . . he went to a hotel in New York with a woman."

It seemed to be the end of the story. "I don't believe it," she said, her voice wavering. "Jerold wouldn't do something like that."

"Well, he did it. He admitted everything when my father told him who it was that saw him. He won't say who the woman is, though, so my father assumes it was one of those . . . you know."

"Yes."

"You won't tell your mother?"

"No."

"I don't want anyone outside our family to know. I shouldn't even have told you. It's really terrible here. Nobody's speaking to anybody. My father says he may not let Jerold go back to Williams this year. I can't . . ." His voice seemed dangerously close to breaking. "Look, will you come to the damned party with me or not?"

"Yes, of course I'll go."

"Thanks, Regina. I just have to get out of this place before they all drive me nuts."

She worried about it, wept over it in the privacy of her bedroom, thought about it endlessly. Sunday morning, when she came back from a short walk, Momma told her Jerold had called to say hello, and wasn't that nice? Such nice boys her brother Willy had, so thoughtful and polite, and Regina knew he had tried to reach her.

She went to the party with Richard and for the first time saw him dance with someone other than his cousin. He was almost nineteen and good-looking the way Uncle Willy was. Girls smiled at him in a certain way. Although she was younger by half a year, she had always thought of him as a slightly younger brother, and now he was growing up, now when there was trouble in the family.

When she awoke on Tuesday morning, she knew what she would do. She had a late breakfast with her mother, then said she would go into New York to look at the stores. It was the first day they were open after Christmas, and maybe she would find a few things for herself.

She had been to Uncle Willy's office only once before, many years ago when he and his partner first moved in and invited Momma to come and see it. It had been a kind of open-house day, with Grandmama coming with Aunt Maude, who was still a young girl. The building had been nearly new back then, and the office large and luxurious.

She found the building with some difficulty and waited until one-thirty to go upstairs. Uncle Willy would not like his lunch disturbed, and she wanted to leave as much of his life in peace as possible.

Uncle Willy's name was on the dark oak door in brass, and she knocked and walked in. A middle-aged woman sat at a desk with a lamp, a telephone, and many papers. A large black typewriter was on a table nearby, a sheet of paper in the carriage. There were doors behind her to the left and right.

"May I help you?" She removed round spectacles as she looked up.

"I'd like to see Mr. Wolfe."

"Mmmm." The woman lifted a clock on her desk and brought it closer to her face. "He's out for the afternoon. May I inquire . . . ?"

"It's a personal matter."

Eyebrows went up, arching expertly. "You are . . . ?"

"Regina Friedmann."

"Mmmm. Mr. Wolfe should be back about five, just for a moment before he goes home. It's a long time to wait." From the tone of her voice it was obvious she would not wait that long for anyone herself.

"Would it be all right? I could just sit quietly somewhere. I won't be in your way."

"He may be in a rush when he comes," the woman sang. "If you could indicate the nature of your problem . . ."

"I'm Mr. Wolfe's niece. I want to talk to him about a family matter."

"Ah. We may be able to help you."

The woman left her chair, knocked at the door to the right, and slipped inside. A few minutes later the door opened and the woman slipped out again. The door, however, remained open, and a second later, Jerold stood in the opening.

They eyed each other like awkward strangers for a few seconds. Then Jerold said, "Won't you come in . . . Regina."

She mumbled, "Thank you," and walked past the desk and through the door he held for her. Inside was the large office she remembered from long ago, a fireplace alight with warmth at one end, windows looking out on downtown New York, a wall of handsomely bound books, a few choice paintings across from Uncle Willy's desk. She stood in the center of the thick Oriental rug, not knowing where to turn or what to say.

"Let me take your coat." His voice was very calm and very gentle, and when he took her coat his hand touched the side of her neck very deliberately.

She stood frozen to the spot on the carpet. He came back as silently as he had gone and took her arm.

"Sit down by the fire." He led her to a group of leather chairs arranged in front of the fireplace, but he remained standing. "Who told you?"

She reached into her bag and drew out the little white linen handkerchief, hand-rolled and -embroidered in Switzerland, that Momma saw to it that she always carried. Holding it to her face, she cried copiously.

"Please," he said.

When she was able to speak, she said, "You mustn't be angry at Richard. I made him tell me. I threatened him." She looked up at him for the first time since she had walked by him into this room. There was a small smile on his lips, as though the idea of her threatening Richard had finally managed to amuse him.

"You were going to tell my father, weren't you?"

She nodded.

81

He pulled one of the chairs closer to hers and sat down. "You can't do that, Regina."

"Richard said he might not let you go back to school. I can't let that happen to you, Jody. I can't let your father think . . . whatever it is he thinks."

"Regina." He sat at the edge of his chair and took one of her hands in both of his. "I feel very . . . It's very good of you to want to talk to my father. I know you're trying to make things easier for me, and I . . . 'appreciate' isn't the word, but let it do for now . . . I appreciate your trying. My father is very angry. I'm not going to be able to see you again this vacation—nothing can change that. A man he knows very well, someone who's known me since I was born, saw us walk into the hotel the other day with the valise. My father is angry that I lied about when I was coming home, he's angry at what I did, and he's angry that I did it with the sort of person that he thinks I did it with."

"But—"

"No." He held her hand tightly. "Listen to what I have to say. He's not going to take me out of school. That's a threat, and he'll come around before I have to go back. No one except you and me knows who I went into that hotel with. No one is ever to find out."

"Jody—"

"Shh. In the end my father will look at what I've done as a schoolboy prank. It's different for a girl. Your parents will never live it down. You'll hurt them more than you can imagine. Twenty years from now, people will remember what you did. They'll talk about it. They'll think of you in a different way."

"I don't care what people like that think."

"I know you don't. But your parents will care. Grandmama will care. And I can't let you do that to yourself."

She sat looking into the fire as if some better answer might rise from the logs with the flames.

"I've thought about it all over the weekend," he went on after a moment. "I'll wait until next year at Christmas to talk to my parents. But until then you're not to say anything, not to anyone, so that if any of this has seeped out, no one will make a connection."

"It's not fair to you. It's not fair that you should be punished when I was as much at fault—if there was a fault."

"Fair is not the question. I don't care what's fair. I care about seeing that you're not hurt and that nothing happens to come between us. I want you to promise me you won't talk about this to my father or to anyone else. Ever."

For the first time in her life she glimpsed the future, a distant time, but this same place. Jerold had inherited more from Uncle Willy than she had ever imagined, and combined his inheritance with his own wonderful qualities. He would do what Uncle Willy wanted him to and he would be happy, because he would do it well. She could see it, looking into the fireplace. The room would change and become his. The glow in the room would be the special glow that came from him.

Looking into the fire, she nodded, promising.

He leaned over and kissed her cheek. "It was the best day of my life," he said, "until I took you home."

While he got her coat, she used the handkerchief again on her eyes.

When they reached the outer office, he stopped at the woman's desk. "I'm going to walk my cousin to the station, Miss Cole," he said. "She came here to discuss a family matter, and I think we've solved it between us. It would cause a member of our family some grief if my father became involved. I hope you'll be kind enough not to mention her visit today to him."

Miss Cole was sitting at her desk, her head tilted up to look at him, her glasses in one hand. "Of course," she said. "There won't be any problem at all." She put her glasses on and turned back to the desk. As they reached the outer door, she called, "Mr. Wolfe!"

They turned. Miss Cole had stood, pushing back her chair. "Please don't go outside without your coat," she said. "It's very cold out." She dashed to a closet, took the coat out, and held it for him. Then she handed him his hat. "That's better," she said with obvious satisfaction. "Now you'll be nice and warm."

8

On a day in February that was not as cold as most of the others, she walked to the library with Shayna, partway down Park, partway down Madison. Uncle Willy's family was moving soon into one of the new, tall apartment houses now being completed on Park Avenue, where a doorman would open the front door and other uniformed men would operate the many elevators. She had written Jerold after Uncle Willy, at the last possible moment, had let him return to Williams, that they must face the reality that they could not marry. Although she was no stronger than he, she seemed in some ways to be the one more ready to accept that unhappy reality.

They turned down Madison in the Fifties and passed, without warning, the little hat shop, another bittersweet reminder that she shared the same world as Jerold.

"What are you going to do when you graduate?" she asked when the hat shop was safely behind them.

"Teach, I suppose," Shayna said. "Aren't you?"

"I don't know. It's what all the girls are doing, isn't it?"

"Probably. Why? What else is there to do?"

"I don't know. I was just thinking." They had reached Forty-second Street and turned right. "I want to do something different."

Shayna laughed. "Since when?"

"Since I was almost thirteen." Her eyes filled and she looked straight ahead. *Since my cousin promised to meet me in Constantinople.* "Don't you have the feeling that if you don't do something now, while you're young, especially before you get married, that you may never do it?"

"I don't know what you mean," Shayna said.

They stopped at Fifth Avenue and waited for the traffic policeman to signal them to cross. "No. I guess I don't know what I mean either."

The policeman turned and flicked his wrist at them, and they stepped off the curb.

"Shayna," Regina said with sudden determination, "would you mind going to the library alone?"

"Is something wrong?"

"No. No, I just remembered I have to talk to my father about something."
She backed to the curb.

"Well . . ." Shayna looked confused.

"It's very important. I'll see you in English tomorrow."

She turned and walked quickly to the subway. She did know what she meant, and now was the time to do it. The building on Park Avenue and the hat shop on Madison had left her with a feeling at once full and empty, full of the existence of Jerold and empty at the thought of life without him. She rode the train to Brooklyn, getting off near Poppa's business instead of going home. He had promised her something once. Maybe she could hold him to it. Somehow she couldn't go on, from vacation to vacation, from summer to summer. Jerold could not move to a place where they would not see each other, but maybe she could.

She got off the subway and walked to the shop. Friedmann Bros., Printers and Engravers. When she was little, he would take her around and show her how everything was done, introduce her to the men who worked there, wearing their long aprons stained with ink. She felt terribly old walking in now and asking for her father, uneasy waiting for him to be summoned.

"Regina!" He looked startled to see her, although he must have been told she was there. "Is everything all right?"

"Just fine, Poppa. I wanted to talk to you."

"Momma's all right?"

"Yes, Poppa. I was just on my way to the library, and I wanted to talk to you."

He adjusted his spectacles, still looking uncertain. "Come to my office."

She followed him through the shop, remembering other times he had saved her life or nearly destroyed it. When he had come home with the news of Aunt Maude. When he had seen her with her hair cut. Her throat tightened as she walked. I'm going to ask you for the whole world, Poppa, she thought, and you're not going to want to give it to me. And then what are we going to do to each other?

"Sit down, Regina." He picked papers up from a chair in his office. "What could you have to tell me that couldn't wait until I came home?"

"Oh, Poppa." She started to cry, surprising herself. She had not known her nerves were quite so raw, not aware that giving up Jerold had pulled her quite so far apart. She took a Swiss handkerchief out of her bag and patted her face. "Poppa, you remember you said when I started Hunter that maybe after two years you would let me go away to school?"

"I remember," he said, leaning forward, his face frightened. "Is that what you're crying about, that you want to go away?"

"I want to go to Paris, Poppa."

"To Paris? To France?"

"Yes. I don't want to be a teacher. I want to see France. I want to do something different. Just for a year. Please, Poppa. I can go to school later, but if I don't go abroad now, I'll never go. I want so much to go. Grandmama used to say—"

"Paris," her father said. He sat back in his chair.

"Uncle Willy's going this summer. He told me once he had clients there. He knows a lawyer there. Someone could find me a place to live. He could arrange it. I'm sure he'd do that. If you let me go, I'll never ask for anything again for the rest of my life. I promise."

"You want to go to Paris, and this is why you've been acting this way all winter?"

She looked at him in astonishment. She had let nothing show. She had been careful not to change even in the slightest way. And with all her efforts, Poppa had seen her misery; he had been moved by her sorrow.

"I'm sorry," she said. "I thought . . ."

"All this because you don't want to be a teacher? Don't be a teacher. Who said I wanted my daughter to be a teacher? I want her to be a happy girl."

"Oh, Poppa, I didn't know how to tell you."

"I thought when you came in here . . . I thought maybe . . . You want to go to Paris? A whole winter like this because you don't want to be a teacher and you do want to go to Paris?" He opened his eyes wide and took a deep breath of relief. "I'll call Willy tomorrow," he said. "We'll talk about it. Maybe . . . A year you want? A whole year?"

She nodded, afraid to say anything.

"Well, a year. We'll have to see. Maybe a few months, maybe till spring, maybe . . ."

"Oh, thank you, Poppa. Thank you, thank you, thank you." She ran to his chair and sat in his lap, hugging him, and he patted her back as though she were the child she had been before the summer.

"Maybe," he said, still patting her back rhythmically, "in Paris the girls will wear their hair a little bit longer."

Momma said nothing. She looked back and forth between them with frightened eyes but said nothing. Regina tried to explain and Poppa tried to placate, but nothing could elicit a sound. Dinner was as bad as the night she had cut her hair. Even cleaning up afterward was done in absolute silence.

Her father read the paper and her mother did some sewing, and then her parents went upstairs. Regina stayed in the living room, reading her history assignment.

Suddenly the quiet was gone. There was a kind of scream upstairs and then the sound of weeping. Poppa's voice, in a kind of undertone, made comforting sounds, but the crying did not stop. Finally, a stream of words became audible.

"The only child I had that lived, and you send her across an ocean. Why, Albert? Why?"

And in the piercing silence that followed, she knew again that what she was doing was right.

She told him one night during his Easter vacation. Like her mother, he said nothing when he heard it. He looked a little thinner. Earlier in the evening, he had said he loved her, but he had said little else. They had walked and kissed, walked and kissed. They had stopped writing to each other, but otherwise, little had changed. The wanting was still there. The feeling still enveloped them.

"Let's have a drink," he said suddenly. "There's a speakeasy around here."

86

"Let's have coffee instead."

"No."

She walked along beside him, hands touching through gloves. She didn't know him to be stubborn, to be unreasonable. She drank as little now as she had when she and Richard ...

"You're still jealous, aren't you? That I went with Richard."

"Yes." They kept walking. "I'm still jealous. I'm jealous of everything you've ever done with anyone else."

"Jody." She turned and put her arms around him. "I have to go. We have to stop seeing each other. I don't know any other way." In the night air, a hint of spring, their last spring.

He held her for a long time, and she didn't look at him when they started to walk again. They were downtown where the streets had names instead of numbers, and when they reached the door, they were let in immediately. Inside it was smoky and a woman with bleached hair was singing. He ordered for both of them without asking her preference, as if he knew it, as though they had been married for a long time and he knew all there was to know about her.

"When will you leave?" he asked.

"After the summer."

"I'll have to work for my father's partner this summer. Three days a week. I'll still be there for market."

She nodded. They could not be children forever. One day there were responsibilities.

"I'll still ... see you."

She felt her mouth quiver, and she looked away, beyond him, through the haze to other tables where people were happier, or seemed so. Suddenly her eyes met those of a man who looked startlingly familiar.

"Oh, God," she said.

"What is it?"

"Don't look. Please, Jody. It's Uncle Jack. He's a few tables behind you. He's with a woman."

The woman was neither young nor old, but she was younger than Aunt Martha and she was handsome. Her hair was fair and short. Tiny diamonds hung from her pierced ears and caught the light as she moved. She smoked through a long cigarette holder.

Jerold took her hand across the table, and a small smile touched his lips. "I'm glad," he said. "Good old Jackie."

"I wish he hadn't seen us. No one's ever seen us before."

"What difference does it make? Who do you think he'll tell?"

"Yes, you're right. He couldn't tell anyone."

"Take a sip," he said, "so I can say you've sinned with me."

She lifted the cup and wet her lips. Licking them, her tongue stung sharply.

"Come on. I'll get you a cup of coffee."

A few days later, Poppa came home with a steamship ticket. On Tuesday the eighteenth of September she would sail for France on the *Suffren*. The next afternoon Regina told her grandmother she was going to Paris.

And suddenly it was the last day of summer. Jerold got the Ford in the afternoon and they drove into town and then he kept on going. It was the last day of all last days. Tomorrow morning they would all return to the city and in two weeks her ship would sail.

He stopped the car and they got out and walked. She had washed when they got back from market and put on a skirt and blouse. The September wind blew the skirt and she held it with her free hand, close to her bare legs. As they walked, she knew the place. It was where he had taken her the summer before, the place where she had told him that Grandmama said they could not marry.

They went through the woods and mounted the hill, Jerold slightly ahead so that she could use his arm for support. They reached the top and stood looking down at the woods and distant farms while the wind blew. At nineteen she was still small and slender, her bust developed and her waist tiny. At twenty-one he was a man, his face stubbly on the way back from Newark.

"I love you," he said, and she nodded because she knew it and she didn't have to answer. That they were here, together, was confirmation of all their feelings.

"Jody . . ." She stood facing the wind, not looking at him. "I don't want to go to Paris. I don't want to go anywhere. I've changed my mind. I don't want to have children. I just want to take care of you. Forever. For the rest of my life."

He waited a while before he answered, standing beside her, holding her hand. "I thought about that," he said, as though he had thought about everything, every possibility. "It wouldn't matter much to me. I don't care about having children. I suppose Richard'll have them someday. It's just that you're an only child. There's no one else in your family to have them. Your mother especially," he said. "I think she'd like you to have them. I think it means something to her."

She stood beside him on the last day of their last summer, the last possibility dissolving in the warm breeze. Two weeks later, with her family and Shayna waving from the pier, she sailed for France.

PART III
PARIS, MAY 1924

1

A knock at the door. "Mademoiselle Régine?" The turn of the door handle before enough time had elapsed for a syllable of answer. *"Voici la poste, mademoiselle."*

"Merci, Françoise." She reached for the letters eagerly. Usually she had already left the house for the day when the morning mail came, and she would find it propped on the dresser when she returned in late afternoon. Last night, however, the family had taken her to the theater and Madame Goldblatt had permitted her to sleep a little longer, although poor Suzanne had had no such privileges; she was in her last year at the Lycée and her attendance record was as sterling as her character. She would be neither late nor absent on account of the theater.

Françoise disappeared silently. Her unobtrusiveness had been perfected early in her employ and had caused Regina surprise and some embarrassing moments in her first days in Paris. A servant in this household was a kind of nonperson. She knocked on a door and entered before the knock was acknowledged. So invisible was she that the members of the family noticed her absence more often and with more irritation than her presence.

There were three letters this morning, the one on top from her father. She opened it without looking at the others. She had written in April with serious questions. Enough time had elapsed for this letter to bring the answers.

She skimmed the first newsy paragraphs: how they missed her still, how well her grandparents were; did she know that Lillian was expecting another baby? that Shayna had come to visit last Sunday, just to see how they were, what a lovely girl—eyes filling, she looked at the date of the letter, wondering what she herself had done on that Sunday—and had she heard that Shayna had gone to the theater with Walter Weinberg, Jerold's friend from college, when he visited last month?

The name, as always, gave her a start. She sat on the edge of the bed and dropped the hand holding the letter into her lap, looking around the room to reassure herself of where she was, that the wounds, though still tender, were healing, that the scars were hers alone to see. Then she went back and read her father's letter.

"We had hoped, of course, that we would have the joy of seeing you by summer's end, but I understand your desire to perfect your French. I was as young as you when I landed in the U.S., and with hard work, I have been able to speak English with little trace of an accent. Mother and I do not feel ready to travel so far this summer, but we have high hopes for the summer after, and if it comes to pass, I shall book a return for three. Most compelling in your favor was the letter written in Madame Goldblatt's own hand. She must surely be as kind, intelligent, and charming as you have described her. To read her letter is to believe that her household will collapse without you, that she will lose a daughter, and that her own daughter will lose the best friend she has ever had. Is it possible that you have achieved all this in half a year? (Although to us the time feels more like a year and a half. I have never seen a house as quiet as ours has become, yet while you were here, I was never aware that you were noisy. I'm afraid we acted rather foolishly when Shayna visited the other day. The poor girl must have thought we would never let her go.) In any case, my dear Regina, you may have your second year. Did Momma write you that . . . ?"

She dropped the letter on the bed, feeling light and happy as the Paris spring. The rest of the letter could wait. If Madame Goldblatt had written the letter Poppa described, it wouldn't do to appear at breakfast when the table was being set for lunch. She took a fresh, springlike dress out of the wardrobe, slipped it on quickly, and hurried downstairs, where the smell of fresh coffee drew her like a magnet to the table set for one tardy American.

The second letter was from Shayna. In the months since Regina's departure, this correspondence had developed into the richest of all the correspondences she maintained. In letters they revealed themselves in ways their conversations had not approached. This letter was full of Walter. He had come to New York in January on a short business trip and written ahead to invite her to the theater. It had been a wonderful evening. Then, in April, Walter had returned to visit Regina's cousin. (She held the letter aside and watched, from her stone bench, the people that passed, always some young and happy couples, now an American and his wife looking bewilderedly from map to tree to sky as though the answer to their question had its origin in heaven.) Again he had written ahead and again she had accepted happily. Walter had invited Jerold to join them, but Jerold had insisted on remaining home to study. Law school was very demanding.

Regina read through the rest of the letter, but the sense was gone from the words. She put it back in its envelope, the top page at the bottom. Tomorrow she would read the remainder, minus the first page. She would like it better that way.

He had written her once, in February, after his first exams were over and he had gotten the results. It had been a long letter, full of news that she welcomed and feelings that still matched her own. He was working very hard and, he knew now, successfully. She had been right; the studies were interesting and challenging. They had helped to ease the pain. He had told his father he was glad he had entered law school. His father was easier to talk to. She should not write, only not forget him.

In a household where servants entered one's room without waiting for permission, one learned not to cry, even in private.

92

The third letter was a potpourri from her grandparents and Millie. Poppi started the letter in his all but illegible hand. Then Millie added a few paragraphs in her large, easy-to-read childish script, and finally Grandmama added some words at the end, not always intelligible but always welcome. Arthur was doing well in school—Millie was unable to find fault with any member of her immediate family, particularly her little brother—and Aunt Bertha had fixed up the house really beautifully over the winter. How clever of Regina to earn money by tutoring English. What would she spend it on? Lillian had mentioned that French perfumes were very fine. Did one smell these fine perfumes as one walked down the streets of Paris?

Regina smiled. Sweet Millie. She would send her some perfume for her birthday. That would please Millie and give her the chance to irritate Lillian, the only member of the family Millie delighted in annoying. But Lillian would get something too, something lacy and fine for the new baby.

She stood, slipping the letters into her bag, and walked slowly through the Tuileries. The gardens were coming to life and she had plenty of time to admire them. It was Friday, the day of the week she reserved for herself. Earlier in the week she took classes and gave English lessons, but Friday was her own.

The English lessons had caused some consternation in the Goldblatt home. Young ladies did not work. What would people think? And did she truly need the money? Finally, after several days of discussion and thought, Monsieur Goldblatt had touched his small mustache and pronounced his decision. What in fact might not be proper for a French girl might indeed be acceptable for an American. Régine could teach English, but she should limit her classes to girls and she should charge a fair price, which he himself would determine.

The lessons increased her acquaintanceships and gave her entrance to homes beyond those to which she was ordinarily invited. And the classes that she had signed up for, guilty for having left Hunter, gave her entrance to an intellectual world she was sure she could not have found on East Sixty-eighth Street. She read the great books of France in French, listened to them discussed in French, sat with a group of students she had gotten to know and drank cheap wine and talked about the meaning of the books, and the meaning of the war they had all painfully survived, and the meaning of everything else they could think of and put a name to.

"Excuse me."

She turned, surprised at being addressed in English. "Yes?"

"You're American, aren't you?" The woman certainly was.

"Yes."

"I thought so. You were reading letters with American stamps. Do you know your way around? We're lost."

"I'll be glad to help you."

"Is this the Left Bank or the Right Bank?"

Regina smiled. "It's the Right Bank. What are you looking for?"

"The other one, I guess." The woman gave her husband a glance indicating the extent to which he had failed her.

"Over there." Regina pointed. "That's the river. The other side is the Left Bank."

"Do you know where we can get a taxi?"

"You don't need a taxi. There are bridges every block or so. Just walk across. You'll be on the Left Bank before you even find a taxi."

The woman turned to her husband with long-suffering eyes. A little breeze blew, and she held a gloved hand to her hat.

"Well, let's start over, shall we?" he asked.

The woman heaved a sigh and took his arm.

"Thank you," the man called back, and Regina waved.

There were regulars in the garden today, an old woman who fed pigeons and talked to them, other younger people she recognized from other Fridays. Some nodded and smiled, some kept secretively to themselves. A woman walked a white poodle, casting seductive eyes at every man she passed. A young man whistled something vaguely familiar, avoiding the eyes of the woman with the dog.

It was past noon and Regina turned and started back. She would lunch in the student quarter, perhaps find some of her friends and sit and talk for a while. It was Friday, and she would have to return early to the Goldblatts' and change for dinner. Tonight the candles would be lit, prayers would be said in Hebrew with a French accent, and ritual wine would be drunk. The Goldblatts were far more religious than anyone in the Wolfe and Friedmann families.

She walked back at the same slow pace, watching the woman with the pigeons, glancing at the paper a man was reading, digesting the headlines easily, almost as if they had been in English. A little boy had stopped to play with the white poodle. His mistress watched the child, looking neither pleased nor seductive. A man sat nearby, his hand covering a closed book, his eyes on the child and the dog, his face expressionless. He had dark hair and his legs seemed very long in comparison with those of other people sitting on other benches. Regina looked at him with faint recognition. He must be one of the Friday people, although she could not remember seeing him here before, as she remembered the old woman feeding the pigeons. She turned toward the Seine and kept walking. She would walk to the Pont Neuf, passing the Louvre. Then she would cross the river to the Left Bank. By the time she stopped for lunch, she would be very hungry.

It was almost five when she returned to the beautiful house on the Avenue du Bois, the sky still bright enough for her to enjoy the opulence of the street in daylight. All the letters that came to the house were addressed with the important XVI. Although Uncle Willy's new apartment was grand and beautiful, Park Avenue would never look like this. This was the Paris Grandmama had promised and Uncle Willy had delivered. It was over six months, and still she could not believe it was hers; still it took her breath away.

She walked inside, pulling her gloves off as footsteps came quickly down the stairs.

"Régine! I've been waiting hours for you." As beautiful as any girl Regina had ever seen, Suzanne, her face one happy smile, took her hand. "It's my English again. Come and help me before sundown so I don't have to leave it for Sunday. What a pretty dress. Have I seen it before?" They hurried up the stairs to Suzanne's room, the monologue continuing. "Did you see your pigeon lady today? See? I didn't even ask you if you went to the gardens. On a day like this, you must have."

"She was there." Regina squeezed the hand that held hers.

"And how many poodles?"

Regina laughed. "Only one. A white one."

"Ah." Suzanne feigned sadness. "Business must be very bad."

"Shh." Regina giggled. "Your mother will hear."

"Not a chance. She's supervising in the kitchen." She said it as though it were a task that usurped all one's energy and senses. Opening the door of her bedroom, she led the way inside. "So," she said, pulling a second chair to her writing table, "who else was there?"

"The man who smells flowers, a rather good-looking student whistling a song I can't recall, a little boy who played with the white poodle"—here Suzanne laughed—"and a man I know from somewhere who watched them."

"A man?" Suzanne's eyebrows rose.

"A rather handsome man. Maybe he's an actor. Come, let's look at the essay before we have to dress."

"Régine?" It was a small hesitant voice from the door.

"Go away," Suzanne said. "We don't have time for you now."

"Don't go away, Marc," Regina said to the little boy. "Come here and give me a kiss."

Still small at twelve, he was, like Cousin Arthur, the baby of the family. Fascinated with Regina since her arrival, he gave her a hug and a shy smile and departed. He was the sweet little brother she had always wanted, although Suzanne assured her he was far less sweet out of her presence than in it. Turning to the essay, she picked up a pencil and began to read.

She dressed quickly. Punctuality was an essential quality if one were to be accepted in the Goldblatt household. Monsieur Goldblatt, it was rumored, checked his watch more often than he checked his investments. A small man who dressed as if color had not been invented, he presided over the dinner table as though it were a board of executives. Formal and proper, he led the conversation, seeking opinions from all the children and discussing them seriously. To the outsider he seemed pompous, lacking in warmth, but Regina knew that he had directed the writing of the letter that had convinced her parents to allow her to stay another year. As much as anyone else in the family, Monsieur Goldblatt wanted her to remain.

She sat to his right at dinner, and to her right was the third child in the family, Maurice, the elder son. Twenty-four and completing his law studies, he was taller by far than his father and his hair was already receding, which his father's had yet to do. Shy, nervous, and bespectacled, he had scarcely spoken to Regina during her first three months in his home except to greet her and exchange polite salutations. Recently he had begun to talk to her about her studies and about New York, and when the question of her tutoring English had arisen, he had volunteered the opinion that she should be permitted to do as she wanted.

Tonight Monsieur Goldblatt allowed the conversation to ramble. Suzanne related Regina's day as though it were her own.

". . . and an actor," she finished, "sitting by himself on a bench."

"An actor." Monsieur Goldblatt's forehead wrinkled.

"I don't know who he was," Regina said. "Probably one of the people I see there when I walk through the Tuileries."

"An actor," Monsieur Goldblatt repeated.

"Americans see the best things," Suzanne said dreamily.

After dinner Suzanne played the piano and then accompanied while little Marc sang a song in his clear soprano voice. They drank strong coffee in tiny porcelain cups, and after a while Monsieur Goldblatt looked at his watch and announced that it was time to retire. The candles that his wife had lighted at sundown were still burning in their silver candlesticks when they mounted the stairs.

Regina closed the door of her bedroom behind her. She was the first occupant of the room in many years. Between Maurice and Suzanne there had been a sister. "My delicate one," Madame Goldblatt called her, her eyes filling. In 1918 she had died of influenza and the room had become empty.

Regina reached around her neck to undo the buttons on her dress. How long ago 1918 seemed. A quarter of her life had passed since then. She had turned fourteen that summer, and now, in a few months, she would be twenty. That was the year the war ended, the year Grandmama had a stroke. She slipped the dress off and hung it in the wardrobe, shutting the door and turning the key. It was the year Aunt Maude had died. She sat on the bed in her underclothes. Imagine, Aunt Maude and Madame Goldblatt's delicate daughter dying in the same year. Suddenly she drew her breath in sharply. The man on the bench had been Uncle Mortimer.

2

"The party is on the twenty-first. I would be honored if you would attend with me." Maurice stood straight and motionless, waiting for an answer. It was almost the longest conversation he had had with her since her arrival.

Regina smiled, hoping his own face might lose some of its stern concentration. "I'd love to go with you. Thank you for asking me, Maurice."

"No, no," he said quickly. "The honor is all mine."

It was the last Friday in May and they were both dressed for dinner. He had been waiting in the hall near her bedroom when she opened the door. She had heard whisperings about this party for nearly a week. The invitation must have arrived many days ago, but it had taken all this time for him to find the courage to ask her. She was glad he had. For years she had enjoyed accompanying Richard to parties in New York. Now she had a kind of second older brother who might take her to parties in Paris.

Madame Goldblatt decreed that she must have a new dress. On Monday they would shop for the fabric and on Tuesday they would go to her dressmaker. The family at whose home the party would take place was one of the fine Jewish families and Régine must be well and appropriately dressed. None of last year's clothes from New York.

Regina found the conversation very amusing. When the sabbath was over, she would write it word for word to Grandmama.

It was a week since she had seen Uncle Mortimer. In the first moment of recognition, she had perceived that he was no visiting American, no transient sightseer. It was only as she realized his identity that she had similarly been aware that he was American. Not his clothes, not his manner, not his actions gave away his mother country. He was not new to Paris. He lived here.

She had consulted the small directory of Paris telephones. There was no "Rush" among the listings, not that she had expected to find out. Besides, if a number had been there, would she have called? What would she say if she met him?

When the weekend was over, she returned to the Tuileries, half-expecting to see the scene of Friday morning repeated—the white poodle, the whistling student. But except for the pigeon woman, the gardens held nothing but strangers.

She did not write her news home. She kept it to herself like a precious jewel, taking it out in solitary moments to appreciate its beauty. Her uncle was alive. He had survived the wars of the world and the war of his own life, even as she was surviving. It was enough to know that.

Madame Goldblatt selected a blue silk chiffon. It was pale and almost glowed. It was light and almost floated.

She shook her head. "No," she said. "Some other color."

"This is your color, Régine."

It was true. She had worn blue to Aunt Maude's wedding, and blue to Lillian's. It was the color Jerold liked best on her. She would not wear blue again for a long time, not this year anyway, not to attend a party with Maurice.

"Perhaps green," she suggested lightly. She held up the end of a bolt.

"Your skin will look too pale." Madame Goldblatt looked troubled. Surely Suzanne never gave her so much difficulty selecting a fabric.

"This is a nice beige," Regina said hopefully.

Madame Goldblatt waved it away with distaste. She would not waste her time on beige. "For old women," she said. "You are young. You are very beautiful. The color must suit you. You must not change to agree with a color."

She looked through the rainbow of colors, the range of textures. An anxious, obsequious saleswoman accompanied her. She found the reds, the roses, the pinks.

"Madame Goldblatt," she said, holding a rose chiffon fabric over her hand. "Look, it's the same silk as the blue. Isn't it lovely?"

Madame Goldblatt smiled. "Beautiful," she said, her eyes alight, and turning to the saleswoman, "You should have showed that to me right away. It's perfect."

They took a swatch to be examined by the dressmaker and left the shop. In the street Madame Goldblatt suggested coffee and they walked to a café and sat at a small table.

"You should not call me 'Madame' anymore," Madame Goldblatt said before the coffee and pastries came. "We know each other too well now. You must call me Aunt Hélène."

"Thank you," Regina said softly, accepting the gift humbly.

"You have many aunts, don't you?"

"Yes."

"Good. Then I will fit into your family as easily as you have fitted into ours. There's always room for one more aunt." Madame Goldblatt smiled broadly. "You're such a pleasure to shop with," she said. "Suzanne never makes up her mind so quickly."

The dress was a work of art, one smooth, flowing line from shoulder to toe. If she had had ballet slippers, the dress would have taught her to dance. Suzanne called it her rose dress and said she looked as though she were in blossom. Maurice seemed thunderstruck.

Before they left for the dance, Suzanne photographed them and then had Maurice take a picture of the two girls, but little Marc insisted on being included. It was a funny picture, Regina in the rose dress, Suzanne in her everyday clothes, and Marc looking like a little schoolboy.

The party was surely the most elegant she had ever attended. Maurice pointed out and introduced to her as many of the guests as he could approach. They all knew him and were friendly to him. He seemed to relax among them in a way he could not in his own family.

From time to time there was an explosion of light as someone with a camera snapped pictures. A few weeks later copies of some of them would be delivered with the compliments of their host, the son of a wealthy manufacturer, who had kissed her hand gallantly at one point and congratulated Maurice on his excellent taste.

When school was over the family went to their summer home in Normandy and Regina went with them. Letters from home told about the farm. It was the first summer in her memory she would not spend there. Richard was now Uncle Nate's chief help. Jerold spent the weekdays in Uncle Willy's office and came out weekends with his father. Poppi worked far too hard, but then, Poppi would listen to no one.

In the fall the family moved back to Paris and resumed residence in the prestigious Sixteenth. Regina registered for a class in drawing. She organized her English students. One day late in September she saw on the calendar that she had been in France for a year. It was that day that she knew she belonged. She rode the Métro as easily as she had ridden the El, and with less fear than she had once had on the subway. She had friends of different kinds, those she knew from her studies and those she knew through Maurice and Suzanne. When she needed a pair of shoes, she bought them in Paris, although Momma wrote from time to time offering to send anything she needed. She spoke the language. She attended the theater. She had new French underclothes. Next week she would go to Madame Goldblatt's dressmaker and have her make a suit that she could wear to synagogue on Saturday morning. She had seen the seasons change four times in Paris and soon she would see them change once again. She thought it would be nice to find a room somewhere, perhaps in the student quarter, and try to earn a small living. There were companies that did business with America now; one of them might use her talents. It would be nice to stay. It would be safe.

She came home from her drawing class late one afternoon and ran into Maurice. He had taken his law exams and now worked in his father's office.

"Ah, Régine, what a nice surprise." Accustomed now to her presence, he spoke more easily to her.

"Maurice, hello. Did you leave early?"

"Yes. Papa asked me to pick up some papers for him, and then it was too late to go back to the office. Where have you been today? History? Literature?"

"I've just come from my drawing class," she said.

"Oh? Have you done something very beautiful?"

"No. I've become convinced that I am completely without talent."

"No, no, that's not possible," he protested. "You are very talented."

She laughed. "Perhaps. But not in drawing."

They crossed the last street to the Goldblatt house. Already she could see its clean white shutters, newly painted this spring.

"I wonder," Maurice said, "there's quite a nice little play I thought you might like to see. I could get tickets—if you would care to go with me. You always seem to enjoy the theater so much when the family goes."

"I'd love to."

"I must warn you, though. My mother doesn't think the play is proper. That's why she won't allow the children to go." "The children" would be Suzanne and Marc.

"Do you think she'll let me?"

"I'm sure she feels, as we all do, that you are quite capable of deciding such things for yourself."

They went on an evening late in October. The theater still presented difficulties in comprehension. Some of the subtler humor escaped her. Had she been with Suzanne, she could have asked for explanations, but she could never ask Maurice. She sat beside him in the dark theater and thought of Jerold. Jerold had never taken her to the theater, but if he had, they would have enjoyed it together, not separately as she and Maurice did. The audience roared with laughter and she brushed a finger beneath her eyes, removing the moisture quickly, before it left the mark of damage. She had powdered her face before leaving the house. A tear would not escape notice. One did not cry at a farce.

After the theater he took her to a café he knew from his student days. The place surprised her. He was so stiff and formal a person, she could not imagine him anywhere less than elegant. But he was here and he was comfortable. He even knew one of the waiters by name although the waiter was rigorously polite and formal to Maurice.

She relaxed with a drink he recommended and they talked about the play and about the theater in New York. She told him about Eugene O'Neill, but he was not familiar with the name. She and Shayna had been going to the theater since high school, sitting high up in the least expensive seats, although Poppa would surely have given her the money for better ones if she had asked. In the spring of 1923, when Poppa was already making arrangements for her passage, they had seen *Abie's Irish Rose,* and along with everyone else in the audience, she had laughed and laughed. Now she tried to explain it to Maurice, who smiled politely but surely understood the situation no better than she had comprehended the innuendos of tonight's play.

She looked around the café through the haze of smoke. The crowd was mixed, students and lovers, elegant two- and foursomes fresh from the theater, "slumming," as Lillian had once described it with distaste. There was something refreshing about the lovers. She felt more kin to them than to the carefully dressed theatergoers of which she was one, most of whom had come to observe, not to be a part.

She watched the waiter make his way through the scarce space between tables, stopping here and there to take another order or pull out his leather purse and settle a bill. A hand raised as he went by, a few words were exchanged, and the waiter disappeared behind a curtain at the rear. Regina held her breath.

"Maurice . . ." she said softly, her eyes on the man at the distant table. "Yes?"

"I must speak to someone," she said. "Will you excuse me?"

100

"I'll go with you."

"No, thank you so much, but I must go alone. It's someone I knew in New York. I'll only be a moment."

She stood quickly before he was quite sure what was happening and made her serpentine way through the café, her heart pounding. Would he know her? What would she say? It had been so long and she had been so young. Would he remember? Would he want to?

She stopped at the little table. "Mr. Rush," she said in English.

He looked at her without recognition, as though he had just awakened in a strange place.

"I'm ... I'm Regina Friedmann." He continued to look at her. "I'm Alice's daughter."

He pushed his chair back and stood, his full height bringing back long memories from a misty past. "You're her niece."

"Yes." She offered her hand across the table, and after a moment of hesitation he shook it.

"Would you like to sit down?" It was less an invitation than a question. She was an intruder in a life that had no room for intrusions.

"Thank you, I can't. I'm here with someone. I have to get back to the table. I just ... I saw you last spring at the Tuileries, but I didn't know it was you until ..." She stopped, trying to think how to say what she wanted to tell him. "I only wanted to say I'm so happy you're all right. I worried about you for years. No one would tell me anything." She opened her bag and took out a handkerchief. "Excuse me. I must go." She touched her eyes quickly and started back, hoping Maurice could not see this far through the smoke. A young man locked eyes with her as she passed, and she felt his gaze after she had freed herself from it.

Maurice stood as she approached. "What is it?" he asked.

"A relative on my mother's side. We haven't seen him for many years." She sat and sipped her drink. "Thank you for being so patient." She turned the conversation back to the theater and from there to her drawing. She could make him smile by describing her attempts at art. She was glad she could talk about it lightly. The attempts had made her want to cry.

"Excuse me."

She looked up. Uncle Mortimer was standing beside their table.

"Oh." In her surprise, she fumbled between two languages. Finally she introduced the men in French. They shook hands formally and her uncle excused himself to Maurice and turned to her.

"It was very kind of you," he said in English. "That you stopped to speak to me."

"May I tell my mother that I saw you? I'm sure she would be happy to know—"

"I'd rather you didn't."

"I won't, then. I promise."

"Thank you. When do you leave Paris?"

"I hope to stay here. I've been here over a year and I'm very happy. I don't really want to go back."

He seemed to consider this. Her eyes stayed on his face. For all that he looked older than she remembered him, he was still the handsome, almost dashing man her aunt had married. The resemblance between him and Philip Schindler seemed very tenuous.

"I usually walk through the gardens you mentioned earlier," he said finally. "About ten in the morning when the weather is good. Perhaps we'll run into each other again sometime. I don't want to intrude now. Good night." He turned to Maurice and wished him a good evening in French. Then he left.

"An unhappy man," Maurice said, surprising her.

"He lost his wife in childbirth."

"I see."

"She was my mother's sister."

"Ah." He frowned as he considered this news. "You must invite him to dinner one evening, Régine. Mama will cheer him. No one stays miserable for long in the company of my mother."

"Thank you, Maurice. You're very kind—all of you. I've had such a happy year."

"And we," Maurice said. "It has been very happy for us too."

3

On Sunday she walked with Suzanne in the Bois de Boulogne and she told the story of her uncle.

"That was the year my sister died," Suzanne said when she was finished. "It was a terrible year."

"Yes."

"Do you think he lives here all alone?"

"I don't know. I didn't even know he was alive until I saw him last spring."

"Poor man." They shuffled through fallen leaves. "How old was your aunt?"

"Nineteen. It's hard to imagine. I'm twenty now. She was so beautiful."

"If you see him again," Suzanne said, "you must invite him to visit us. Mama will talk to him."

She kept her promise and wrote nothing of him to her family. On nice days when she had a free morning, she walked through the Tuileries at ten, but the weather made those days infrequent. In November it rained. In December it became cold. It occurred to her that he did not really want to see her again. He had left the States because of his connection with the Wolfe family, and he would not want to renew an acquaintanceship that would inevitably also renew old memories. It was something she could understand readily. If Walter Weinberg arrived in Paris, how much time would she want to spend talking about mutual friends and old times?

At the end of December a letter from her mother brought news of a second daughter for Lillian. A very pretty child, her mother wrote, and even the handwriting had a wistful look. How fortunate Aunt Martha was to have two lovely granddaughters.

Classes were over for the Christmas vacation, so she decided to shop for a gift for her new cousin. Suzanne was busy, requiring a last fitting on a dress for a holiday party they would both attend, so Regina went alone. It was a delightful excursion. She had never shopped for anything for a baby before. Lillian's first daughter had been born just after Regina arrived in Paris, and Momma had sent a gift from all of them.

She looked through masses of tiny delicate clothes, white and pastels, exquisite crocheting and embroidery. There were christening gowns as fine as any dress she had ever worn—or longed for. She decided finally on a carriage cover. Lillian had a beautiful English carriage. Now she would have a French cover for it.

She paid for the cover and asked the shop to send it. Outside, the air was bright and crisp and the day was hers. She turned toward the river. She had stopped near the Place Vendôme, and the Seine was not far. It was afternoon, but she would do without lunch. When she returned, Françoise would make her a pot of coffee and find something sweet to go with it. Perhaps Aunt Hélène and Suzanne would have returned from their fitting.

She turned into the Tuileries and saw him almost immediately. She stopped where she was, and he stood so that she knew he had seen her. He tucked a book under his arm and walked toward her.

"Miss Friedmann."

"Yes. Hello."

"It was very kind of you, that night last month."

It had been nearly two. "I must have behaved very oddly that night. It's just that we all worried about you so. I was glad to see you alive. We all wondered about you."

"We?"

"My cousins. No one would say where you'd gone."

"I joined the army."

"Then you've never been back."

"No."

"I've just been buying a present for Lillian's new baby," she said because there didn't seem much else to say.

"Lillian?"

"My cousin. Uncle Jack's daughter, and Aunt Martha's."

"Yes, Martha. It would be hard to forget Martha."

"I know."

"Would you like to walk? You look cold."

"Yes." It was an answer to both questions. They started to walk, slowly. "You used to make me laugh," she said. "Now, when I see you, I want to cry."

"There's nothing to cry about." A young man who looked vaguely like Jerold walked briskly by them. The wind made her eyes tear. "I'm really quite happy here."

"Are you?"

"Where do you live?"

"In the *seizième*. With a family named Goldblatt."

"Goldblatt? The attorney?"

"Do you know him?"

"Of him. You made a good connection."

"My Uncle Willy arranged it."

"Willy, yes. He's a nice fellow."

"He's my favorite uncle."

"He has a son, doesn't he? A little boy about . . . a boy about your age?"

"There's an older one too. He's studying law."

"It's been a long time."

"Do you have a car?"

He looked at her, and there was something of the old Uncle Mortimer. "You mean like that car."

"Yes."

"That was some car." Something of the old glint. "She loved that car."

But she could see that he had too. "My grandfather sold it after . . . after you went away."

"Your grandparents are still living?"

"Oh, yes. Half in the city, half in the country. My grandmother had a stroke just before the war ended. It was too much for her." She could see them in her mind, after Aunt Maude's wedding, Grandmama glowing with happiness.

"I once got it up to forty miles an hour," he said.

They walked for a while without saying anything. Then she asked, "Does your family know you're here?"

"I do some work for my father. He visited me last year."

"Doesn't he want you back?"

"Doesn't your father?"

She laughed. "Touché," she said.

"I do things for him that he needs done abroad. I don't work very hard. I enjoy Paris. Last month I went to Germany, next month England. There's some equipment there we may buy. My father makes woolen fabric, good-quality stuff. Rush Woolens. Have you heard of it?"

"No."

"I worked for him for several years, until . . . until I went into the army."

"You've been away so long."

"I like it here. I couldn't go back now. Your family . . . some of your family . . ."

"You should think of your own family, not mine."

"She didn't have to die, you know."

"I know that."

"Your grandmother—"

"Please." She stopped and looked up at him.

"I'm sorry. I'm very sorry." He shifted the book to a hand and she thought she saw the hand tremble slightly. "I appreciate your concern. I appreciate it very much. You're a kind and lovely girl, Maude always said . . ." It was the first time her name had been mentioned. Saying it seemed to drain him of the last of his energy. "Please don't cry. I'm sure you understand why I can't go back." He took a deep breath of the cold December air and looked around the garden. "One of the nice things about Paris is that I don't run into people I know."

Stung, she moved back a step. "I'd better get home," she said.

"I didn't mean you, Miss Friedmann . . . Regina. It's very gracious of you to stand out in the cold and talk to me. It reminds me that I once had a warm home I could have invited you into." He said it with a small smile, as if the anger had passed.

"I'm sure you still do." She tightened the silk scarf under her collar. Perhaps Françoise would make her chocolate and drop a large spoon of whipped cream into it.

"Perhaps." He put the book back under his arm. "Since you live in the *seizième,* do you go home with a taxi?" The question was slightly taunting.

"No. I earn very little myself, and I'm careful with it. I use the Métro."

He turned and they started walking in that direction. "You said your cousin had had a baby?"

"Yes, Lillian, her second. She married someone who looks a little like you, but he's not as nice, although I don't think she knows it." She smiled up at him, and he watched her with interest. "We were all in love with you, you know. My cousin Millie said she would quit school and marry you if you would only have her." He made her feel terribly young, as though she were twelve or thirteen again, and she could see he enjoyed her youth, her openness.

"Millie—the sweet one with the high voice?"

"Yes. She takes care of my grandparents now, but I think she'd be happier with a family of her own. May I tell you a secret?"

"Yes, by all means, tell me a secret."

"It's about my Uncle Jack. I'm the only one in the family who knows. I was in a speakeasy last year—"

He laughed. "A speakeasy!"

"Yes. You see what you're missing being away so long. Anyway, I saw Uncle Jack there with another woman."

"Did you." He seemed delighted.

"A beautiful woman. Much younger than Aunt Martha. Much . . . well, more sophisticated." She embellished the story zestfully. "I told one of my cousins about it, and you know what he said? He said, 'Good old Jackie.'"

"I agree with your cousin. Yes, good old Jackie. I agree with him a hundred percent."

"Well, good-bye." She held out her hand. "It's good to see you laugh again."

He pulled his glove off and shook her hand. "Good-bye."

She hurried down the stairs, shaking her own glove above her head as she ran.

On New Year's Eve Suzanne fell in love. The match, if not made in heaven, certainly had the blessings of her parents, whose glee at the auspicious meeting was scarcely concealed. The young man's parents were known to the Goldblatts and admired. The couple had met at various times earlier in their lives, but something magical had happened on the last night of the year and Suzanne awoke on New Year's Day in a haze of love. He had invited her to the theater on an evening two weeks later and she knew there would never be another man in her life.

She crept into Regina's room early on New Year's morning, when the sun had barely risen and there were hours more to sleep before a large, late breakfast would be served.

"Régine?" she whispered loud enough to wake Marc, who slept next door."

"Oh, no. What is it?"

"I'm going to marry Étienne."

Regina pulled herself up under the satin comforter and peered through the darkness. "That's wonderful," she said. "Did he ask you?"

"Of course not, silly. We only met last night. But I will, you'll see."

"Good. I'll go to the dressmaker tomorrow and—"

Suzanne giggled. "It will be out of date by that time. He has his medical studies to finish. Isn't he wonderful, Régine?"

"Yes. I had my eye on him myself."

Suzanne laughed her lovely tinkling laughter. "You didn't."

"No, I didn't, but he seems very nice."

Suzanne took her robe off and crawled into Regina's bed. "Mm, nice and warm. Have you ever been in love?"

"Once, just a little."

"How did it feel?"

"Wonderful."

"Why didn't you ever tell me?"

She shrugged, but it only moved the pillow a little. "I never told anyone."

"What happened?"

"Nothing."

"He didn't marry another girl?"

"No."

"Then . . . ?"

"We stopped seeing each other."

"But why?"

"We . . . we couldn't marry."

"Ah. He wasn't Jewish."

"Yes, that's right." She accepted the convenient explanation gratefully.

"Here that's not so important, at least not for the girls." She giggled again. "But then, it's the men that always do it. I couldn't, of course. My parents wouldn't allow it."

"I know."

"Do you still love him?"

"Yes." The conversation had become very painful.

"It's why you came here, isn't it?"

"Yes."

"My poor Régine."

They lay in the darkness, thinking separate thoughts.

"It wasn't just a little love, was it?" Suzanne asked.

"No. It was a big, wonderful, unforgettable . . ." She wanted a dozen adjectives, but they eluded her, and besides, if she had them, they would be unspeakable, as the love was.

"I'm so glad," Suzanne said, touching her arm. "At least someone in this house will know how I feel."

In January Uncle Mortimer wrote her a short note from England thanking her for her kindness. Étienne became a regular visitor on Sundays, and having lost her weekend companion, Regina began accepting invitations from her university friends to visit museums, climb the steps to Montmartre, sit in little cafés and talk about where their lives were going. Visiting the museums with her friends was as different from visiting them with the Goldblatts as Paris was from New York. Aunt Hélène thought all artists should paint as Renoir had. The test of a good painting was whether one would hang it in one's living room. Picasso, for her part, had lost his ability to paint when he had come to Paris, and as for his morals . . .

But her friends showed her where Picasso's first studio had been when he had arrived in the year in which she had been born, and then where he was working at that very minute. Once they saw him leave the building, all by himself, walking with quick strides down the street and then turning a corner and disappearing. Another time she saw the Russian woman he was married to leave the building with a small boy and enter a waiting car. She wrote about it to her parents, and they responded enthusiastically.

What they didn't say was whether they would visit in the summer, and for some reason they stopped talking about her coming home. Letter after letter arrived, and there was nothing on the page or between the lines. It was as though they had forgotten that she was halfway through her second year or else they were waiting for her to say something and she didn't know what to say.

In February Lillian wrote an effusive thank-you for the carriage cover. Baby Celia looked like a princess sleeping in such luxury on their walks in the afternoon. Now that there were two children, she was looking for a new apartment, but the right one was terribly hard to find. There would have to be a maid's room, of course, and she didn't want anything drafty or too far from Phil's subway and she did want to live among the right kind of people. She hoped they could be settled by May because her most exciting news was that she and Phil would be visiting London and Paris in the spring and they *definitely* wanted to see Regina.

Later that month, a year after his first one, a letter arrived from Jerold. Richard would graduate in the spring and was considering a job with someone in publishing, a friend of their father. Not only that, Richard had expressed the rather firm desire to live in a place of his own, preferably down in the Greenwich Village area. Aunt Eva was heartbroken but Uncle Willy was giving it some thought. He ended the letter "I never forget you," and she put it away with the other one, the 1924 letter, and went into Marc's room and helped him with his English, immersing herself in his questions, grateful that he was there, that they all were there, that they all loved each other.

She gave up the drawing class and signed up for one recommended by a friend at the university. Here she could work with color and the teacher was modern and experimental. Aunt Hélène raised her eyebrows at some of the work she did, but she enjoyed it more than anything else she had tried. She invented patterns and mixed colors and won the instructor's approval. He took some of her attempts and gave them to a colleague who transferred them onto various fabrics—silk, cotton, even the kind of burlap used to bag potatoes. The results were exotic and exciting. She wanted to learn the techniques involved in transferring the patterns herself, and her teacher suggested a course of study for the following fall. She left the studio one afternoon in March and ran into her uncle.

He was carrying a bread under his arm the way the French did, and a few groceries.

"Hello," she said exuberantly. "You must live near here."

"Down the street. How are you?"

"Bursting. I'm so glad I ran into you. I want to tell someone all about it in English."

"I'm in something of a hurry," he said.

"Oh. I'm sorry. I didn't mean to presume." She juggled the folder of papers so that she held them more comfortably. "It was nice to see you. Take care of yourself."

She turned and started down the block toward the Métro station on the Boulevard Rochechouart. She would be home in half an hour and she would tell Suzanne. Suzanne thought her new work was beautiful. Maurice didn't think so but, very politely, he told her he did.

"Regina . . ."

She turned. Her uncle was almost beside her.

"That was very rude of me. I'm really not that pressed for time. If you'll give me a minute to put these things away, I'll take you somewhere for coffee. A drink, if you'd rather. I can't offer you a speakeasy . . ."

She laughed. "That's very kind of you. The speakeasy is a secret. My father would never understand."

"I wouldn't think so."

They began walking. "That's my teacher's studio," she said, pointing. "On the top floor. I paint there. It's the best afternoon of the week. Have you ever painted?"

"No. Maude did."

"I didn't know that."

"She was very talented." He stopped at a door painted a shiny dark green. Where the paint had chipped near the edge, an older brown showed through, layer upon layer of color thickening the surface, generations of history buried on a single door. "This is where I live." He looked up and down the street. "Do you mind waiting? I'll only be a minute."

"I don't mind."

He opened the door and started in, then stopped. "Look, why don't you come up? I'd rather you didn't stand down here alone."

"All right."

They walked up two dark flights and he unlocked a door. Inside, the room was sparely furnished and very tidy. A wooden table and two chairs stood near a window, and in the corner beyond, a small kerosene stove rested on a cabinet. On the opposite wall, near where she had entered, there was an old couch and two heavy chairs. He went to a stove with a bucket of coal on one side and a pile of briquettes on the other and got a fire going.

"If you look out that window to the right, you'll see the Sacré Coeur."

"How marvelous." She put her things on the table, unlatched the window, and pulled it open. Below, a tiny courtyard waited for spring. Off to the right, the great church sat majestically on its hill. "It's beautiful. No wonder you live here."

"It pays for a handful of inconveniences. You were very excited about something when I met you in the street. Is it your painting?" He closed the stove, put his groceries away, and brought a bottle of whiskey up from a cabinet.

"Yes." She pushed the window closed, latched it, and brushed her hands together. "I like what I'm doing and my instructor likes what I'm doing. In the fall I tried drawing but I was terrible." She walked back to the center of the room.

"Drink?"

"No, thank you. I'd prefer coffee." She started to unbutton her coat, turning toward a dresser set in an alcove that the door had hidden as they entered. The top of the dresser was covered with framed pictures: Maude as a bride, Maude in her traveling suit, Maude and Mortimer on a beach, Maude and her friend in summer dresses almost down to their ankles, Maude and Poppi sitting in the front seat of the Pierce-Arrow, an oval formal portrait of Maude, even Maude in a laughing side view ostentatiously projecting an obviously pregnant midsection.

A match was struck and she smelled kerosene as the stove ignited. Somewhere nearby water ran briefly into a metal container. She stood transfixed, her eyes moving from picture to picture and then again to the first one.

"You were saying?"

"You can't live like this." The words just came out.

"I can't . . . ?" He took a few steps and looked toward the dresser. "Oh, Yes. Well, now you know how I live."

"My aunt was the happiest person I ever knew."

"She had every right to be. Her family let her think she was in perfect health. They told her a fairy tale as if she were a small child. One deception followed another, and here I am and there she is." He nodded toward the dresser. "Will you take your coat off or will you leave now that I've insulted your family?"

She looked at him briefly, then unbuttoned her coat. He took it from her, carrying it through a door on the far wall. Beyond the door she could see a tiny room with a bed and little else. He returned and closed the door behind him. In the stove the fire crackled. The room was starting to warm.

"There were other things too," he said. "Maybe your Aunt Martha will tell you about them the night before you marry."

"You mean about the other brother?"

"Are they spilling their secrets now?"

"No. I found a book of family pictures and the envelope with all the ones that had been removed. I asked my Aunt Eva about it. It took her two months to tell me." Steam issued from the kettle on the little stove. She watched it, fascinated. "There was a second brother with the same problem. After my mother was born. I don't think Martha even knew about that one."

He looked surprised but said nothing. Moving to the kettle, he took it off the flame and began to make coffee. The aroma filled the room. She walked to the table, removed her things, and sat in one of the chairs. He put two large ceramic cups and saucers out and filled a pitcher with milk from a half-liter bottle he had brought in with the bread. He poured the coffee and left the pot on the table.

"Is that why you came to Paris?" he asked.

She said nothing. Her reasons, like his, were bound up with the Wolfe family. They were not easy to talk about. He could escape them by moving. She would carry them with her as long as she lived.

110

"Forgive me," he said. "I shouldn't have asked. We should talk more about cars and less about personal things."

"I thought I would like living here," she said, not looking up. "Grandmama told me about Paris from the time I was very young. She knows us all very well and she knew I would be the one who would want to go. Sometimes I think she knows what we want before we even think it ourselves." She tried the coffee. It was strong, the way the French made it. "It's good," she said, smiling at him. "She was right. It's a wonderful place."

"You seemed very happy when I met you in the street."

"Paris makes me happy. Don't you think the sun shines brighter in Paris?"

"I'm sure it does," he said, "for you." He uncorked the bottle of whiskey. "Would you like a little in your coffee?"

"No, thanks."

He lifted it as if to pour, then, changing his mind, recorked it.

"You don't have a car, do you?"

"No."

"I bet you miss it."

"I wouldn't know what to do with it here."

"I missed it. That first summer, I used to imagine I heard it sometimes, but it was never there. Uncle Nate got a Ford."

"Model T?"

"Uh-huh. They got very cheap around then. He only paid about three hundred dollars."

"A Model T is different. It's not a real car. It's just something you drive around in."

"I can drive one."

"Maude was learning. When we came back to New York after we were married, she said . . ." He looked at her and put his cup down. "I never talk about her, you know."

She put her own cup down and went back to the window. In the courtyard, a beautifully decorated communal tap dripped steadily, the water running off to nourish the shrubbery.

"My father would like Paris," she said. "It never changes. You can be born, live a long life, and die here, and all that will happen is that someone will add a coat of paint to the door."

"Do you like that?"

"I don't know. You wouldn't recognize New York, it's changed so much. It's a city that keeps moving. Still"—she looked down at the tap with its beautiful wrought-iron flying fish—"it destroys its relics, doesn't it?" She moved away from the window and looked at a shelf of books in a bookcase he must have constructed himself. "Oh," she said admiringly, "you have it." She pulled one thick blue-and-white volume out carefully. It was a copy of *Ulysses.* "Have you actually read it?"

"Twice."

"How wonderful."

"I can't say I understood it either time. You're welcome to borrow it. In fact, why don't you take it? I'd like you to have it."

"Thank you, I really can't. I went down one day to get myself a copy, but in the end I didn't. I think Madame Goldblatt would be upset if she knew it was in her house. She's a very proper lady." She giggled. "You should hear what she says about Picasso's morals."

"You don't agree with her."

"I don't think his morals make him a worse painter. Maybe I think the opposite." She put the book back in its place, and when she turned around, she saw the pictures again. "I knew Maude very well, you know. She lived in our house for a long time, all the time she went to high school. We were almost like sisters, although I always called her Aunt. I couldn't speak for her, of course. No one can. But if I loved someone and something happened to me—if I wasn't there anymore—I would want him to be happy. I would want him to have as full a life without me as he would have if—"

"You can't know what you would think."

"But I do. I do know." She thought of Jerold living in a small room somewhere, putting a log on a fire to keep warm, Jerold going out and dancing with a beautiful girl, like the one at Lillian's party that time. "I think I ought to go. Aunt Hélène will expect me for dinner."

"You have aunts everywhere."

"Yes, and none better than this one."

"Even with her rigid sense of morality."

Regina smiled. "She never said I shouldn't read it. She only said she wouldn't like it in her house. There's a difference."

"I suppose there is." He got her coat from the other room and helped her on with it.

"Thank you. Thank you for everything. For the coffee, for the view, for the Joyce." She turned to open the door, and there they were again, Maude in 1917, Maude in 1918. "Uncle Mortimer . . ." She stood with her back to them. "You knew, didn't you? About her heart? Why didn't you tell her? She would have listened to you."

His eyes darted to the dresser behind her and then returned. "I've been a little hard on your family," he said. "I'm as much to blame as they are—more, if I'm to be honest. I tried to tell her, but there was never a right time. She was young and sweet and beautiful, and one day she was pregnant and it was too late."

"I see." Too late. Like an echo. Too late.

"Maybe now you understand what I'm doing here. Maybe it's a little clearer to you why I can't go back."

She reached up and kissed his cheek, as she might have when she was twelve and helping him polish the car. Then she ran down the stairs, her heels thudding on the old wooden treads. She was already out on the street when she remembered she had left her folder of artwork up in his room. Under the circumstances, she decided not to go back.

The folder was delivered without a note two days later while she was out. The following morning when she left the house, her uncle was standing beside a tree near the front gate.

"Good morning."

She stopped inside the gate. "Hello."

"Classes this morning?"

"Nothing on Friday."

"Care to walk?"

She stood watching him through the bars.

"If you'd rather not . . ."

"I don't know what to call you."

"Morty."

She unlatched the gate and swung it open. "I'd like very much to walk."

He started down the street toward the *bois,* walking with long strides so that she had to hurry to keep apace. They went for two blocks without saying a word, and finally she stopped, her thighs aching. It took him a moment to realize she was no longer beside him. Then he turned around and looked back at her.

"I can't keep up with you," she said defiantly. "You said 'walk,' and I've been running. I can't run."

He looked at her as though assessing the challenge. Then he came back to where she waited. "I suppose I'll have to make an accommodation," he said, and when they started out again, he walked distinctly more slowly.

"Did you get the pictures?" he asked.

"Yes. I'm sorry I put you to so much trouble."

"No trouble. I looked at them after you left."

She felt her cheeks warm.

"I can't say I understood them any better than I understood *Ulysses,* but I liked them."

"Thank you. That's really all they're for, to be enjoyed. If I'm still here in the fall, I'm going to learn how to screen patterns on fabric."

"Are you thinking of leaving Paris?"

"I don't really know what my father has in mind for me."

"How old are you?"

"Twenty."

"Twenty." They walked for a while. "How did you get Albert to send you here in the first place?"

"I caught him in a weak moment."

They reached a corner, and he stopped and looked around, getting his bearings.

"We can turn left here and get back to the Seine. Or we can go on to the *bois.* What do you think?"

"I think it's a little cold for the *bois.*"

He took her arm and crossed the street. "Can you hold out till we find a Métro station?"

"I don't mind walking. I walk anywhere."

"Then we'll leave the *bois* for another day."

She had thought there was something he wanted to tell her, something about their meeting earlier in the week, or about Maude, or perhaps a message he wanted passed to someone in the States, but if that was the point, he did not get to it. He seemed content simply to walk, mostly in silence, often speeding up without being aware that his pace had changed, and then making a conscious effort to slow down, to accommodate.

About noon he asked, "Do you have plans for lunch?"

"Nothing out of the ordinary."

"What's ordinary?"

"I meet friends at the university."

"The university." He said it like an echo. "You live two lives, don't you, one in the *seizième* and one on the Left Bank."

"I live as many lives as I can."

"Yes, well, that's because you're twenty. Will your friends on the Left Bank miss you if you don't show up?"

"It's a very loose arrangement."

"I could take you to lunch." He said it as though it were one of many possibilities.

"Are you inviting me?"

He stopped and looked at her with something between surprise and irritation. They had reached Trocadero, and the Eiffel Tower loomed close across the river. "Yes, I'm inviting you."

"Thank you."

"You have a most beautiful smile. Your family has produced some beautiful women. Well, let's see where we're off to. I think I'll take you somewhere you haven't been. I'll show you how the working classes eat. Will you mind being the only woman?"

"Probably, but I'll do it anyway."

"Good. It's another new life for you, right?" He took her arm and they started across the street.

It was a hearty lunch, and although she enjoyed it, she was glad to be outside when they finished. The sun had warmed the air and he took her to Montmartre and they sat in a café.

"Whiskey?" he asked.

"Thank you, just coffee."

"I like to have a drink in the afternoon."

"Please do."

The waiter came, and he said, *"Deux cafés,"* and turned back to the table. "It's warming up. We'll have a good spring."

"Is this how you spend your days?"

"Sometimes."

"So do I, sometimes. Especially on Fridays. I've organized my week so that I can do whatever I please on Friday."

"I've organized my life so that I can do whatever I please any day."

"No you haven't, not really."

"I've done it the best I'm able."

She sipped her coffee and put the cup down. "If I have to go back, I'm going to take some of Paris with me. Like the coffee, the wine, some of the food. If I get rich, I'm going to buy a Monet and sit and look at it all day."

He looked out at the street, which Monet could never have painted, and then called the waiter over and ordered something which she could not hear.

"I've ordered you an Armagnac," he said. "I want one for myself and I'd like you to join me."

"Armagnac." She laughed. "That's very strong, isn't it? I won't find my way home."

"I'll take you home." The drinks came and he lifted his glass in salutation without touching hers. "I thought we might have dinner together."

"Oh, I'm sorry. I couldn't do that. It's Friday, and Friday is very special at the Goldblatts'. We dress and light candles and Suzanne plays the piano after dinner."

"Idol worshipers," he said under his breath.

"That's very unkind of you. I understand how you feel about my family, and I sympathize, more than I can tell you, but you don't know the Goldblatts. You don't know anything about them as people and you have no right—"

He put a hand on her wrist. "You're right," he said, interrupting her. "It was unkind. Will you be good enough to accept my apology?"

"Yes, of course." She felt suddenly defensive, as though she had been the one to make the unkind remark.

"My mother used to light candles. If she'd lived, I suppose we would have kept it up, but Pop didn't care much. She had a pair of pretty silver candlesticks she'd brought over with her. They're mine if I ever go back to claim them."

"She left them to you?"

"More or less. I was pretty much the one who was home with her when she was sick. Well, are you going to drink it? I want to get you home before sundown."

She took another taste and pushed the stemmed glass toward him. "Thank you for slowing down to my pace," she said.

He smiled and looked more relaxed than he had all day. "Thank you for not reminding me of my obligation to self, family, and country."

Lillian wrote giving the dates in June that they would visit Paris. They would start their trip in London, continue to Paris, and then travel east to Berlin and Vienna. She had never been so excited about anything. Most of her time now was spent assembling her wardrobe.

The letters from her parents continued, cheerful and newsy, and still with no word of an impending visit and no request that she return. Perhaps they meant to surprise her. Perhaps they were still debating whether she should be allowed another year, but she could scarcely believe that. Well, Lillian would be here soon and perhaps her questions would be answered then. In fact, as she thought about it, it began to seem likely that Lillian would deliver the message.

He was waiting for her the following Friday when she left the house, and she said "Hello" and they started to walk, this time in the other direction, toward the Étoile, and when they reached it, east. He pointed out interesting old facades, an iron grillwork here, a hidden gate somewhere else. He walked slowly, and she had no trouble keeping up with him.

"I should have written you a note," he said when they had walked for about two hours. "I wanted to have dinner with you tomorrow night. I suppose it's too late to ask now."

"It's not too late. I don't go out much, except with my friends, and that's not very formal."

"I would think lots of people would take you out. Alone."

"I don't accept very often."

115

"I start to think Albert sent you to Paris to get you away from someone in New York."

"Poppa didn't send me anywhere. I asked to go. I quit college to go. I had two years at Hunter, and now I probably won't finish."

"You sound very indignant at my suggestion."

"I feel indignant. I do what I want to do. Nobody sends me. I hope you've invited me to dinner, because I accept."

"Yes"—he looked at her in an odd way—"I've invited you, and I'm grateful that you've accepted."

"You're teasing me."

"Indulge me a small pleasure. It's been a while since I teased a pretty American girl. Do you like jazz?"

"Yes. We go sometimes at night."

"There's a new Negro group just over from the States. I heard them the other night. Maybe we'll go tomorrow, after dinner. Now"—he turned and looked down the street—"why don't we think about where to have lunch."

He would not meet the Goldblatts. He waited for her outside the house at seven. She told Aunt Hélène she was meeting her university friends, but Suzanne, dressing for an evening with Étienne, raised her eyebrows.

He had dressed carefully and well, and the April night had a fresh smell to it. They took a taxi and had dinner and he asked her about Hunter, what she had studied and what she had read. Later they took another taxi to a crowded, smoky club where the new group was playing.

"I apologize," he said. "Word must've gotten around. Let's try another place, and we'll come back here during the week." They came out to the street. "Or we could go back to my place," he said, "and have some coffee."

"Let's hear music."

"All right."

He rattled off suggestions. He knew the groups, where they were and the kind of music they played. The way he described them, it was like choosing a flavor for an ice-cream cone. They all sounded delicious.

"Take me to the one that has the best bass."

"Ah." He narrowed his eyes and concentrated. "Life is always a challenge, isn't it? Can you walk?"

"Sure I can walk."

"If you . . ." He stopped speaking and walking abruptly.

"What?"

"Nothing. Where did you get the name Regina?" He started walking again, slowly.

"It was somebody's grandmother's name. I forget now. Is anything wrong?"

"No. Maude was named for someone. I was too, I think. I should ask Pop someday. I suppose it's something I should know."

"No one will ever forget her, Morty."

"No."

They walked slowly without saying anything, but she could sense something happening within him, sense it because she had felt it herself more than once, something she had always associated with Jerold, a feeling of endless devotion and agonizing hopelessness.

116

"If you would take your glove off," he said slowly, "I would hold your hand and keep it warm."

She stopped walking and looked up at him, her eyes open wide and her lips not quite together.

"Are you afraid to hold my hand?"

"No." Faintly, because she was. She didn't hold hands with men, she shook hands. She talked to young men in bunches about the meaning of life, and then she went home to live hers alone. She started to pull the fingers of her glove, the smallest one first. The gloves were new and of black kid and they clung. Pulling them off was somehow like undressing, a long, emotional process marked by small milestones. She took the wilted glove and stuffed it in her pocket and offered her hand, palm up, a small white left hand that became lost in his large one.

"A good bass," he said, holding her hand hard against his hard thigh. "Around the next corner." He took a very deep breath. "I think you'll like it."

She did like it. Her eyes burned from the smoke and even her throat smarted slightly, but the music was invigorating; it was subtly arousing. The bass player was a tall heavy black man who seemed to match his instrument in shape and intensity. His small head moved in time to the rhythm. Watching him, it was hard not to move in sympathy.

They said very little. The place was noisy, the music loud, and something she had not expected had happened. Now that it had happened, she did not know what to say.

"Has my touching you upset you?"

She shook her head. It had upset her terribly. Only a short time ago she had thought of him as a kind relative, someone in whom she might confide her own griefs, her impossible hopes. She had thought of telling him about Jerold. She had considered asking his advice about a number of things. A month ago he had been much older than she. Tonight suddenly the gap in their ages and experience had narrowed to practically nothing. The touch of his hand had an unmistakable effect on her, and he knew it. He knew she was not a Suzanne having her first carefully prescribed attachment to a young man.

"It upset me," he said.

She looked at him and then away. A very small and very important fact of life had just been revealed to her, and the revelation was nearly overwhelming. She had thought, when she left her home almost two years ago, that she was forever immune to the feelings that Jerold stirred in her. She knew now there was no such immunity.

"Would you like me to take you home?"

"I wish"—she heard her voice faltering unexplainably—"I wish you wouldn't ask me things I can't answer."

"Let's go."

He stood and put her coat over his arm. At the door, he helped her on with it. Outside he stopped the first taxi and instructed the driver to take them to a corner off the Étoile. At their destination they began to walk. It was still some distance to the Goldblatts', a distance she walked regularly when she returned from classes. Tonight she would not walk it alone.

117

"Cold?"

"No."

He put his arm around her as though she had answered yes to his question, and they started walking. He was not wearing a coat, although it was only early April. The trees were at that point where they were neither entirely bare nor yet in leaf, but somewhere in between, somewhere in the budding stage, as she was at that moment, walking in her second April in Paris, her heels echoing on the pavement of the *seizième*. He stopped suddenly and kissed her, and she knew he missed the feeling of kissing as much as she did, more perhaps, because he had been married. She had never before been out with a man who had been married, never thought about what it would be like. Surely he would not be satisfied with a kiss on the street, any more than she would.

"You'll come out and hear some music with me next Tuesday or Wednesday."

"Yes."

"And we'll walk to the *bois* on Friday if the weather's nice."

"Yes."

"I must be a foot taller than you." He rubbed his cheek on her hair.

"More." She laughed. "An inch for every year."

He put his arm around her again, cozily, as if they knew each other now, and started walking. "How do you know how old I am?"

"I can guess—or figure. Maude told me once. Thirty-two?"

"Does that seem very old?"

"Not since you kissed me."

They had reached the wrought-iron fence.

"Maybe I could bring it down a little further."

She had never dreamed a month ago she would want to be kissed.

They listened to music together. They picnicked in the *bois,* both of them forgetting glasses and they had to drink wine out of the same bottle—like sailors, he told her, drinking rum.

In May she asked him if he would like to meet the Goldblatts.

"They know about me?"

"I was with Maurice the night you stopped at our table. He was the first to invite you. They don't know I've seen you lately."

"Give them my regrets. The Goldblatts are too much like . . ."

"Family?"

"With all the civilized urban trappings."

"I don't think you mind the trappings so much."

"I can't get back into it. It's too late for me."

She turned her head so he would not see her eyes glistening with new tears. They were sitting in the Tuileries Gardens, where she had first seen him a year before. "Then what will you do?"

"I don't know."

"It's not too late." She said it softly, speaking to the bench.

"Let's go somewhere for lunch."

"I said—"

"I know what you said. Why do you bother?"

"Bother what?"

"Crying. You see that I'm not unhappy. I live a nice life. I indulge a great many of my desires."

"You argue magnificently."

He took her hand and kissed the back of it. "You haven't heard from your father, have you?"

"No."

"I want you to be here in the fall."

They spilled over and she brushed them away angrily as a white poodle leading a mistress with brassy hair passed before their bench.

"Let's have lunch," he said gently, putting his hand on her shoulder, "and not worry too much about Mortimer Rush finding eternal happiness."

They went out for dinner every Saturday. "I'm going to England next week," he said as they finished coffee early in June.

"For how long?"

"A few days, maybe a week. Something for Pop." He smiled. "I'll be back."

"I'll miss you."

"We'll do something special when I get back."

"We always do something special."

He settled the bill and they left the restaurant. Outside it was warm and almost fragrant. "Pop's doing well," he said. "I'm kind of proud of him. It's his own little baby. Ever been to a woolen mill?"

"No."

"Pop's is in Brooklyn. It's not like one of those monsters up in New England, but it's a good size."

"Did you work there?"

"Not right there. My brother does. He's the machinery man. Pop and I did most of the selling. The offices're in Manhattan."

"Were you good?"

"Sure I was good." He laughed. "But they didn't really start making money till I left. Why don't we go up to my place?" He said it so offhandedly she knew he had been waiting for some time to insert it in the conversation.

"I don't think so," she said.

"Is it because of the pictures?"

"No."

"Well?" He sounded slightly irritated.

"For the usual reasons women don't go to men's apartments."

He took a few steps away from her and then turned and addressed her across the space between them. "Regina, I need to be alone with you somewhere, somewhere with four walls and a roof."

She shook her head.

"I thought you might come to England with me."

She said "No" very softly, but her heart was breaking.

He waited a moment, then came back and took her hand and started walking.

"Well, I shall invite him." Aunt Hélène was sitting at her writing table. "Write his address down for me, Régine. I can't think of anything more foolish than your uncle living in Paris and not coming here for dinner."

It was the week he was away. Aunt Hélène wrote a long note on her fine

119

thick writing paper and had it mailed the same day. The answer arrived a week later. It was lying open on Regina's dressing table for her to read. Written in correct polite French, it declined the invitation and intimated that other commitments would keep him busy for the foreseeable future.

"You mustn't worry," Aunt Hélène said, coming into the room as she finished reading the note. "One day he will change his mind, when he knows there are people who care. And when he does, our door will be open."

He was there on Friday when she left the house. It had been nearly two weeks since she had last seen him. She looked at him through the tall bars of the gate.

"Are you angry with me?" He stood on the street side.

"I'm never angry with you."

"Maybe you should be." He approached the gate. "We could take a train to Versailles." He said it like a question.

She unlatched the gate and walked outside. "I haven't been there since last year."

He took her hand and they started to walk. "I'm planning a trip in August," he said.

"I'll be away too."

"Oh?"

"I'll go to Normandy again with the Goldblatts. It's very peaceful there, very refreshing."

"All summer?"

"We'll leave as soon as Marc finishes school."

"I'm planning to visit the north countries. I thought you might come with me."

"You mean . . . ?"

"I mean exactly what you think I mean."

"I can't, but you're very tempting."

"I or my offer?"

She felt her cheeks heat and cool. "You. Very, very tempting. I couldn't spend a month with you and then have Poppa call me home and know I would never see you again. Even now—"

"Stay in Paris, Regina. Stay with me."

"Why do you do this to me?"

"Because I want you. Here. Close. With me."

"I have a family, Morty. My mother cried when I left. I'm their only child. One day my father will tell me to come home, and I'll go. Do you understand that? I'll go."

They had reached the Métro station but remained standing on the street beside the stairs.

"Let's take a taxi," he said, signaling a shiny black one that was nearing the curb.

They got in and he put his arms around her, cradling her like a baby, shielding her from the family that would take her away from him.

"Don't leave me," he said as the taxi took them to the train station where they would go to Versailles, where the gardens were all in bloom, but she knew that when the time came, there would be no choice.

* * *

120

Shayna wrote that she would graduate in a few days, and after a summer of some work and some vacation, begin to teach. Regina felt not a flicker of envy. She was safe and happy, and later, in the summer, she would speak to the Goldblatts about moving into a room of her own, somewhere where she could paint and teach English and continue her studies. She had already bought a small compass made in Germany so that she could tell exactly what direction the light came from in her future home.

Then, in the last week of June, Lillian arrived. She had written that they would visit on Wednesday at two, and exactly at that hour a taxi pulled up. Seeing it from behind the curtains upstairs, Regina went down to greet them.

"Lillian!" She hugged her cousin warmly. "You look marvelous. Phil." She offered her hand. "Both of you. Come in. It's so good to see you. I think I'm suddenly homesick. You're the first people from home I've seen in almost two years."

"What a *lovely* house," Lillian said. She laughed delicately. "And here we thought you were living in some hovel somewhere with a bunch of unwashed artists."

"We're very well washed. Come inside."

Phil left his hat and they went into the living room. Aunt Hélène had whispered upstairs that she would come down after a quarter of an hour.

"And you," Lillian said, sitting on the silk-covered sofa. "You look like a little French girl, like a regular coquette."

"Paris suits me. Tell me, how are my parents? What did they say to you?"

"Just the usual, didn't they, Phil?" She looked sideways at her husband. "Much love, lots of kisses. Are you eating well? What else did they say, Phil?"

Phil seemed more interested in the room. "That's about it," he said off-handedly.

"They didn't tell you to put me on a ship and send me home?"

Her cousins looked at each other, and Phil shrugged.

"And they didn't say anything about visiting here themselves?"

"I'm sure they're not doing that," Lillian said. "They talked about the summer when we saw them. I think Uncle Albert said something about Maine in August."

"I see. Well, maybe I'll get to stay another year. Tell me about your beautiful daughters."

At twenty after two, Aunt Hélène opened the door and the conversation turned to dinner the following evening. Then Françoise served tea and little cakes, and after that the Schindlers left.

They returned the next evening for dinner. Except for Marc, all the Goldblatts spoke at least a little English and the conversation stayed mainly in that language, although there was a great deal of explaining and translating as the evening went on. Lillian kept remembering tidbits of news and dropping them as they occurred to her, regardless of the topic being discussed.

"I suppose you know Adele started normal school last fall. It isn't like a degree from a good four-year college, of course, but I suppose it's all she can manage."

"I'm sure she'll make a good teacher," Regina said. "She's an excellent disciplinarian."

And a little while later, "You should *see* what Aunt Bertha's done to the house. You'd think electricity was invented just for her. Lamps everywhere. She has the lightest house in New Jersey."

Salad was served, and Lillian looked up. "You'll never guess what I heard," she said, speaking directly to Regina. "Someone told Momma that Uncle Mortimer lives in Paris."

"Really?" Regina looked around to see if the others were following the conversation.

"Mm. Gone all to seed, I hear. Drinks a lot. Lives in a shabby place somewhere. Doesn't do anything. Just a wasted life."

"I'm sure it's an exaggeration," Regina said carefully. "People who don't live in Paris seem to think the worst of those who do."

"Momma seemed quite certain," Lillian persisted. "Just think how many years it's been. Surely any normal person would have gotten hold of himself by now, don't you think? A shame, really. He seemed so fine when we knew him."

And afterward, when they were eating dessert, "You've heard about Jerold, of course."

She could feel her skin prickle, feel herself submerge in something cold and liquid and unbreathable. "What about Jerold?"

"That he's getting married. *Some*body must have written you."

The sensation of drowning, of feeling one's internal temperature plummet. "No." Keeping her voice very steady. "I hadn't heard."

"Well, he hasn't given her a ring yet, but he will soon. What was her name, Phil? We met her that time at Uncle Willy's."

"Harriet something," her husband said.

"Well, I know 'Harriet.' It's her last name I can't remember."

"I don't know her last name, Lil. How can I keep track of everybody's girlfriend's last name?"

Lillian laughed delicately, as though her husband had just said something amusing.

"That's very happy news," Regina said as though she had just heard of the death of someone she loved. "I'm surprised Richard didn't write. I get letters from him . . ." She stopped before her voice failed her.

"And of course my brother is doing very well," Lillian said. "My brother is going to be a medical student," she explained, and Suzanne's face lit up.

"My special friend is a medical student," she said.

"Oh, how *won*derful," Lillian gushed. "You must be so proud."

The conversation around her had become a mélange of languages and voices. It struck her that she could not distinguish one from another, male from female, French from English, Suzanne from Lillian. She had to be alone, but she could not leave the table. She wanted the comfort of someone close to her, but she could not share her secret. She wanted to drink something cold to soothe the pain that had sprung inside her, but there was only coffee now, hot and strong, and it burned.

Somehow the evening ended. Her cousins had loved the dinner and adored seeing her, but their schedule was full and they would not see her again this trip.

She went to her room and closed the door. The bed was turned down and she switched on the lamp. She had told Morty once, months ago, if she couldn't have the man she loved, she would want him to be happy. She did want him to be happy, but could she survive his happiness? He had written in February that he never forgot her, and now it was June and he was getting married. She would never go back. She would find a place to live, work at her painting, make a career for herself, earn some kind of a living. But first she must get undressed, lie down in bed, and cry.

The next day was Friday and she knew he would be waiting.

"What's wrong?" he asked, opening the gate as she approached it.

"Lillian came to dinner last night."

"They want you back?"

"No."

"Then what is it?"

"Just little bits of gossip. Lillian always seems to know how to touch your most sensitive points. I think I'm a little homesick."

"Come with me."

"No. I just wanted to tell you I can't come today. I'm going back upstairs."

"To do what? To lie down and cry because your bitchy cousin couldn't keep her mouth shut?"

She couldn't answer. He took her hand, and she walked with him to the Métro. She had left the house without her bag and with her hands empty she felt strangely dependent on this man beside her. They got on a train, rode, got off, and she knew suddenly where they were when they passed her art teacher's studio. They were going to his apartment.

They climbed the stairs and he unlocked the door with a large key. The room looked the same except that the coal scuttle was empty and the window open. He closed the door behind her, crossed the room, and opened the door to the bedroom.

"I won't touch you if you don't want me to," he said, "but I want you where I can look after you. I don't want you crying alone."

She went into the bedroom and crawled onto the bed, the foot of which grazed the open door. The room was scarcely larger than the bed itself. There was something comforting about its smallness. She lay thinking about Jerold, whom she loved, and about Morty, whom she had wanted to love in the same way, thinking mostly about how he had changed. He came in after a while and lay down beside her, holding her, protecting her from Lillian, who, like her mother, always brought the awful truth and dropped it where it would hurt most.

She could feel him next to her as she had never felt him before, a sexually eager adult man who desired her, and she wanted to be made love to that day more than she had ever wanted to before, but there seemed no point in it; she would only hurt herself and she would hurt him, and maybe that was worse. And late in the afternoon, when she was finally back at the Gold-

123

blatts' getting ready for the sabbath, she couldn't remember if the pictures of Aunt Maude had been on the dresser in the alcove.

A few days later, they were on their way to Normandy.

She didn't stay. She told Aunt Hélène she had work to do, and if she stayed in Normandy, she would not do it.

"Something is wrong," Madame Goldblatt said.

"No, of course not."

"Since your cousins visited. You miss your family, don't you?"

"I always miss them a little, but nothing is wrong. I promise you, the minute I feel lonesome, I'll take the next train back here."

"An absolute promise?"

"Absolute."

She left before the second week was over. Etienne was arriving that night, and she knew they could use the extra bedroom. Besides, she could not bear to watch Suzanne and Étienne together.

She got back to Paris and understood why the natives fled in August. Even now, in July, the heat was oppressive. Riding the Métro in late afternoon was nearly impossible.

With Françoise's help she set up a small studio in a light corner of the attic, but by afternoon the heat had built up to such an intensity that she was unable to continue her painting. Even opening the window, which was not true north or anything near it, did little to alleviate the discomfort.

In the evenings she dined with Maurice and his father, but during the days she kept to herself.

On Friday, the last day of July, father and son departed early for Normandy. The house became utterly quiet, like the evenings she had eaten at Grandmama's when no one was home, like the evening three years ago when Jerold had come to tell her he could not see her anymore and instead he had taken her upstairs to the room where the moon was.

Françoise was to spend the first part of August in the house, then leave to visit her family. Others on the staff would fill in for the rest of the month. The house was always occupied; it was never closed completely.

On the first Saturday she was alone, she wandered around after a morning of painting. Her university friends had left for homes around the country when the semester ended. Even those most reluctant to go, most at odds with their bourgeois parents, were no longer at the old hangouts. The city was drained. Students and teachers, parents and children, readers and writers, all were gone. Even the Americans, famous and not so famous, who caroused in Montparnasse through the cool and colder months, had left behind a mass of empty chairs at their favorite cafés.

When she came home, it was already dark. She had left word that she would not have dinner. It was cheap enough to eat out, and she enjoyed it. The franc had dropped precipitously in value since her arrival, and Poppa's monthly check provided far more than it had two years ago. In New York prices only went up after the war; here the cost of everything seemed to be going down.

The house was dark and she used the key Françoise had given her. A single light burned in the foyer. She left it on and made her way back to the kitchen to find something cool to drink. In the kitchen everything shone. The cook was away, but she had left her premises honorably.

There was nothing but water to drink. Regina went to the little room beyond the kitchen, the pantry, where the fruits and vegetables were kept. Entering, she heard a sound. She stopped at the door, at first curious, then frightened. It was a woman's voice, young and in pain. She advanced a few hesitant steps into the pantry, trying to determine the source of the sound. She heard it again, and then, a moment later, a man's voice.

It was Françoise. The servants' rooms were behind the pantry, and Françoise was there with a man and they were making love. Pivoting silently, Regina tiptoed out of the pantry and back through the kitchen to the foyer, where she let her breath out in a rush. She had known Françoise almost two years, and this was the first she had ever been aware that the girl had a life beyond the Goldblatts' home, that she knew men, that she entertained them in private. It seemed a doubly sorrowful message, that she had not been aware and that her own love was irrevocably lost.

Monday was a little cooler, and she painted until two and then came down to wash and change her clothes. The previous evening Françoise had insisted on serving her in the dining room, although she had particularly asked if she might eat in the kitchen. Tonight she would eat out. Anything would be better than being served in that large, ornate room alone at the long, empty table. More than she had ever believed in it herself, Françoise was convinced of a distinction between classes and was intent on its furtherance. Regina would not willingly facilitate those ends.

She went to the bathroom in her slip and splashed water on her face and neck, rubbing soap into her paint-stained hands. Being alone in the house gave her a comfortable feeling of privacy and independence. She would enjoy living alone if only she could find a place with minimal comforts. A bathroom down the hall at the Goldblatts' was not the same as a toilet down the hall in Montparnasse.

Rubbing her face dry, she went back to her room barefoot and closed the door. From the clothes cupboard she selected a light summer dress she and Suzanne had made together in the spring, using Aunt Hélène's sewing machine. It made her look boyish in the way the French girls were now dressing, clothes falling straight from the shoulder, allowing scarcely a curve. Of course, coming from the Wolfe family, she was not quite flat enough in the chest to carry it off successfully.

She sat at her dressing table and adjusted the mirror, picked up the brush, and began to pull it vigorously through her hair. It was shaped differently from two years ago, cut so that it fell closer to her face, almost like a cap. Suzanne thought she looked marvelous.

There was a knock at the door. She called, *"Entrée,"* without looking around. It was time for the afternoon mail. She continued to brush her hair, but no one came in. After a moment, there was a second knock.

She put the brush down and stood up. Françoise in love was Françoise losing her mind. Since when did she need an invitation to enter a bedroom?

She went to the door and pulled it open, a sentence in French starting from her lips. It never came out. At the door, standing hatless and wearing a light summer suit, was her cousin Jerold.

125

4

"It's good to see you." It was clear that he meant it. He looked happy and admiring. "You look wonderful. You look . . ."

Two years of steady healing and she could feel the wounds open with a wrenching tear. "Hello, Jody." Someone else's voice where her own should have been.

"May I come in?"

She stepped back, making no move to shut the door after him.

"You'll let me kiss you, won't you?"

"No . . . please." She stepped away from him quickly.

He dropped his hands, a look of surprise on his face, mixed, she thought, with pain. "You've spoken to Lillian, haven't you?"

"Yes."

"What did she tell you?"

She swallowed painfully. She would never be able to say it. She could believe it, and somehow she would live with it, but she would never be able to speak the words. "She said . . . she told me . . . she said you were going to be married." In a rush so that it would be out, so that she would never have to utter it again.

"Regina . . ." He touched her arm where it was bare, his cool hand burning her skin. "You know Lillian, don't you? Don't you know me even better? Do you think I would do that without telling you first? Do you think I would let Lillian be the one to tell you?"

Her eyes filled. Hot tears on her clean, cool cheeks.

"She really told you that?"

Regina nodded. She would never speak again, not in his presence anyway.

"She was just a girl I took out, Regina. I saw them talking together after I introduced them. I suppose I should have guessed Lillian would manufacture a romance. There wasn't any romance. There haven't been any romances. There's never . . . I haven't cared for anyone—not since you left. Not this year, not last year. Regina . . ." He put his arms around her tightly,

126

and she cried heavily, her tears wetting the shoulder of the very crisp suit he had worn for this special day in Paris when he would see her again.

He held her all the time she cried, as though that was what he had come for, to comfort her, to reassure her, and it worked; she felt comforted; she felt reassured. But nothing more. She would never heal again. It would be futile to try.

"Oh, Jody," she said when she was finally calmer, "I don't know what to do. It's two years and I still love you and I don't think I'll ever stop."

He took her hand and kissed her cheek. "We'll talk about it," he said. "We have lots of time, till the end of the month. Then you're coming home with me. They asked me to bring you back."

She had merely mistaken the messenger. Of course Momma would not allow Lillian to bring the word. Lillian would have informed her archly that on such-and-such a day she was to leave France. Jerold might coax, but he would not coerce. She could talk to him about it. She could make up her own mind. At this moment, she could hardly believe the relief she felt, simply knowing they wanted her back. And how foolish of her to think they might not.

They went for a walk, holding hands, along the coolly shaded avenues of the *seizième*. All his news had a vitality Lillian's had lacked. The messages that he carried from home were intimate and personal. Richard wanted to talk to her. In fact, when she returned, he wanted her to set aside three whole days when they would just talk. Uncle Willy was going to set him up in an apartment in Greenwich Village for a year while he worked on a biography of some obscure Frenchman he had become interested in, and then, perhaps next summer, he would go abroad.

"But you should have the apartment, Jody. You're older."

"It doesn't matter. He wants it more than I do. I don't need it—unless you come back."

"No."

They walked all the way to the *bois* and then back again.

"I had no idea how beautiful it was," he said. "There really isn't anything in New York that looks like this."

"Have you seen much of the city?"

"Nothing. I came in from Brussels this morning. I just changed and came to see you. I haven't even had lunch."

"I haven't either. I was up in my 'studio' painting. It's what everyone does here—if they aren't writing poetry."

"We'll have lunch together." He pulled a watch out of its pocket. "Or dinner."

"I never saw you with a watch."

"Graduation. From my parents." He took it out again to show her. It was reddish gold, richly engraved. "I didn't wear it that last summer. There isn't much use for a watch on a farm. And I wasn't much in the mood for anything that summer."

"No."

They had almost reached the gate to the Goldblatts' house.

"Regina . . ." He stopped with one hand on the gate, the other still holding hers. "How do you feel about hotels?"

"Hotels?"

"I mean"—he looked down for a moment—"I took a double just on the chance . . ."

A hat with a feather, and all around them the rush of Christmas.

"If you cry again, you're on your own. My last handkerchief is still soaked."

An August day in Paris, rarely cool. He had not even kissed her on the lips yet. A longing that spanned years and oceans.

"Only if you really want to, dear. You mustn't ever do anything you don't really want to. You were so awfully honorable back there when you opened the door and thought I was engaged. You wouldn't kiss me, and I've been afraid to try ever since, although God knows I want to."

"I'll pack a bag," she said.

Françoise made no secret of being pleased that Regina was leaving. She realized these must be days the poor girl looked forward to each summer, having the house to herself, entertaining her lover as she pleased.

They moved into the Grand Hotel in early evening, a room with a large bed and a bath for thirty francs, overlooking the opera, and they stayed a week. It was like something she had never had the courage to dream about, having him to herself every moment of the day and beside her all the night. She took him everywhere in Paris she had ever been, the gardens, the museums, the Eiffel Tower. They had a drink at a café in Montparnasse where she had once seen Fitzgerald and his wife drinking and laughing with a group of Americans, and another where she had seen Hemingway early in the day alone at a table, apparently writing. They walked down the Odeon, stopping in at Shakespeare and Company, and she told him in carefully chosen words about Uncle Mortimer and tried to persuade him to buy a copy of *Ulysses* to smuggle back to the States, but he wouldn't; he was a law student and that was precisely the kind of trouble he could not afford.

Afterward, he asked how Uncle Mortimer was.

"Not bad," she said. "Quieter. Not happy, but not unhappy."

"He must be past thirty now."

"Thirty-two, I think."

"Did you ask him to come home?"

"I suggested it."

"Tell me why."

"His family. You know the reasons."

"Will you come home?"

She shook her head.

"The same reasons are there. They want you."

"I know. I'm glad they want me. I wish they had come this summer. But there's so much I want to do here. I started so slowly. It's really taken until now for me to know what I want to do."

"You can come back again someday."

"No. Paris isn't a place you leave and come back to. It's a stage in your life."

At the end of the week he asked her where she wanted to go.

"Wherever you want, Jody. I can go anywhere."

"Berlin? Vienna?"

128

"If you'd like."

"But if you were choosing . . ."

"I'd go to one of the little villages in the south on the sea and just stay for a while. Then we could swim and it would be cool at night. There are lots of places on the coast between Italy and Spain."

"Let's go."

They went down toward Italy and found a good beach that was half-empty and moved into a small hotel.

"I can't believe your mother let you come," she said. They lay on the beach on a large blanket he had bought in a local store.

"She insisted."

"I don't believe it."

"Richard wanted to come. Desperately. He said this was the place writers came to, that I didn't even want to come to Europe, I was only interested in China. My mother was very adamant."

"Do you think she thinks that Richard and I . . . ?"

"I think she does."

"Thank goodness. That means no one really knows."

"Except Uncle Jack."

She laughed. "Right. Except Uncle Jack."

Love on a large French bed in the middle of the night and halfway through the day. Conversations on the sand early in the morning and late in the afternoon.

"Your birthday's tomorrow."

"I never thought I'd spend it with you."

"I want to do something special for it."

"You already have."

"I mean very special."

It was ten in the morning and they were lying on the beach. Only a few minutes ago she had awakened from a nap. She caught her sleep at odd times in small amounts now. There was no schedule to obey and few clocks to watch, only periodic hungers that were satisfied as they arose, followed with sleep and then, perhaps, a swim and a drink of something sweetly alcoholic.

"I thought we might get married."

A yacht flying the American flag floated across the water from left to right, headed for Nice or Cannes or Marseilles, or perhaps for the Strait of Gibraltar and the Panama Canal, continuing around and around so that one day it would float across this very horizon again as the moments of her life passed, receded, and returned in later years.

"We can't." She turned on her side to face him.

"You'll be twenty-one."

"Everything we said two years ago is still true. Truer. Everyone we love would be hurt and angry."

"What about us?"

"We'll manage."

"I won't."

She leaned over and kissed his cheek, rubbed his head. He had thick hair, still light brown. He would keep it as his father had. Uncle Jack's had begun to disappear twenty years ago, but Uncle Willy had all of his and he was only two years younger. "You will. We both will."

"I can't spend a month with you like this and give you up again."

"Jody, darling, it isn't giving up. It's . . ." But she couldn't put a name to it. "You know . . ." She sat up, seeing the yacht in the distance to her right, so far it was hard to believe something moving so slowly had achieved so much. She turned her back to the water, facing him. "When Lillian told me you were . . . you were getting married, I thought I would die. I thought I would just forget how to live. It isn't that I didn't expect it. I knew it would happen someday. It's just that when it did, it was such a blow. I couldn't sleep, and when I did, I had awful dreams."

He took her hand and said, "Stop."

"But I never hated you," she went on. "I was never angry at you. I never felt the way Shayna told me she felt once when someone she liked very much stopped seeing her. I still loved you, and I always will. I'm sure now—I know—we won't have Paris or the beach anymore, but we'll have what's important. We'll have this feeling. Not just me, both of us."

He pulled her down beside him and held her. The sun had moved over their umbrella and she could feel it on her exposed arm, hot on her skin. Everything this month was hot, the sand, the sun, the tears, the love.

"Do you remember what you said to me that morning after our first night at Grandmama's?" she asked.

"If you were all right," he said, rubbing her back. "I was afraid I'd hurt you. I didn't hurt you, did I?"

"You asked me if I was still happy."

He caught his breath.

"I am, Jody. Very happy. That's what you give me, more than anything else."

At night there was a breeze. Sometimes, if they had a late dinner, the room was even cool. They came up on her birthday and he shut one of the windows to keep the wind off the bed.

"Suppose I stay in France with you," he said.

"You can't."

"Why not?"

"I'm going to put you on that ship myself. Tuck you in. Wave good-bye."

"You want to save my life again, don't you?" He sat on the edge of the bed and touched her as she stood beside him, the bare neck and shoulders, the breasts not nearly well enough concealed by the constricting under-clothes. In a moment or two he would take them off her and she would breathe again. She would do more than breathe.

"You don't need to be saved. You're doing fine."

"What'll I do when you're not there for me anymore?"

"Someone will be. Someone will always be there. It's because of the kind of person you are. You're easy to love and you love back."

"Come home with me."

"No."

In Paris she had asked him to return the steamship ticket, but he had re-fused. They were booked on the *Paris,* which was to sail from Le Havre on the twenty-sixth. On the twenty-first they had a long talk about going home. She told him why she wouldn't and what she was planning for herself.

"I want two more years," she said finally. "I need two more years."

"They want you home."

"They can come next summer. Tell them that, Jody. They can spend a month in Normandy, and I'll travel with them the second month. Anywhere they want to go."

"Regina ..." He stood and walked away from her, looking out over the Mediterranean. They were at a small round table on a patio outside a bar that backed on the beach. She had never drunk so much, loved so much, talked so much, eaten so much in her life. She had never wanted less for it to end. It was a day's travel to reach Paris and then a separate trip to Le Havre. Another day or two and it would all be over. "You can't have your two years, darling." He was back, standing beside her, a hand on her bare back.

Something in the way he said it made her uneasy. A small eddy whirled in the pit of her stomach. "What do you mean?"

He pulled out the bistro chair of twisted wire and sat down, taking her hand. "Your father is ill," he said in a very low voice.

The August heat evaporated. She was struck by a blast of air so cold that it set her entire body shivering. She tightened her hold on his hand like a clamp, squeezing it, willing his strength to seep through her skin. It was the first moment of her life she thought she might be sick.

"They didn't want you to know." He moved his hand across her back. "Let me get your wrap."

She shook her head, and he stayed. "What is it?" she said finally.

"They're not sure. They want to operate, but he won't let them till you're back."

"Oh, Jody." She let his hand go and rested her face in both of her own.

He pushed what was left of his cognac toward her. "Drink this."

She took a sip, and then another one. It made her feel better because someone had once told her it was supposed to. "I would have gone home in the spring," she said.

"You know your father. He said he'd promised you a second year and he didn't want to go back on his word."

She sat for a long time while everything settled and a measure of warmth came back. But the summer was over. More than that was over. Poppa was sick.

"Please don't leave me, Jody," she said at last.

He kissed her cheek and mumbled something about wild horses.

It was all a rush. First they found the post office and wired her parents to expect her aboard the *Paris*. The next morning they took a train to Paris and the following day went on to Normandy to say good-bye to the Goldblatts. They returned on the twenty-fourth and spent half the night packing her things.

She watched the city slip by as she made her last trip through it in a taxi. All the people she would never say good-bye to. All the places she had left little bits of her youth. In the fall the students and writers and artists would come back and she would be gone. Looking out the window, she thought about Poppa, who had given her all this. In the end, it didn't matter anymore that she was leaving Paris, because she couldn't see it anyway.

5

The shock was seeing her mother. She had always been small and pleasant-looking, easy to smile, easy to love. In her whole life she had never spanked a child, although she had admitted to Regina that once she had been tempted to give Arthur a small reminder where he would remember it best. Now she looked wasted. Seeing her, Regina knew her father would die.

The operation was scheduled for September 15, and he insisted on working through the entire week before, coming home early and sinking into a chair, pale and out of breath, but otherwise looking better than Momma.

In the days after her arrival and before the operation, she visited her grandparents, sitting in the living room with her audience of three and telling from experience stories like the ones her grandmother had fabricated years before. She described the house she had lived in, the clothes, the cafés, her art teacher. Millie said that Jerold had visited the night before and told them about London and Amsterdam and Brussels.

"He said you could tell us more about Paris," Millie said. "I showed him the perfume you sent. It's so nice, Regina." She giggled. "I showed it to Lillian when she came to visit once, and she turned green."

Poppi laughed. "She got her trip," he said. "A nice trip it sounded like. She said you lived in a palace."

"I did. It was wonderful." She smiled at Grandmama, realizing she had kept their secret, doing nothing to stop Jerold from making his trip.

"Now, you take care of your poppa," Poppi said. "It's good to have you back. We got to walk on that boardwalk they got now in Coney Island. You ever been there?"

"Not yet. After the operation, Poppi. I haven't breathed any good air for two years."

The doctors said the operation was a success and Mother seemed cheered. Relatives from both sides of the family visited in the evening after the first few days had passed.

One night in the second week of his stay, Regina looked up to see Jerold at the door. Like the days when she was fifteen and shy, she felt herself pale, but she reached out her hand and he held it briefly.

"Look who's here, Poppa," she said, standing quickly.

"Jerold. Well, isn't that nice."

Poppa's sister-in-law, Aunt Dorrie, sat in the second chair and Poppa made introductions as Regina slipped out. She waited down the hall. The hospital had very strict rules about the number of visitors. Momma would come only for the last half-hour tonight, and then they would go home together.

He came out twenty minutes later, and they kissed when he reached her chair.

"How are you?" He took her arm and they went down the stairs.

"Better."

"He's in very good spirits."

"But he's so thin. He looks worse than before."

"So do you. You've lost all that weight I put on you." He pushed open the door and they walked outside.

"Better for my clothes."

They walked to the street and stood under a lamp.

"You must have a lot of work," she said. "It was awfully nice of you to come."

"I didn't know you would be here."

"I know." She opened her bag, pulled out one of the new handkerchiefs she had brought back with her, and held it in her hand. "But I'm glad I was."

He kissed her again. "Me too."

When she got back to the room, Aunt Dorrie was just preparing to leave.

"What a nice family Alice has," she said, tucking her scarf into her coat.

"Every one of them," Poppa agreed. "The best."

He came home on the thirtieth and began to improve. He ate better and began to put on weight. He sat in a chair except to sleep, saying the bed was only for sick people. Cautiously, Momma began to shine again.

In the middle of October a Mr. and Mrs. Gerstman came to visit one Sunday. They were people Regina had never seen before, but they seemed very friendly toward her parents. Mrs. Gerstman was stout and wore a rather old-fashioned large hat and a dark dress, but her fingers were covered with rings. She asked Regina many questions about Paris, seeming sincerely interested. She had had the chance to go once but had not taken the opportunity. She was glad to meet a girl with more sense than she had had. Both she and her husband spoke with noticeable accents of their native Germany.

Mr. Gerstman spent most of the visit talking to Poppa about Coolidge and business, but before he left, he turned to Regina and asked some of the same questions his wife had asked.

"I suppose you're glad to be back," he said finally. "What do you think of New York after all this time away?"

"It's expensive, and they seem to be building everywhere I look."

"Elevator apartments," Mr. Gerstman said. "Even here in Brooklyn. Pretty soon I think they'll be putting them in private houses."

"I suppose that would help Albert," Mother said.

"Albert doesn't need help," Mr. Gerstman assured her. "Look, there's color in the face. That's a good sign."

She knew it was one of the things people say to be nice, but hearing it encouraged her. "I think so too. We'll be going out for walks soon if the weather holds."

"You're a pretty girl," Mr. Gerstman told her, "very pretty." The R's rolled. "You look a little Frenchy."

"It's just my clothes. And my hair. Poppa wants me to let it grow." She stole a look at her father, who was absorbing the admiration for his daughter happily.

"Not at all, not at all," he said. "I changed my whole mind about that a long time ago. I like having a little French girl around the house. She's so light on her feet in those shoes, she almost floats."

"My goodness, Poppa." She blushed in a very un-French, unsophisticated way.

When they were gone, Mother beamed. "Aren't they lovely?"

"Yes, they're very nice. I've never met them before."

"Oh, Poppa knows them a long time. Mr. Gerstman is a manufacturer. He does a lot of business with Poppa."

"Oh." She sat on the sofa to catch up with the Sunday paper.

"What does he manufacture, Albert?"

"Tools," Poppa said. "Right here in Brooklyn. A big factory. You would be impressed, Regina."

"Yes."

"Started with nothing twenty years ago."

"So did you and Uncle Max, Poppa."

"What we did is nothing compared to Mr. Gerstman."

"What you did is wonderful," she said. "What you did is the best I've ever seen."

Poppa looked at her, and she picked up the paper and started turning pages.

"Maybe they'll come again," Mother said brightly. "Maybe another Sunday soon."

On a Saturday she visited Shayna in the little apartment she shared with her sister above the one their parents occupied. They ate sweet cakes her mother had baked the day before and sipped her mother's vishnik. Regina had brought gifts with her, bought on the last hectic day they were in Paris before leaving for Le Havre, a silk scarf, some perfume, and a book of French poetry.

"I can't believe you really went and you're really back," Shayna said, still admiring the scarf. "I remember that day we walked to the library and you said you wanted to do something different. I had a feeling that was the day you made up your mind to go."

"It was." She sipped the vishnik, coughed, and laughed. Somewhere in her memory French brandy burned its way through her body on a hot beach.

Shayna laughed at her. "I bet it's not as bad as absinthe."

"Different."

"You didn't . . . ?"

"Once. Just a sip. Don't look so shocked. You'll give me a conscience. Tell me about Walter."

"Oh, Walter." Shayna drew a deep breath, and her shoulders rose and fell. "Walter, Walter, Walter."

"You've been seeing him."

"He comes into New York every month or so on business, and when he's here, he takes me out."

"And?"

"And nothing. He's terribly polite, takes me to the best places to eat and the best shows. He kisses me good night." She looked at Regina from under dark lashes. "And then he goes back to Boston."

"What do you think?"

"Well . . ." Shayna pushed the plate of cakes across the table between them. "Am I a realist?"

Regina laughed. "I don't know. I thought you looked a little like a cubist."

"Hardly. I'm a Hunter College graduate with a job teaching fourth grade. That qualifies me as a realist if anything does. I think if I lived uptown where your cousin lives, everything would be different. Your cousin hasn't . . . said anything, has he?"

"No. My cousin Jerold is very discreet. I don't think he would."

"I suppose not. Anyway, I met a dental student over the summer and we've gone out a few times. He's very sweet and I think I like him, but he doesn't exactly have Walter's savoir faire. Not that you can live on savoir faire."

"No." She moved a crumb along the tablecloth until it disintegrated. "But wouldn't it be nice to try?"

"You see?" Shayna said. "That's why you went and I stayed."

She met Richard for lunch one day, and they talked about Paris.

"I wanted you to meet the daughter in the Goldblatt family," she said. "She's really lovely, but I think it's too late. She fell in love with a medical student."

"There'll be others. But thanks for thinking of me."

"I hear you're writing."

"Feverishly. Want to see the place I live?"

"I'd love to."

They took the train downtown and climbed to the top floor of his narrow deep building. Inside, a large room with a sleeping couch led to a bright kitchen, almost as large. Entering the kitchen, she drew in her breath.

"Richard, you have my skylight."

"It's nice, isn't it?"

"It's wonderful. It's just what I was looking for in Paris."

"It's not that great," he said. "You don't get much sun. It's at the north end of the house."

"Oh, Richard, if you only knew."

She stayed for almost an hour, admiring his accomplishments—the apartment, his new typewriter—and talking.

"I know you've been out of touch," Richard said at one point. "I still tell people about my gorgeous cousin. If you'd like to meet someone . . ." He waited and then continued. "There's a guy who lives just downstairs. You might find him interesting."

136

"Thank you, Richard. When Poppa's feeling better, I promise I'll take up your offer."

In the middle of November the Gerstmans returned for another Sunday visit. It was two months since Poppa's operation and he was planning to go to work the next day for a few hours for the first time. The Gerstmans made elaborate assurances that they would not stay long so that Albert should not be overtired for his first day of work.

Mother served coffee and several kinds of cake and after a while Regina excused herself to go upstairs to read. As she stood, there was a clamor of four distinct voices, insisting that she stay. She looked from one anxious face to the other and sat down again.

"Without your company," Mr. Gerstman said with a smile, "the afternoon is not so bright."

Fifteen minutes later, there was a knock on the door.

"Looks like more company for you, Poppa," Regina said.

"Why don't you answer it, dear," her mother suggested.

She opened the door expecting to see her grandfather, rather looking forward to a walk with him. The conversation had grown dull, two men talking business and two women trying to draw her into a womanly talk about prices and gossip. The man at the door was not her grandfather. She looked up at him questioningly.

"Good afternoon," he said. "I'm Martin Gerstman. I've come to pick up my parents." Behind him at the curb stood a new car.

"Yes, of course. Come in."

He took his hat off and she put it on the hall table and led the way to the living room.

"Martin," Mrs. Gerstman said with theatrical surprise, "how nice of you to come for us. Come and meet Mr. and Mrs. Friedmann. I see you've met Regina already."

He said a brief how do you do and greeted her parents while she stood aside watching the carefully arranged little drama unfold. She felt choked with a childlike gratitude. They had worried about her. She had been home two and a half months and had not gone out with a single young man. Friends had called inviting her to parties, but she had declined; Poppa was too ill. She didn't dare to take the time. Someone had to see Momma home from the hospital.

"You'll have a cup of coffee, won't you, Mr. Gerstman?" Momma offered eagerly.

"Well . . ."

"Of course you will, Martin," his father said. "There's no rush, is there? Sit down, Martin. How's the car running? Martin's just got himself a nice new Essex. Eight hundred dollars. Wonderful machine."

Regina smiled. She felt a little sorry for Martin, who had obviously walked in unaware and unprepared.

"Sit down, young lady," Mr. Gerstman said.

"Right here, Regina," Momma said. "You'll have some coffee too, won't you?"

"I'll get it, Momma."

"No, no. I'll be right back."

For a moment she was afraid she would laugh. It was all so obvious, so heavy-handed. She was awash with coffee, saturated with nonsensical conversation. The thought that these four adults had concocted this meeting was so ludicrous she could scarcely keep her face sober, but she feared that if she allowed herself to smile, Mr. Gerstman would comment on how bright and happy she looked and what could have happened to provoke such pleasure?

It was necessary, of course, when the Gerstmans left, for the Friedmanns to stand outside the front door and observe their departure in the new Essex. All six cylinders roared to life, failed, then roared again. Hands waved and the car moved down the street.

Momma was glowing. They washed and dried the dishes together while Momma talked about the lovely afternoon they had had.

"They're very nice people," Regina said, stepping up on her special stool to put a pile of saucers in the cupboard.

"And their son especially," Momma said. "So well-mannered. What luck that he came to the door."

"Yes."

"Maybe he'll come around again sometime."

"Careful, Momma, that one's chipped. Here, let me switch it with a good one."

He telephoned on Tuesday evening, introducing himself formally and then inquiring after her father's health.

"He's fine, thank you. He's been to work the last two days and he looks healthier than I've ever seen him."

"I'm glad to hear that. I wonder if you'd care to go to the theater on Saturday night?"

She could almost feel her mother's presence through the doorway to the kitchen, the sudden silence when the conversation began. "Thank you, I'd like to very much."

"Is there any show you'd specially like to see?"

She thought for a moment. "I've been away," she said. "I'm afraid I don't even know what's playing."

"May I come for you at a quarter to seven?"

"That would be fine."

She passed the news to her mother, who made a quick excuse to go upstairs where Poppa was resting. Alone in the kitchen, she cleaned the sink and wondered how she would spend an entire evening with a stranger.

Martin Gerstman was a quiet man who had reached the age when he believed he should settle down. He was twenty-seven and about Jerold's height. He looked a little like both his parents, but while he was not thin, he had not attained their girth. He worked in his father's factory, which he would someday take over completely. He had two sisters and no brothers. Both sisters were younger and both were married.

He recited the details of his life as though anticipating an immediate evaluation. She did not know how to reciprocate. She was unwilling to settle down. She would not inherit a factory. She had neither sisters nor brothers.

Instead, she asked polite questions about his family. When he left her at the door a little before one, he said he would like to see her again.

During the following week, Mother sat and talked to her about Martin.

138

"It was a nice evening, Momma."

"He's the right kind of young man for you, Regina."

"There'll be other young men, Momma. I haven't seen anyone because Poppa's been sick, but now, maybe things will change. I'm going to take an art course next semester, and I'd like to keep up with my French."

"You should think about settling down."

"I'm only twenty-one. It's not as if . . ." As if what? What did twenty-one have to do with anything?

"Poppa and I would like to see you settled, in your own home."

It was a cold feeling. There had been more behind the arrangement to meet Martin Gerstman than just seeing that she got out of the house for a pleasant evening. "I will someday."

"It should be soon." Momma looked very serious. "Especially with Poppa not well."

"Poppa's so much better now."

"Regina, the time has come. You didn't finish college. You can't teach the way Shayna can. You should have someone who can look after you. Martin Gerstman can look after you the right way."

She went out with him a second time, and then Richard called.

"I'm having a party," he said. "I'm inviting everyone I know, including the guy downstairs. Will you come?"

"When is it?"

"December nineteenth. How's your father?"

"Really fine, Richard. Can I let you know?"

"Since when are you so cagey? All my friends say yes and all my relatives act as though they'll wait and see if they get a better offer. Would you believe my own brother isn't coming?"

She started to say something, but nothing came out.

"I couldn't believe it either," Richard went on. "Don't you disappoint me too."

"I won't," she said. "I'll be there. I just checked the calendar, and it's a good night for a party."

When Martin Gerstman asked her out for dinner on the nineteenth, she said she had a previous engagement.

Poppa was angry. "How could you do that to him?"

"I only said I was busy on the nineteenth."

"After he takes you out for three weeks, you just say no?"

"Richard invited me to a party. I wanted to go. I had nothing else planned when Richard called."

"You couldn't invite Martin to go with you to the party?"

"I wanted to go alone. Richard says someone will be there that I should meet."

"Meet?" Poppa said, raising his voice. "What kind of person are you planning to meet?"

"A friend of Richard's. Richard says he's very interesting."

Her father looked at her for a long time and then shook his head. "For this you turn down Martin Gerstman?"

She hated to hurt him. He was feeling so much better, enjoying his return to work. She didn't want to defy him, but after three evenings with Martin, she was ready for Richard's party. The night she went, her father was pointedly absent from the living room.

The group was an incongruous mix of girls in skinny, supple silk dresses, young men in starched shirts and well-tailored suits, and a small group of men and one woman that Richard obviously knew from his new neighborhood. The woman was tall with dark hair pulled back from her face and she must have been in her late twenties. There was something in the way she and Richard spoke that made Regina wonder, but Richard played the host all evening, favoring no one.

The interesting man from downstairs was named Timothy McGuire —Richard introduced him as Mac—and he was a refreshing change. Dressed in rumpled clothes, he pulled his tie away from his collar soon after he arrived, letting it hang there as a conspicuous sign of his rebellion and disdain.

"Rich says you lived in Paris," he said, swirling bootleg gin in a water glass. She had never heard her cousin called anything but Richard.

"Yes. I just came back in September." She liked the fact that he had said "lived." She hated the word "visit." It made her sound like one of those Americans who were forever looking for taxis to take them back to their hotels so they could rest.

"Could I afford it?" He asked the question with no qualifying information.

"If you can pay the passage. Paris is cheaper than New York if you're spending dollars."

"Why did you come back?"

"My father was ill."

"I haven't seen my father for ten years."

She nibbled some salted nuts, letting his statement drift in the smoky air. "Richard says you write."

"I have a novel half-finished. I'd like to give up my job and just write, but I don't have enough saved to get by in New York. I don't have your cousin's independent income." He said it without malice. It was simply a fact of his life.

"You'll never regret going," she said. "You can get a good lunch for less than a quarter now that the franc is down. You can always come back, you know. But if you don't go . . ."

"I know. I think about that all the time." He drank from the glass, then drank again. "Are you sorry you're back?"

"No. One day in August I realized my parents wouldn't live forever."

"I'm sorry. I've been sounding like an inquisitor. Sometimes I leave all sensitivity to my characters. Would you like to come downstairs to my place? It'll be a little quieter."

It was the first invitation of its kind she had received since leaving France. She remembered afternoons and occasional evenings in people's rooms, keeping warm by a stove, talking about the meaning of life and the meaning of meaning. She would enjoy doing that again, even in a room with steam heat. He reminded her nostalgically of some of the people she had known at the university. He worked, he created, he was unconventional. The composite was very attractive. He oozed a magnetic sexiness. She could go downstairs with him and they would talk and drink and he would ask to see her again and then one night in a week or a month he would want to take her to bed and she would have to say yes or no, and either decision would be painful for different reasons.

"Thank you," she said, "not this evening."

His glance flickered toward Richard. "I understand. Let me fill your glass. It's looking kind of empty."

He came back with her glass and they talked for another hour, when she decided she ought to go home. He offered to take her, but she said it was all right, she would take a taxi. They went downstairs and walked to the corner, waiting in the cold for one to come along. Finally he saw one and waved it down.

"How much are the whores in Paris?" he asked as the cab pulled up to the curb.

The question startled her for a moment. Then she looked up at him and grinned. "About the same as lunch," she said. "In Paris it's an even choice."

He called her the next evening, dropping nickels into the telephone box as the conversation progressed. From time to time her mother poked her head out of the kitchen to see if she was still on the phone. Her father was upstairs resting.

He wanted to see her, and somehow it was the most encouraging, the most optimistic thing that had happened since Poppa went back to work. When he finally put the question to her, would she come down to his place on Saturday for dinner, she turned him down. His name was McGuire. Her father was already deeply distressed about her apparent defection from his plans. To anger him further was needless and unkind. McGuire would be only a passing fancy if, indeed, he would even be that. She wished him well and told him she would give him names and addresses if he made the trip. Hanging up, she threw in her lot with Martin Gerstman.

Martin didn't call until after New Year's. She heard furtive conversations both on the phone and off that she was sure concerned her cavalier treatment of him. Finally he invited her to a party in Brooklyn and she accepted.

She signed up for a class in designing fabrics at the Art Students League and a course in the nineteenth-century novel in the cluster of brownstones on West Twenty-third Street that were the New School, and once a week she had dinner with Richard. She explained about McGuire and he said he understood, but she kept Martin to herself. Saturday after Saturday he picked her up in the Essex and they went to dinner or the theater, once to the opera, occasionally to a party at the home of one of his friends. In March he began to visit on Sunday afternoons, and finally Momma invited him for dinner on Friday night. The whole weekend had become Martin.

She found that she liked him as a person. He was an honest businessman and a sincere person. He admired her accomplishments but he remained skeptical of the benefits two years in Paris could have in the life of a young lady. He himself had little desire to travel.

One evening at the theater, a scene on the stage touched her curiously. Images of her father and Jerold obliterated the actors caught in their fictional crisis a few rows ahead of her. She reached to take hold of Martin's hand, craving a touch, a feeling of warm comfort.

"Please," he said in a low voice that carried its unmistakable irritation, and removing her hand, he placed it firmly in her own lap. There was a time and place for demonstrations of affection, and she had miscalculated on both. She came from a family of hugs and kisses; she had loved someone who kissed her in the street when he needed to kiss her. Sitting in the theater with her hands primly in her lap, she knew she would have to learn a different, and less desirable, way of living.

She called Richard one night to make arrangements for their weekly dinner, and after he answered, there was a long pause.

"Uh, you called at a bad time," he said finally, and from somewhere not too far from the telephone came a distinctly female sound.

"I'm sorry," she said. "Call tomorrow," and hung up. But she wasn't sorry; she was glad, very glad for Richard.

She tried to talk to her mother about Martin. She explained that although he was very kind, very decent, something that she wanted was missing.

"Regina," her mother said, "that will all change after you're married. You'll grow to love him. Especially after the children come. You mustn't worry about it. You'll see that I'm right."

"But I want to marry someone that I love now."

"You're much too young to understand, Regina. Life isn't one of those plays you see on Saturday night. Life works itself out slowly. It doesn't come ready-made like dresses in a store."

But all she could think of was a shawl dropping on the grass and a room on the Riviera on a night in August.

The conversation left her drained and unhappy, not on her own behalf but on her parents'. She had always thought they had married for love. Aunt Eva and Uncle Willy had. Uncle Jack had, for all that he might have later regretted it. Hadn't her mother? Was it possible that Momma had married Poppa because it was the right thing to do, because he was a promising man with a good business? Could Grandmama have promoted such a match? Could she have *allowed* it? Poppa was the most lovable man she had ever met. How could Momma not have loved him the first time she laid eyes on him? What did Momma mean?

But she could not ask and she did not want to know.

On the last Monday of March, everything exploded. It happened suddenly, at the dinner table. She looked at her father and knew something was wrong.

"What is it, Poppa?" she asked as her mother turned to look.

"Nothing, nothing. Eat your dinner."

"Poppa." She felt a panic far beyond what the apparent situation should have evoked. *"What is it?"*

"A little pain. It's nothing. There, it's gone."

"What do you mean, a little pain?" She had stood and gone to his place at the table. She put her hand on his shoulder. "When did you start getting little pains?"

"This minute," he said. "This is the first little pain I ever had."

"Momma." She walked around the table to where her mother sat staring at Poppa. "Where's the doctor's number? Quickly. I want to call him."

It turned out, of course, that it hadn't been the first time, and it hadn't been so little. The doctor thought Poppa should go to the hospital for a few days, just for a rest and to let the doctors have a look.

At the end of the week the doctor told her "the problem" had returned. There was medicine they could give him to help with the pain, and Poppa could go home, but there was little else they could do.

She called Martin and said she couldn't see him Saturday night and explained why. He visited the hospital and took the morning off when Poppa was released, driving him home slowly in the car. The next Saturday night, apologizing for the haste—they had known each other such a short time, but surely she understood the reason—he asked her to marry him.

She told him she was too upset about her father to give him an answer, that she would have to think about it. She let a week go by while she saw Poppa decline from one Sunday to the next. Then, when she knew Aunt Eva would be out of the apartment, she called and left a message with the maid asking Jerold to telephone.

He called that evening and she ran from the kitchen to answer before Momma did. Since Poppa had come back from the hospital, friends and relatives called day and evening.

"Regina. I got your message."

She wondered if she would ever hear that voice without an inner turmoil, a shattering of calm. "I have to see you. Please, if you can possibly make it."

"When?"

"It doesn't matter. As soon as you can."

"I'll call you back."

"Thank you."

Half an hour later, he was back on the line. "Richard's place Thursday night at six o'clock. Is that soon enough?"

"Yes. Will we be alone?"

"Of course we'll be alone. Do you want me to call for you?"

"No. I'm fine, Jody."

She got there a little early and walked up the stairs wondering if he would be there. On one landing she heard a news broadcast from a radio, on the next, music. McGuire at work. Everyone in America had a radio now. When she had left for France, they were still rather new. In 1926 the radio had become a necessity of everyone's life.

He opened the door when she knocked, and kissed her, holding her very close, a man who loved and could show it, a man who could return affection.

He took her coat and hung it in Richard's closet, sat with her on the couch in front of the windows that overlooked the street, Richard's southern exposure.

"I don't know how to say it, Jody."

"Is it your father?"

She nodded her head. She would never be able to say it. Putting it in words was almost more terrible than accepting it.

"We heard he was back in the hospital. We were hoping—"

"There's something else." She spoke rapidly. The words would come out before she had a chance to reconsider, to ponder their meaning for either of

143

them. "They want me to marry. Now. Very soon. They've picked him out, the man they want me to marry. I met him in November. He asked me to marry him over a week ago, and I can't put him off any longer. I have to tell him. I have to say yes."

His expression did not change, but his face lost its color. "I never thought it would happen," he said, "not so soon anyway."

"They want me to marry him while my father is still . . . is still well. I can't refuse them. They want me settled." She had never thought that so simple a word could be so ugly. "I've thought about all the things I can do, and it turns out there's nothing. My father's done everything in the world for me."

He put his arms around her and she could feel his convulsive intakes of breath. They had reached the ultimate impasse; neither could save the other, and they both needed saving. She reached up and loosened his tie, unbuttoned his shirt, and laid her hand on his bare neck. She wanted to tell him how lucky they were, that she would never forget, that part of her would always be there for him and maybe that was the part that mattered, but she couldn't say it. Her voice was gone and the words were somewhere else, in Richard's typewriter maybe, but not here.

He let go of her suddenly and stood, taking off jacket, tie, shirt, undershirt, taking her to Richard's bed and undressing her, not asking, because his words were gone too, and besides, he didn't need them; they were two people who knew each other; they would always know each other. Once, in Paris, she had not kissed him because she had thought he was engaged, but tonight in New York there was no engagement, only an offer floating somewhere in Brooklyn, hanging, waiting for acceptance. Tonight they were still free and his offer was more tender than the other.

He made love to her, satisfying her easily, quickly, too quickly, perhaps; she wanted this night to last, to burn with such heat that the embers would glow forever. She heard: I will always love you—and she didn't know who had said it, wasn't sure either of them had. She lay beside him, recovering from the ordeal of telling him, loving him, giving him up.

"I got us something to eat." He got out of bed and brought her his shirt.

She put it on and they went to the kitchen and made sandwiches. Then he turned on Richard's radio and found music and they danced on bare feet, and finally, when it was getting late, he made love to her again.

They stood on the corner looking for a taxi. He wanted to take her home, but she said no, he had work to do and it would only make it harder for both of them.

"It always seems to happen when you're in your last year of school," she said, seeing a taxi and knowing it would be hers.

"I'll be all right. Anyway, after this year there's no more school."

"After tonight there won't be any more crises."

"No."

The taxi stopped and he opened the door. They looked at each other a moment. Then he kissed her. A minute later she was on her way to Brooklyn.

The next afternoon she went to Manhattan and told her grandmother she was getting married. It was a short conversation, with Grandmama doing most of the listening. When it was over, she said, "You're a good girl, Regina. Both of you, you're both good."

On her way out, Regina met Millie on the stairs, and when Regina continued on her way down, she caught the scent of French perfume.

That night, when Martin came to dinner, she told him she would marry him. A week later, in front of her parents, he gave her a diamond ring.

A letter came from Suzanne. Her parents would announce her engagement to Étienne in June when he completed medical school. They would be married a year later, and Régine must plan to attend.

She told Shayna about Martin, and Shayna listened in amazement. "You never told me," she said. "I see you all the time, and you never said a word."

"I was waiting till I was sure."

"Regina, did something happen to you in Paris?"

"Nothing I haven't told you about."

But Shayna looked as though she didn't believe it.

Plans were made for a small wedding. Parents and grandparents would attend, but no aunts, no uncles, and no cousins. Regina was very firm about this, and Mother concurred. They must make everything as easy as possible for Poppa.

In the evenings she and Martin looked at apartments. As soon as they found something suitable, they would set a date. New buildings were rising everywhere, but many of them would not be available till fall. The best apartments always seemed to be in those buildings.

She was willing to compromise, but Martin thought compromising was a bad idea. If they continued to look, they would find exactly the right place.

It was May and her classes were coming to an end. She refused to give them up. Tuesday she painted and Thursday she learned about the novel. On those two nights she would not look for an apartment.

Since her engagement she had stopped having dinner with Richard. He had been surprised by the news, but very pleased. He told her McGuire was leaving for Paris at the end of May. He was working his way across the Atlantic on a freighter.

She had dinner at home on the second Tuesday in May and she lingered, talking to Poppa, so that when she left it was past seven and the painting class was at eight. She put on a light coat and pulled gloves on, admiring her large round diamond. She called good-bye and hurried out the door. It was starting to get dark and she didn't want to be late.

She walked down the steps, looking briefly at her gloves. They were French kid, one of a dwindling number of relics of a happy time now past.

"Regina."

She knew the voice but she couldn't match it to a person. Wondering, she turned slowly.

"Morty!" Tall, healthy, and well-tailored, Mortimer Rush stood before her. "You came back." Looming in the dusk like a mirage, but so much more solid. "You really came back. I don't know whether to laugh or cry."

"Don't cry."

"You look wonderful, you look absolutely wonderful. I can't tell you how happy I am. When did you get back?"

"November."

"November! You've been here all this time . . . ."

"I wanted to give it six months and see how it worked out before I came to see you. I'm back with Pop."

She grinned at him. "Are you still good?"

"I'm damn good."

"I knew you would be. I just knew all you had to do was try."

"I went to see the Goldblatts in September."

"Oh, Morty, I'm so glad."

"I wanted to apologize. I was unforgivably rude when they invited me to visit."

"You weren't rude, and anyway, we understood, all of us."

"They told me . . ." He looked toward her front door.

"Yes. He's very ill."

"Well, they made me stay for dinner and we talked a lot. We talked for hours. I was afraid I was going to have to move in."

"They're wonderful people. I told you they were."

"Well, you were right." He took a breath. "So I came back."

"I'm so glad you did. Everything was so awful that last time I saw you."

"I brought you something." He took a small package from under his arm. It was wrapped in white tissue paper.

She took it from him and felt it with her fingertips. The blue showed through the fine layers of paper. "It's the Joyce, isn't it?"

"Yes."

"That's very kind of you." She looked up at him and smiled. "I didn't know you were a smuggler."

"Only as a sideline."

"I'm so happy to see you." She felt suddenly shy, full of wistful memories in a drawer long closed, the fragrance of a small love in the *seizième*.

"I really went to the Goldblatts' to see you," he said.

"I left in August."

"I had a hellish summer. I missed you every day of it. When you weren't there in September, I decided to give it a try. I got some new clothes." He glanced down at his very correct suit. "I'm making an honest living. Have you ever felt a little crazy?"

"Not since I left Paris."

"I came back to marry you."

It had become dark. She was holding the copy of *Ulysses* against her chest, right hand over left. Through the gloves she could feel the pressure of Martin Gerstman's diamond ring boring into her right palm.

"Would you like to come up to my place and talk?" he asked. "I live in Greenwich Village. It's not very big—bigger than the one in Paris. I promise I'll watch my manners."

"Yes, I'd like to." Feeling a little dizzy, a shift of continents, a displacement of spirits.

He found a taxi and they rode into Manhattan, not speaking. His apartment was not far from Richard's, a little larger and on a lower floor. It was as neat as the one in Paris, but less bare. Half a dozen framed watercolors decorated the walls—Sacré Coeur, the Pont Neuf, bookstalls. There were no photographs in the living room at all, but there were papers on a desk, a bottle of blue ink, unmistakable signs of labor.

She removed her gloves carefully, pulling Martin's diamond ring off at the same time and letting it fall into one of the fingers. She felt the lightheadedness of a raging fever, but it was something else that was raging. She remembered the first night he had kissed her in the Sixteenth. She remembered the night she had tasted absinthe.

"I'm afraid I don't have the view," he said.

"The view is inside." She looked around, turning only her head. "The best views are always inside."

"You can't really be surprised." He took her arm and led her to the sofa. She was dressed for her design class, overalls and one of Poppa's old shirts. Poppa loved to see her like this. "You knew in Paris how I felt about you."

She shook her head. "I'm just trying to think how I'll tell my parents," she said.

It was almost eleven when she got ready to leave. She had stayed nearly three hours, sitting across the small table from him in the kitchen, drinking strong coffee and talking. They had had Paris together for a little while; now they would have New York. More than that, they would have each other.

He helped her on with her coat, and she reached into her pocket and felt the glove, heavy with obligation, and left it there. Tonight she felt weightless. Some law of science had been repealed; gravity had been rendered invalid.

"I'd like to get you something," he said. "A ring. Something with a pretty stone in it, maybe something French. You have the delicate quality of a French girl, even in overalls."

"I don't need a ring, Morty. It's hard to paint with rings on. You know what I think you should do? Buy a car, something really gorgeous."

He seemed almost stunned by her suggestion, looking at her as if expecting her to withdraw it if only he would give her a moment to reconsider.

"It would be more fun," she said, "don't you think? You'd have to let me drive it, you know. I mean, just because you talked me into marrying you in three hours and five minutes, you can't expect to sit in the driver's seat all the time."

He put his arms around her and kissed her. Four walls and a roof over them. He had been right; it made a difference.

"I'd better take you home," he said, "while I still want to."

He locked the door behind them and took her hand as they went downstairs. "That's better," he said, looking at her bare hand. "Much better. I think we'll have a hell of a good time together, Regina."

"I think so too. I feel as crazy as you do."

And sitting beside him in the taxi a little while later, she knew this was one time she would not call Jerold and tell him what had happened.

There was a note for her that Martin had called. He had found an apartment and perhaps they could look at it during lunch tomorrow. She called him at the factory in the morning and he picked her up at exactly noon. As they drove, she told him she had decided not to marry him. It turned out to be the hardest thing she had ever done, harder than a hundred evenings when she and Jerold had reviewed the facts of their lives and the bleak outlook they portended. This time she was inflicting uninvited pain, and she suffered an opposite but equal remorse.

He pulled the car to the curb as she came to the point of her little monologue and sat white-faced as she finished. They were somewhere on Flatbush Avenue, surrounded by traffic, pedestrian, motor, horse-and-wagon. The car was a little island in a mercantile sea.

"I see," was all he said. Then he just sat looking at the dashboard.

She had nothing more to say, but he seemed to be waiting for something. Suddenly she remembered the ring, took it out of the change purse in her bag, and gave it to him.

"Thank you," he said, put the car in gear, negotiated a difficult U turn, and drove her home in silence.

Telling her parents was quite different. They were finishing lunch when she returned. Poppa had tried to work for a few weeks after getting out of the hospital, but gradually he had stopped. He still dressed each morning, and Regina walked with him when he felt able, but he no longer went farther than the square block on which the house stood.

She sat at the table, keeping her hands in her lap. "I told Martin I'm not going to marry him," she said.

Eyes pierced her, and Momma gasped.

"Regina," Poppa said sternly, "Regina, you have given your word."

"I know, Poppa. I shouldn't have. I didn't love Martin."

"Love," Momma said with exasperation. "I told you about love." Her voice had a hysterical quality.

"Alice," Poppa said, "I feel so tired. Everything is such a rush, a rush to meet, a rush to get married. Nothing moves slowly anymore." He looked around the table with sad eyes. "Except me. Only I move slowly."

Mother was crying quietly, holding a table napkin to her face. "We tried so hard," she said. "I don't know what's going to happen to you now."

"I'll be fine, Momma."

Poppa pushed his chair back. "I need to rest," he said.

Regina put her hand on his. "I'll go up with you, Poppa. Wait."

She waited till her mother's tears had abated. "I'm going to marry Mortimer Rush," she said quietly.

Poppa said, *"What?"* and Momma said, "Oh, my God," and then both of them talked and nothing was very clear.

"He came back last fall," she explained. "He's been in Paris since the end of the war."

"Paris," Poppa said, looking at her with stern, questioning eyes.

"He must be forty," Momma wailed.

"Thirty-three."

"He isn't a well person," Poppa said.

"Very fit and looks wonderful." She knew she was smiling. "Let me help you upstairs, Poppa. After you sleep on it, we'll talk about it some more."

They went up the stairs and she took his jacket and hung it up, pulled his shoes off, and covered him with a quilt. She sat on the edge of the bed and held his hand.

"I never say no to you, do I, Regina?"

"Of course you do, Poppa. It's just that we know each other very well. You wouldn't want me to marry someone I don't love. Momma didn't, did she? Shouldn't I be as happy as Momma has been?"

"Everything is being happy." He closed his eyes. He still had his glasses on.

148

"Yes. Everything is."

"Regina . . ." He opened his eyes. "You don't have to get married if you don't want to. We wanted you to be settled, but we want you to be happy too. All this running around—a little college, a little Paris. It had me worried. Do you know that?"

She nodded.

"Now, suddenly one day you're marrying this one, the next day you're marrying that one. Are you doing this for me? Is it because I'm sick?"

"Martin was for you, Poppa."

"And Morty Rush?"

"Morty is for me."

"You knew him in Paris?"

"Yes."

"So many things you never told us. I wish I could be here in twenty years to see what becomes of you."

"You will, Poppa."

He took his eyeglasses off and handed them to her. "No. Twenty weeks if I'm lucky."

He closed his eyes, and when he was asleep, she tiptoed out of the room.

They were married a month later at Temple Emanuel on Fifth Avenue. Morty sent flowers early in the morning and a car to pick them up in Brooklyn at eleven, and he opened the door himself when they stopped and helped Poppa out. Morty's father came, and his brother, Stuart, with his wife. Shayna was the only friend, Millie the only cousin. She came with Poppi and Grandmama, whom Morty had insisted on speaking to without Regina present. When Regina made her own private visit a day later, the photograph of Aunt Maude had disappeared from its shelf in the living room and Grandmama had a glint in her eye that Regina had not seen for years.

They had a small celebration in the rabbi's study after the ceremony, with champagne from France, because Mr. Rush knew a man who could get it and how could you have a wedding without champagne?

Poppa insisted that they have "a few days together," although Momma was against it. She wanted Regina to visit daily; how would she get along for four or five days without her? But Poppa won out, and after the champagne, they all kissed good-bye, Shayna promising to see her parents home and visit for a little while.

As they prepared to leave, Poppa handed her a small envelope from his business with something very hard inside and she put it in her bag and threw them all a kiss. The essence of marriage was not the bed, which she already knew, but the coming and going. She had arrived in one car with her parents; she would depart in another with Morty. It was an experience she had never shared with any other man, walking out a side door and leaving her parents behind to travel in another direction. It was what made marriage different from the other, the leaving behind.

At the curb was a new 1926 Mercedes-Benz, the spare tire tucked aristocratically in the front fender. He handed her the key so that she could unlock the door. She sat down in the passenger seat and he bent over and kissed her.

"It fits better than a ring," she said, stretching her legs.

"Needs more polish, though." He closed the door and went around the car. "Do you like it?" He started it with a key.

"I love it. I've never been in anything like it. Where are we going?"

"Uptown." He turned right at Fifth, avoiding an old Ford that stood, undecided, halfway through the intersection.

"Uptown? Aren't we going to the apartment?"

"Not till after the weekend."

"You didn't tell me."

"You didn't ask."

It was true. She had been so delighted to be granted a short respite from the cares and responsibilities in Brooklyn, she had never thought to ask where they would spend the days.

She pulled Poppa's envelope out of her bag and unwrapped the tissue paper inside. In her hand lay two engraver's dies, the letters on each in mirror image. RFR and RR, the former with Poppa's fancy curlicues, the latter rather plain, more readily legible.

"What is it?" he asked.

"My monograms. My father made them. He went to the shop the day after we said we were getting married. I had no idea." She wrapped them carefully and put them back into her bag, wishing she could turn back for one last kiss, but they would be gone now, on their way home.

They passed the last of the Marble Row houses on the right and then he turned left at Fifty-ninth, circled around the fountain, and stopped in front of the Plaza Hotel, the car facing Cornelius Vanderbilt's monstrous mansion.

"Want it?" he asked magnanimously.

"Huh-uh."

"Not your taste?"

"Too big and too many strangers in it. I like the apartment and I like the Village. How could I wear overalls on Fifth Avenue?"

The hotel doorman had reached the car and was opening the door. "Try the Plaza for a couple of nights?"

"I'll try anything."

The room was large and bright, rich in fabric, with heavy, dark furniture. The bellboy opened the window and the late-spring breeze made the room smell fresh and new. Outside she could see miles of Central Park.

Morty arranged the valises, moving hers so that it would be more accessible.

"It doesn't weigh anything," he said.

"It's all summer things, silk and cotton. Nothing weighs more than an ounce or two. But it's full."

"I suppose Alice got you a very beautiful, very expensive white nightdress."

"Dozens," she said, laughing. "I had to pull her away from the counter. Half the clothes in the valise are nightgowns."

"You know"—he held up the hand with the thin gold band shining brightly and rubbed it with his thumb—"in the afternoon you hardly need one."

"Show me," she said.

And looking rather pleased with himself, he did.

6

She sat in the middle of the bed, wearing a slip and nothing else. It was the end of July and she could see sweat on Morty's face but she was so cold that she held a blanket around her shoulders. The room looked unfamiliar. It was almost a week since she had seen it.

"I could warm up some soup," he said.

She shook her head.

"Did you sleep at all?"

She shook her head a second time, and her shoulders quivered with cold.

He adjusted the blanket and she felt the warmth of his hand through the wool. Human warmth was different from solar warmth. They were right to want her married before Poppa died. She could not have stood it alone in that house with Mother. They were beyond comforting each other.

"It's going to be at two o'clock tomorrow," he said.

"I can't go." Her voice sounded odd, unused. She had not spoken since he had taken her home.

"We'll go together."

"I don't have a black dress." She wouldn't go. She would stay here, and he would stay with her. She was sure today was a Monday, but he had not gone to work. Tomorrow he would stay with her too.

The telephone rang and he got up to answer it, the lifting of his weight causing her almost to lose her balance. She sat with her legs folded under her as only children and Indians were able to. She knew she was not an Indian, so she must be a child, and children were accorded special privileges; they did not have to attend funerals.

Morty spoke in a low voice on the telephone so that she could barely hear him in the kitchen. "Early this morning . . . no . . . she needs a black dress."

It had rung all day as she lay on this bed trying to sleep or at least just not to think. She had been doubly unsuccessful. That she was here and not in Brooklyn was success enough. Aunt Eva had arrived early in the morning with Uncle Willy, taken one look at her, and said, "Take her home, Morty. I'll stay with Alice," and they had left. Her place was with her mother, but she would not go. She would stay here.

He came back to the bedroom with a cup of tea and a slice of buttered toast, but before he could say anything, the telephone rang again and he left her. Earlier in the day Richard had come to call, and she had heard them talk in the living room. She hoped no one else would come. She had heard enough voices. Now she wanted only to sleep.

Morty came back and sat down on the bed. Her legs had begun to ache. She lay down and he tucked the blanket around her. There was lots to spare. Her body was pulled in a tight ball, a small body made even smaller. No one looking at her would imagine she was even human—no one, perhaps, except Morty.

There was a knock on the door, and he left her, closing the bedroom door behind him. She heard a man's voice speaking quietly, a voice she knew. It was Jerold. She closed her eyes and slept.

It was bright when she awoke. She must have slept twelve or fourteen hours, but it had not been long enough. She had not slept through the funeral.

She got out of bed and walked in bare feet to the kitchen. Morty stood quickly.

"You look better," he said, but she knew it was a lie. She was rested, but she felt worse. A day had passed. She could no longer say: It's two hours since Poppa died. It's six hours. Now it was more than a day, and today they would bury him.

"I'm not going," she said.

"Come and sit down."

The table was littered with cups stained with coffee and tea, plates with rinds of meat and dried mustard. A newspaper opened to the financial page lay folded next to his place. She sat.

"I'll run a bath for you."

She started to cry, leaning her elbows on the table and holding her head. A moment later she felt the blanket across her shoulders. She could not stop crying.

She felt his hands on her shoulders, felt him leave, heard the bath running. After a few minutes she could smell the hot water, but she had not stopped crying. He came back to her, lifted her out of the chair, and carried her to the bathroom, which was just off the kitchen, set her down on a mat on the old green linoleum, took her slip off, and helped her into the tub. Kneeling beside the tub, he washed her, letting the hot water run over her body again and again, the liquid warmth calming her. He held the wet cloth against her eyes, using his hand to soap her back. She could have been his child, but she was someone else's, and the someone else had died.

When she was clean, he pulled the rubber plug out of the drain and swung the chain over the edge of the tub. A small whirlpool sucked at her feet. He helped her out, wrapped her in a large towel, and carried her to the bedroom. At the most, she had weighed little more than a hundred pounds. Today she could not have been much more than ninety. He put her down on the bed and started to dry her.

"I'm not going," she said.

"We'll go together. I'll be right next to you. When it's over, I'll take you home whenever you want."

"I'm not going."

There was a knock on the door. He wrapped the towel around her and went to open it. She heard him say, "Thank you, thank you. I can't tell you how much I appreciate it."

There was some whispering, and then the door of the bedroom opened and Lillian walked in, carrying a large box. She was wearing a black dress and hat and could have posed as a stylish matron on her way to a funeral. She kissed Regina, put the box on the bed, and opened it. Regina watched her lift out a black dress and hold it up.

"Thank you, Lillian." She looked at the dress, admiring it. "I'm not going."

"You're going, dear. We're going to take you. Let me help you dress."

Regina shook her head and drew the damp towel closer around her. Lillian coaxed, but she would not move. After a while, Lillian left the room, and then Morty was on the phone.

She heard the footsteps heavily on the stairs. The sound contrasted strongly with the sounds of the last three quarters of an hour, Lillian's hushed whispers and Morty's rumbling voice. She had thought they would leave, but instead, someone else was coming. A door opened and closed. Whoever it was was coming for her. This time she would not escape.

The bedroom door opened and Grandmama came in, Lillian right behind her. Grandmama turned and whispered something, and Lillian retreated.

"Come," Grandmama said, sitting heavily on the bed. "Now you get dressed."

"I can't go."

"We all go." Grandmama got up, opened the closet door, looked around, and pulled out a pair of black shoes. They were the last pair she had bought in Paris and they still looked almost new. Aunt Hélène had told her there was no substitute for quality, and Aunt Hélène had been right. Grandmama held out her hand. "Come."

She sat up, the damp towel still covering her nakedness. "Don't make me go."

"I don't make. We all go."

She let her grandmother take the towel from around her shoulders. "He gave me Paris, Grandmama."

"A good man, your poppa." She opened drawers, looking for underclothes, tossing them on the bed as she found them. "Paris was yours, your Paris. It waited for you."

"He let me go."

"Stand up. That's right." Grandmama pulled the dress over her head and straightened it. "A good poppa. He let you go." She stood away and looked at Regina through narrowed eyes. "Good. Now you're back in New York. Now we all go together."

She stepped into the shoes and looked down at the dress. It was a perfect fit. She could not have made a better selection if she had gone to the store herself. Grandmama handed her the hair brush and she pulled it through her hair a couple of times without looking in the mirror.

Grandmama nodded. "Now," she said, "everyone is ready."

They were all there, Uncle Nate and Aunt Bertha, whom she had seen only once since her return from France, the uncles, the aunts, the cousins. Richard hugged her and Jerold held her hand and kissed her on the cheek. Adele said how sorry she was. Millie cried. And when the service was over, they all drove out to the cemetery where they had buried Aunt Maude, and they said a last good-bye to Poppa.

PART IV
FALL 1926

1

She walked north on Third Avenue from shadow to light and back again to shadow, the small, angular areas of light like bright oases in a dark forest. She reached one of them and stopped, lifting her head and shading her eyes from the brilliant late-fall sun, looking beyond the El to the very blue sky. It was good to feel good again.

For two months she had felt like this street, more shadow than light. Quite suddenly, at the end of September, the pattern had reversed. As though the previous night's dinner had contained a magic potion, she had awakened one morning feeling something of her old self, something of the delight of getting out of bed in Paris or the almost floating sensation of completing a design that pulsed. She had asked Morty if they could spend the weekend at the Plaza and he had answered yes very quickly, as though he had been waiting for the question. It was a good weekend, and when they drove back downtown on Sunday, she sensed the beginning of her own recovery.

For her mother it had been almost exactly the opposite. Mother had coasted through the summer and early fall, relieved of the long months of responsibility, the sleepless watching. In October she quietly collapsed. Persuaded to move in with her parents, she began slowly to mend. Now she was back in Brooklyn and Regina was on her way to her grandparents' apartment.

Just up the street she caught sight of Millie leaving a bakery, her hands full. Regina could feel her mouth water as though she were still a child, as though the plate of little cakes could still reward, bribe, and calm an injured spirit.

"Millie," she called, lengthening the last syllable in an effort to attract her cousin's attention.

Millie turned, and her face brightened. "Oh, hello, Regina," she said as they met. "I've just been getting something for tea."

"Let me help." She took a large, heavy box from her cousin. "This can't be bread."

"No. I got a cake."

"We're all getting lazy, aren't we? Pretty soon we won't need ovens."

Millie blushed deeply. "Oh, I still bake. It's just . . . well, someone in there always insists. I don't really . . . I mean, it's something like a present."

"A present! She sounds like a good person to know."

"It isn't a girl." Millie stopped walking. Her large eyes looked very wide and her face suddenly very somber.

"Millie!" Regina's face lit up. "You've never said a word. Who is he? How long have you known him?"

"Almost two years, but I couldn't tell anyone. Grandmama would be very upset and Poppi would throw him out on his ear."

"He would not, not a friend of yours, not if you've known him two years. What's his name, Millie?"

"Izzy." She waited, expecting a reaction. "He's not from a family like ours, Regina. He's very religious. He wears one of those little . . ." She giggled and patted the top of her hat with her free hand. "And he talks with an accent, and you know how Grandmama is about accents. But he's very sweet and he works very hard."

"I'm sure he's a wonderful person if you like him, Millie, and I'm sure Poppi would like him too." She wasn't sure; in fact, she was rather certain of the opposite. "Maybe you could bring him to our place for dinner one evening. I'd love to meet him."

"Oh, he couldn't eat at your house," Millie said.

"No, I suppose he couldn't."

"I've been to see his rabbi." Millie said it tentatively, as if testing cold water.

"You're very serious, aren't you?"

"Oh, no," Millie said lightly. "It's just a silly thing. I know nothing can ever happen."

"What did the rabbi say?"

"There are lots of things I would have to learn. You'd be surprised, Regina. I would have to cook differently, and you need two sets of dishes. I couldn't even eat in my mother's house anymore. I don't know if I could do it." It was almost a question.

"You could do it. Mmm, Millie, you smell like Paris."

"It's almost gone now. I wear it whenever I go to the bakery. I think Poppi guessed a long time ago. He's always teasing me. I'll miss it when it's gone."

"We'll ask Suzanne to send more. Come, let's go eat some of this good cake."

At night she told Morty about it.

"Sounds like Granny's going to have something to arch her back over," he said. He always called Grandmama that, knowing it irritated Regina.

"I don't like to see Grandmama hurt. She's suffered a lot, and she still isn't well from her stroke. Still, it seems so unreasonable. Millie's devoted so much of herself to them."

"Millie would die for your grandmother," Morty said seriously. "Maybe it's time Granny let Millie live a little."

She was glad he was on her side. His concept of family was very different from hers, as was the family in which he had grown up. His mother had died twenty years before, at a time when his father was necessarily occupied with a growing business. His brother, Stuart, was six years older, already in his father's business when their mother died, and something essential was missing between the brothers. Between his mother's illness and her early death, he had raised himself, taking a rather cavalier attitude toward school when it pleased him, and once or twice toward women, he admitted, until the day he met Maude Wolfe. By the time he was twenty-five, he had lost a mother, a wife, and a child.

She talked to Millie over the phone before her next visit, and Millie said if Regina were there, she would tell Grandmama about Izzy. A few minutes after Regina arrived, Millie came up the stairs.

Poppi sniffed the air theatrically. "French perfume," he declared. "I think Millie has a secret from us, maybe this Valentino."

"Oh, Poppi," Millie said, "Valentino died last summer."

"All I know is, when Millie goes out with the perfume, she comes back floating."

"With cakes," Grandmama said perceptively.

"I have a friend at the bakery," Millie said in a wavering voice.

"What kind of friend?" Grandmama asked.

"A young man, Grandmama. He's twenty-six." She reached out a hand and grasped Regina's as Grandmama's eyes followed the hand. "He came here just after the war."

"He works in the bakery?" Poppi asked. "Or does he own it?"

"He owns half of it."

"What's his name?"

Millie looked quickly at Regina and then back to her grandfather. "Izzy," she said forthrightly. "Izzy Benetovich." She pronounced the third syllable as though it rhymed with "tub."

Poppi made a sound in his throat and turned away. "You couldn't find maybe a Schindler like Lillian did?"

"Poppi," Regina said sternly.

"You think Millie should leave her Grandmama for this Izzy?"

"We'll find someone to take care of Grandmama if that's what Millie wants to do." She moved her gaze from her grandfather's eyes to her grandmother's. The old woman looked at her unblinkingly.

"You bring him here, Millie," Grandmama said. "Then we see."

The news darted through the family like electric current. Mother called to say her parents had met a young man Millie wanted to marry.

"Did they like him, Momma?"

"My father's not very happy with him."

"Poppi will come around."

"What do you mean, Regina?"

"Millie's twenty-three and she's known him for two years. He works hard and he sounds like a nice young man. If she wants to marry him, I think Poppi should tell her he's in favor of it."

"Really, Regina, sometimes I think you don't understand the first thing about families."

"Don't you think Aunt Bertha wants her daughter married? Don't you think Uncle Nate does?"

"Of course they do, but it should be someone they can call their own."

"Momma, all they have to do is say it. Just open the door and say, 'You're ours.' There's nothing else to it."

Lillian was more pointed. "I hear he doesn't speak English," she said over the phone.

"Of course he speaks English, Lillian. What else does Millie speak?"

"You don't suppose we'll have to invite his family, do you? I mean when we have our family affairs."

"I'm sure you don't have to if you don't want to. Besides, your girls are hardly out of diapers. By the time they're ready to get married, Izzy may have bought and sold the whole Wolfe family."

"My goodness, Regina. Aren't you optimistic? I just think of poor Millie stuck for the rest of her life with someone who works in a bakery and talks with an unpleasant accent. I'm sure there must be worse things in life than not getting married."

The following week Regina met him when she went to visit her grandparents. A round-faced young man with curly hair and an incipient potbelly, he obviously adored Millie.

"You're her cousin, am I right?" he asked with the Yiddish accent Lillian would never get used to.

"That's right. I'm very glad to meet you."

"And you gave her that perfume? That good stuff from France?"

"Yes, but it's gone now. I've asked someone to send more."

"Now I see why Millie tells me you're so sweet. You've got a sweet face too, you know that?"

"Thank you." His own could have been the gingerbread man's. "Take care of my cousin, Izzy."

"You bet," he said. "You bet I will."

Early in December Izzy visited the farm on a Sunday. He came back enthralled. His mother had kept chickens when he was young, the dog had taken to him like an old friend, the house that Aunt Bertha had electrified and refurnished was like a palace. He had even discovered on that brief outing that there was a shul a few miles away, a pleasant walk on a Saturday morning.

There was no word from Uncle Nate for almost a week. Then Poppi received a letter asking him to travel to the farm.

Sensing that he was about to be compromised, he railed against the invitation. Millie's place, he said to Regina, was in his home.

"Millie's place is in her own home."

"With him? With *him?*"

"Poppi!" Grandmama said sharply.

He gave her a quick glare and turned back to his granddaughter. "These ain't Jews like us, Regina," he said, pleading his case. "You see them taking over?"

"Poppi, they're trying to make a living."

"They're ruining the city." He looked half-ruined himself. "Everywhere you go now you hear them talking in that . . . that . . ."

"You're being unfair. Izzy speaks English."

"That's English? Fifty years I live in this country. My granddaughter should marry into the right family or she should stay here. Things could be a lot worse than living here."

"Poppi, she loves him. Be kind to them. Don't make Millie give up the first person she's ever loved."

Her grandfather stared at her. "You're crying?" he said in amazement. "You? For what?"

For the day she had sat in a chair in that other living room, drunk tea from a china cup, and told her grandmother the best news of her life, her great love. "Grandmama," she said through tears, "please."

Grandmama looked at her with eyes that had seen everything. "Poppi," she ordered, "tomorrow you see Nate."

"Tomorrow? I'm not ready tomorrow. Maybe the next day."

"The next day is too late. You go tomorrow."

That night she told Morty she thought it would all work out for Millie.

In November Morty had taken her to someone his father knew to have a coat made, something with a fur collar. She had declined a fur coat, saying she was too small to wear fur; it would overpower her. She decided on a design with a large fox collar.

It was made up in gray wool with a deep V at the neckline, the fur extending along it. When it was cold, she could pull the fur around her neck so that her face was half-buried in it. The feeling was indescribably luxurious.

He took her to dinner the day the coat was finished so she could wear it.

"We should have a better place to live," he said, running his hand over the fur.

"I like where we live."

"It's a lot better than when you moved in."

It was true. She had had curtains made and chairs covered. Gifts had arrived from her family, silver from Uncle Willy and Aunt Eva, crystal from Grandmama, hand-worked table linens from Aunt Martha. There were nights when they stayed at home, using their gifts, and on those nights she felt married. But on other nights they drove up to Harlem to hear jazz, often on the spur of the moment, always on Morty's suggestion. Sometimes he took her to a speakeasy where there was good music or a singer he had heard about. Sometimes they danced. On those nights they came home late and the next morning, when the alarm sounded, he would kiss her cheek and say, "Don't get up." Those were the times when she felt deliciously sinful.

In the middle of December he came home one evening with a bottle of champagne. "It's six months," he said. "I thought we should celebrate."

She kissed him and pressed her cheek against his cold one. "We've been celebrating all winter." She laid the bottle carefully on the ice, although she could feel that it was already cold from the out-of-doors.

"This is different. There's daily celebrating and then there's special celebrating. How would you like to have a honeymoon?"

He had a way of showering sparks that never failed to ignite her. There was something she wanted that she had not asked for, that she wouldn't ask for, something special and costly and totally unnecessary, and she wanted it desperately. "We had one," she said. "A good one. We even had a second one in September." She grinned. "That one was even better."

161

"Would you like to go to Suzanne's wedding?"

"Oh, Morty."

He reached into his vest pocket and handed her a large envelope. The booking was for an outside stateroom. She read the name written in a heavy hand in black ink: Mr. and Mrs. Mortimer Rush.

"It's not the best time of year for a business trip," he said, "but that'll be a good excuse for making it mostly pleasure."

"I can't believe you guessed."

"You got a letter last summer from them, after you wrote that we'd married. Seemed like the wedding would be a good time for a trip."

"The best time." She looked down at the papers in her hand. "It'll be almost two years by then. Sometimes I can almost taste Paris."

"I'll take you to London, too. You've never been there, have you?"

"No."

"Maybe Berlin. Maybe a little rest in Switzerland." There was a contagious excitement in his voice. He looked around the kitchen. "Where's the champagne I brought?"

"I put it on ice."

"Bring it out. I'll get the glasses down." He went to the cupboard and reached them easily. "We should drink more champagne," he said. "We should do more of everything."

"There are only twenty-four hours—"

"I know, I know. People keep telling me that." He took the bottle out of the icebox and set to work carefully on the wires holding the cork. "My father's getting old and wants to keep things the way they are. My brother has no ambition for enlarging this business of ours, and he resents mine. And you, my dear girl"—he aimed the bottle at the ceiling and the cork flew out with a classic pop—"tell me there are only twenty-four hours in the day." Foam erupted and coursed down the side of the bottle, covering the fingers of his large hand. He said, "Oops," and poured into the two saucer-shaped glasses, handing her the first one.

She took it and leaned over to the hand holding the bottle, kissing the wet fingers and licking the dripping liquid. He put the bottle down and slid his arm around her, kissing her forehead.

"Well, then, I forgive you." He took her to the living room, still holding her. "I forgive you everything." He touched his glass to hers and they drank. "Besides, you added six months to my life."

"I did? How?" They had sat on the sofa, his arm around her.

"I didn't expect to be accepted quite that fast last May, or with quite so much enthusiasm."

"I was very glad to see you."

"Even so. Being optimistic, I didn't think we'd do it till about now. I started to change my mind when we left the apartment and you didn't put your gloves on. I remember you used to do that in Paris."

"I couldn't put them on that night. I had someone else's diamond ring in the left one."

He put his glass down next to hers and didn't say anything for a while. "I was just in time, then."

"Yes."

"An old flame from before Paris?"

"No. My parents introduced us just a year ago. There was no flame at all."

"Why didn't you tell me?"

"I wasn't sure how honorable you were. I mean, I was afraid you might be too honorable."

He finished his champagne, set the glass down, and sat looking at it. "I think there may be a place for you in the business world," he said.

Regina laughed. "I'm much happier printing my designs."

"You really didn't want a ring then, did you?"

"No."

"I've had pangs about that car."

"I love the car."

"My father thinks I haven't treated you well." He glanced around the room.

"You've treated me wonderfully. No one else ever brought me champagne or took me to Paris for Suzanne's wedding or held my hand without gloves. Your father doesn't know how well you treat me."

He stood up and circled the coffee table. "More champagne," he announced, heading for the kitchen. Halfway there, he turned around. "Any more secrets?" He looked peculiarly vulnerable.

"No. Anyway, that wasn't a secret. It was just an event in my life that shouldn't have happened. I'd almost forgotten it."

"Well." He smiled at her and was the old Morty again. "It's my own fault. I should have asked you in Paris."

A few days later Millie called. "Regina, we're getting married." She sounded ready to fly.

"Millie, that's wonderful. I'm so happy for you. I knew Poppi would come around."

"It was my father that did it," she said proudly. "He thinks Izzy is wonderful. He wants Izzy to give up the bakery and come work the farm with him."

"Will he do it?"

"Oh, yes. We're going to build our own little house, between Momma's house and Uncle Willy's. There's some land for sale across the road, and Poppa's going to see about buying it. It'll be good to get out of the city, Regina. It's so noisy here with the El, and so crowded, and the cars don't watch where they're going. I saw an old man run down in the street the day before yesterday. Out in the country, people care more about each other."

"Millie, you sound so happy. I'm so glad it's all working out. Have you set a date yet?"

"We have to talk to Izzy's rabbi, but I'd like to get married in June."

"June is a lovely month for a wedding." She felt a flicker of relief. In June they would be in France. She could send her best wishes and avoid the reunion of all the cousins. She would not have to see Jerold.

"You can come in June, can't you?" the high-pitched voice at the other end of the line asked.

"I'm not sure. I'll have to check with Morty. We may have to be away."

"Then I'll change the date," Millie said promptly. "You have to come, Regina. I couldn't get married without you there."

For Shayna it was a winter of indecision. She brought her persistent admirer, Morris, now a dentist practicing in the Bronx, for a visit one evening. He declined dinner for dietary reasons although he had recently begun riding on the sabbath, but accepted Regina's coffee and cake from Izzy's bakery. It was obvious that he was very fond of Shayna, proud of her accomplishments. A pupil of hers, a young child, had written her a note with a small Christmas present and Morris recited it from memory. Shayna watched him, pleased at his attention, but Regina knew that Morris was only second best. Two weeks later, Walter Weinberg came to New York, telegraphing his arrival in advance, and Shayna went to the station to meet him.

Millie's wedding was scheduled for the second weekend in June, and Millie moved out of Grandmama's apartment in January to prepare herself for her new life. She moved in with Izzy's sister, who lived on East 118th Street and who would teach Millie how to keep a kosher home. Poppi refused to talk about it. Grandmama began to cook again, but she had difficulty standing. Regina increased her weekly visits, and her mother began traveling from Brooklyn several times a week to make up the empty days. Sometimes, when Regina had spent an afternoon with her grandparents, Morty would pick her up there and take her out for dinner. Usually on those evenings she was tired. Usually on those evenings Morty was irritated.

"Visiting is one thing," he said at dinner after calling for her in mid-February. "You're not visiting anymore. You're taking care of them, and that's not your job. Let the family get someone to take Millie's place."

"Morty, 'the family' is my mother and my uncles. Uncle Jack doesn't visit often, and when he does, he's oblivious. Uncle Nate probably feels he donated his daughter for eight years and nothing more is required of him, and I think he's right. Last time Uncle Willy was over, Poppi lied to him about where Millie was and Momma didn't want to tell her brother that their father is a liar."

"What a family." He shook his head. "But I want you out of it. No more keeping house. Promise?"

"Well . . ."

"You could spend the time painting. You missed one of your classes last week because of them, didn't you?"

She ignored his question. "Morty, I think my mother is going to move in with them."

"Permanently?"

"Yes. She wants to sell the house. She says she's lonely and the house is too big." She sighed and put her fork down next to the almost untouched cake.

"You don't want her to."

She shook her head. "I seem to feel a greater attachment to that house than she does. They've had it so many years. Going back to take care of her parents seems like such a defeat to me. I don't like to see my mother defeated."

"Suppose I talk to her."

"Thanks, Morty." For the thousandth time in less than a year she was glad she was married, glad she had married Morty. It was easy enough to have all the rest of it, the champagne, the jazz, even the sex, without being married, but it was this—suppose I talk to her—that made her happiest, the taking on of the family with its sometimes overwhelming responsibility, its decisions.

But Mother had made up her mind. Poppa had left her quite comfortable, a house, savings, and an income from the business. Uncle Willy had drawn up the will and would see that things went well for his sister. In the spring, he found an apartment in a new building in the East Eighties with a large sunken living room, two bedrooms, and a modern kitchen and bathroom, and after the house was sold, Momma moved in with her parents.

In March Richard telephoned. He had become almost reclusive and Regina was happy to hear his voice.

"Looks like we have a wedding this spring," he said jovially. "Will you be there?"

"Yes. It's a few days before we leave for France. We've got a second wedding when we get there."

"Sounds like a good year to get married. I've got one to tell you about too."

She held her breath a moment. "You, Richard?"

"Oh, no, not for a while, anyway. Remember my brother's old friend Walter?"

"Yes, of course. He used to visit at the farm."

"Well, it looks like the wedding of the year in Boston. Next fall, I hear. Jerold's going to be best man."

"Really."

Richard laughed. "I've never heard you less enthusiastic."

"He was taking out my friend Shayna on and off."

"I'd guess that's off now. You know Walter, a girl in every port, or maybe at every station."

"I didn't know."

"He's marrying very big money," Richard said. "Her name's O'Brien or Flanagan or something like that."

"I see."

"You're not going to tell me you're surprised?"

"No, just disappointed."

"Don't be. I hear she's quite a girl. Walter's taken out a lot of nice girls. I seem to remember he had his eye on you some years ago."

"She probably is very nice. I can't imagine Walter marrying someone who wasn't."

"That's the spirit. After all, just because a girl is beautiful and rich doesn't mean she automatically has two strikes against her."

Regina laughed. "You sound very chipper, Cousin. You must have gotten something published."

"*Saturday Evening Post.* How's that?"

"It's wonderful. What is it?"

"An article on the Village. I worked on it all fall. It won't be out for months, but I'm feeling good."

Regina felt less than good when she broke the news to Shayna. She had hoped Walter would do the gentlemanly thing and tell Shayna himself. But nearly two weeks passed, during which time they met twice to attend an evening class in French literature. When Shayna failed to say anything, Regina told her while they had a bite to eat before class.

Shayna's face scarcely changed as she heard the news. Her eyes widened momentarily and her fair, delicate skin paled, but she never moved, never said a word until she knew she was ready to speak.

"It's a shock," she said, "but not really a surprise. I've always been the realist, haven't I?"

"I'm sorry."

"So am I. I guess I'll marry Morris now, won't I? And live happily ever after."

"I like him, Shayna, But you don't have to do anything."

"I'm twenty-three and he's the only man I've gone out with in the last year. Except Walter."

"Twenty-three isn't old. Twenty-three is just starting to be exciting."

"It's easy for you to say. Your knight in shining armor crossed an ocean to win you."

Regina looked down at the table. "It was a little more complicated than that." She had never told Shayna the whole story of Morty. Sometimes, in a solitary moment, she thought about it, the Wolfe family and its little secrets.

"Everything's always more complicated. But it's wonderful to be swept off your feet, isn't it?"

"Yes."

"I suppose it's even better in Paris." Shayna shrugged her coat over her shoulders. "That's the way Walter was. When you were with him, you could believe you were the only girl he had ever treated so grandly. I expect it's just the way he always is."

"I expect so." She had never dreamed she could feel so depressed about her friend's being tossed over by a man like Walter.

"Do you mind if I don't go to class tonight? I'm not up to love poems in French." She rummaged through her purse for the correct change.

"Shayna, don't do anything right away. Think awhile. Take the summer and go somewhere."

Shayna dropped several coins on the table and stood up, buttoning her coat. "I don't believe it," she said in amazement. "You're crying. You're crying about me. That's silly, Regina. I knew from the start this wouldn't lead anywhere. We live in different worlds. I'm just lucky that every once in a while they overlapped."

She got home after class and found Morty reading the paper. On the night of her class he came home late, having dinner with his father first. He unwound himself from the chair as she opened the door. "Good class?" he asked, kissing her.

"Morty." She put her books down. "I haven't regretted for one minute that I married you."

"I didn't think you had."

166

"I wanted to tell you. I wanted you to know."

"What the hell happened tonight?"

"If you hadn't come back from Paris—I just realized—I would have gone back to find you. I would, really."

"With someone else's diamond ring in your pocket?"

She looked up at him with surprise. It was barely a year, and she had almost forgotten her ill-fated engagement. "I would have managed," she said. "Somehow or other, I would have managed."

"That must have been one hell of a class," her husband said.

It was a Sunday in April and they were driving up Park Avenue. Someone Morty knew had invited them for two o'clock and they were running late. They had heard sirens and now they could see, a couple of blocks ahead, an ambulance, a crowd, and a police car.

"Better turn off here," Morty said, winding down the window. They were in the left lane and he put his hand out and slowed for a left turn.

Regina looked out the window to her right. A gray-haired woman had just lifted a fine-looking carriage to the curb and she leaned over and adjusted something inside, a proud grandmother exercising her Sunday privilege.

Peripherally from her right she saw an automobile draw alongside theirs, and she turned her head to get a better look. It was magnificent in a way that theirs was not, a shiny midnight-blue Marmon, chrome gleaming. At the wheel sat a young, immaculately uniformed chauffeur, his eyes straight ahead, his face expressionless, as though traffic and ambulances were as much a day's work as the open road. She started to say something to Morty, to call his attention to the vehicle as it began to pass them, but something made her stop. In the backseat, a young, beautiful girl, a bit of fur on the collar of her suit, her fair hair held in place with a small cloche, glanced at her with an empty gaze, while beside her a man leaned forward, his face moving into view, a face Regina had known all her life, but not like this, not filled with such apprehension, such awful solemnity. Her cousin Richard's eyes met hers, glistened with recognition, and the fairytale car rolled across the intersection as Morty moved into his turn. Ahead of them, the small rear window of the blue car protected its occupants from the curious world outside.

She felt almost dizzy. Bits of remembered conversation tumbled in her head. From the confusion a kind of unexpected sense emerged. Richard had meant to leave for France last summer. Richard had been working on a biography but he had not spoken of it for many months. Richard had scarcely been seen recently; Poppi had grumbled about it once.

Something quite terrible was happening to Richard this afternoon.

A few weeks later they drove uptown to Grandmama's new apartment. The wedding was only a month away and a party was being held in honor of the bridal couple, catered by a kosher cook who had supplied dishes, silver, pots and pans, as well as the food, while Poppi walked the streets to avoid the ignominy of it all.

It was the first gathering of the family since Poppa's funeral, and Regina looked forward to seeing the New Jersey branch. She had been out to the farm only twice the previous summer, to take Momma out and bring

Momma back. Morty would not go, and his quiet but firm insistence had surprised her. Worse, Momma would not ride in a car her daughter drove. Her daughter could attend college and live in Paris, but Momma would not sit in a car with Regina behind the wheel. They had gone the old way, starting with the Tubes and ending with a taxi from Caldwell. Regina had made both trips in one day. She had not wanted to be away from Morty overnight.

She had heard in advance that Jerold would not be present today. Aunt Eva was sure he could have tried harder to change his arrangements with Walter, but Jerold had assured his mother he was expected in Boston this weekend and no alternative would suffice.

They arrived a little early to visit, but guests began filling the apartment and then food was served and it became crowded and noisy. Introductions were made in two languages, English and a kind of singsong parody of German. The guests divided quite naturally, the speakers of English, dressed fashionably with an occasional glitter of a precious stone or metal, in one area and the speakers of Yiddish, the older ones awed, almost intimidated, huddled in another. Between the groups Millie and Izzy moved like mediators in a strike, drawing the opposing sides together momentarily, to have them fade back to their respective strongholds when the engaged couple had passed to another group.

Morty found Uncle Willy early and they retired just inside Grandmama's bedroom door, talking earnestly. Lillian arrived late and confided to Regina that she was just not sure she would attend the wedding.

"Is the date inconvenient?" Regina asked with feigned innocence.

"Look at them," Lillian said, tossing a hand in the direction of Izzy's relatives. "Do you really want to spend a whole evening with them? Besides, I hear they're serving boiled chicken."

"I'm sure Aunt Bertha will seat us with people we know."

"Mmm." She bit into a small round object she had taken from an offered tray, made a face, and dropped what was left into a napkin, patting her red lips daintily. "How's Morty doing?"

"Fine, thanks. We're going to France next month. Suzanne's being married."

"How lovely. Say hello to them for us. Such fine people. I take it Morty's prospering, then?"

Regina laughed. "I haven't asked him lately. In fact, I don't think I've ever asked."

Lillian's eyebrows went up and then settled back. "You know what I mean," she said in a confidential tone.

"We're very happy."

"That's all that matters, isn't it?" She looked around the assemblage. "I'd better say hello to Grandmama. I think we'll be on our way soon."

"You look very lovely, Lillian. Your fur piece is beautiful."

"Thank you, dear. Wasted on this crowd, don't you think?" And smiling, she wriggled away through the guests.

Regina stood by the wrought-iron railing that separated the large deep foyer from the living room. She had spoken to Henry briefly when he arrived with his parents, bearing the good news that he would attend medical school in Washington, D.C., in the fall. Aunt Martha had refused to eat anything. She had not been well lately, and from the smell of the food she could tell it would only disrupt her already delicate digestive system. Uncle Jack had smoked a cigar and bragged about his granddaughters and his son who would be the first doctor in the family.

The door to the apartment opened and closed, but Regina could not see who had entered. She descended the two steps to the living room and said a few words to her mother and Aunt Eva. Turning, she saw Richard a few feet away. His face, usually full, seemed drawn and his skin was pale, as though he had risen from a sickbed. Their eyes met over the head of a tiny woman, and Richard turned his head deliberately, right, left, right, then reversed direction and made his way out of the living room. It was the last time she saw him that afternoon.

The wedding was late on a Saturday night at a large hall on St. Mark's Place in Manhattan that catered kosher affairs. Although Uncle Nate was nominally hosting the wedding, he had let Izzy's family make the important decisions. They had selected the menu and the music, as they had provided for Millie's new education. Before the marriage, Izzy's sister had taken Millie to the mikvah for the required ritual bath. In a way, the Wolfe family would be mere spectators at tonight's ceremony.

Regina sat watching the couple under the maroon canopy. Millie had done poorly in school, but this lesson she had learned well. Although little of the ceremony was comprehensible, the joy of the bride and groom needed no translation. Regina pulled off a glove and reached out for Morty's hand. He took hers and squeezed it, touching her bare arm with his other hand. Two rows ahead of her and slightly to the left she could see the unmoving heads of Aunt Eva, Uncle Willy, and their two sons. It was a meeting that could no longer be avoided, and she had slept poorly the previous night anticipating it.

The mood after the ceremony was extravagantly high, the movement of people almost a whirlwind. There was food to be eaten before the food that would be served at the tables, whiskey more available than water. Morty picked up a glass and sipped it.

"I haven't taught you to drink yet, have I?" he said, taking her hand and making his way to their table.

"Next year."

"Maybe on the ship."

"Here we are."

The Schindlers had just arrived, and Lillian rolled her eyes significantly at her cousin. Morty shook hands with Phil and struck up a conversation. Regina, standing behind a chair, looked around the table. It was set for eight.

Morty pulled out a chair and offered it to Regina. "Would you mind if I left you for a minute? I see Willy over there, and I want to get him while my head is still clear."

"Kiss him for me."

He kissed her cheek. "Kiss him yourself," he said, and ran off.

She watched him walking between tables, reaching Uncle Willy after a great number of detours, saw them shake hands. Uncle Willy talked and nodded, gestured with his hand and moved away, returning with Jerold. She saw them meet and shake hands, her husband and her cousin. Her own hands were sweating. She took the second white kid glove off, pulled the beaded bag on her lap open, stuffed the glove in, and drew the cord. To her right, to her great relief, Lillian sat two chairs away and Phil sat on her far side. At least he would not be next to her. She prayed for Richard to sit to her left. That would be most comfortable, her husband on one side and Richard on the other.

"Hello, Regina."

"Henry, how nice to see you. Congratulations again. All we've been talking about lately is your acceptance at medical school. You must be walking on air."

"I am. It's a great feeling."

"I bet you'll love Washington."

"I probably won't get to see much of it. They tell me it's a tough four years."

"It won't be for you." She felt a warm pride in his accomplishment. There was something shining about him. Going away was the best thing that could ever happen to him.

"Save all your ailments."

"Oh, I intend to. A lot longer than four years."

He laughed, and she reached up and pulled his face down to kiss him. There was something reassuring about knowing that a boy brought up by Aunt Martha in the same home as Lillian could turn out the way this one had.

She turned back to the table and saw Morty and Jerold approaching, still in conversation. They stopped when they reached the table, and Morty said, "I'll take care of it Monday," and walked around to the chair between Regina and Lillian.

"Ah," he said, sitting down, "a place to sit, a drink, and my wife. What more could I ask?"

"Something to eat," Lillian answered. "Do you have any idea how late it is?"

"I hear there's at least half an hour of praying before they serve the food," Morty told her in a whimsical tone.

"I wouldn't be surprised. And then I suppose it'll be overcooked."

Across the table Jerold took the place beside Philip Schindler. It was the farthest empty chair from where Regina sat, and she knew it was the distance, not familiarity, that had led him there. A moment later Richard arrived and sat to her left.

"Good to see you," he said.

"Hello, Richard."

"Sorry about the party at Grandmama's. I looked for you, but you were gone. Ah, the eighth cousin arrives."

It was Arthur, still round at seventeen but dressed smartly. "My sisters got head table," he said, "but I like this one better. Keeps me out of the limelight." He had a glass of whiskey with him and he raised it to the occupants of the table and drank half the contents. "Wow," he said, and coughed.

"The cousins," Morty said under his breath.

"Yes, the cousins."

Morty was right about the prayers. It was nearly midnight before food

170

was served and even later when the dancing started. The two married couples at the table danced the first dance; then Phil disappeared. Arthur joined in a rollicking circle inside of which the bride and groom were carried aloft in chairs. Arthur never returned to the table after that. Henry went off to dance with his mother, and Jerold walked away. Morty talked quietly with Lillian, who was smarting at being deserted.

"I'm going abroad," Richard said in a low voice.

Regina turned. "When?"

"As soon as I can book passage. Next month, I hope."

"For how long?"

"I don't know."

"France?"

"After a while. I want to try England first. Someone in my class is living in London now."

"I'll give you the Goldblatts' address. We'll see them in a couple of weeks and I'll tell them about you. They're wonderful to talk to. They made Morty come home."

"You made Morty come home."

"Richard . . . is there anything I can do?"

"Thanks, nothing. Just, about that little scene last month . . ."

"I won't say anything."

"Thanks." He looked up. "Uh-oh, I see my most unfavorite cousin coming this way. Do you mind if I disappear?"

"Run."

At the same moment, Morty murmured something about Lillian being alone, and he stood and escorted her to the dance floor. Regina looked across the empty table. Jerold had just returned and was standing behind his chair. Her heart was pounding furiously.

"Hello, Jody."

He looked at her a moment before he spoke. "Would you care to dance?"

"Thank you."

She stood and waited for him to circle the table, then started for the dance floor, feeling his presence close behind. A trio of violins was playing a slow tune. Above the heads of the dancers she could see Morty moving gracefully with her cousin. They started to dance, his hands holding her lightly, almost gingerly.

"You look very beautiful, Regina."

She met his eyes and looked away without saying anything. If she was beautiful, he was extraordinary. His suit was dark and finely tailored. A gold chain hung across his vest. His face had aged in the last year just enough so that it had the solid, dependable look of his father. He was twenty-five now. It was ten years since Aunt Maude's wedding.

"Blue is your color, isn't it?"

She nodded. The dress was blue and embroidered with beads in several shades of the same color.

"I thought I was the only one who would be nervous."

"I didn't sleep last night."

"There's no need for that."

"You aren't angry with me, Jody? You don't hate me, do you?"

171

"We don't hate each other, Regina."

She felt her eyes fill.

"I like Morty very much."

"I know. He's hard not to like." Something of the same pride she had felt for her cousin Henry welled up in her. He's mine and he's wonderful and even Jody can't help liking him.

"I'm glad it worked out this way for you."

"Thank you." She could feel the pressure drop. "I am too."

"He wants us to handle the legal work for his company."

"Oh." The tangle of the families, not merely at weddings but now at law offices too.

"I'm sure we'll work together very well."

The music stopped and almost immediately struck up a Hebrew dance tune. She turned and started back toward the table, feeling his hand low on her back, touching fabric, not skin, very lightly.

He took her to the table and pulled out her chair.

"Thank you, Jody," she said.

"It was my pleasure."

The next day Shayna called and said she and Morris would marry in December, and a few days later they sailed for France.

2

The crossing was the most relaxing week of her life. Left to his own devices, Morty turned the clock around, much to the consternation of the cabin steward, who never seemed able to find the right time to make up the bed. Morty liked to be awake at night, especially on the sea. Like Poppi, he enjoyed the salt air. Like Regina, he liked to talk in the dark. In evening clothes after a late dinner they walked the deck while he sketched his plans for the company he owned a third of, as she had sketched designs on paper once in an attic in Paris, filling in the details with bright, optimistic colors.

Only his brother seemed to threaten the realization of his designs. At forty Stuart had lost whatever small ambition he might once have possessed. Born in Germany in 1886, he still recalled the crossing with his pregnant mother, the reunion with the father who had left months before, the subsequent birth of the little boy who would be the last of the Rush babies to survive. When their father, after several faulty attempts at business, had begun to manufacture woolen fabric, Stuart had joined in the venture. It was the war that had made them, if not rich, at least more comfortable than they had ever imagined. Uniforms of heavy wool were required for the soldiers. Someone had to produce it, and Rush Woolens had acquired lucrative contracts. Father and both sons had worked night and day, and their rewards had been plentiful. Then came the marriage, the deaths, and Morty had gone to war, leaving the business and forfeiting his generous salary. When the war was over, his father had sent checks each month to Paris out of Morty's share of the profits, putting the rest in savings against the day he would return, but Morty had relinquished his voting rights in the company to his father. The return of the second brother had been an unforeseen shock to Stuart. That his younger brother, after so long away, had asserted his desire to reenter the family business, had fomented a quiet resentment that appeared now and then to be on the point of eruption.

"But it's your right," Regina said. "You're equally your father's son."

"But a ne'er-do-well," Morty said, his voice teasing.

"You've done well by me."

"It's been the best year of my life."

It was a hope she hoped fervently. "Mine too."

"Not all of it, I know, but I think it's been a good spring. You look like I remember you in Paris."

"You're incurable, Morty."

"Well, if I am, I'd like to put it to good use. I keep thinking of leaving the business and going out on my own."

She felt a tinge of the excitement he always seemed to generate. "Why don't you?"

"I hate to give up the name."

"Rush Woolens."

"It's established. We have markets. You see it in the stores." He looked out over the dark ocean. Sailing east, every night was shorter than the one before, as though time itself cooperated in speeding the trip. On the return, all the nights would be long. "If I could only get it through Stuart's head," he said, "that this doesn't have to be a business that just supports a father and two sons. You wouldn't believe the struggle I had to get them to accept Willy. The lawyer they've been using is older than my father and he's been practically retired for years. Everything he handled was small. Stuart thinks small. My father thought big, but big has changed in the last ten years." He looked at his watch. He was the only man she knew who had worn a wristwatch for years. "Want a sandwich?"

She laughed. "You eat six meals a day on the ocean."

"I'm hungry. It's almost two o'clock. That means three. It's hours since we ate. Let me find the night steward."

He took her hand and they went indoors and he ordered a sandwich and a glass of beer. When it came, they went back on deck. A group of glittery young couples had usurped their spot, and they passed them, looking for another. Behind them there was laughter, then the sound of glass breaking and more laughter.

"You did something to me," he said. He had finished the sandwich and stood leaning against the side of the ship, his back to the ocean, the glass of beer in his hand. "I gained a generation when we got married. I got younger. It made me feel different, marrying a kid like you."

"It's not me. It's all you. I could see it that night you came back last year."

"Whatever it was"—he set the empty glass on the deck—"it made me think there was still time."

"There is."

"I hope you're right. I thought maybe it was just that it was four A.M. and that's when my juices start flowing." He put his arm around her and they went back to their stateroom.

The return to Paris was a homecoming. They had arranged to arrive several days before the wedding in order to see Suzanne and Étienne, who would leave for a month after their marriage. In spite of the attention given to the bridal couple, the Rushes were made to feel like visiting royalty. No one else had traveled so far; no one who was not related came closer to being a member of the family.

The wedding was the most lavish Regina had ever seen. The gowns, the jewels, the music, the food gave it the air of a grand ball. Cousins came from Frankfurt and Berlin, from Amsterdam and Luxembourg to attend, giving the event an international flavor. There were people Regina had known from her years at the Goldblatts', young people now marrying and starting families as her own cousins were.

They taxied to the hotel in the early morning, passing through familiar streets. Paris, as always, had not changed. All the landmarks were still there, solid and dependable. At the cafés, the writers who never grew up had not yet stopped drinking.

"I'm so glad we were there," Regina said, leaning back.

"You missed all that when we were married."

"I didn't miss it. I asked not to have it. I enjoyed being a guest at this one, and last year I liked being married and getting away after a glass of champagne."

The taxi stopped and they got out. Up in the room she slipped her shoes off and flexed her toes, rocking on the flat cushion of the rug. Morty had gone to the window and pulled it open.

"It's a nice place to visit," he said, looking out over misty rooftops.

"Paris?"

"But I wouldn't want to live here. You said it once, the way it never changes. It's a nice place to come back to. You can find your way around as if you'd never left. But New York is a place where things happen, where I believe things can happen. It gives me a certain kind of feeling I can't quite describe."

She joined him at the window, not reaching his shoulder without her shoes. He slipped his arm around her.

"It must be almost four," she said. "Your juices are running."

"Is that what it is? Here I thought I'd made some great philosophical discovery, and all it turns out to be is the hour of the morning and too much good champagne."

"Maybe that's all it takes."

He took a deep breath and pushed the window back so that it was open only a crack. "Wouldn't that be nice," he said.

They went to Switzerland and he bought her a watch decorated with diamonds. They traveled to Germany to see Berlin, came back through Holland and crossed the Channel to England. In London they went to the theater; then, while she shopped, Morty talked business.

It was late July when they sailed back, their trunks filled with all the things they had waited until this summer to buy for their home.

"We ought to look for a bigger place to live," Morty said on the afternoon of their first day out. Only a little while ago England had faded into the horizon.

"I'll start looking when we get back."

"Finally lost your enchantment for our little hole in the wall?"

"I think I'm pregnant."

He had been on the point of saying something, but he stopped. It was as complete a surprise to him as she had hoped. He seemed neither to notice nor to care what the days of the month were, and he was always just a little surprised when she had her period, as though it were an inconvenience he could not have foreseen. She had suspected in Berlin, been fairly sure in Amsterdam, and by London almost certain. She had been married a year, and neither of them had done anything to prevent a pregnancy. It had simply not happened until now.

"Say something," she ordered, grinning at him. A wooden slide from a nearby shuffleboard game overshot its target and came to a stop near her shoe. "Sorry," a man's voice called.

Morty stood facing her, not touching her, as though she had suddenly become as fragile as the china they carried in their trunks.

"Now," he said slowly, "we start a dynasty."

He telephoned her from work late in August. It was miserably hot and she was in the apartment waiting for the iceman. A letter had arrived in the afternoon mail from Suzanne, three lovely pages describing their travels, their apartment, and their plans. She reached for the telephone from where she sat drinking iced tea at the kitchen table and answered.

"Regina, I think I've bought a house."

She turned her head away from the phone and started to laugh.

"You still there?"

She turned back to the mouthpiece. "You think what?"

"A house. It's not very big, but it has a garden. And two bedrooms. Can I pick you up in half an hour and show it to you?"

From the stairs came the sound of the iceman. "I'll be downstairs waiting. Morty, you didn't spend a fortune, did you?"

"Of course I spent a fortune. How are you feeling?"

"Hot, but just fine."

"See you in half an hour."

He drove her farther downtown and parked in front of a small apartment house. They walked in the front door, through a narrow, dark hall with mailboxes on the wall, and out a back door. In the middle of a large square of very green grass stood a small house like something in a child's picture book, two windows upstairs, two windows downstairs, a door in the exact center.

"They moved out a week ago. I've got the key."

"It looks like a fairy tale," she said.

"Wait till you see it."

Inside there were a kitchen and living room on the first floor and two bedrooms on the second. Between them was a bathroom with a chain pull on the toilet.

"Is it all right?" He seemed much less sure of himself than he had when he had telephoned.

"You can buy all my houses," she said.

They moved in just before Labor Day, having had the kitchen divided into two rooms and the house painted inside. The day after Labor Day a new refrigerator and a modern stove were delivered and Morty dragged the ages-old icebox and stove out to the curb to be taken away by the garbage collectors. It was 1927 and they would live in style.

Mother brought her parents out to visit at the end of the week. They had returned from the farm just after Labor Day. Even with electricity, the comfort of the farm could not compare with the new apartment.

Mother was clearly disappointed. "It's older than our house in Brooklyn," she complained. "They're building such lovely new houses. Shouldn't you have looked at those?"

"We didn't want a new house, Momma."

"And it's so small."

"It could be made bigger," Poppi said. He had walked around the outside, looking at it carefully. "A little work is all. I could do it with you, Morty. Call me up when you're ready, maybe in the spring."

"Poppi," Grandmama said in her most derisive voice, "you build houses now at seventy-seven?" She looked at her daughter. "Or maybe he's eighty-seven."

"Grandmama," Regina chided, "he isn't even seventy-seven. Poppi could still build a house from scratch if he wanted to."

"Right," her grandfather asserted confidently. "From the bottom up."

"A nice house," Grandmama said, looking around. "A good place to begin."

She had not told her mother about the baby, partly because she wanted to keep it a secret, partly because she didn't want Grandmama to know quite so soon. In August she had gone to her family doctor in Brooklyn, the only doctor she had ever known, and he had confirmed her pregnancy. The baby would come in the middle of April after the snow and the cold weather were gone. It would be a good time to have a baby.

She kept a second appointment soon after they moved and made a third for October. Leaving the office, she felt remarkably happy. Having a free afternoon, she made a small detour and visited her Uncle Max at the printing shop. He had made her stationery with Poppa's traditional monogram when she had married. Now she asked him for some with her new address.

Two days later she lost the baby. The discomfort started soon after Morty left in the morning. Two hours later there was a little blood. She lay on her bed, holding the phone awkwardly, and asked for the doctor's number, trying to stay calm and not managing very well. The office answered and told her the doctor was making his morning calls and might not be able to call back until afternoon. She hung up and lay quietly. If she believed strongly enough, it would turn out all right. She closed her eyes and willed herself to believe she could give birth to a perfect baby.

She would not call her mother. A tiny, razor-sharp memory from 1923 made her keep this secret. *The only child I ever had that lived . . .* She thought for a moment of calling Lillian. Lillian had had two children and could talk with great authority on the subject of childbirth and its complications, but she didn't want to talk to Lillian.

She wanted Morty and she could not call him. If she rested, she might feel better by evening, and he could be spared her panic, her dreadful fear.

A little before noon the cramps began. She waited, hoping, then called Morty's number.

"Rush Woolens."

"Mrs. Murray? Is my husband there?"

"Good morning, Mrs. Rush." The delightful Irish accent she had carried across the Atlantic with her. "He's just left with his dad, I'm afraid. Lunch with someone very important. Is there something I could do for you?"

"No. I'm just not feeling very well."

"Oh, y'poor thing. I could run over on my lunch hour, dear."

"No. Just tell him I called."

"I'll do that. You take it easy now, Mrs. Rush."

177

"Thank you."

By the time the door burst open at two-thirty and he called her name, it was all over. She had spoken to the doctor and lain down again, and all that was left was to tell Morty what had happened, tell him he shouldn't worry, it would be all right.

When she felt better, she went back to the doctor and asked him why. He examined her and then sat down behind his desk and lit his pipe. She remembered the smell of the tobacco from her childhood. Hours after he had left her house, the sweet smell lingered in the rooms he had walked through. It was a reassuring smell; the doctor had come and now the disease would fade. For a moment, sitting opposite him in this quiet, familiar office, she could almost feel the old reassurance.

"You're in good health," he announced. "A little on the thin side. Why don't you build yourself up?"

"I feel all right."

"A few pounds wouldn't hurt. I wouldn't try to have another baby for a while. You could wait a year. You're still young."

She couldn't explain to him that she had not waited to have this one, that she had not planned, that her husband's wife had lost one almost ten years ago. "Why did it happen?" she asked.

"These things happen." He puffed and she inhaled, but the smoke failed to give her her answer.

"But it doesn't happen to everyone. Why did it happen to me?"

He laid the pipe in a large ashtray. "Sometimes the body makes a mistake," he said. "Then the best thing it can do is get rid of the mistake."

"You mean there was something wrong with the baby?"

"We don't know."

"What . . . what sort of thing might have been wrong?"

"We can't tell." He said "we" as though there were a whole committee involved in his thinking, as though any blame that might be his would have to be shared by the nameless others.

"It could happen again, then."

"Could, but probably won't. Many women have a miscarriage and go on to have healthy babies the second time."

But she had a family history, a mother and a grandmother whose bodies had made mistakes. "Thank you," she said, gathering her bag and gloves for the trip home.

"Take yourself a good rest," the doctor said, walking around the desk and patting her shoulder.

She said she would, but it was only to get away.

In October she heard that Millie was pregnant. In November a long letter from Richard arrived from London. He had sailed while they were still abroad and she had missed seeing him again after Millie's wedding. Now he was working on a new article, which he would soon finish and send to magazines in New York. After the new year, he would leave for the Continent.

She walked into the empty bedroom one day in the fall and decided it would make a perfect studio. One window faced north and the other west. With the proper curtains and shades, she could keep the afternoon sun from glaring in. Morty helped her set up the room, hammering fixtures in the wall

178

for curtain rods and picking up an easel in an art-supply shop. She began to paint in earnest at home as well as in class, taking her finished work to school and bringing home designs on cotton that she had screened herself. One of them Grandmama liked so much, Regina had it framed and gave it to her as a gift.

In December they attended Shayna's wedding and in January visited her in her new apartment on the Grand Concourse in the Bronx. All up and down the beautiful boulevard, new buildings rose, clean and solid and modern, with elevators and large rooms. Morris showed them around proudly and Shayna looked equally happy, as though this was what she had always wanted. It occurred to Regina as they left that she had not heard about Walter's wedding, but then, how could she have? Only Jerold would have told her, or Richard, perhaps, and Richard was across an ocean.

She never told Morty what the doctor had said about waiting a year. It had taken her over a year to become pregnant the first time; why should she waste another when her body had its own private arrangement with nature? Her body resumed its womanly cycle and she and Morty returned to each other freshly, making promises about the future that were an end in themselves. In April she missed her period.

She told him almost immediately this time, and he set down rules requiring her to rest. He bought a second radio for the bedroom so she would not be bored. And this time she found a specialist in Manhattan and on her first visit she confided the story of her brief first pregnancy and her long family history.

He was the most reassuring man she had ever met. When she left his office she was convinced she could conceive and give birth to a healthy child.

In May Millie gave birth to a boy, the first great-grandson. He was given a name almost unpronounceable in Hebrew, but Millie said he would be called Harold in English. A number of Izzy's relatives traveled out to the farm for the required festivities, but none of Millie's relatives took part except for Poppi, Grandmama, and Regina's mother, who were already at the farm when it happened.

In June, when she was safely past the point of her first miscarriage, she told her mother and grandparents. Lillian telephoned one day to congratulate her. Aunt Martha called to ask how far along she was, and when she heard it was past three months, she said, "That's nice. You'll probably carry it all the way, then."

Morty refused to let her visit the farm. The roads were bumpy, and riding them was a risk she should not take. He bought a fan to cool off the second floor, pulling the cooler north air into the studio and out through the south window in their bedroom.

In the fall they both began to relax. The baby was due in January 1929 and by October Regina was round and wearing the hideous tasteless wrap dresses that neither concealed nor enhanced a pregnant body. They merely covered it. Cut from fabric of drab, dark colors, the wrap was edged with hooks that fastened onto rows of eyes stationed progressively along what once had been a waist. Every few weeks, when the hooks failed to reach a set of eyes, they fastened on the next looser set.

In early November, having already expanded her dress one large notch,

179

she took a taxi up to Thirty-fourth Street to indulge a desire to look at baby clothes, to add to her mental list, to touch the soft, pretty things that would soon belong to her baby. She got out of the taxi holding her coat together. It was the one with the fox collar she had had made two years ago, and while she could still button it, it was difficult to sit with it buttoned. She stopped on the sidewalk in front of Altman's and closed the top two buttons. Then she went up the steps to the row of doors and walked headlong into her cousin Jerold as he exited.

"Regina!" He held her arm to steady her as they separated from their near-collision.

"Jody." She laughed, regaining her precarious balance. "What good luck it was you. How are you?"

"I'm fine. You look"—his glance went rapidly down her bulging midsection—"lovely, absolutely charming."

"Thank you."

He looked very pleased, as if this special way that she appeared was special to him too. "Do you have time for a cup of coffee?"

She hesitated, thinking more about propriety than what she wanted. She had all the time in the world.

"Come," he said, taking her arm. "I'd like to sit and have coffee with you."

She smiled and nodded, and they walked carefully down the stairs. Diagonally across from them the Waldorf-Astoria loomed with all its ghostly memories.

"Can you manage two blocks?"

"Easily. Grandmama thinks I should do more exercise, but Morty worries."

"I'm sure you do enough just being you."

They walked the two short blocks to Park and turned into the Vanderbilt. Jerold checked his hat and they were led to a small table set for tea. All around them ladies dressed in fashionably clinging dresses sat and talked intimately with men and other women.

"They'll all look when I take my coat off," she said, sitting down and unbuttoning it.

"Ignore them. Just look straight across the table. I feel very virtuous this afternoon. I've just bought a birthday present for my mother. When I do that, my father winks at the time. How have you been? When is it due?"

"January, and I'm fine."

"Coffee, dear?"

"Yes."

"And some pastry? I'm sure Grandmama would approve of a piece of pastry?"

She nodded and he ordered, turning back to smile at her. "I hear you live in a fairytale house."

"The outside is made of gingerbread, but it's very comfortable inside. It's got fireplaces and the people we bought it from put in electricity. I wish Richard could see it."

"Not likely. He finds the other side of the Atlantic very congenial. Did you read his article on London?"

"Twenty times." It had been titled "London, A Passing Glance."

"There'll be one on Paris soon, and he's in Rome now, so we know what to expect. I think he's found his métier. Have you found yours?"

She touched her solid middle, feeling a tiny, precious squirm near the surface. "I hope so. We lost one last year."

"I'm sorry. I didn't know."

"We didn't tell anyone." She looked down at the starched white damask cloth and back up at Jerold. "I didn't want them all to know."

"You can always trust your lawyer."

She nodded. A waitress appeared at her side with a tray of pastries in individual crinkled papers in a variety of colors. The cakes had swirls of buttercream, decorations of red cherries, and sprinkles of nuts. She selected one that looked especially rich. Like a treasured childhood memory, the thought of Jerold would always taste sweet.

"You look better than I've ever seen you," he said.

"I hope it's true. I feel wonderful now. Since summer. The first few months were such a worry, after what happened last year."

"Are you still painting?"

"Yes. We set up a studio, which my friend here"—she touched the bulge—"will usurp soon. Morty got me a high stool so I don't have to stand." She tasted some of the mocha-colored cream. "You're doing well, aren't you, Jody?"

He nodded. "And enjoying it. Someone once told me I would."

"Someone guessed right."

"Someone knew me better than I knew myself." He poured more coffee from the pot. "I'd like you to see my office sometime. I think you'll appreciate it more than anyone else I know."

"Someday."

He walked her back to Altman's when they were finished, and he took a cab from there downtown. There wasn't much time left to the afternoon but she went on with what she had come for, feeling very peaceful as she touched the little dresses and hats and coverlets. It was the first time she thought she would like to see him married, like to see him happy. She was happy. This afternoon she was immensely happy. Even now she could still taste buttercream.

She watched herself expand, felt the activity inside her increase, reached a point one morning when she gave up painting because she could no longer climb onto the stool and sit with any comfort or feeling of stability. She realized, cleaning the brushes for the last time, covering her work no longer in progress, that she felt no regret. Soon they would push the easel and stool aside and prepare the room for its original purpose, for the little fighter in her expanded womb. Setting the work aside gave her, rather than a feeling of regret, a feeling of moving forward. She left the room with pleasure, looking forward to the day she would reenter it with her child.

December came and she walked awkwardly, holding the heavy old banister tightly as she trod the stairs. Well into her eighth month, the skin across her abdomen was pulled taut and the child inside moved deliberately as she moved to make herself comfortable. It felt, it sensed, it was capable of loving. Even now it was a special person in her life.

The doctor had told her she would know instinctively when labor began, and he was right, she did, but it brought with it a wave of panic like nothing she had ever known. It was still December. The date the doctor had told her the baby was due was five weeks away. She had not yet begun her ninth month.

Mrs. Murray answered the telephone on the first ring.

"It's me, Mrs. Murray. I need my husband. It's the baby."

"Oh, no," Mrs. Murray murmured into the phone. "Oh, Lordy. You sit there and don't move. I'll fetch him for you."

She sat without moving, praying she had made a mistake, that her overactive instincts had played a trick on her, but knowing all the while that it was no trick; it was the real thing and it was too early.

"I'll be right there."

"All right."

"Don't move." He hung up abruptly and she replaced the receiver.

She had not yet packed a bag, but she didn't want to lift it from its storage place. No lifting, no bending, no stretching. Grandmama had been very specific. Perhaps she should have paid attention. Perhaps Grandmama's archaic ideas on pregnancy had some validity.

She laid clean clothes in piles on the bed so that when Morty came she could drop them into the valise. When she had everything in order, she lay down to rest for the ordeal that was surely before her. As she made herself comfortable, she realized she had forgotten to call the doctor.

He stopped the car at the hospital entrance, turned off the motor, and took her hand. She knew what he wanted to say and she didn't want him to say it, didn't want him to feel that he had to. A few listless snowflakes blotched the windshield, and for no reason she thought that in a closed car it was hardly a windshield anymore. It was very much a window like the rest of them.

"I'm glad you found me in Paris," he said.

She nodded and tightened her hold on his hand.

"I never crossed an ocean for anyone else."

She smiled, remembering the place and the moment, *Ulysses* in white paper and someone else's diamond ring under a glove.

He leaned over and kissed her cheek. "I'll be there when you wake up," he said.

It was a boy, very tiny with dark hair like Morty's. He was frail and they were worried about him and they would neither bring him to her nor let her out of bed to see him, as if now that she had given birth, she had relinquished all control. Two days after he was born he died. She had never held him but that seemed to make little difference to the people who cared for her in the hospital. Her breasts ached, but that was a consequence of childbirth that she must live through. During visiting hours happy people walked back and forth before her door, laughing and spreading congratulatory messages. She asked the doctor to let her go home, but he said she needed rest and the hospital was the best place to get it. She felt too demoralized to argue, and her mother agreed with the doctor. So she rested.

3

It was only when she lost one that she realized how much she had wanted a baby, not merely for Morty but for herself. She had misspoken at nineteen; now, five years later, she paid the price.

It was a bleak December and a bleaker January. She asked her mother to stop coming to cheer her up. She closed the door of the room that was neither studio nor nursery and spent her time reading in the living room. Once or twice she went walking in the Village, looking in on the small shops that used to excite and tantalize her, but with money to spare, she bought nothing.

On a Saturday afternoon, Morty walked with her, stopping at shop windows with handmade silver and copper jewelry, pointing to pieces he liked, coaxing her in vain to pick something. Finally, on Eighth Street, he said, "Look," and she saw a string of green glass beads of odd, irregular shapes on a fine gold wire. She said, "Oh, they're pretty," and he took her hand and went inside and had her put them on, and while she was still looking at her reflection in the oval mirror on the counter, he pulled his wallet out and paid for them.

She kept them on all day, although they didn't match her dress, but when she got home she saw that she had nothing to wear them with and she folded them away in a drawer.

Grandmama came one afternoon, carrying a large pot of stew still warm on the bottom.

"This is a big trip now," she said, sitting at the kitchen table while Regina transferred the stew into her own pot. "I got old."

"You're hardly more than seventy. That's not old. Look at Poppi."

"Poppi's crazy. A man gets to be eighty, he gets crazy."

Regina laughed. "He was always crazy, Grandmama. You just never noticed it."

Grandmama raised her head. "You think so?"

"I know so." She put the pot in her refrigerator and turned on the water to let Grandmama's soak. Then she sat at the table.

"You're a smart girl," Grandmama said. "You do something now. No more babies this year. You understand?"

"Yes."

"Another year, you have yourself a baby, a good one. I promise you."

She said, "Yes," and turned away. That was the trouble. The best anyone could do was to promise her another one.

It made getting up in the morning difficult. It made one day seem like the rest. It made her see very keenly how Morty was covering up his own unhappiness to spare her more.

She got out of bed one morning late in January and everything looked exactly as it had the day before. Nothing in the house had changed since the day in December that Morty had taken her home. There was nothing to do except read another book, think about the little baby she should only now be carrying into the house plump and healthy, shed a few tears and keep them secret.

She would not go into the room with the northern and western windows. The thought of painting gave her no pleasure. You do something now, Grandmama had said. But Grandmama had lived on a farm where there was always something to do. Here there was nothing.

She went upstairs after lunch and opened the drawer with the green glass beads Morty had bought for her and she had not worn. In the closet everything was old. She had begun the fall season with ugly wraparound dresses. Everything else she owned was from last year. She took out a brown wool two-piece dress and slipped it on. Morty had liked this one. She had bought it about a year ago when she was walking on Fifth Avenue in the upper Thirties and gone into Bonwit Teller. She dropped the beads over her head and stepped back to look at herself in the full-length mirror on her closet door. You do something now, Grandmama had said.

She took a taxi to Canal Street, went in the door and up the stairs, shunning the elevator. Morty had brought her here once, just after they were married, to show her the sales offices, and while here, he had introduced her proudly to the staff. She walked down the hall, hearing a typewriter clack, a telephone ring, her father-in-law speak loudly on a phone as though he still did not trust the wires to carry his message without some extra assistance. She stopped at a door with a frosted glass panel with "M. Rush" in black letters that needed repainting. She knocked on the window and opened the door.

Morty looked up in surprise and stood. "Regina! What brings you here? Are you all right?"

"Fine. I want to do something. Anything." She unbuttoned her coat. It was the coat with the fox collar and it fit her well again. "Preferably something very simple where I can count how much I've done at the end of an hour."

"All right. I can find something like that."

She opened her coat to take it off, and his eyes fell on the necklace. "Nice beads."

"A present from a tall dark stranger. I opened my drawer this morning and there they were, so I came down to show them off. You will find me something to do, won't you?"

He kissed her and took her coat. "Sit down. I'll be right back."

He returned quickly with a pile of unevenly sized papers. "Invoices," he said. "We check the arithmetic before we pay. It's just multiplying and adding. Want an office?"

"Yes."

"I'll give you Stuart's. He doesn't use it. He spends most of his time in Brooklyn at the mill."

They walked two doors down the hall and into an office that lacked any evidence of habitation.

"How's this?"

"I'll take it."

He pulled the chair out for her and she sat down and took the sheaf of papers from him.

"You're sure you want to do this?"

"Very sure. You can leave me. I know what to do."

"Mrs. Murray'll come by with coffee later."

She adjusted the gooseneck lamp on the desk and turned to her work. The top invoice was for the rent for the Canal Street offices. It was a flat sum and there was nothing to check. She turned it over, starting a second pile. The next was for raw wool, a handwritten bill for a sum that startled her. It was difficult to read and there was an error in the second line. She corrected it in pencil and started a third pile. By the time she turned her attention to the next invoice, she had become curious about the content, the source, and the figure at the bottom of the right column. In a drawer she found some scratch paper and she jotted down the final figure from each invoice. When she came to the end of her original pile, she added the column of figures on the scratch paper. The sum was staggering.

"How're you doing?" Morty stood in the doorway.

"Sit down a minute."

"Am I in for a lecture on how to run a business?"

"Just some questions." She lifted the pile of invoices. "Morty, this is an immense amount of money."

"Uh-huh."

"And the payroll isn't even here. How many men do you have at the mill?"

"We're over two hundred now." He pulled a chair nearer the desk and sat with one foot up on the radiator behind her.

She calculated rapidly. "That's hundreds of thousands of dollars a year in wages."

He said, "Uh-huh," again and leaned back in the chair, watching her.

"How much business do you do?" she asked softly, as though the answer were a secret she might not be entitled to, as though she were not yet part of the inner circle.

"Well, we do over a thousand pieces a week," he said, musing. "Most weeks. That's over sixty thousand yards. In a year that comes out to"—he looked up at the ceiling—"well, it was about two million last year. Little more maybe."

"I can't even imagine that much money."

He put his foot down on the floor. "It could be more."

"There's an error on this one," she said, switching abruptly to the task she had just completed.

He looked at it and smiled. "There always is. They're a good supplier, but you have to watch out for them. Count everything twice. Check the figures. Everything else all right?"

"Yes." She handed him the invoices. "Why isn't it more?" she asked.

"The business? Stuart says anything beyond what we're doing now involves expansion. He doesn't want to expand. He's wrong, of course, but I'm tired of arguing. I want to go out on my own."

Her heart skipped a beat. "Doing what?"

"Well, to start with, without getting into the milling ourselves, we can convert fabric. We buy cotton from a mill, send it out to have it dyed, printed, and finished, and sell it to the people who make apparel."

"Print it? You mean stripes and flowers and patterns?"

"Uh-huh."

"Could you tell me about it?" She heard herself sounding like a schoolgirl, hesitant, and a little anxious.

Morty looked at his wristwatch. "Would you like to have dinner with me?" he asked. "You remind me of a kid I once knew in Paris."

It was like being on the ship again. They stayed up late and she asked him questions. What they did now was manufacture woolens. Starting with the wool tops, the raw wool which they spun into yarn, they wove woolen cloth on looms. Some of it went into blankets, some into coat and suit fabric. What they produced was good. Morty wanted to expand the good into better. He had looked into importing cashmere but Stuart said there wasn't a big enough market for cashmere. The truth was, Stuart didn't wear it, and if Stuart didn't, there wasn't a market for it.

"I wear it," Morty said.

"I know you do." She had accompanied him in the fall when he had bought the cashmere coat he was wearing. She rubbed her cheek on the sleeve. "There's nothing like it."

"That's what I tell my brother."

But it was the printing that aroused her interest most. Cotton mills produced fabric that was good for very little in its original form. Before it could be sold for dressmaking or tablecloths or bedsheets, it had to be converted from "gray goods" into finished material. Designers produced patterns, converters bought the gray fabric, sent it out to be bleached, printed, and finished, and then sold it to the garment manufacturers.

"We have something very special to offer that other people in the industry don't have," he said. He unlocked the car door and opened it for her. It was late and cold. They had just left a club where Morty liked the music. They had danced for the first time in months and she had appreciated the closeness in the way she had appreciated it last year and the year before. He took his place behind the wheel and closed his door.

"We do?"

"We have you. You're a designer. You've studied in Paris and New York. You're good—you're very good. You have a full portfolio right now. We haven't danced for a long time, have we?"

186

"No."

He slowed at the corner and turned right. A car coming down the street from the left faster than it should have sounded its horn and passed them, swinging widely. Mother complained that they only put up traffic lights after someone was killed at a corner. They followed the angry fading yowl of the horn down the dark street. "Will your doctor mind if I exercise my marital rights tonight?"

"No." She had visited him for the last time a week ago. He had probed and spoken and reassured.

"Will you?"

It was the first night in months she could have faced the question. It was the first night he had asked it. All evening she had felt an excitement growing as they talked about the business—their business: they could do this, they could do that. She had felt elevated by a champagnelike effervescence and she had thought it sprang from their conversation, from the ideas that might grow into plans, but now she saw it was the same excitement he always generated in her, the same that she had felt the first time he had touched her in Paris, taking her hand as they walked in the seizième. It was neither the business nor the place; it was Morty. He was the source of it all.

She said, "No, I won't mind," and then, hastily, "I mean, I would mind if you didn't."

The car accelerated and a few minutes later they were home.

He kissed her when they walked inside the front door, the lights still out. Then he turned them on, took her coat and tossed it toward the sofa, missing, and kissed her again. She knew there would be no leisurely shower tonight, no filing of fingernails, no brushing of hair. She would descend in the morning to a scattering of clothes, and seeing them, she would feel the tingle of warm recent memories.

They went up the stairs closely, his fingers unbuttoning the back of her dress. At the top of the stairs she saw the closed door of the room that had lost its purpose and she stopped.

"I'll get you a studio," he said.

"No. It's a nice room. I'll use it. Open the door for me."

He turned the cut-glass knob and pushed. The door swung slowly open.

"Morty . . ." She looked into the dark room without moving toward it. "Was he all right? Was there anything wrong with him?"

"He was perfect."

"Are you sure? I didn't ask. I wanted to but I couldn't."

"I asked. There was nothing wrong with him. He just came too early. That was all. That was absolutely all. He was as perfect as you." He pulled the top of the unbuttoned dress and exposed her shoulder. He bent and kissed it.

Perfect. She had been afraid to ask, but if the baby had been perfect, if it was really only the earliness, then she could wait a year and try again. She could go through it again. She would. There was no question about it. He had been perfect.

She took Morty's hand and led the way to the bedroom.

She spent the next day walking through the large department stores, looking at dresses, tablecloths, and fabrics made of cotton. Starting at

Macy's, she continued across Thirty-fourth Street to Fifth Avenue, stopping in at McCreery's, then Altman's, then turning up the avenue to Best's at Thirty-fifth, Franklin Simon, and finally at Thirty-eighth Street, Bonwit Teller. For a quick respite she ducked into Tiffany's at Thirty-seventh and looked at some glitter, but when the overbearing man behind the counter offered to show her some diamonds, she laughed and left the store.

At dinner she told Morty about it.

"How did the fabrics strike you?" he asked.

"They're all right."

"But . . . ?"

"I can do better."

"I know you can. Shall we work up some samples, have some cards printed, and see if we can make a little money?"

"I don't know." It made her feel queasy to think about it.

"I'll rent some space from Pop for an office and we'll make the rounds together. There are printers and finishers in New Jersey. I'll make some calls, get some prices, put something together that looks good. Shall we give it a try?"

"I'm scared."

"It's better than being overconfident, the way some of us are."

She stood up from the table, took her plate, and walked around to where he sat to get his. He put his arm around her. "Better wear high heels when we make our calls," he said. "I don't want anyone looking down on you."

He knew his family. Pop Rush had a glint in his eye when Morty told him about their idea. Milling cotton was up and down these days, but maybe there was steady money in converting. They could sell a quality product, like their woolens, without the heavy investment of the spinning and weaving machinery. Perhaps, Pop said, his head nodding slightly, they should think about silk too. The best dresses were made of silk, and that new stuff, rayon, would never replace it, even if they did call it artificial silk.

But Stuart was furious. No only did he disapprove of the whole scheme—he never called it a suggestion or idea—he felt his brother had acted underhandedly. Morty's place was with Rush Woolens. His time should be spent selling, not wasted on a new business. And involving his wife was unforgivable. A wife had no place in a business venture.

"You know," Pop said as they sat at dinner a few nights later, "Stuart could be right. Some of those guys in the cotton mills are losing their shirts."

"We're not milling cotton, Pop," Morty said.

Pop Rush sighed. He was a gray-haired man of medium height with a graying black mustache. If Stuart was nearly forty-three, Pop must have been nearly seventy. "I can't take sides with you boys," he said, as though his sons were children fighting over a point in a game. "You do what you think is right, Morty. You work hard, and times are good. Nineteen-twenty-eight was our best year, and right now twenty-nine looks to be even better. You'll make a good living for yourself."

"Thanks, Pop," Regina said.

"And don't borrow any money," her father-in-law went on. "I don't spend anything anymore. Let me give you whatever you need."

"You don't have to do that, Pop," Morty said in a low voice.

"Sure I don't have to. What else am I going to do with my money? Besides, I'm not giving it to you. I'm giving it to Regina."

She said, "Thank you," and smiled. Since she had lost the baby, everyone she knew had been nice to her in special ways.

"And I'll tell you who to see," Pop went on, pulling a piece of paper out of his wallet and a pencil from his coat pocket. He wrote something on the paper and pushed it across the table to her. "Federman," he said with something like triumph. "You tell him you're my daughter-in-law, he'll buy from you." He turned to Morty. "You remember Federman? You were just a little boy then."

"I remember." Morty was enjoying the scene. His father was more animated than usual, and Regina could see that it pleased him. "You helped him fill a big order."

"Big? It was tremendous. It made him rich, that order. And it cost me with someone else. You never heard the whole story. You go see Federman, Regina. He'll buy from you."

They saw Federman and they saw so many other people that she lost track of the names—printers of cotton and buyers of printed fabric. They went through all the designs she had collected since her days in Paris and picked out the ones Morty thought would be the best to start with if they were to develop a clientele that wanted more. They worked out costs and schedules and arranged to meet with Uncle Willy to sign papers for a partnership.

Federman gave them an order, and other buyers gave them other orders. She watched Morty as he talked to the men who would be taking their fabric and making it into dresses or skirts or shirts, listening to what he said, to the questions he asked: What are you looking for this year? We can't give that to you now, but we will next spring. One day she would be doing this alone.

And she watched the faces of the girls and women who welcomed them and led them into cluttered offices, saw how they looked at Morty with a combination of pleasure and flirtatiousness, wondered how the looks might be different, less ambiguous perhaps, if she were not along.

She went to visit her mother and grandparents one day in February after everything had been decided and before anyone had been told. With enthusiasm she described their plans, leaving out the conflict in the Rush family, being fairly general and very optimistic.

"We've sold some of my designs," she said. "Not the best ones, we're saving them, but we've got a lot of good comments. People who said they couldn't use anything for the fall told us to come back when we're ready for next spring."

"Regina," Mother said skeptically, "is this Morty's business or yours?"

"Ours, Momma. We're in it together. I'm learning everything—how to sell, how to order, how to get samples ready. Pretty soon I'm going to—"

"I don't see why you want to do this," Mother interrupted. "You should be—"

"Alice!" Grandmama said sharply, silencing her daughter. Then, turning to Regina, she smiled. "I like it," she said. "You work together. Like Poppi and me in the old days."

"Yes, that's just the way it'll be." She liked the image, Poppi behind the plow, Grandmama and the children harvesting the vegetables. Grandmama and the children. . . .

"There's lots of money in textiles if you're smart," Poppi said. "Old man Rush made plenty during the war. And later he made even more."

"Old man Rush," Grandmama said derisively. "He's ten years younger than you, old man."

"Come, Momma," Mother said. "Don't get excited about nothing."

Regina laughed. "The three of you. I don't know how you do it."

"My good nature," Poppi said, and they all laughed.

A few days later they went to Uncle Willy's office to sign the papers. She had asked Morty to go without her, but he had insisted, saying it would only take additional time for him to bring the papers home and send them back. They went up in the same wonderful old cage of an elevator and through the heavy door with its brass plates to which one had been added, Jerold Wolfe, at the bottom of the column. Inside, the same woman with the same on-again-off-again eyeglasses sat at the same desk with the Underwood nearby. It had been so many years. She had been so young and so unhappy that day, so full of a special love and a special anguish.

"Oh, yes, good morning, Mr. Rush," Miss Cole said, removing her glasses and letting them fall to her breast, where they hung from black ribbon. Miss Cole's hair was long and knotted in the back. She had not heard about the changes in fashion. The twenties had come and almost gone and they had passed her by and she had not noticed. "In Mr. Jerold's office this morning, if you'll follow me."

The door was opened and Regina was the first to enter. She drew in her breath as she saw the interior. On top of a bookcase with glass doors was a large cloisonné vase with a serpent winding around it, a glass lotus bowl beside it, and a jade carving beyond. On the floor was a large Chinese rug in pale colors, mostly ivory and blue. A group of Chinese paper cuts of traditional theatrical characters hung on the wall framed in dark wood.

"It's very lovely," she said softly.

"Thank you."

They had not said hello.

Relinquishing her coat to Miss Cole as Morty and Jerold shook hands, Regina was suddenly aware of the slenderness of her figure. He had seen her three months before, when she was bursting with child.

Uncle Willy came in and they signed the papers and exchanged bits of family gossip. Richard was in Rome, and Uncle Willy and Aunt Eva would visit this summer.

"Well, I expect you'll be our largest corporate client one of these days," Uncle Willy said, looking at Regina. He still spoke to her as though she were his young niece, while he addressed Morty as a client. Morty was almost exactly halfway between Uncle Willy's age and Regina's.

"We hope so," Morty answered for her. "We just need a couple of good years. If this goes, we may start milling our own cotton."

"Not too fast," Uncle Willy cautioned. "Lot of problems in cotton these days."

Morty said something, and Regina left them to look around the office. On a shelf a small community of carved ivory animals held one another at bay.

"How are you feeling?" Jerold stood near her.

"Better."

"I was very sorry."

"Thank you."

"I told Richard about it last time I wrote."

"Thanks, Jody. I keep putting those letters aside. I had to write to Suzanne. She's expecting in the spring."

"Walter's wife had a baby in December. They're raising him Catholic. And spoiled, I think."

"It's probably the right way   spoiled, I mean. When do you have time to indulge your Oriental taste?"

"An afternoon now and then. I have quite a collection of books at home—and some other pieces. When I get started talking, I toss around the names of dynasties rather recklessly."

"Not recklessly, I'm sure."

"Time to go, love." Morty put a hand on her shoulder. "Good to see you, Jerold. I didn't know you were an Orientalist. Pop's got an old piece of silk embroidery somewhere—dragons or serpents or some damned thing. Got it about thirty years ago so Mom could make a pillow."

"I hope she didn't," Jerold said.

"No. She said it was too old, it'd fall apart if she tried to put a needle through it. I'll send it over one of these days."

"I'd appreciate that. Good luck on your new venture."

In the car Morty handed her the envelope from Uncle Willy. "Did you read what you signed?"

"Huh-uh. I trusted you."

"Never do that."

"If you expect me to flinch, I won't."

"Open it up and see what you signed."

She pulled the papers out and began to read. "Oh, Morty." She rested the sheaf on her lap. The name of their fledgling company was Regina Rush Fabrics.

It was a spring of destruction and new life. The beautiful temple in which they had been married was already gone, razed to make way for something newer and less beautiful, and now the Waldorf-Astoria was taken down, to be replaced by what they were told would be the tallest building in the world, with clean pure lines and a dock for dirigibles near its top. But like the new temple a mile north of the old one, it would arouse no memories. One would walk by it and the air would not pulse.

Suzanne gave birth to a son in March and telegraphed the news. In a subsequent letter she said Maurice would marry in August. Richard wrote that his friend McGuire had found a publisher for his novel and expected to see it in print in the fall. Adele announced her engagement to a fellow teacher and set a date for spring of 1930. Mother said she had heard Jerold was "seeing" a very fine girl who was a student at Vassar. Regina Rush Fabrics went into production, and after all the accounts were settled for fall, Morty paid his father back the small amount he had borrowed.

But between Morty and his brother a great silence grew.

"He was waiting for us to fail," Morty said. "He was hoping for it."

"Maybe he wants to be part of it," Regina suggested.

"I offered it to him a long time ago."

"He's your brother. Offer again."

"Never."

"What happened between you two?"

"Nothing."

He pushed his chair away from the table and walked to the window. The lone tree in front of the house was richly in leaf, and around the house annual flowers had begun to bloom. He stood looking out the window as she cleared the table. Discussions about his brother seemed invariably to unnerve him. Usually they ended before Regina's last question. Usually he swallowed a visible anger and acted as though the subject were forgotten.

"It goes back to my cavalry days," he said from the window, speaking euphemistically of his brief service in the war. "He thought I shouldn't have enlisted, and when the war was over he thought I should have come home."

"You did come home."

"But not the way he planned it. I'd been away seven years. Stuart wanted me to come back as a junior partner until I proved myself. He felt I should serve an apprenticeship and get paid that way. Pop said nothing doing. Pop put away my share of the profits while I was in the army and sent me checks out of it. When I wrote that I wasn't coming home, they threw most of my salary into the kitty."

"You did work for him over there."

"Not that much." He pulled his tie and unbuttoned the collar of his shirt. "When I came back, he took me in as a full third partner. Stuart was . . ." He started to say something and stopped. A volatile anger she had never seen before had begun to surface. "He was sore as hell," he said, modifying the flavor of his original sentence. "And then there was the nest egg Pop had put away for me. Pop's always felt guilty about me, since Mom died."

"It isn't guilt. You're his son."

"It's guilt." He took his jacket off and folded it over the back of a chair and watched her for a moment. She was rinsing the last of the dinner dishes, the fine French porcelain with which she set the table every night. She placed each piece carefully on the drainboard. "Stuart thought it was bad for Pop to give me any salary at all, and worse for me to take it. He was probably right—about my taking it."

"He wasn't right about anything. My father sent me to France, and yours put some money aside. Stuart knew why you went away. Did he think you should be punished beyond what you had already been through?"

"Who are you shouting at?" His own anger seemed suddenly to have dissipated at the onset of hers.

"Maybe if he'd listen to you once in a while, he'd earn back some of the money he thinks you took from him."

"That's another thing," he said, and he was himself again now. "He's jealous that in ten years I managed to find two beautiful wives while in fifteen he's only had the one prissy one."

She could only agree. She had tried unsuccessfully to be friends with her sister-in-law and had finally given up. There were fifteen years between them and outlooks on the world that could not be accounted for only by the difference in their ages.

"Morty . . ." She hung the damp dish towel on the rack near the back window. "There's space available on Worth Street. Let's move RR out of Canal. It'll cost a little bit but it'll be easier to keep our accounts separate. I think we should keep everything as separate as possible. Then no one can say we're not paying enough for the services we get from Rush."

"Sounds like you're taking over." He looked as though it wouldn't bother him a bit.

"Subject to approval," she said.

"I approve without reservations. Let's do it right away." He pulled his tie off, picked up his jacket, and laid it over one arm. "I want to buy him out, Regina. I'm just waiting for the right time."

"You're the most gorgeous man I've ever laid eyes on," she said, watching him prepare to go upstairs and change his clothes.

He looked startled, as though he had been confronted with shocking information. "How would you know?" he said evenly, recovering. "You aren't even twenty-five yet."

They moved the office in June and began looking at cars. The Mercedes was three years old and starting to give Morty trouble. He had a yen for something new and different. When they walked, he stopped and looked at cars parked on the street, appraising their design. Then they would drop in to look at new models and talk to the salesmen. He told her to listen to what they said and how they presented it. He was interested in the cars, but you could always learn something about selling by observing people who did it for a living.

Around their anniversary he bought a Packard, and the first week in July, when the mill closed down along with the rest of the industry for its annual vacation, they drove upstate to a house he had rented in the mountains and had a good rest. When they came back, she began working on samples for the spring of 1930.

She woke up on her birthday to the smell of brewing coffee. It was hot with the thickness of August. A week ago she had traveled to the farm to visit Mother, and while there she had met Adele's intended and played with Millie's smiling little boy, now walking at fifteen months. In the afternoon she had taken a dip in the swimming hole, flexing muscles whose use was scarcely required by city living. It had been a good visit but she had returned home gratefully, almost with a feeling of relief. Here it was quiet and very orderly. They set their own schedule, altering it at a whim, moving at a pace they determined for themselves. It was the meaning of comfortable.

She put slippers on and went downstairs. She could hear the sound of the exhaust fan in the kitchen and mutterings from the unaccustomed chef. It was a Wednesday but he had taken the day off to spend it with her. He looked up from the stove with some dismay as she entered the kitchen.

193

"Either I've lost my touch or you've spoiled me." There was a feast before him on the stove, some of it smoking threateningly.

"I've spoiled you." She stood on tiptoe to kiss him and took over the eggs while he did something to the bacon and turned the flame off under the coffee.

"There's even caviar in the fridge," he said, draining the bacon deftly. "I thought it would go well with eggs. Happy birthday." And before she could answer, "I forgot to squeeze the oranges. Do you think we could have that with dessert?"

"It'll taste wonderful with dessert."

"I have something for you out in the living room. I guess it'll have to wait till we've eaten." He made a helpless gesture with his free hand. "I just couldn't make it come together at the same time."

He hurried her through the meal so that she could see her present. When they were nearly through, he put more coffee on the stove and took her to the living room. On the rug lay a large white box tied with blue ribbon. Just under the bow was an envelope. She pulled it out and read the card: "This is one you can drive yourself." She looked at him questioningly.

"Open it carefully," he said. "It's in parts and you don't want to lose any of it."

She knelt on the floor, pulled the ribbon off, and shook the top till the bottom dropped to the floor. It was quite heavy, and inside the contents were covered with white tissue paper. Curious and excited, she pulled the paper away.

"Oh, Morty." She ran her hand across the dark brown fur. "It's beautiful. It's absolutely . . ." She lifted it out of the box.

"Careful," Morty said, and she saw something glittery roll away across the rug and stop near the screen in front of the fireplace.

"What is it?" Holding the coat over her left arm, she crawled a short distance and reached for the glitter. It was a ring with a large round diamond that picked colors out of the air as she turned it.

"Put it on."

She slid the ring next to her wedding band. It was slightly large and she had to hold her fingers together to keep it in place. Her heart was pounding furiously, and as she stood, she felt almost dizzy. Her arms slipped easily through the silk lining of the sleeves. When she had buttoned the coat, she looked down to see the white peignoir falling beneath it to the floor. She turned slowly, aware of a strange sound from the kitchen.

"Morty, the coffee!"

"Hang the coffee. I'll clean up the stove. One of these days. Turn around again. What makes you think you can't wear a full-length fur?"

"But mink," she said, stroking it with her newly bejeweled hand. "We haven't even turned a profit yet."

"We will," he assured her. "Wait till fall."

She would have remembered the day anyway. At seven-fifteen, while they were sitting down to breakfast, the phone rang. It was Morris, bursting with pride and happiness.

"It's a boy," he said, shouting into the phone. "Two-fourteen this morning. Seven pounds, six ounces. Beautiful. Looks just like Shayna. There'll be a brith next week. Can we count on you?"

"Of course you can. Morris, that's wonderful. How's Shayna?"

"I haven't seen her yet. They said she'll be up soon. I wandered around the hospital half the night and then decided to come home and shave. Can she call you at your office?"

"Anytime. Morris, I'm just delighted."

"Well, I'd better get downtown and see my mother-in-law. Don't forget the brith. I think the date comes out to be November fifth."

She glanced at the calendar on the kitchen wall. It was October twenty-ninth.

There were a few cancellations. One of the small dress companies to whom she had personally sold a group of floral prints for summer dresses went out of business. The owner had invested heavily in the market earlier in the year on a tip, buying on margin. After the crash, he could not meet his payroll.

The phone began ringing at their two offices, jittery buyers, sellers, competitors, and mere onlookers. At Christmas the stores were full, just as she remembered them from past years. Fifth Avenue from Thirty-fourth to Thirty-eighth, the center of the retail industry, was thronged.

But early in January Mother told her that her cousin Phil Schindler had begun working for Uncle Jack.

"He was with that company a long time, wasn't he?" Regina asked. "I think he was working there when they got married."

"It went broke," Momma said simply.

"Oh."

"Before Christmas. It had something to do with the crash. He looked around a little, but . . ."

"It's lucky Uncle Jack has a place for him."

Momma looked somewhat uncomfortable. "I'm not sure he does," she said.

The wedding plans for Adele were suddenly scaled down. It wasn't that Uncle Nate couldn't afford it, Mother explained carefully. It was just that things didn't look very good for the future and he was a cautious man. There had been enough of these big weddings anyway. Millie's had been very extravagant and Uncle Nate didn't need to do something like that every two years. But it was clear that she was worried.

Buyers that spring bought timidly, but they still bought. Cotton was cheap and there was a good profit in converting it. The demand for the bottom of the line began to soften, but their fabric, all of it very fine quality, continued fairly strong. Morty picked up an account with a company that made expensive men's shirts. Regina sold pastel stripes to a company that made women's golfing outfits.

On Park Avenue and Fifth Avenue young women were introduced to society at expensive debuts, wearing expensive clothes. On the lots, unsold Fords, their prices reduced, began to pile up. Once in the *Times* a small, square paragraph about a company she had never heard of mentioned Jerold.

They sat one spring afternoon in the Worth Street office. On her left hand Regina's ring picked up the light from the window and made colors of it. It had not left her finger since the day it had been made small enough to fit properly.

"It's been a good year," she said. In front of her were notes she had made. This was the "meeting of the board" that they had from time to time, and she knew that today was an important one. They had both reached the point where there were too few hours in the day, and they had decisions to make.

"I wish we'd sold more of your designs."

"It doesn't matter. We've sold, and that's what's important." Macy's had bought two designs in bolts to be sold for home sewing, and they had reordered both. Regina had signed the fabric with her RR and she was trying to get several other stores to carry her designs.

"It does matter. That's your special place, and one day women will look for a Regina Rush design the way people ask for a Rush woolen."

"We have time for that, Morty. Things are so shaky since the market crash. Right now we have to think about whether we want to add a salesman."

"We do."

She had known he would say that. In the little more than a year they had been in business they had built a small clientele that might well support them without Rush Woolens. There was an edginess among buyers, and raw cotton was selling for record low prices, but manufacturers were still in business and customers were still buying in the stores. When the country recovered, and President Hoover seemed to feel recovery was imminent, the same clients would buy more. But to increase the scope of their market, they needed to depend on someone other than themselves. Morty had to spend time with Rush, and she had to have time to design.

"Do you want to advertise?"

"No, we'll be deluged. Let me make some phone calls. There're plenty of guys out there who know fabrics, but the truth is, anyone who's smart can learn. I'd like to get someone I can really trust."

She crossed a line off her notes. Morty never wrote anything down and never forgot a thing.

"I was wondering," she said, looking down at her papers. "About the printing. How would you feel about our doing it ourselves—I mean buying our own equipment? I've been doing some figuring, and it seems to me . . ." She stopped, surprised at the look on his face.

"You are something," he said in obvious disbelief. "You really are something. And here I thought I was still one step ahead of you."

She laughed, pleased at his reaction. "Then you think we should?"

He pulled his foot off the radiator and sat up straight. "Next year, love. Next year you can have anything you want."

In the middle of June they traveled to Newark to attend Adele's wedding. The ceremony was in a temple, and afterward they drove to the hall where the dinner was. Walking out of the temple, they met Lillian and Phil.

"An awful fuss," Lillian grumbled, "for a handful of people. I don't see why they couldn't have just done the whole thing in one place."

"I understand the Bergmans wanted a temple wedding," Regina said, repeating the family gossip. "And they didn't like the banquet facilities here."

"I don't know why it's always our family that has to accommodate. Stuffy in there, wasn't it? I didn't like the smell."

"Well," Morty said genially, "going from one place to another gives you a chance to have a breath of fresh air."

Druing the short drive he said, "That isn't the guy you once told me looked like me?"

"It's hard to believe, looking at him now. Back in twenty-one, when they were married, I could have sworn there was a resemblance, but he looks pasty and old now. He can't be more than thirty-two or -three. I wonder how Uncle Jack is doing. If he goes down, Uncle Nate'll go with him. And Izzy. It's a lot of families."

"I didn't see Granny."

"She was probably up front. Uncle Willy sent a car for them."

"Willy's the prince of the family," Morty said with admiration. "I'm always amazed at what he has his finger on. Remember what he said about cotton the day we were up there last year? It could have been anything. He knows what's going on everywhere."

"You should hear what he has to say about railroads," Regina said.

They milled around in the outer room until the bride and groom arrived and a receiving line formed. Everything they said about brides was true. Adele was at her most beautiful tonight. A plump girl with a plain face, she seemed nevertheless a long, almost slender beauty in the floor-length white silk dress and veil. Even her disposition had changed for the night of her wedding. She radiated warmth. "Regina, he*llo!* Morty, how good to see you. I don't think you've met Stanley yet." A ring of bright gold on her left hand and the world was hers.

They passed along to the room where the tables had been set, stopping at a small buffet, greeting Henry, newly home from medical school, and Aunt Martha, who was concerned about her granddaughters alone in New York with a maid.

"They're very grown-up," Aunt Martha sniffed, "and better behaved than people three times their age in this family. I don't see why Bertha left them out."

"It's nicer without children," Henry said. "They squeal a lot."

"You didn't squeal. I wouldn't have allowed it."

Morty groaned, took Regina's hand, and they wandered away. "Not everything improves with age," he said. "Hey . . . look who's here."

She turned and caught her breath. "Richard. *Richard!*" They wrapped their arms around each other. "Three years and you never wrote that you were coming. Oh, Richard, I'm so glad to see you."

"I didn't know until I got on the ship. I've called a couple of times, but you're never home during the day."

"I work. Morty and I work together. You should have called at night."

"I've been busy." He looked apologetic but not sorry.

"Tell me everything. I read you more than I talk to you now. Richard, you look wonderful. Where's Morty? I think I've lost him. Never mind, I'll find him later. Talk to me."

He still had an arm around her and she slipped her own along the back of his jacket.

"Are you back for good now?"

"Not a chance."

"My expatriate cousin."

"More like the man without a country. But I like it that way. I like it more than I can tell you."

"How's McGuire doing? I read his book last fall."

"Hell of a time for a book to come out, wasn't it? What did you think of it?"

She considered carefully before she spoke. "I think he's going to be a good writer," she said. "His next book'll be better than the first. He worked too hard on this one. He should have let it go sooner. I suppose he couldn't because it was his first. What do you think?"

"I think I don't want you taking up literary criticism. I hope when you read my stuff—"

"When I read Richard Wolfe I turn to mush. I'm just carried away by your writing."

"My best cousin." He looked at her with appreciation. "I see Morty has you in diamonds."

"Pre-crash diamonds. It gave me a funny feeling at the end of October."

"You weren't hit, were you?"

She shook her head. "Thank God. Stocks aren't Morty's vice. But cotton mills may be. I may be left one day with nothing but a diamond, a house, a car, and the memory of all those mills somebody else is making money on." She didn't sound unhappy at the prospect.

"Well, that's better than McGuire's been left. He's well into his second book now, but he's going to have to give it up. He's about out of funds."

"He's not coming back here, is he?"

198

"There's nothing for him in Paris."

"There's nothing for him here either, Richard. Everything's down and getting worse. Morty's woolen factory is doing much worse than last year. They've cut production for fall and they've laid men off. I keep hearing that Uncle Jack's got problems too. I don't know what McGuire can do to make a living."

"I tried to lend him some money, but he wouldn't take it. His advance was a pittance and they haven't sold many books. Hell, let's talk about something else. I think we're at table seven."

There were cries of "Richard!" as they approached, and she watched the cousins greet him, feeling strangely moved. Like a magnet, the wedding of his least favorite cousin had drawn him back to the fold as such occasions would draw them all, all their lives.

"Let's see," she heard Richard say as he looked around the table before sitting, "who've we got tonight? The Schindlers, the Benetoviches, the Rushes, and the four incomparable bachelors of the Wolfe family. How are you, Arthur? My God, I hardly recognize you. You must be twenty by now."

"Morty," she said quietly, "would you mind if I wrote a check for five hundred dollars that we'll never see again?"

"A check?" He looked confused. "Write anything you want."

"It's a lot of money."

He reached into his vest pocket. "Need a pen?"

"Thanks, dear." She left the table and after she had said hello to the uncles and aunts and her grandparents, she asked Uncle Willy to see to it that Timothy McGuire, at an address in Paris she would send on Monday along with a check, received five hundred dollars in the most anonymous way he could think of.

"You're the client," Uncle Willy said. "Imagine if someone had done that for my father fifty years ago. He might be a rich man today."

"He is, Uncle Willy. You just never noticed it." And she went back to the table.

"How does it taste, Izzy?" Arthur looked at the dish in front of his brother-in-law with skepticism. The special meal had been brought in wrapped in cellophane and guaranteed kosher.

"A feast," Izzy said, patting his mouth with the large napkin. "A chicken so fresh it could still lay an egg."

"Izzy!" Lillian said with obvious revulsion. Her own plate looked scarcely touched.

"So how many companies do you own now, Morty?" Phil asked.

"Haven't counted lately," Morty said. "We're putting our big effort into our converting operation, but I'm still part of the woolen business."

"Sounds like you don't know there's been a crash."

"We know. The mill's been hit, but we'll get back. I think next year'll see an upturn."

"You're a lot more optimistic than my brother," Richard said. "To listen to Jerold, you'd think this is going to go on for years."

Morty looked with interest at Jerold, who sat across the table from him next to Millie. "It's good to have a pessimist for a lawyer. Keeps me in line."

"I think my father's business is on the slow side," Henry said, looking through glasses at his cousins.

"Henry!" Lillian's voice rose and fell theatrically. "That's not true at all. Poppa's doing very well. We're doing better than we've ever done before, aren't we, Phil?"

"Much better," Phil mumbled.

Izzy looked at Phil quizzically but said nothing.

"We certainly eat better than this," Lillian murmured as though speaking exclusively to herself, but Millie heard and glared at her.

"Well, I think I'll be the first in the family to get rich," Arthur announced, his voice thick with alcohol and his eyes glazed. "I've got a scheme."

"He won't stay sober long enough to count it," Lillian said under her breath.

Millie laughed. "My brother has a new scheme every day of the week. But I think Henry'll be the first one in the family to get rich. People need a doctor even when times are bad."

"You see?" Izzy said. "My wife got her head on right. She knows what's what. A doctor you always need, and food you always need too. Pretty soon we all get rich together."

The music started and Morty stood so quickly he startled Regina.

"Dance," he said. "Now. On your feet."

She left the table laughing. "My family does things to you."

"Gives me indigestion. How could that nice old lady have been responsible for that table? I don't think your cousin Arthur is going to do an honest day's work in his life. Henry is the soul of gentility and Lillian can't let anything pass without a bitchy comment. Even the brothers surprise me. Willy gets up at dawn and goes to work and Jerold's just like him, but what the hell does Richard do?"

"He writes."

"That's not a living, Regina, an article on London and an article on Paris."

"It's the way things worked out for them."

"Richard's damned lucky."

"Maybe he has a father like yours."

She watched his face change. "Touché. I'm not long on memory, am I?" He drew her a little closer and they danced in silence for a few minutes. "What was the five hundred for?"

"For someone who has a different kind of father."

He handed her over to Richard later and went to dance with her mother.

"How long will you stay, Richard?"

"Through the summer."

"You'll come and visit?"

"Anytime. I want to see that house of yours. Grandmama thinks you're Hansel and Gretel."

"It's a wonderful house."

"You've had some tough times."

"They're over. I'm fine now." She had learned to talk about it with a measure of equanimity.

"You actually go to work every day."

"Yes." She laughed. "I don't think you believe it."

"It isn't what I pictured. Nobody's what I pictured—except Lillian. I could have designed Lillian ten years ago."

"But you wouldn't have put your name on the design, would you?"

"What a bitch."

"She has her good moments, Richard."

"Like an asp." He looked disgusted, then moved his head. "There's my mother."

Aunt Eva was dancing with Jerold, and when they came close, Aunt Eva said, "Let me have my son back, Regina," and in a moment they had switched partners.

"Hello, Jody." She smiled at him, full of amusement at Aunt Eva's perennial misunderstanding. "It's good to see you."

"Come and talk to me," he said. "Outside."

They left the room and walked out a side door.

"This is Newark," she said, looking around, up at the night sky. "I used to think Newark was a place to go to market. I wouldn't know how to get here without a horse and wagon."

"I hear Uncle Nate's having problems. Prices are way down."

"There are no flowers on the tables. Did you notice?"

"Flowers? That's why it was easier to see everyone."

"Aunt Bertha's wearing the same dress she wore to Millie's wedding."

"Why do they have to do it? You didn't have a big wedding."

"No, but I think my mother would have liked it. Poppa would have. He would have liked knowing he could bring them all together like this, tables and tables of them, from Grandmama down to the little ones. It would have been the first time in his life that he could have shown everyone he knew that he had come as far as they had, that he could feed them more than they could possibly eat."

"Symbolism," Jerold said.

"It's more than that. Richard came home for this wedding. He left after Millie's and he came back for Adele's. It's something more than symbolism. Look at how happy Grandmama is tonight. She's got every one of us here."

"And we're all still at the same table."

"The table's growing up. I think I saw it tonight for the first time. We're going to grow old together there, the eight of us. We'll have a doctor, a lawyer, a farmer, a writer, a manufacturer . . ." She laughed at her ego which had inflated her own accomplishments.

"A schemer," Jerold picked up, and laughed with her. "A teacher."

"And all of us still together. It's thirteen years since . . ." She broke off, barraged by a conflict of memories. "There's a day in May every year that Morty goes off by himself. I didn't make the connection until we'd been married two years."

"We all have days like that."

"I'm glad Uncle Nate had a wedding for Adele. Even with no flowers on the tables. I'm glad Richard came back for it."

She turned away from him. Down the street in a small wooden house, an upstairs light went off and the house was entirely dark. A dog howled, although she could see no moon. Perhaps, like herself, he was howling at the memory of the moon.

"You don't mind if I still love you a little?" He sounded uncertain, like the boy he had been at bygone weddings.

"How could I mind?" Almost half her life was wrapped up in loving him. "We'd better go in."

"Yes." He pulled the door open. "Without our two sane voices, there's likely to be mayhem at the table."

Late that night Grandmama suffered what they called a massive stroke and by morning she had died. The bridal couple, uninformed, had already boarded a train, but since Richard had come home for the wedding, all the grandchildren but one were present at the funeral.

5

For still another season the clothes that fall looked as depressed as the country. Hemlines had dropped and shoulders had squared. It was as though the music had gone out of fashion. Regina bought herself two tweed suits and a few silk blouses, wearing them with high heels, dropping a string of something bright around her neck, sometimes the green glass beads that she credited with putting her in business. In the stores there were silk dresses with long sleeves and large collars and deep V necklines. The twenties were over and everything had changed.

Richard returned to the Continent. Before leaving, he showed her a letter from McGuire with amazing news. She told him she was very pleased but admitted nothing. The woolen mill produced less because there was a smaller market, but Morty pointed out (again and again to his brother, who refused to listen) that the top of the line was still selling well. People with money were spending it, and they should be catering to those tastes.

A manufacturer of women's daytime dresses bought several of Regina's designs, and Macy's continued to order—cautiously—in bolts. The new salesman, Karl Handelman, an old friend of Morty's from the days before the war when they used to kick around the streets together, worked longer and harder than either of his employers had, and with promising results.

Poppi turned eighty and spent his days looking out of the window morosely while Mother spoke to him brightly and tended his every whim.

In December, shortly before Christmas, Regina received an unexpected long-distance call.

"This is Henry, Regina. I'm calling from Washington."

"Henry! Is anything wrong?"

"Oh, no, we're fine . . . I'm fine. I need . . . I'm sorry to impose, but I wonder if you have room for a friend of mine to stay with you over the vacation?"

"Of course. We have an extra room. When is he coming?"

"Uh . . ." There was some static on the line and then he came back. "It's a girl, Regina. Does that make a difference?"

"Of course not. When can we expect her?"

"Tomorrow night. And could you keep this kind of a secret?"

"Whatever you say. I'll even move out if you ask me."

"Oh, no." He sounded flustered. "I wouldn't want you to do that. I just need a room and a hotel is so . . ."

"Will you both come for dinner?"

"Gee." There was another silence. "I think that would be very nice. The train comes in at five. We should be there before six."

"Come hungry."

They fixed the extra room up that evening, pushing artistic equipment aside and making up the extra bed they had installed almost two years before to accommodate transient family and friends. Regina came home early the next afternoon and prepared a feast.

The girl was almost as tall as Henry and about his age. Her name was Margaret and there was a certain forthrightness about her that was very appealing. She had lived in Washington since graduating from college, working for the federal government and earning a nice salary. They had known each other for two years but Henry had never mentioned Margaret at home. He had a lot of reasons for his silence. The main one was Aunt Martha.

"What do you think, Regina?" he asked as they were having dessert. "I'm not worried about Pop, although I'm not altogether sure about him. It's my mother. How much difference do you think it'll make to her, that Margaret isn't Jewish?"

"Run away," Morty said before Regina could answer. "I'll give you the car for the week. There's a house upstate Regina and I rent sometimes. No one'll be there over Christmas."

"We couldn't do that."

Regina looked at Margaret, who had not spoken. She was looking steadily ahead of her, meeting no one's eyes.

"Why not?" Regina asked.

"You know my mother. Her health has always been so delicate. I couldn't walk in on her and say, 'Here's my wife.' "

"Why couldn't you?" Morty persisted.

"Morty, he's got to do what he thinks is right."

"I couldn't be responsible for anything that happened," Henry said. "Not that I think anything would, but I've seen her when things were bad. She fainted a couple of times and scared hell out of us. Sometimes she can't catch her breath, almost like an asthmatic. I can't convince her to see a specialist. She sticks with the doctor she's known all her life, and he can't treat her. I know it's her nerves, but it doesn't make what happens less real—or less frightening. Even Pop gets shaken when she has a fainting spell."

"How do you plan to tell her?"

Henry took a deep breath and looked unhappy.

"Henry's going to speak to his mother tomorrow," Margaret said in a clear voice. "If she agrees to meet me, I'll go uptown. If she doesn't, I'll go back to Washington."

"You won't go back to Washington," Henry told her in a low voice.

"Why don't we all move to the living room?" Morty suggested.

"I'd like to help Mrs. Rush clean up," Margaret said, standing and carrying her dishes to the kitchen.

204

Regina whispered, "Go," and Morty took Henry with him.

"Why don't you call me Regina, Margaret? We're almost the same age, I think."

"I was surprised when I first saw you. Henry talks about you as though you were much older. You went to Paris for a few years, didn't you?"

"That was a long time ago, in the early twenties."

"But you went."

"Yes."

"I've dreamed about that sort of thing." She smiled, almost for the first time. "I've never met anyone who actually did it. I hope you'll excuse me for intervening this way in your plans, but I wanted to speak to you alone. Mrs. Wolfe is your aunt, isn't she?"

"Henry's mother? Yes. She's married to my mother's oldest brother." She was aware that she was placing a certain distance of relationship between herself and Aunt Martha.

"What do you think she'll say—tomorrow, when Henry talks to her?"

"I can't be sure."

"Is Mrs. Wolfe's health as delicate as Henry believes?"

"I don't know, Margaret. I've never been a sick person. I've never fainted. I've never been short of breath. She's given her family a great deal of anxiety about her health."

"I'm sorry. I shouldn't have asked. I've put you in the position of compromising your loyalty to your family."

Regina turned the water off and rubbed her hands on her apron. "If you asked my husband," she said, standing with her back to the sink, "he would tell you that Martha's health is no worse than anyone else's, that she uses it to control her husband and her children. He may be right. He's not the only one in the family who feels that way."

"I see."

"On the other hand, I remember when I was young Aunt Martha would never take the Tubes to come out to the family farm because they ran through a tunnel under the river and the tunnel made her feel claustrophobic. She used to take a ferry instead." Regina laughed. "That made her seasick. She almost never came out to the farm. Uncle Jack used to come out with the children. That was a long time ago."

"Henry told me about it—the swimming hole and going to market in a wagon."

"Margaret, suppose I take a day off tomorrow—it's very slow just before Christmas anyway—and show you New York?"

"Thank you." Margaret shook her head. "I'd rather stay here and wait for Henry's call."

The call didn't come. Regina came home at three to find Margaret sitting in a big chair in the living room with a magazine open on her lap. They looked at each other without speaking, and Regina put her groceries on the floor of the foyer and took off her coat.

"No," Margaret said, standing. The magazine slipped to the floor as though she had long ago forgotten its existence. "He hasn't called."

Regina hung her coat up and turned to look at herself in the mirror opposite the closet. Momma had said you had to have a mirror there so you could adjust your hat, and it was useless to explain to Momma that she never wore hats.

"Margaret, would you like a glass of sherry? I can get a fire started and we can sit and talk."

"No." She was standing like a statue in front of the chair. "The fire would be nice, but if Henry calls, I shouldn't have alcohol on my breath when I go up to see his mother."

"No, you're right. That would make a bad impression." She picked up the groceries. "I'll be back in a minute."

In the kitchen she filled the refrigerator and measured coffee and water into the percolator. She could feel a cold emptiness inside her, like a haunting memory for which she had no referent, an ache that seemed to have transplanted itself from the quiet girl in the living room.

"He isn't going to call, is he?" Margaret stood in the doorway between kitchen and dining room.

"He'll call, Margaret. I know Henry. He'll call."

"Why do you think it's taking so long?"

"He probably didn't want to bring it up till he'd been home for a while. It's not the sort of thing you walk in the door and announce just like that."

"It's what I would have done."

"Yes, I know. It's what I would have done too."

"She's going to say no, isn't she? She's going to say no, and that'll be the end of it. He'll finish medical school and I'll never see him again."

"I don't know," Regina said. She turned and looked out the window. Their little lawn was covered with unmarked snow. "I wish my grandmother were alive. She would have made everything come out right."

"Only Henry can make it come out right," Margaret said, and Regina knew it was true.

The phone rang finally at eight as they came to the end of a tense quiet dinner. As Regina left the table, she could see a shudder run through Margaret.

"It's for you," she called a moment later, and Margaret walked white-faced into the kitchen. Regina shook her head at Morty and he muttered something under his breath.

"He's just a few blocks from here," Margaret said, returning. "I'm sorry to run like this."

Morty reached into his pocket and took a key off his ring.

"Thank you," the girl said breathlessly. "Thank you very much."

It was past midnight when she returned. They lay awake like parents waiting for an errant child, talking about Martha and Henry and the girl who was their guest. The front door opened and closed and there was no further sound. Henry had not come in with her. She mounted the stairs so quietly, one could have believed she was a dancer.

Regina slid out of bed and put on a robe. In the space between the two bedrooms the light was on. They met at the top of the stairs and looked at one another. Margaret had her coat over one arm.

"How can someone reject a person without meeting her?" she asked with an unsteady voice.

"Some people are that way. I know that you're not." Regina touched

206

Margaret's cheek. It was icy and white. Her fingers looked withered. They had walked and walked in the midnight cold, reviewing their agony as generations before them had, all of them believing they were alone. "Let me run a hot bath for you." She went into the clean white-tiled bathroom, stepping on the cold hexagonal tiles, and ran water in the large footed tub, breathing the steam that rose from it.

"I should leave," Margaret said.

"Sleep first."

"What's the use? I'll only have to get up again tomorrow."

In the morning Regina had breakfast with Morty and then waited for Margaret to come down and made breakfast all over again.

"He's going to try again today," Margaret said dully. "Nothing'll come of it, but I couldn't very well discourage him."

"You can still decide what you want to do. You're both old enough to think for yourselves. You've got a good job. That would keep you going for the next few years."

"There's nothing to decide. Mrs. Wolfe told him if we married, there would be no tuition for medical school. Henry's in his last year. He can't give it up, and I don't make enough to cover it and support us too."

"You can borrow."

"You don't understand, Regina. Henry is his mother's son. He will never be my husband. I see that now. Even if we married, he would be her son first." She stirred sugar into her coffee and put the spoon down carefully. "He wanted me to go there last night. He thought that if she met me, she'd change her mind. I wouldn't go. I couldn't subject myself to that. He can go back again and again and beg for her permission to do something he shouldn't have to ask for in the first place, but I can't. Henry may come from a close family, but I come from a proud one." She picked up the spoon and stirred the coffee for a second time. "Do you think I was wrong?" she asked in a small voice.

"No, I think you were wonderfully right."

She went to the Worth Street office and tidied up some paperwork. It was Christmas Eve and the telephones were silent. Karl Handelman was on vacation and Morty would be home early. They had planned to go out that evening to visit friends, but now it looked uncertain. She got back to the house at two and opened the door to find a valise in the foyer.

"I was just waiting to say good-bye," Margaret said, rising from a chair in the living room.

"Has Henry called?"

"No, and I don't want to wait anymore. Nothing's going to change. I'm going to visit my parents for Christmas. It's better than being alone—or imposing on you."

"You're not—"

"Thank you, Regina," Margaret put in quickly. "This is your husband's key. That's really why I waited here so long. I forgot to give it back and I was afraid he'd be locked out. I wouldn't want to be remembered that way."

"Let me take you to the station."

"I'd rather go alone."

They shook hands and Regina kissed her. Standing in front of the door,

207

she watched Margaret make her way along the narrow walk and enter the building that opened onto the street. When she went back into the house, the phone was ringing.

She didn't see Henry again during the vacation or for a long time afterward, but the Sunday before the new year, Aunt Martha called.

"How are you, Regina dear?" the voice in her ear crooned. "We hardly see you anymore, now that Mother Wolfe is gone. It was wonderful the way she held the family together. I suppose they'll all go their separate ways now. That's the way it is with big families; they don't last. It's the small ones that stay together." The voice droned on and on with its murmured accusations and half-spoken innuendos. Regina pulled a kitchen chair near the window, sat, and looked out. ". . . should really see the girls now. Rosalie is just seven and little Celia had her sixth birthday this month. You were in Paris when she was born, weren't you? Funny the way you went off to Paris and never finished college, but I suppose it didn't matter in the end. What would you have needed college for just to go into business with your husband? How is Morty, dear?"

"Just fine, working hard."

"That's good to hear. So many of the businesses are doing so badly these days. It's nice to know someone's doing well. Of course, we're doing nicely ourselves. Uncle Jack was just saying . . ."

Regina yawned and moved her left hand so that the diamond picked up the sunlight and flickered pink and violet. He never asked if she wanted anything; he just bought it and brought it home and everything he gave her had a halo of quality around it, an aura of good taste. They were going out tonight and she would wear the mink coat, appreciating it more for its warmth than for its luxury, and even more because he had given it to her.

She could imagine him if they had a child, imagine the effusiveness of his joy, the car piled above its windows with soft little objects of pink and white. Funny how she always imagined them pink when the one they had had, had been a boy. Two years. A year of being careful and a year of not, and still no pregnancy. A letter yesterday from Suzanne telling her that Maurice's wife would have a baby in the summer. Babies everywhere.

". . . and then the internship. We're hoping for a hospital here in the city so he can live at home. It's nice to have the children around. I'm sure your mother is happy to have you so close, especially now that Mother Wolfe is gone."

"Yes."

"Henry says his friend stayed with you last week." The voice stopped abruptly and Regina realized that an answer was expected.

"Yes, last week."

"So nice of you, Regina. It must have been an imposition."

"It wasn't. It was a pleasure having her. I was sorry to see her go."

"I'm sure she was a lovely girl."

"She was."

"But a different family, if you know what I mean."

"Yes."

"They all want to marry Jewish doctors, don't they? Not at all our kind of people. Did you find that, Regina?"

"Yes, I did. You're right about her. She wasn't your kind of people at all."

"It's good that she left when she did," Aunt Martha said smoothly. "I wouldn't have wanted to see her hurt. It would have disturbed Henry, too. He's a sensitive boy. He'll make a wonderful doctor."

When she hung up, she sat looking at nothing, the window on her right, the telephone in front of her, seeing neither.

"What's wrong?" He filled the space that was the doorway to the dining room.

"Nothing. Just thinking."

"Who was it?"

"Martha."

"Sorry I didn't pick it up."

"It doesn't matter." She stood, returning the chair to the kitchen table. "I didn't give her anything to feed on."

"Why don't we take a ride uptown and see Alice and Poppi?"

"That would be nice. I'll just run upstairs and change my shoes."

"Wear your coat," he said, meaning *the* coat. "It's cold out."

6

They kept their expenses to the bone, drew their salaries, and showed a modest profit. They paid Rush Woolens to do their bookkeeping and they and Karl Handelman did the selling. A small business not unlike their own closed its doors, leaving an empty office in the Worth Street building, an office a little larger than their own. Regina talked to the owner of the building and got him to compromise on the rent, and in March they moved. They had room to breathe now. They could move without touching shoulders. Two weeks later Lillian called.

"It's just so long since I've seen you," she said brightly. "I hear about you whenever we visit Poppi. Aunt Alice is so proud of how well you and Morty are doing."

"We're working hard. Every time I sell one of my special prints I get a wonderful feeling."

"I'm sure you do. They're so beautiful. You're not busy all day, are you, Regina?"

"Well . . . no, not all the time."

"Because I'm going to be down your way on Thursday and I thought maybe we'd meet for a long lunch."

A long lunch would be the end of the day. "I tell you what. Come to the house at two-thirty and we'll have tea together."

"What a lovely idea. I'll see you then."

She came home at two and set the coffee table in the living room, made a fire, and boiled water for tea. As she was closing the pot to let it steep, Lillian arrived.

They hugged and kissed as though they were displaying familial affection for an uninitiated audience.

"*So* charming," Lillian said, looking around. In the three and a half years they had lived there, the Schindlers had visited only twice. "And what you've done with it, Regina. You have such *taste*. I always seem to need outside help to decorate, but Aunt Alice says you've done this all yourself."

"I remembered what I liked in France. When I come in here I think of that lovely house and the wonderful people I lived with."

210

"Weren't you lucky to have the chance?" Lillian was all smiles. "And now I hear Richard's left Rome to settle down in Paris. Such a coincidence, don't you think, both of you running off to France?"

"Why don't you sit facing the fire, Lillian? I'll bring the tea in. I'm sure it's ready now." Both of you running off to France.

She went to the kitchen and checked the tea, wondering what the point of Lillian's visit was and how long she would have to wait to find out. She was afraid it had something more to do with Henry, and she could not bring herself to discuss the Christmas affair with his sister any more than she had talked about it with his mother. Returning to the living room, she poured for both of them and sat down, waiting for Lillian to turn the conversation in its intended direction.

The chatter went on for an hour while the fire across the room flared and subsided.

"I don't know when those two boys will marry," Lillian said, and Regina caught herself half-asleep from the monotony of the conversation. "Richard and Jerold," Lillian prompted, as though she had seen her cousin drifting off. "I can scarcely imagine what kind of women Richard must be seeing in Europe," using the word "women" as a kind of pejorative. If they had been nice, surely they would have been "girls."

"Very nice women," Regina assured her. "I liked the ones he knew when he lived in New York."

"Did you?" Was she questioning the information or questioning Regina's judgment?

"Very much. He had a group of very intelligent, very artistic friends."

"I didn't know you'd been that close to his friends."

"Not close." Regina smiled. "I met them sometimes at parties."

"And of course Jerold is just the most eligible bachelor in town. So well off and still so handsome. He must be thirty now."

"Twenty nine." She said it quickly and regretted it. She knew his birthday as well as her own.

"Mm."

"Yes. You and Jerold are almost exactly the same age."

Lillian smiled and moved one hand very delicately. "I'll have to be careful around you, dear. You know all my secrets. Anyway, he always seems to be seeing someone, and nothing ever comes of it."

"He'll marry someday."

"Well"—Lillian looked around the room with eyes that appraised, little price tags popping up as her gaze fell on each article of furniture—"you certainly married well."

Regina moved to her end of the small French love seat they shared in front of the coffee table and pulled her silk-clad legs up along the light blue silk that covered it. "We all did. We've all been very lucky."

"I hear your business is thriving."

"It isn't thriving. Nothing's thriving nowadays. We're coming out ahead, and that's very satisfying."

"You're too modest. You don't want to admit how clever you've both been."

"We've worked very hard for two years. I don't usually take an afternoon off like this. My tea-party days are behind me."

"Or ahead of you, as the case may be. It's a lovely tea. The cakes were just scrumptious. I'll have to diet tomorrow with all I've eaten."

"You never need to diet, Lillian. You're just as slim as you were the day you married." The conversation had become so dreary she was afraid, with a few more exchanges, she would have nothing more to say.

"Have you heard Phil is looking to make a change?"

The question prickled her mind, sharpening her faculties. "No," she said quietly, "I hadn't heard."

"Poppa's business is so dirty," Lillian said with distaste. "And it doesn't really let Phil use his talents."

His talents. Which talents, Lillian? The ones you've been told about, or the others, the ones he exercises in your absence? "In times like these," Regina said carefully, "I would think staying where he is is the best course he could follow."

"He can't stay, Regina." Lillian's voice was icy with something that sounded like fear.

"I see."

"That awful place they have over on West Street. There are rats walking around. I don't know how Poppa stood it all these years."

"He had a good business that he built up from nothing. He goes home to a lovely apartment at night. Maybe that's how he's done it."

"Maybe." Lillian looked down at her lap, then raised her eyes. "You could find a place for Phil, couldn't you, Regina?"

The question brought on a feeling of emptiness that was almost nausea. "I don't know . . ." She faltered. "I don't see—"

"You employ so many people at the mill."

"Lillian, a lot of them have been let go. The mill doesn't produce what it did two years ago because there's no market now."

"Even so. Phil did very well, you know, in his old company. It was a terrible misfortune that it went under. Heaven only knows what some of those people at the top were doing with the money. But Phil did a splendid job there. Any one of them would give him a recommendation."

Regina stood and went to the fire. It was hardly more than a glow. With all her practice, she could never get a fire to last as long as Morty could. The mill was out of the question. Even if they could hire—and they couldn't— the strain between Morty and Stuart would preclude hiring someone at Regina's request. There was only RR, and she found herself full of a prideful resentment against Lillian. They were making a living by working hard and cutting corners. Karl Handelman needed and deserved a raise. He had a wife and three children and he had done well in the twenties. To take on another person now would be to deprive him of what he had earned as well as to dissolve whatever profit they claimed for themselves.

Still, this was her cousin, her cousin's husband. Beyond all the fictional trappings of Lillian's story, one could detect the bittersweet smell of rot. Uncle Jack's business could not support two families. People still had to eat, but food prices were low and the margin of profit for the farmer, the distributor, and the grocer was minimal. Like their own fledgling business, there was a living if you worked hard, but it couldn't be spread very far. Phil would never find anything today comparable to what he had had in the twenties.

212

"I'll have to talk to Morty," she said.

"Of course you will. I knew you wouldn't let me down, Regina. I remember how touched I was when you sent the carriage cover from Paris when Celia was born. Some people hardly saw fit to send a card. You always know who you can count on."

"Yes, well, I'll call you after we've talked."

"Phil doesn't know anything about this." Lillian spoke in a clipped, instructive manner. The arrangement had been made; she was giving the orders now. "It would be nice if Morty could call him, you know, out of the blue, so to speak. As if he was looking for someone and Phil came to mind."

"Yes, I'm sure that's the way we'll work it out."

"Thank you so much, Regina." Lillian looked down at a diamond wristwatch. "Oh, my, I've stayed forever. I'll have to send Momma home in a cab when I get back or poor Poppa won't have any dinner tonight, and we can't have that, can we?"

Regina went to the closet and took Lillian's coat down.

"Thank you, dear. Cold for March, isn't it?"

"How's Henry, Lillian?"

"Studying furiously for his exams. Did you hear he's been given an internship in Brooklyn?"

"No, I hadn't heard."

"We're so pleased. He's been gone four years now. It's time he came home. Well"—she kissed Regina's cheek—"for the tea and for everything. I'll wait for your call."

It was the first time in their marriage that she hesitated to talk to Morty about something. Before he came home, she called her mother and had a long conversation about the family, settling once or twice on Uncle Jack. Mother was at the hub of family gossip. Everyone came to visit Poppi, and every guest added something to the repository of family lore. Mother loved it. She knew everything and repeated what she knew with a kind of poetic license. The story she told Aunt Martha varied significantly from the one she told Aunt Eva, although both were essentially true. Her brothers were somewhat closer to God than her sisters-in-law, and Aunt Eva was far more a model of perfection than Aunt Martha. It was necessary to distill Mother's information and add carefully selected ingredients to emerge with facts. The fact about Uncle Jack was that business was very bad.

She told Morty about it before dinner. Keeping it from him turned out to be more painful than telling him. He sat listening, nodding a little, anticipating the end before she had reached it.

"She wants us to hire him."

"Yes."

"Did she dictate what we pay him?"

"I think she thinks that's men's talk. She's a little too ladylike to indulge in money."

"We don't owe him, you know."

"She's my cousin, Morty. Momma says Uncle Jack isn't doing well."

"He did well enough in the twenties."

"I suspect that's how Lillian got her trip to France and some of the other necessities of her life."

Morty sat back in his chair and closed his eyes. He came home tired now.

He worked harder, much harder, and each month the books looked worse. He, Pop, and Stuart were making a living, but at the mill the ranks had thinned, the machines were sometimes quiet. It took a personal toll on him.

"You'll have to break him in yourself," he said, opening his eyes and sitting up in the chair, "the way I did for you. Take him around. Train him. There's a hell of a lot, but I don't have the time."

"I know."

"You don't like him, do you?"

"No."

He paused, choosing his words. "Something specific, or just that scent of malevolence I always smell on him?" A small smile played on his lips.

"A little of both."

"If he touches you, you can let him know I'll kill him."

"He won't touch me, Morty. He needs a job."

Morty made the calls during the day and told her about them the next evening.

"He lies, you know. Found out by a fluke. He told me what he was earning and who he worked for before the crash, Kastner, a real-estate developer. I know Kastner, met him before the war. I called him up this afternoon. Your cousin has more than an inflated ego."

"Let's just put him on salary and forget what he told you."

"Kastner said he works hard," Morty offered as a kind of apology. "Maybe he'll pay his way."

"I hope so," Regina said fervently, but less fervently than she felt.

He started work the last Monday in March, and Regina tramped around the city with him, making introductions Morty had made for her two years before. Morty took Karl Handelman out to dinner one night to explain what had happened, and Karl, in his gracious way, took it like a gentleman. Several evenings Karl stayed late and taught Phil what he had to learn about fabric.

"He's coming along," Karl told Regina from time to time. "If things don't get worse, we'll all make it."

But it was the spring of 1931 and Morty had stopped making optimistic predictions, although the President hadn't.

At the beginning of May they all met at Poppi's apartment. Poppi was anxious to go to the farm, and the family, or most of it, had come to say good-bye. It was a Sunday afternoon and all the Schindlers were there with Uncle Jack—Aunt Martha had stayed home to nurse a lingering spring cold—and Uncle Willy had come with Aunt Eva. Morty sat and talked to Poppi while Regina helped her mother get the dinner ready. The next day Uncle Willy would drive Mother and Poppi to New Jersey and look over the houses that had not been used much in recent years, his own and the Friedmann house. Regina suspected there was more to his visit than an inspection, but she asked no questions. The filtered news about Uncle Nate's and Izzy's livelihoods was not ecstatic.

When the meal was over, Regina sent her mother off to the living room and tackled the dishes herself. Lillian joined her in the kitchen soon after she started, and began to dry and put away. When Aunt Eva poked her head in the door, Regina shooed her away, and her aunt obligingly disappeared.

"How's everything going?" Regina asked conversationally, thinking she would really have preferred Aunt Eva's company to her cousin's.

"As well as can be expected."

Regina looked up from the sink to see Lillian's mouth set in a tight straight line. It occurred to her that there had been little said between them during the afternoon, a signal that something was surely awry, and looking at Lillian's face, Regina could feel the weight of responsibility falling upon her, although the reason for it eluded her.

"Poppi looks well, don't you think?" she asked to divert her cousin from whatever was troubling her.

"Everyone looks well," Lillian said tightly. "You look especially well."

Regina glanced at her cousin and then away without responding.

"And you should," Lillian went on. "You don't have to wear last year's clothes. You don't have to worry about children outgrowing their shoes and needing new ones."

Piercing like a dart tipped with poison. It was the one allusion she could not bear, that she was incapable of having a child and therefore inferior, unworthy, that being childless rendered her insensitive, when in fact every nerve ending had been sharpened since that day in December 1928. She turned back to the dishes and scrubbed as though she cared, as though it were crucial that this procelain gleam.

"I thought we had an understanding," Lillian went on, her voice low and frigid. "I thought Phil was going to be paid what a man needs to maintain a family. I didn't think he was being taken on as an apprentice, as if he were nineteen years old with no experience in the business world."

Regina turned the water off and found a clean dish towel. If Morty were here, he would tear Lillian to bits. If she allowed herself to say what she was bursting to say, Lillian would never speak to her again, and she could not have that.

"We pay Phil what we can afford to pay him," she said with extreme calm. "He may be worth more—lots of people are worth more than they're getting nowadays—but the money isn't there. When times get better—"

"There are two of you," Lillian interrupted her icily, "and four of us." The "us" hissed. If Richard were here, he would make a slimy comparison.

"Lillian, Karl Handelman has three children and he's been with us over a year. He deserves more than he's getting too. I wake up in the morning and go to sleep at night thinking about how little we pay him and how much he needs."

"Karl Handelman is a thief. He picks your pockets and you don't even see it."

"He's not a thief. He's an honest and loyal—"

"How would you know? You sit in an office all day. If you walked the streets with him—"

"Listen to me, Lillian," Regina interrupted, the rising anger overflowing, "I walk the streets. I take the orders. I know what the people who work for me do and don't do." She held on to the edge of the sink so that Lillian would not see her hand shaking. Why was it always this way with Lillian? She could laugh at Adele, shrug at Arthur, love all the others, but with Lillian there was always an undercurrent of hostility that erupted periodically

215

into rage like a volcano, and why could she never retaliate the way she wanted to? Why did something always hold her back? If Jerold were here, he would take her by the hand and lead her out of the building, away from the conflagration.

"The people who *work* for you," Lillian hissed. "No one should *work* for you. You should be home with children the way I am, the way normal women are, instead of taking a man's job away from him. Two of you in one family making a living, and only your two mouths to feed. You should be ashamed of yourself, depriving families of what they need, keeping it for yourselves when others who work harder need it more. They should pass a law—"

" 'Bout ready to go?"

Morty stood in the doorway, a knight in woolen armor, offering her salvation.

"Yes," she said without disguising her eagerness. She slipped Momma's apron over her head and thrust it at Lillian, whose hand reached for it almost in a reflex action. "Quite ready. Lillian can do the pots. Everything else is finished."

"I thought we'd take a run down to the new Empire State Building and see if we can go up to the top. It's a nice day to look down on the world."

"Perfect," she said, afraid she might giggle. "So long, Lillian. Give my best to your mother."

And outside in the street, just standing, her hand on his arm, catching her breath while her heart slowed down, laughing finally—it was such a relief to be out of that kitchen—while Morty waited for an explanation. "Oh, God, where did she come from? How did she get into this family?"

"You look ravaged."

"I feel ravaged. Let's go, anywhere, just fast. Can I race you to the car?"

"You're standing next to it."

She laughed again, feeling very good now, very light. The air was so fresh, even Poppi would love it. She got into the car and stretched her legs. "I shouldn't laugh," she said, catching her breath. "It's really terrible. I mean, down deep I feel awful. They're not making ends meet, and it's terrible for them. Oh, Morty, I left her with the pots." She had never laughed so hard in her life. "I didn't plan it, I just walked out and left Lillian with the pots." She sniffed, reached into her bag, and pulled out a handkerchief, pressing it to each eye. "All those crusty, dirty pots. When I saw you there, it was like the day you came back from France and saved me from marrying that . . . that . . . I've forgotten his name." He put his arms around her and she collapsed on his shoulder, laughing and crying at once. "Morty, I wish we had a child. I wish it so much, but if we can't, I'm so glad I have you. I'm so glad."

Later, when they talked about that afternoon, they called it the day they didn't go to the top of the Empire State Building.

They celebrated their fifth anniversary in June, and when the industry closed down the first week of July, they rented the house in the mountains and stayed on a second week, leaving Karl in charge at RR. They were not displeased with Phil as his first quarter-year ended. His presence relieved Regina enough that she had more time to spend designing, and he began to pay for himself.

216

In the fall she assembled a group of samples for a dressmaker who sold regularly to Best's. She had tried him before, tried several times, and he had not bought from her, but she had watched him and knew she was close. This time she would have him. She wanted to see her fabric made up in the simple elegant dresses he sold to Best's. She wanted to see those dresses in the women's department. She wanted to see them in the window on Fifth Avenue and Thirty-fifth Street. She wanted everything, but she wanted to talk to Karl Handelman first.

Like Phil, he came in punctually every morning before making his calls. She spoke to both of them briefly and asked Karl to come to her desk.

"You know Feldman?" she asked.

"Of him. He's on your list, isn't he?"

"Yes, but I never get anywhere. He likes this, he likes that, and he never buys."

"Half of them are that way."

"This is different. I think he wants to buy. I watch him when he looks at what I show him. He's not comfortable with me. I think he won't buy from me because I'm a woman."

Karl looked at her appraisingly. "I couldn't say."

"I want him to buy, and I don't want to take another chance and lose him again." She handed him the folder. "He's yours."

He hesitated a moment, then took it from her. "I'll do my best."

"That's all I want."

He called late the next afternoon and said he had done it. It was a good order. She would see her fabric next spring at Best's.

"He would have bought from you," Karl said. "It was the designs that did it."

"He wouldn't, and it doesn't matter. I wanted the sale and we got it. He's yours now, Karl. I'm going to run through my list and see what else you can help me out with."

There was a silence, and she thought she had lost the connection. Then Karl's voice came back. "You run a good shop, Mrs. R."

"Thanks, Karl. That's what I want to do."

He came in the next morning and shook her hand warmly. She had always liked him, and today she liked him even more. He was thirty-nine, as Morty would be soon, and they had been friends since earliest youth. When Morty outlined his great dreams, Karl had a place near the top of the pyramid.

As they talked, Phil walked in looking somewhat agitated, hurried to his desk, and made a call, dropping his hat on a chair as he waited for an answer and shrugging out of his coat as he spoke. There was something odd about his looks this morning, but Regina could not put her finger on it, and she had other things to think about, things that were important, and by the time he left the office a little after nine, she had forgotten the incident.

A little later in the morning, Morty called. "I think we may want to go into the printing business," he announced.

"Now?"

"A guy in Paterson ordered some new machinery in better times and he just got word of delivery. He's got to get rid of what he has or he can't pay

217

for the new stuff. I think the price may be right. Want to take a drive over?"

"I'm certainly not going to let you go alone. You may come back owning half of Paterson."

"I thought you trusted me."

"With my life, darling. Just not with our checkbook."

He was right about the price. She stood watching printed cotton fabric, the third color of the design newly applied, emerging from the copper roller like so many miles of newspapers. She felt nervous again, as she had two and a half years before when they had put together RR. Karl had told her she ran a good shop, but this was a different kind of operation; they would need someone to manage it, men to run the machines. On the top floor of this building there was empty space, and Morty was already talking to the owner of the building, negotiating the rent, setting a date to take over and move the machinery.

"Do we do it?"

She turned and saw him beside her, raising his voice over the din.

"Sure we do it."

They walked out of the story-and-a-half-high printing area and back through the steamy bleaching room with its unpleasant smell of chemicals. Here five thousand yards of gray fabric were bleached white, spread, dried, and rolled for printing. In still another room a woman used a pentograph to engrave a copper roller with tiny dots in the shape of one color of a design from which she worked. Other rollers would print the other colors to produce the final, perfect product, after which the fabric would be pressed between the finishing rollers.

"Come on," Morty said, taking her hand, "let's celebrate. There must be a place in this town where you can get an illegal drink."

They took over the printing and finishing of their fabric and started to look for more work from other converters. A second telephone was installed on Regina's desk with a different WOrth 4 number, and when that came, all the phones were changed to dial. Now you could lean back in your chair and talk instead of leaning forward to speak into a mouthpiece. Now you needed an operator only to call long distance.

A week or two after the new telephones arrived, the strange early-morning scene with Phil Schindler was repeated, the hasty dash to his desk, the hat flung aside, the rapid dialing. He turned self-consciously away from Regina, which was unusual. Ordinarily he spoke a little too loudly on the phone, as if to assure eavesdroppers that he was doing his job with enthusiasm. Now his back curved so that his head was barely visible, forming a private retreat in the least private of offices. After a few minutes he slammed the receiver onto the hook, took his coat off, and straightened his tie. For the second time Regina had the feeling that there was something wrong with the way he looked, something about his clothes or the way he was wearing them.

And then it struck her. She had noticed his tie the previous day, admired it, in fact, and complimented him on it. This morning he was wearing it again on a white shirt that looked more rumpled than fresh. He was a man who took special pains with his clothes, who wore good clothes and wore them well. He was not a man who would get up in the morning and put on yesterday's shirt and yesterday's tie. Unless . . . unless . . .

A snatch of conversation overheard the previous late afternoon: "Hey Lil, I'll be late. Don't bother . . ." Waiting dinner? Waiting up?

He had not gone home. A shudder passed through her, an ache of sympathy for her cousin who had heard from her husband only a minute or two ago, her cousin who had spent the night with her two children and without her husband.

Regina thought back to those early months of 1929 when Morty had made the rounds with her to potential customers, calls she now made alone, but in those days Morty had been with her and she had observed with occasional flickers of jealousy the exchanges between him and the girls in the offices. There were always girls in offices, frequently young and unattached girls for whom a wife at home was as significant as a pet dog—and less to be feared.

There was nothing she could do. Ironically, the decade-old memory of Lillian's engagement party had blinded her to the possibility of other, more serious infidelities. She had attempted never to be alone with Phil in this office, had turned down even invitations for coffee, thinking foolishly, childishly she saw now, that it was she who was the object of some desire, when in fact it was women. Phil did not discriminate.

They had their brisk daily chat, and he departed, leaving her with paperwork, decisions, orders to fill, purchases to make, shipments to expedite, and a heavy, almost tearful feeling that her cousin Lillian bore a great burden, that perhaps the scene in Poppi's apartment last spring had in some way been related to this, and for the thousandth time in her life, Regina forgave her.

The country did poorly but the business did better. They specialized in high-quality fabrics for the more expensive women's clothes, and they sold. At Rush Woolens Pop began to look his seventy-two years and Stuart blamed the decrease in their sales on Morty's involvement in the converting business.

"Maybe he's right," Pop said at dinner one night in January. "Maybe you should spend more time with us."

"Regina's been running the converting business by herself for almost two years," Morty said, exaggerating only slightly. "We get together on it in the evening. You know what I do all day." She could hear the incipient anger just below the surface in his voice.

"I don't know. We made so much money a few years ago. It seems like things should be better." Her father-in-law sounded old and discouraged, as if something had failed him and he hadn't deserved it.

"Why don't you retire, Pop?" Morty suggested gently. "You can afford it."

"What would I do with myself?" he asked almost plaintively. "Sit around the house all day? Grossman's gone now, you know. Weissberg. It's hard to get up a game of *skat* nowadays."

"Take a trip. Remember how much you liked Paris?"

"It wasn't Paris. It was you I went to see. No, I need my work. How come"—his eyes moved around the room—"how come you never moved uptown? You could live in a better neighborhood. With two businesses, you could afford it, no?"

219

"We're hanging on to our money for something else," Morty said. "When the time comes, I want to have it ready."

Pop shook his head. "Another business? You got too much already. You take one thing, you work at it, you make a living. Like I did. Even when things are bad, we make a living, don't we?"

"It could be better."

"Nah." Pop shook his head. "Stuart says your head is full of crazy dreams. I think maybe he's right. I don't know why. I brought you boys up the same."

"They have different personalities, Pop," Regina said. "It's not the way they were brought up."

"And different wives," Morty added under his breath.

His father glanced at him but said nothing, and Regina had an odd feeling about the conversation, that his father had been telling him something, but she wasn't quite sure what.

Suzanne wrote that she was expecting a second child in the summer and that her father, who had recently returned from a trip to Germany, was concerned about the political situation there. Fortunately in France they had nothing to worry about, and she and Étienne and the baby were fine. They were making plans to move into a large apartment on the Avenue Foch, not too far from her parents' home. How lovely it would be if Régine could visit. Reading the letter brought pangs of nostalgia. Trees would be leafing out in the *seizième*, blossoms in the *bois*, and best of all, babies in Suzanne's house.

They went to visit Momma one weekend and heard that Jerold was seeing a lovely girl who would graduate from Barnard in June.

"It's about time," Poppi grumbled. "What's the matter with those boys?"

"They're just taking their time, Poppa," Mother said, pacifying him as though he were a child. "There isn't a girl in New York who wouldn't marry Jerold."

"I'm tired of waiting," Poppi said. "Eighty years I was patient. Now I'm not so patient anymore." He shifted in his chair. "You talked to Willy about this girl?"

"I told you all about it," Mother said with exasperation. "She goes to college and she's going to graduate in June."

"So they get married in July?"

"No one's said anything about getting married."

Poppi made a sound deep in his throat. "I met this girl already?" he asked.

"No, Poppa, you haven't met her. You would remember if you met her."

"Sometimes I forget."

"You pretend that you forget," Momma said.

"You think she's the right kind of girl?"

"I'm sure she's the right kind of girl, Poppi," Regina interjected rather sharply.

"Ah . . . look, suddenly someone has something to say."

"Plenty to say. You're browbeating Momma." Her mother turned away. "One of these days I'm going to spank you. Pretty soon I'll be big enough."

Poppi looked at her uncertainly. Then his mouth broke into a mostly toothless grin. Momma complained that he refused to wear his teeth except to eat. "Come here," he ordered, and Regina obeyed, standing beside his chair while he patted her arm. "The best one," he said to Morty, as though imparting the most intimate of secrets. "You got the best one of the whole lot."

Later, in the kitchen, Momma wept into a handkerchief. "He's so . . . so difficult sometimes," she said, blotting away the embarrassing tears. "Since Momma died. He never stops missing her. He sits by that window all day and thinks about her."

"And makes things hard for you."

"Oh, no," Momma said, sniffing. "It's just that he's getting old and he misses Momma and he wants everything to be the way it used to be."

Morty had been standing just inside the kitchen. Now he turned and left, and Regina heard him say, "Listen to me, Poppi . . ."

She patted her mother's shoulder and walked to where she could listen unobserved.

"I want you to lay off Alice," Morty said, and the old man's head jumped to attention. He looked stubborn and alert. "You know, I can take your guff, but she can't."

Poppi made a sound in his throat. He looked ready to pounce.

"Tell you what I'd like to do," Morty went on smoothly. "Who's your barber?"

"Romano," Poppi said, prolonging the syllables. "Down the block. Nice fella. Speaks with a little accent." He grinned toothlessly.

"Suppose I ask him to come up here in the morning and give you a shave?"

"Up here?"

"Why not? A man your age should have a few comforts."

"You get him here every day?" Poppi looked incredulous.

"Sure. I'll come up during the week and talk to him. You don't mind, do you?" She had never heard him sound quite so crafty.

"Nah," Poppi said, as though he were doing Morty a big favor, "I don't mind. He'll give me the towels too?"

"The works. Whatever you want. But you better put your teeth on. Regina tells everyone what a handsome guy you are. I wouldn't want Romano to be disappointed."

It was a year of ups and downs. The Lindbergh baby was kidnapped in March and in May they found his little body. They didn't talk about it much, but they didn't have to. It was everywhere, every newspaper, every newscast on radio. Shayna called to say she was pregnant again, and in June word came that Adele would have her first child at the end of the year. She would not return to her teaching job in the fall. Suzanne gave birth to a daughter. Governor Roosevelt was nominated by the Democratic party to run for president, and suddenly everyone Regina knew had become interested in politics.

Business slumped. Large orders became medium, and medium orders were canceled. Nothing was reordered. Karl Handelman came into the office on summer afternoons dripping sweat and sat at his desk looking defeated. They had given him another raise, and he acted as though he had yet to earn it.

"Take it easy," Regina cautioned one day in July, looking at him anxiously. Her own cotton dress looked as wilted as his shirt, and almost as damp.

"It's bad out there," he said, and he could have meant the business world as much as the weather.

"Break earlier. You just kill yourself the last couple of hours of the day. No one buys after two o'clock in this weather anyway." She moved the floor fan slightly so that he would benefit from its dubious value.

"Department-store sales are way down."

"I know. You're not going to change that single-handed."

"There's gotta be an end." He looked as though he didn't believe there would be. "Where's Schindler?"

"Probably quit for the day."

He faced the fan and closed his eyes for a minute. "You know he's playing around."

She nodded. Every once in a while, in the middle of the week, he came in rumpled, hurried to the phone, and went through the familiar charade. She could not watch it, not think of it, without feeling Lillian's anguish. At thirty she had a bleak life to look forward to, full of a desperate uncertainty. How did she explain to her girls that their father had not come home last night? How did she explain it to herself?

"It's none of my business," Karl said. "But I know he's married to your cousin."

"Yes." She shuffled some papers on her desk to make the topic change. She wanted to think about something else. She wanted to go away somewhere with Morty, somewhere cool, be alone with him without thinking about department-store sales that were down, orders that were canceled, machines that were idle.

The door burst open and Morty appeared, an unexpected breath of fresh air.

"Karl, hey, good to see you." They shook hands warmly, as though, she thought absurdly, there were any other way to do it on a day like today.

"Hello, sweetheart," Morty said, turning toward her desk. "Happy birthday."

She looked at him with dread. "What have you done?" she asked in a low voice. Her birthday was still three weeks away.

"I just got you a present," he said, undaunted. "I bought you a silk mill this afternoon."

"Oh, Christ," Karl said, putting his head in his hands.

"Silk, Morty?" The temperature had suddenly dropped about twenty degrees. Her skin prickled. "Darling, we can't even sell cotton."

"You're *crazy*," Karl shouted, lifting his head. "There's a depression out there. Don't you read the goddamn papers? There is no one out there *buying* anything."

"What the hell is this, a funeral?" Morty looked from his friend to his wife. "I was high as a kite till I walked into this mausoleum."

Regina swallowed. "We were having a depressing converstion. Until you walked in, I mean. Tell me about . . . Why silk?"

"Your designs'll go better in silk. They'll be terrific in silk. Look, the price was right. I took something off somebody's hands and made us both happy.

222

I've been dickering with him for weeks. I thought I'd get it down to rock bottom by your birthday, but this was the day. I drove over to Paterson and gave him a check. I have a lot of ideas. We'll have to sit down, the three of us—not today, it's too hot—but soon. I think things're going to turn around after the election."

"What you mean is, they can't get worse." Karl had taken out a large handkerchief and was pressing it to his neck.

"They could get worse." Morty pulled a wooden chair away from the side of Karl's desk and sat facing them. "We could go out of business. Prohibition could stay forever. Things could be a lot worse." He looked as though he were contemplating the possibility. "But they won't be. We'll have a good spring in thirty-three. Want to take a trip to Paterson and see your new toy?" He looked at his watch. "Well, maybe tomorrow. Go home, Karl. It's too late to work any more today."

Karl shut his desk drawer with a bang, waved, and left with his jacket over his arm. "Have fun, you two."

"Give my love to Lucy. Tell her I'm going to make you a rich man." The door closed on Karl's laugh, and Morty looked across the room at her. "You aren't angry, are you?"

She said, "No," softly and shook her head.

He patted his thigh and said, "C'mere."

She stood up, feeling the fan on her neck as she moved, and went to where he sat waiting for her. She sat on his lap and put her arms around his neck. It was so hot, so terribly, uncomfortably hot. He held her as though it were winter, as though he needed to know she was with him, and she felt a small shudder ripple through him the way it always did when he enclosed her.

"It's a wonderful present," she said, kissing his cheek and tasting salt. "Did you have to borrow much?"

"Not much. The owner's holding the mortgage. It's a small mill, but it's big enough for us."

"You're right about the designs. We'll have to go through the Paris ones again. They're different from what I've been doing lately."

"They're more you. You were doing what you wanted to do then, not what the market wanted. I've always liked those the best. You'll do more of them now. You were just ahead of your time."

"Like you."

"I'm way behind," he said, and there was an echo of regret. "I lost so much time. I don't want that to happen to you. I want you to do what you want to do, sit in a studio somewhere and paint all day if you feel like it, not push papers around and talk to greedy men on the phone and coax them to do what they already promised and what you paid them for in the first place."

"I do what I want now."

"I know you do, but I want to make it better for you. I don't want you to work so hard. I want you to come and have lunch with me sometimes."

She laid her head on his shoulder and kissed his neck just above the collar. One would think he had just sold a factory, not bought one. One would imagine he had this moment freed her of all responsibilities, not added a big one on top of all the rest. She felt like laughing.

223

"Hey, pig," he said softly, "you're sweating on my collar." His hand lay damply on her bare arm.

"It's not sweat, I'm crying," she told him. "Can't you even tell the difference?"

She learned about silk. It was far stronger than wool or cotton and could be woven more quickly without risk of breaking. They produced cautiously, converting some themselves, and tried to sell to a new market. They had some success, and even Karl sounded optimistic. Manufacturers were interested in blouses and skirts for the spring season, especially jumpers, which were suddenly in demand.

The call came in September, just after Labor Day. It was Momma and she was almost breathless.

"Uncle Willy called himself," she said. "Jerold's engaged. Isn't it wonderful? I'm as happy as if it were my own son."

She felt a sudden sharp pain somewhere between her shoulders, and then a kind of emptiness. "It is wonderful, Momma."

"A beautiful girl," Momma was saying, as though Regina had not spoken. "Dark hair, lovely, just lovely. She graduated from Barnard last June and her father sent her abroad for the summer. Willy said it was to test her feelings. Well, she came home last week and now they're engaged."

"When will the wedding be?" She had to clear her throat before the words came out.

"Oh, June, I think. They're planning a big wedding. She's an only child. You know how it is with an only child." Momma laughed. "Edith French. Pretty name, isn't it?"

"Very pretty."

"Jerold's thirty now. He's waited such a long time, but I think he knew just what he was waiting for. You'll have to send them something, Regina. Don't forget. I don't know if there'll be an engagement party, but you should send something."

"I'll send something very nice, Momma," Regina said.

She hung up feeling ashamed and angry that she felt human instead of happy. Someone would take care of him now, someone beautiful, someone he had waited years and years for, someone he loved.

They met by accident at Poppi's the following Sunday, entering as Jerold and Edith were preparing to leave. She was very beautiful. She was more than beautiful; she glowed. Regina could not imagine this girl anything but happy. Her face was radiant, framed with dark curls. She looked like a picture Regina had once seen of Lady Hamilton. There was a great delicacy about her, and a delightful warmth.

"Regina Rush," Edith said, shaking hands. "You're Mrs. Friedmann's daughter."

"Yes. She's Aunt Alice to the family."

"I'm so glad to meet you. You two are the first of Jerold's cousins that I've met."

"These two don't make trouble," Poppi said, out of his chair at last and standing near the couple.

Edith laughed. "We won't either," and Regina could see how pleased Poppi was.

"Not for a while, anyway," Jerold said. "We have to run now, Poppi. Edith's uncle and aunt are coming over to meet me. I have to stand inspection."

"They don't like you, you send them to me."

"Better stay home, then. Edith says her uncle is a tough customer."

"Oh, Jerold, of course he'll like you."

She was so young, not quite twenty-two, such a fresh, wonderful age. Edith drew on gloves, and a diamond glittered on her left hand.

Jerold pulled a watch out of his pocket. "We'd better go, dear." He slipped the watch back and took Edith's arm, moving his hand slightly along the sleeve, as though touching her through the silk was a source of pleasure.

"Good-bye, Edith." Regina took her hand, leaned forward, and kissed the pink cheek. "I'm so glad to have met you."

"Thank you. Thank you very much." The cheeks reddened slightly.

"Come back soon," Poppi called as the couple went out into the hall, and as though they had practiced, they called back in unison, "We will," and left laughing.

Later in the day they left to go out for dinner.

"Nice little girl Jerold's marrying," Morty said, pulling the car away from the curb.

"Very nice. I think she'll be good for him."

"Very good. She'll get him out of his shell."

"Shell?" She could feel a small anger fomenting.

"He's a guy with limited interests, a nice guy but not very easy to talk to."

"I don't think his interests are so limited."

"Take it easy. I'm not tearing him to pieces. I said he's a nice guy. I'm just trying to tell you I heard him say more this afternoon than I've heard him say in the last five years outside his office. Maybe five years from now I'll even be able to have a conversation with him."

"I'm sure if you wanted to have a conversation with Jerold"—she heard her voice turn to ice—"all you would have to do—"

"Hey, Mrs. Rush . . ." He reached out a hand and covered her gloved one. "You don't expect me to admit your cousin is way ahead of me, do you?"

The ice began to melt. "I didn't say "

"How many people could I have had a conversation with in 1925?"

It trickled warmly. She swallowed. "I talked to you."

"That's all I'm saying. We still friends?"

She slid across the seat until they almost touched. "Yes."

He squeezed her hand and let it go, taking hold of the steering wheel. "Damned family loyalty," he teased. "If I'd had any sense, I would've been born your cousin."

The engagement was unsettling. It was hard to imagine Jerold married to someone so young, someone no older than Cousin Arthur, the baby of the family. It was strange to look at this beautiful girl, six years younger than Regina, and see her as Jerold's wife. There was a kind of perfection about Edith that was reflected not only in her looks and manners. At twenty-one she had had a degree from Barnard. It was the first time Regina had felt an omission in her own life, an incompleteness. She had wanted an education and gotten one of sorts, but now she felt the lack of a degree as a visible mark of failure. She had wanted a child but she had not been able to bear one that would live, and now she seemed incapable even of becoming pregnant.

Their childlessness affected them in small ways that she had only recently come to notice. Three-quarters of their house was pristine in its neatness and cleanliness. Aside from an occasional newspaper, a book, or an empty glass, the house looked scarcely lived in. In a kind of retaliation, she allowed her studio to accumulate debris. She let paint drip on the drop cloth. She kept the cleaning woman out and only rarely tidied the room herself. Still, she enjoyed the sleek unblemished look of the living room. It was a place for adults to enjoy themselves. When she visited Shayna, she stepped over wooden toys, kept her voice down occasionally so that little Hershel could fall asleep, and when she left, she stepped outside feeling relieved and free and pleased that she lived a life that avoided all that inconvenience. But sometimes at night, after Morty made love to her, she would lie beside him with two fingers of her left hand crossed and say to herself: Please, this time, let it happen. Or she would awaken knowing her period was due and she would think: Not today. Please not this month—and she would get out of bed and know she had failed again as she had failed thirteen times each year since 1929.

They became exclusive and caring in a way they might not have had time for if they had had a child, and they both liked it. Sometimes in the morning Morty would tell her not to cook, they would go out for dinner. He liked to bring her flowers, and now and then he would go shopping with her and insist that she buy an extravagant dress. If the house they rented in the mountains was available, they would take it on a whim and spend a weekend in the country, packing quickly and running off with only the door to lock behind them. They belonged to each other more completely than any other couple she knew, and she liked it. It was almost a substitute for the other.

His birthday was in October. She had planned a small surprise party for the following day, Saturday, giving the key to the house to Karl so that his wife could set things up while Regina took Morty out of the house on a pretext.

He seemed utterly undisturbed at the prospect of being forty, but it bothered her. Now he would be forty-one years older than any child they might have, or forty-two, or forty-three. Some bright prospect that had glimmered in their lives six years ago had burned out. Jerold would marry and have children, Adele would have a baby in December, Shayna would give birth momentarily, Suzanne would have a large family, but Regina was a barren woman.

She awoke on the Friday of his birthday with all the feelings pulling at her.

"Happy birthday, I love you," she said.

"Ah." He turned toward her. "It can't be that day already."

"It better be. I got you a present."

"Just for turning forty?"

"For turning it here."

"You taking me to dinner?"

226

"Uh-huh."

"You have to treat me nice today."

"I will."

"Very nice."

"I promise."

"Give me my present."

She reached into the drawer of her night table and pulled out the box.

"Tiffany," he said, raising his eyebrows. "I thought I was supposed to buy you diamonds there."

"Next year."

He pulled the ribbon off and opened it, saying "Mmm" as he saw the gold buckle engraved with an R. "Worth about forty years." He kissed her forehead. "I'll need a belt."

"I thought we'd get it together."

"Tomorrow," he said. "Boy, that's heavy." He hefted it a few times. "Imagine that, gold, and I'm only forty."

He drove her to Worth Street and went back up to Canal. Karl came in and they talked about the surprise party the following evening. Karl had turned forty earlier in the year, and the Rushes had taken him and Lucy out more extravagantly than he had expected. Although Regina had insisted on paying for tomorrow's party, he was taking great pains to assure its success. While they talked, Phil came in and hurried to his desk to make his apologies to Lillian. As always, the little scene put a damper on Regina's morning.

She had an appointment at ten with a dress manufacturer Karl had originally contacted. He wanted to speak to the designer herself, wanted something special that he could have exclusively, a slight modification of a pattern and his choice of color. There was a lot of hesitation this fall among buyers, and Regina Rush Fabrics would barely break even this year. The election was less than three weeks away and the people she dealt with were thinking six to nine months in the future, to a time when there might be a new president, when there might be an end to the depression, or when things—God forbid, they always said—could be even worse. She took the folder and her notes and left the office, thinking about Phil and Lillian, about Morty turning forty, about an election that might put prosperity just around Mr. Hoover's proverbial corner.

"Mrs. Rush," her client said effusively as she entered his office, "give your husband this from me." He shoved a fat cigar at her. "I got another grandchild yesterday."

She said congratulations, put the cigar in her bag, and sat down to do business.

On the way back, she stopped at a delicatessen where she was a frequent customer. They would make her half a sandwich instead of the usual whole, which she could not finish. She took it with a paper cup of coffee and went up to the office to eat it and read the paper. Morty called and thanked her for the present. He lingered on the phone in an uncharacteristic way so that she could almost feel their fingers touching. She hung up feeling more depressed. Why should she feel this way about her husband turning forty when he didn't feel this way at all himself? She wished the day would end, but it was just after noon and scarcely begun.

She looked over the financial page, prices of cotton and wool tops, the stock market, which they had never invested in but which affected their lives nevertheless. Then back to the beginning, to the news from Germany, which had gone from depressing to frightening, to the latest report on Franklin Roosevelt, to the same about Herbert Hoover. The coffee tasted stale. Morty had told her to buy a hot plate and perk her own, and one of these days she would have to listen to him. He knew how to make himself comfortable in uncomfortable surroundings. He had lived in Paris and New York; he had been in the army; he had been in business for years; he had learned everything he could learn everywhere he had been. He was forty.

He called for her at a quarter to six. Phil and Karl had left and she was finishing her paperwork when the door opened. She threw him a kiss and organized her papers for Monday morning. He came to her desk, bent way over, and kissed her.

"Lose my balance doing that one of these days."

"It's the last thing you'll lose."

"Think so, huh?"

"I got Feinberg."

"I knew you would. He likes to be babied. You know how to do it."

A cigar in her pocketbook. She would leave it there till later. "Stuart remember your birthday?"

"Forget Stuart. You remembered."

"Morty . . ." She looked around the one-room office that she knew better than any room in their home. She loved being here alone with him, loved their meetings of the board and meetings of their minds. Sometimes she thought there was more intimacy between them here, in front of this window, than anyplace in which they cohabited. They had shared moments of triumph here and hours of hard work. They had reached agreements, approaching from different directions, arguing and listening, giving advice and taking it. In this room they were partners. She reached out and took his hand.

"What's wrong?"

He was forty and the balance of years was tipping. On her desk the paper was folded to a story of Germany, a story she had read, unfortunately, while she was eating.

"Morty . . ." She swallowed. "I need to have a child."

7

"How's March?" he said.

"March?"

"The *Aquitania*. It lands in Cherbourg and we can visit the Goldblatts."

"I'd love to."

"It's confirmed."

"Thanks. Really. You move too fast for me."

It was the day before Election Day, two and a half weeks since his birthday. He had taken it the way he took everything if it came from her, with calm and understanding. She had not meant a baby, she had meant a child, a young one, perhaps three or four years old. There were anti-semitic incidents in Germany now; one read about them almost daily. There must be children there that needed homes, families, children that could be saved. It was one of those that she wanted.

He had contacted an agency immediately and Uncle Willy after that. There were children available, and pictures and biographical information would be sent shortly. Bringing a child in would pose no problem. German citizens had no difficulty immigrating. Once here, there was a set procedure for becoming a citizen. Uncle Willy could foresee nothing that could stand in the way of an adoption.

The best time to go, from the point of view of the businesses, would be December or January, but the agency wheels moved too slowly. June was out because of the wedding. Ships crossed the Atlantic with less frequency in the winter, so Morty's choice was something of a compromise. The *Aquitania* left the night of March 17 and they would be on board.

They stayed up late the next night listening to the news of the election on the radio. Although nothing would be definite for a long time, they went to sleep certain that there would be a new president.

She sold silk to a company that made evening dresses for Bergdorf Goodman. It was one of the Paris designs, corrected and altered. She had learned a lot since 1925, and what she had learned was paying off.

They heard from the agency Morty had called, but she found she could not look at the pictures. She started one evening at the dining-room table, got to the second one, and pushed them away.

"I want a boy born in twenty-eight or twenty-nine," she said, and never looked at them again. But in her sleep that night she saw the faces, saw herself trying to make a choice, and awoke shivering. One could not choose among children.

Morty rented the house in the mountains for the week from just before Christmas to just before New Year's. No sooner had he made the arrangements than they received an invitation to Jerold's engagement party on Christmas Eve. Morty looked disappointed.

"We don't have to go," she said.

"It's your cousin. You won't be forgiven."

"We're going to the wedding. If we stay home for this, we'll miss two days in the country. You need a rest, Morty."

He looked undecided. "Willy's done so much for us."

"Leave it to me."

To her surprise, he agreed. He was more tired than she had suspected, more in need of a rest. She wrote her regrets to the Frenches, telephoned Aunt Eva and explained their previous arrangements, making a point that they had booked a March passage to Europe so that they would be home for the wedding. Aunt Eva was most gracious in understanding.

Pop Rush got thinner. There were times when he seemed almost confused. The great mill that had provided so abundantly for himself and his sons in the twenties was operating far below capacity and only marginally in the black. His sons scarcely spoke to one another and, he thought, perhaps there lay the true problem. Restore family harmony and perhaps there would once again be lavish profits. The worse things became at Rush Woolens, the harder Morty worked to sell what they produced. By the time the end of December came, he too seemed thinner and certainly more tired than Regina had ever seen him.

"Why don't you let me drive?" she offered as they carried groceries to the car.

"I'll drive."

"I know the way. You could rest, Morty. You were up again last night."

"I'll sleep when we get there."

It was Friday morning and they had given everyone a long weekend. She sat beside him and looked at the paper. Germany was erupting. Names like Hitler and von Papen were suddenly as familiar as Roosevelt and Lehman. Now when she read about the turmoil abroad, there were other thoughts that pierced the anxieties. She would take one of those little children whose pictures she could not look at and give him a new life. Someone who today had nothing to look forward to would grow up healthy and happy in her home.

She watched Morty anxiously as they drove north, grateful that they were getting away. He was not merely tired; he was angry and worried. Pop was getting old, and he was relying on Stuart more and more. Nothing would ever improve between the brothers, and now, very slightly, Pop seemed to be taking sides.

Morty yawned and she offered again to take over, but he shrugged her off. They were out of the city now, on the open road, riding along the Hudson. This was the kind of driving he enjoyed most. He would not relinquish the wheel just because he was overcome with fatigue.

They pulled into the gravel drive a little before noon. Morty turned the motor off, put the key in his pocket, and leaned back in the seat.

She put a hand on the sleeve of his coat. "Go inside and lie down. I'll make a fire and bring the groceries in, and when you wake up I'll have something for you to eat."

He took a deep breath and exhaled, almost with relief. "Know what I want to do?"

"Hm-mm."

"I want to take my clothes off, lie down on that bed, and . . ." He leaned over and whispered a syllable in her ear.

She felt her cheeks redden.

"You're not gonna tell me I shocked you."

She shook her head and grinned at him. "I thought you were tired," she said, putting her arms around him.

"I am. I'm tired of my brother and engagement parties and your cousin Schindler and business being lousy. Will you come inside or do I have to carry you?"

"I'm on my way."

In January Mother called to say the wedding plans had been changed. "They decided it was silly to wait until June, so they're getting married before Passover."

"Before Passover? When will that be?"

"The end of March."

"We'll be away, Momma."

"You should try to change your plans, Regina."

"Momma, I talked to Aunt Eva in December and I told her we had arranged to go in March so we wouldn't miss the wedding in June."

"Well, Jerold says he sees no reason to wait that long, and they were able to make new arrangements. You should try, Regina. He's your cousin and he's always been very good to you."

She didn't try, and she told Morty there was no need to. It was better this way. She was the last person Jerold needed at his wedding.

At the end of January the office phone rang and a woman said she was trying to locate the designer of Regina Rush fabrics.

"I'm Regina Rush and I do the designing."

"Well, I'm just delighted to talk to you," the voice purred. "We've been noticing your fabrics for several seasons now and we're very excited about them. They have such freshness and originality, there's something almost French about them. Now my sources tell me you've gone into silk?"

"Who is this?" Regina asked, puzzled.

"Oh, I'm sorry. I forgot to introduce myself. I'm calling from *Vogue* magazine."

When she got off the phone, finally, after several minutes of flattery and an appointment for lunch, she called Morty at Rush.

"What's up?" he said when they found him.

"Oh, Morty, I think 1933 is going to be a wonderful year."

It wasn't a wonderful year for Lillian. Although the day varied, by early 1933 the morning phone call home had become a regular weekly event. By January he had stopped disguising his actions. "Look, Lil," Regina would hear him bluster into the telephone, leaning back comfortably in his chair, "I couldn't make it. You're carrying on like an idiot. You've got nothing to worry about. My insurance is all paid up." Eventually he would slam the receiver down in anger or disgust and start to organize papers for his day of work.

By February his work habits had changed. His expenses had crept up, but he was visiting fewer clients. It was something Regina did not want to talk to him about and wanted even less to discuss with Morty.

"Take it easy," Karl said to her one day when they talked about it. "He's still paying his way."

"Not the way you are."

Karl shrugged. "Morty never told Schindler he'd make a rich man of him."

Their trip was only a month and a half away and she hated to leave Karl with problems. They had wanted to keep the trip a secret from Phil until the last moment, but the family grapevine could be counted on to prevent that. Aunt Martha seemed to pick up gossip before it had even been formulated, and pass it on in its embryonic stage. They didn't talk about the trip openly, but they assumed Phil knew.

Halfway through February it was all finally resolved. It was a cold Wednesday and when she unlocked the door, Regina hurried to the radiator to thaw her fingers. Even with a new longer coat and a fur hat, it was bitterly cold. She was still at the radiator when Karl arrived.

"Better learn to get the blood circulating if you're going to run after a kid," he teased. They had told him the reason for their trip, although they had discussed it with almost no one else.

"He'll just have to learn to love radiators," Regina said. Thinking about it, about the child she would bring home, warmed her more than the steam. She had never looked forward to anything with more enthusiasm.

"You'll do all right," Karl said. "You run your family the way you run your shop, no one'll have any complaints."

She pulled her hat off and hung it on the tree, then her coat on a hook nearby. "I'm talking to *Vogue* tomorrow," she said.

"Nervous?"

She laughed. "I've never worried so much about what I should wear."

"You look fine like that." She was wearing a wool suit and a white silk blouse, very businesslike but far from imaginative. "It's what you do that matters. Without people like you, *Vogue* has nothing to write about."

"I'm going to show her some of my really daring designs. Morty thinks I've been too conservative. Maybe with a new president there'll be more excitement in fashion."

"Let's hope so."

"I'm feeling very optimistic." She went to her special file cabinet and pulled out a large folder. "We did some strike-offs in Paterson. Want to look?" She displayed one piece of fabric after the other. "It was expensive," she said, "but if *Vogue* prints any of them, they'll be beating down our doors."

"They're wonderful." He sounded awed. "Where have you been hiding these?"

"In my studio-soon-to-be-nursery. I wasn't sure they would sell."

"I'll sell them. Give me anything *Vogue* doesn't walk away with. Give me the watercolors. I know who'll buy them."

"Flattery will get you everywhere."

"No, really. I think these are the best—"

He stopped short as the telephone rang.

"Don't forget the rest of that sentence," she said, laughing as she dashed for her desk to answer the call. "I want it all when I get off the phone. Regina Rush."

"Regina, this is Lillian."

Her heart dropped a thousand feet. "Lillian . . ." She glanced at her watch. It was nine-thirty. In two years, Phil had never walked in that door late.

"Is Phil there?" her cousin asked in a calm, ordinary voice, the way Regina might have said "Is my husband around?" when the phone was answered at Rush.

"No, uh, he hasn't come in yet . . ." She sensed that it was over, that he had made his decision, that he had walked through that door for the last time.

"Well, I just wanted to check with him about something. If you'd ask him to call when he comes in?"

"Yes, of course, the minute I see him." Her own voice a register lower than her cousin's, her heart pounding against her ribs.

"Thank you, Regina. Bye-bye."

She dropped the phone in the cradle and looked up. Karl was standing several feet away, watching her. "She must be going through hell," Regina said. She felt her eyes fill.

"She's seen it coming."

"It can't make it any easier."

She went to Phil's desk and pulled open the top drawer. There were pencils, paper clips, rubber bands, all the usual paraphernalia. Other drawers contained folders of business papers, stationery, envelopes. There was nothing personal, but she had no way of knowing whether anything personal had ever been there. It was the first time she had ever opened his desk.

She pushed the last drawer shut and looked again at her watch. "You'd better get on with your day," she said woodenly. "I'll take care of this."

"I'll call in later."

She nodded and watched him go. Slowly she put the strike-offs back in the folder, looking at each with diminished pleasure. Phil was gone. He would never come back.

She waited an hour and called Lillian. Her cousin answered the phone anxiously.

"It's me, Lillian, Regina. He's not here yet and he hasn't called."

"I see. Well, he must have made an important stop on his way."

"Yes, perhaps that's it. I wonder . . ." She didn't know quite how to phrase it, but there seemed only one way. "Did Phil come home last night?"

There was a pause, and then Lillian's voice, frosty with rage, pierced her ear. "How dare you," she hissed. "Where else *would* he be?" And the receiver slammed down, severing the connection.

Regina hung up. Lillian had never visited this office. Perhaps she imagined—or had heard—that Phil had a private office, that none of their conversations were overheard. Perhaps she thought she was the only person besides her husband who knew of his philandering. Perhaps she was trying to protect her own tottering tower of respectability.

The morning passed and he did not appear. After lunch Regina took the subway uptown and went to Lillian's apartment. The door opened and Lillian, her thin face drawn and white, looked at her from the foyer.

"What do you want?"

"I thought you might like some company."

"I wouldn't, thank you. My daughters will be home from school soon, and I don't want you here when they arrive."

Regina said, "I'm sorry," and started down the hall.

"Come back here a minute," Lillian ordered, and when Regina had returned she said, "The bank account's empty, in case you wanted to know."

"I didn't want to know. I wanted to know that it was still full." She walked away for the second time, and this time no one called her back.

She went home, walked through the narrow lobby of the old apartment house, out the back way, and along the snowy path to their little pixie house on the snow-covered green. A man she had never seen was standing at the door as though waiting for someone to answer.

"Looking for someone?" she called as she approached.

"Good afternoon, ma'am." He turned toward her and took his cap off. He looked old and worn and seedy, but she was sure he was not much older than she.

"Can I help you?"

"Well, maybe just a bowl of soup," the man said deferentially.

She stopped and looked at him more carefully. He was thin but surely very strong. His eyes were clear. "Come on in," she said, taking her keys out. "Maybe you'll have time to stay for a sandwich too."

She heated last night's leftovers while he washed, and set a place for him in the kitchen. She watched him eat for a few minutes, then excused herself and went into the living room. Sitting in a deep chair, she thought about Lillian and Phil and the man in the kitchen.

The man cleared his throat, and she looked up in surprise.

"Sorry, I must have been . . . Are you finished so soon?"

"Yes, ma'am. It was very good, thank you. Anything you have that needs fixin'?"

"Let's see. The kitchen window sticks, but it's so cold now, I wouldn't want to try to open it."

"Yes, ma'am. I'll come by this way again in the spring and take care of that for you."

"Only if it's not out of your way."

"No, ma'am. Not out of my way at all. I'll be going now, and I thank you for the supper."

"Wait a minute."

She got her bag and took out her wallet. There was a five and three ones. She took the five and handed it to him.

He stood looking down at it as it rested on the palm of his hand. "Thanking you very much, I can't take it, ma'am. If I have that much money in my pocket, they won't give me a bed tonight."

"You could spend some of it," Regina suggested.

"That would be wasting."

"Will they let you in with three dollars?"

"Yes, ma'am."

She made the trade and said good-bye and watched him make his way to the building that led to the street.

The next day a package arrived from Uncle Willy. Inside was a new novel by Timothy McGuire. It was dedicated to his benefactor.

On Friday morning she telephoned the bookkeeper at Rush who kept their accounts and asked to have a check for four days' work sent to Lillian Schindler. She didn't tell Morty about it until the following Thursday evening. "He's not coming back," she said, "and he walked off with everything they had in the bank."

"I gather you're planning to do something about it."

"I sent her four days' pay last Friday. I want to keep doing it until something works out."

"You know it's not your responsibility."

"It's Phil's responsibility, and Phil's gone. Who else is there? Uncle Jack can't help out anymore. Henry's still in his hospital training. I don't see how she'll manage."

There was a long quiet moment and then Morty said, "Write it out of your personal checkbook. This isn't a business expense."

"Thanks, Morty."

"I hope she thanks you. I hope once in her life she does something nice for you."

"She already has," Regina said.

The *Vogue* article would appear in the spring, well after their return, but already there were rumors and inquiries. Regina had toyed with the idea of retiring after they adopted the child, but she knew now she would not. She would design and Morty would work half-time at Rush and half-time at RR. The woolen mill was scarcely breaking even now, and they could use his half-salary. With Schindler gone, there was a need for another person. The new trio was high on optimism.

Until Roosevelt was inaugurated. They turned on the radio the following day and heard about the bank holiday.

"Oh, Christ," Morty said. "Oh, Jesus Christ. We're sailing in two weeks." He looked at her where she lay in bed shedding the last of her Sunday sleep. "What the hell are you laughing about?"

"I just think it's funny. How could you pick a date in October and have it come out a few days after a March bank holiday?"

"Regina, if they don't reopen, we may leave this country without money."

"It's the best way to see Paris."

"When you're young and single, not when you're old and adopting a child, not when you have to pay out bribes to little people who facilitate your passage."

"We'll manage. I think it's a good omen. Everything will go wrong before we leave and everything'll be wonderful once we get there. It's like breaking the glass at a wedding. It satisfies the evil spirits and then they leave you alone."

"If you say so." He didn't look convinced. "I'd better cable the Goldblatts and ask if our credit is good."

She stretched and laughed again. "I wonder if we can pay for the cable," she said.

Ten days later, shortly before they were to sail, the phone rang during dinner. Regina went to the kitchen to answer.

"Regina, how are you?"

There was a second while she connected the ebullient voice in her ear with a face. "Richard! Where are you? Richard . . . oh, Richard."

"Can I see you? Both of you. I really want to see you."

"Tonight? I still have the dishes to do."

"Hang the dishes. I have to see you. I want you to meet my wife."

8

She was almost as tall as Richard and her name was Jeanne-Marie. Her hair was long and dark and pulled severely back from face and forehead. She had a warm smile and a strong handshake.

"We came in on the *Aquitania* this morning," Richard said, relaxing in an armchair.

"I hope you left it seaworthy," Morty said. "We're sailing on it Friday night."

"Ah, so soon." Richard leaned forward. "That doesn't leave much time."

"For what?" Regina asked, pouring coffee.

"I need a favor, a big one. I want you to use your charms on Mom."

"What's wrong?"

"We haven't been accepted."

Regina met Richard's eyes and then looked at Jeanne-Marie. "Not your mother, Richard."

"It's a combination of things. We've been married awhile and didn't let anyone know. Jeanne-Marie comes from an old French Catholic family and has no intentions of changing—any more than I would—and that seems to have hurt Mom more than I anticipated. So here we are, back for Jerold's wedding, and I think I've been disinvited. Hell of a thing for the best man, wouldn't you say?"

"I think she is only confused," Jeanne-Marie said in accented English. "She will change, but the wedding is so soon."

"Have you talked to your brother?" Regina asked.

"Only on the phone. I asked him not to say anything at home. I don't want him to jeopardize his position in the family. Everything's kind of frantic right now. You've always been kind of special to Mom, and maybe you'll know the right way to talk to her. I'm afraid I'll make a mess of it if I try again. Jeanne-Marie says I sounded pretty arrogant when I called this morning." He looked over at his wife and smiled in a way that little Richard Wolfe used to smile during the summers of their childhood. "She has to know I'm not Cousin Henry. I can't ask for permission to do something I've made up my mind to do anyway."

"Richard!" Jeanne-Marie said sternly and they all laughed.

"Arrogant," Richard said. "I think it's my new phase. Depression arrogance. We're only staying a few months, you know, and I really can't see this sort of thing splitting up the family."

"I'll talk to her, Richard. Tomorrow morning."

She was announced by the doorman, and a maid opened the door as she stepped out of the elevator into the small private hall. Inside, the space was overpowering. Their little house could fit easily in this room, and again in this room, and maybe there, down the hall.

"Good morning, Regina."

"Hello, Aunt Eva."

They kissed and Regina gave her coat to the maid. It was bitterly cold for March and it would take a few minutes to warm her fingers.

"You don't look well, Regina."

"It's the cold, and we're sailing Friday night. Everything we hear about Germany nowadays is very frightening, but we have to go."

"Yes, the news is very bad." She led the way into the living room and they sat. "Your mother tells me you're adopting a child."

Regina nodded and smiled. Even if Uncle Willy had told her, Aunt Eva would not have admitted it. "A little boy probably. It was a boy that we lost."

"Yes, I remember. It's a few years now, isn't it?"

"Four."

"Oh, my."

"The orphanage in Frankfurt has a little boy about that age. If he's still there when we arrive, I thought he would be the right one for us."

"Have you looked into his background?"

"His background? What sort of background could a four-year-old child have?"

"His parents, dear," Aunt Eva said. "We're all born with a family tree, whether we know it or not."

Regina smiled. "It does sort of get in the way sometimes, doesn't it?"

Aunt Eva looked away toward the windows, which were heavily curtained. "What does he look like?" she asked.

"I think he has dark hair. I couldn't . . . I had a lot of trouble looking at the pictures. It seemed too much like buying a dress. I don't know how to choose between children. I just thought, for myself, I'd like a child that wasn't too young. I'm not sure I could manage a baby."

"It comes easily," her aunt said.

"If he's older, I'll be able to talk to him."

"They say the older ones often come with ready-made problems."

Regina took a deep breath. "Then we'll all be even, won't we?" She glanced at her watch. Too much time had elapsed since her arrival and she had not begun to plead Richard's case. She had a long trip back down to Worth Street, and surely Aunt Eva had much to do with a big wedding less than two weeks away. "Aunt Eva—" she began.

"What is she like?"

"What?"

238

"Richard's wife. What is she like?"

Surprised, Regina met her aunt's eyes. "She's one of the nicest people I've ever met. She does photography—not portraits, but very artistic things. They may do a book together. They seem so . . . I've never seen Richard quite so happy."

"Yes." Aunt Eva stood and crossed the room slowly. "Where are they staying, Richard and his wife?"

"At Delmonico's. They're just down the street."

"Yes." Aunt Eva consulted her watch. "You'd better run along, dear. I know you've taken time off from work to come up here. It was very nice of you. I'll call Richard at Delmonico's."

"That's wonderful. I'm so glad."

"Have a good trip, Regina."

"Thank you."

"I'm sure you'll make that little boy very happy," Aunt Eva said, and kissed her good-bye.

It was a terrible crossing. Winter lingered over the ocean as though pushed from its shores with nowhere to go. It was stormy and cold and Regina was sick for the first time in her life. The weather did not calm until they were within hours of Cherbourg.

Relieved and happy to arrive, they stretched a weekend in Paris into several days, staying at the great house with all its empty bedrooms. Only Marc remained with his parents, little Marc, now tall and twenty-one. They visited Suzanne and saw her children. Maurice and his wife had them to dinner. They even managed to steal some time to talk to people in their industry. The last word was always Paris. What was new in Paris was still undreamed of in New York.

Finally they boarded a train early in the morning and traveled east to Frankfurt. She entered the country with a feeling of fear. She had lived her life in a world that was largely Jewish—her family, her close friends, many of the people with whom they did business. There were places one did not go because Jews were not wanted, but that was a fact of life. Now she was in a country that did not have a place where Jews were wanted. Every day the Times reported new incidents. On the day they sailed, they read that police in Leipzig had banned a concert conducted by Bruno Walter. Even music was not immune from the new regime. Negro jazz would be heard no more in Germany. The music she and Morty had learned to love in Paris, had listened to for hundreds of hours in two countries, would not be played again in this one.

They stepped off the train in Frankfurt tired after the long trip and somewhat apprehensive. Morty went to find a porter while Regina waited with the luggage. Across the track on the next platform a family waited for a train heading west. They stood like an island surrounded by trunks, valises, and packages, the woman a young, erect, well-dressed modern counterpart of Grandmama, her hand on the youngest child's shoulder, the father staring across the track without seeing. A traveler moving briskly along the platform bumped the woman's shoulder unnecessarily and continued without offering an apology. When he had gone, the woman gathered the children a little closer and bent to say something to one of them. In three more minutes their train would arrive and they would board, leaving Frankfurt for the last time, a new Exodus in its infancy.

Outside the station they got a taxi and drove to their hotel. Brown Shirts in the streets and here and there a swastika. Morty had booked them at the Frankfurter Hof, a large, grand hotel that reminded Regina of the Plaza in New York. She watched nervously as the desk clerk flipped pages in their passports. As Americans with a thoroughly Americanized name, they were accorded full respect. No one would bump Regina's shoulder in this magnificent lobby. There were bows, scrapes, and smiles, and finally they entered their large room with its heavy furniture and thick draperies.

"I didn't know you spoke German so well," she said.

"My mother never learned much English. I never talked anything else to her."

She opened her valise and began taking things out. "Everything seems to be flourishing here. It's hard to believe what we saw in the station."

"What we saw in the station is more the truth than all the smiles you see in the street."

"I hope it doesn't spread to France." She could see Suzanne with her beautiful children, Aunt Hélène presiding in her dining room, a way of life as solid as a fortress and as fragile as a crystal goblet.

Taking a handful of Reichsmark notes with him, Morty went downstairs to buy a newspaper, and when he returned he translated a paragraph here and a sentence there. All the outrages in Germany were caused by communists in one place, socialists in another place, and Jews everywhere. They ordered dinner sent to their room and they did not go out again until morning.

The taxi stopped on a corner and they got out. They still had a block and a half to go, but the man from the agency had instructed them to walk. They were in a residential area some distance from the hotel. A woman in a dark coat and black hat came down the street, walking a small dog. She nodded and smiled as she passed, not considering the object of her salutations, not stopping to wonder whether they were worthy of her smile.

The address was a larger house than the others but identified only with a number. A pane of glass in the front door had been broken and crudely mended, and Regina wondered at the cause.

"Ready?"

"Yes. Are we on time?"

He looked at his watch. "A few minutes early. I don't think it matters. He said we'd be expected."

He knocked on the door and a moment later it was opened by a graying woman in a dark uniform with a large white collar.

"Mr. and Mrs. Rush," she said, "won't you come in? I am Mrs. Gelber." Behind them the door was locked. "Did you have a good trip?"

"Very pleasant," Regina said.

"We thought you would come yesterday, but it was just this morning that Mr. Steiner called."

"We stayed an extra day in Paris with friends."

"Yes, Paris is so lovely. Would you like to talk about the children first, or would you like to see them?"

Morty looked at her and she said, "I'd like to see them. Are they all together?"

"Yes. Come with me. You can watch them without disturbing them. They are in the kindergarten now. We have four at the moment. You should keep your coats. It is a little cold in the hall." She spoke a comforting accented English, as though she had learned it in England. "There is only one girl now. She is a little older. The girls always seem to be taken first, especially if they are young."

They climbed the stairs and walked what must have been the depth of the house. From beyond the wall to their left came the sounds of children.

"Here we are," Mrs. Gelber said, stopping at the end of the hall. "You can look through this window, and the children will not see you."

Regina stopped before she reached the window.

"You all right?" Morty asked.

"You are very nervous, Mrs. Rush," Mrs. Gelber said, coming to her and taking her arm. "Come and sit on one of the chairs and I bring you a cup of tea. It must be difficult for you after so long a trip, and our country is not what it used to be."

Regina sat and waited until Mrs. Gelber had left before she raised her eyes. Behind the glass was a large playroom with toys, books, and small furniture. A beautiful tile stove was built into one corner of the room. A woman sat near it with a little boy, while three other children occupied themselves separately.

"He's over there," Morty said quietly, sitting on a chair beside her, his hat on his lap, one hand reaching to cover hers.

The little boy had dark hair like Morty's but he was small. He was taking something apart with great concentration, a toy of some sort.

"I want to take him and go," Regina said.

"They won't let you."

"I know."

He clasped her hand. "I've never seen you like this. Are you sure you're all right?"

"Yes. Morty, what will happen to the others?"

"You can't save the whole world, Regina."

"I know, but I can still worry about it, can't I?"

"And here is a nice cup of tea." Mrs. Gelber, on rubber soles, had materialized with no warning.

"Thank you." Regina sipped it gratefully. The little boy on the other side of the glass had put his work down and was watching the other lone boy. "It's very good, Mrs. Gelber. I feel much better now." He walked to the other boy and said something. "How long has he been here?"

"Since September."

"When was he born?"

"In twenty-nine. Let me see. February, I think."

"That would be just about right. His name is Ernst, isn't it?"

"Yes. He's a very sweet boy, Mrs. Rush. He should eat a little more, but

241

the doctor says he's very healthy. If you like, you may see him this afternoon when he wakes up. We have a nice little room where no one will bother you. Then, when Mr. Steiner comes at five, you can talk to him."

She looked at Morty.

"Whatever you say."

She said, "Fine."

"Maybe you would like more tea," Mrs. Gelber said with a note of victory, as though she had just arranged a difficult match.

"Thank you, I'd just like to watch for a while."

They walked out into the street at noon. The children would have dinner and a nap and they would return at three.

"Feeling better?"

"Much. It was a lot easier getting married. It was even easier selling my first designs. The tea helped. She must have put something in it for nervous mothers-to-be."

"You're pregnant, aren't you?"

She looked at him with more embarrassment than surprise. "Yes."

"How long?"

"A few months. I think it was that torrid week around Christmas."

"Have you seen a doctor?"

"No. I just have an extra glass of milk with lunch."

"Why didn't you tell me?"

"I didn't want anything to get in the way of the trip. First there was the wedding and then the bank holiday and the weather was so rotten. And the agency people in New York seemed so concerned about my working. I was afraid if they found out I was pregnant, they'd say no to the whole adoption. The first three months are so touchy anyway. I was going to tell you the minute we signed the papers. You aren't angry, are you?"

"Not angry. I just wouldn't've let you work so hard after Schindler left."

"I thought maybe if I toughened myself up a little . . . Anyway, if I'd told you, we would have talked about it, and I didn't want to think about it. I thought if I could just forget it was happening . . . It didn't happen this time until I'd given up, until after we'd talked to the agency. I know I sound silly and superstitious, but—"

"Mrs. Rush?"

They turned and saw Mrs. Gelber walking out the front door.

"There isn't anything wrong, is there? I saw you from the window and I was afraid—"

"We're just talking about where to have lunch," Morty said easily.

"Ah, that's good." Mrs. Gelber smiled with obvious relief. "I have already told Ernst someone will see him this afternoon. We like to prepare them, you know. Yes, I should have told you where to eat. If you go always straight ahead down this street and then right at the corner for two blocks, you come to a nice little *Weinstube,* they make you anything you like. It is a Jewish family, you know? Would you like me to walk with you?"

"Thank you, I'm sure we'll find it. You'd better go inside. It's very cold out."

"Yes, Mrs. Rush. Thank you. We see you at three then?"

"Three sharp," Morty said, and Mrs. Gelber returned to the house.

It was an excellent lunch, and after the place had emptied a little, Morty struck up a conversation with the proprietor, a man in his forties who seemed to know half his clientele intimately. They talked for over an hour, and finally, when they left, Morty gave his card to the man and told him to call if he got to New York, suggesting strongly that he should leave Germany.

Then they went back to the orphanage and met the child.

It was less frightening and less emotional than Regina had anticipated. The kindergarten teacher, Miss Silberberg, brought him into the room where the Rushes waited, a small sitting room warmed by an old coal stove. He was very polite and shook hands, withdrawing immediately to the safety of Miss Silberberg's presence. A few minutes later, milk, coffee, and cookies were brought and Regina watched the little boy drain the glass.

"It must taste awfully good," she said, looking at the dark eyes that watched her over the rim.

"There is sugar in the bottom," Miss Silberberg said in her heavily accented English. "That way they always finish."

Morty asked him in German if it tasted good and the dark head bobbed. Miss Silberberg said Ernst could count to ten in English, and with a little coaxing and some help from Regina, he did. They made hesitant conversation and after three-quarters of an hour Miss Silberberg told the boy very casually that she had to look after something and he watched her leave with frightened eyes but without voicing an objection.

It was an awkward ten minutes, with Morty doing the talking for both of them and the little boy listening and watching, his glance moving now and then to the door. Finally, sensing a moment, Regina left her chair and took his hand, walked him to the sofa, and sat with him. He looked at her watch and listened to it, admired the diamond ring, and stroked her fingernails. When Miss Silberberg returned, all three of them were on the sofa and Morty had promised the little boy a watch if he could learn to tell time.

At five Mr. Steiner arrived. Properly addressed "doctor," he was a lawyer who served the agency. He went rapidly through the biographical information: mother died at birth, father died August 1932 after a visit by Nazi storm troopers to the shop he had owned in a town in Bavaria. Health apparently good but no records predating September 1932. He droned on. Child available as soon as staff approved, probably by week's end. Today was Thursday.

When they left, it was nearly six and dark. Mrs. Gelber had whispered that Ernst's favorite toy was a fire truck, and they hurried to a store that was still open and bought one for him and one for the orphanage. Morty picked out other things with enthusiasm until they realized they were keeping the store open. Back in their room Regina sat on the bed and looked through their purchases, remembering toys in Richard's room at the farm when they were young, cars and trucks he guarded jealously against the encroachment of Adele, toys he had shared only with his most favorite people, with his brother, with little Regina, who would dust off the dirt when they were finished playing, and suddenly she was in tears, terrible cumulative tears spotting a bright red fire engine.

"I wish Grandmama were still here," she said, wiping the truck. "I miss her so much."

They gave him the fire engine the next morning and they all had lunch together at noon. They came back after his nap and he was already waiting in the sitting room when they entered. His eyes opened wide when he saw Regina. She was wearing the mink, now cut down from a coat to a long jacket to accommodate the longer skirts of the new decade. He approached her gingerly and stroked the fur. Turning to Morty, whom he now acknowledged as interpreter, he asked if it were a dog and they all laughed and Regina picked him up and let him rub his cheek in it.

Mrs. Gelber hinted that after Saturday they might take him. Saturday morning they bought some clothes before they made their visit. In the afternoon Mrs. Gelber said Mr. Steiner would come to see them at four, and later she called them away and they went to the office on the ground floor.

"Mrs. Gelber is satisfied to let you take the boy," Mr. Steiner began, "and I have checked that everything is in order. You are staying in a hotel here in Frankfurt?"

"Frankfurter Hof," Morty said laconically, and she sensed he had had his fill of the slow pace of the proceedings.

"Yes, a pleasant hotel. One can eat well there."

"When can we take him?" Regina asked, suddenly equally tired of all the formalities, the requirements, the prerequisites to continuing their lives.

"Very soon, very soon." Mr. Steiner smiled across the desk at his clients. "There is one small problem, however, but you need not trouble yourselves about it. Because of the family situation, the documents for Ernst are not quite in order. We feel you could have some trouble taking him out of Germany, so we are prepared to arrange it for you."

"Can you explain that a little better?" Morty asked with a touch of irritation.

"We have people who will take him across the border for you, and you will find him in Amsterdam next Tuesday."

"Amsterdam?"

"Yes. There is a house there, a very fine lady, Mrs. Kuipers, who has helped us before. There will be no trouble."

"Do we have a choice?"

"No, Mr. Rush, I think you do not have a choice. I cannot permit you to take the child across the border yourself. It is my responsibility to deliver him safely out of this country. I must decide on the method."

"It means he'll be with more strangers," Regina said. "It'll be very unsettling for him."

Mr. Steiner smiled. "Yes, Mrs. Rush, you are right. It will be unsettling, but for everything there is a price. To leave this country and find a new home in America, for some people the price is very great. They leave homes and businesses and families. They must learn a new language. Your child will spend a few days with strangers and he will be frightened. To a mother this is very unsettling. You will have many years in which to make things calm again."

When they left a little while later, they took with them the name and address of the woman in Amsterdam, and Morty left an envelope thick with greenbacks.

The instructions were to wait until ten on Tuesday morning. They arrived in Amsterdam on Sunday night and spent Monday shopping and sightseeing to pass the time. Monday night they scarcely slept.

The address was on a canal, and they walked from the hotel after a large Dutch breakfast, trying to make time stretch out, not wanting to arrive early. It was ten after when they rang the bell of the tall narrow house; the woman who answered expected them. She was in her sixties and wiry, and her English was good.

"Yes, someone is waiting for you," she said, leading them into the living room, where Ernst sat alone on a sofa, his eyes lighting with recognition as he saw them.

Regina kissed him and he patted her jacket.

"Such a nice boy," the woman said, "but very tired this morning. It was very late when they arrived, after midnight. But look how bright his eyes are." She sat next to him and patted his hand as though she had known him a long time and their acquaintanceship had just been interrupted by the arrival of the Americans. "You want to take him now, don't you?" she said, and there was a note of sadness. She would suffer a small loss when he left her.

"Yes, I think so," Regina said gently. "We have to make arrangements at the consulate."

"Yes, of course. So many things to do. *Komm, Ernst. Ich zieh Dich an.*"

She got a coat and a woolen hat from a cupboard and put it on him, buttoning the buttons and pulling the cap over his ears. She picked him up and said something to him in German and then kissed his cheek. Watching, Regina felt a surge of excitement, a combination of all the great moments of her life. This kind woman was about to hand her her child. All the preliminaries were over. The disappointments and the years of waiting had passed.

"You will come back and visit perhaps?" Mrs. Kuipers asked Regina. "I like to see what happens to my children."

"We'll come back. Another year or two, when things get better in Germany."

"Then I give you your boy, Mrs. Rush."

Regina started forward to take him, then turned to look at Morty, and stopped. "Give him to my husband," she said, and she watched as Morty lifted the little boy and gave him a hug of welcome.

9

"He has a Dutch passport?" The man was blond and about thirty and spoke with a midwestern accent.

"No," Morty said, trying to keep the irritation under control. It was the third time he had explained it. "He's not a Dutch citizen. He's German." He went back over the facts, slowly and carefully.

"Right, I understand all that," the man said. "But I need papers to prove it. You don't have a record of his entry into Holland."

"No, I don't have it because there isn't any record. Look, I don't have to tell you what's going on in Germany. A problem was circumvented in getting this boy out of the country. I'm sure you know how to circumvent whatever problem you're faced with in issuing a visa."

"We don't operate that way, Mr. Rush. In order to process a visa, this office requires—"

"Mr. Hardy, I know what your office requires and I can't produce it because it doesn't exist. Give me an alternative."

"The alternative is for the person to establish residency here in Holland."

"How do we accomplish that?"

"Well"—the blond man gave a little laugh—"it takes eighteen months."

"I don't have eighteen months. I don't have eighteen days. I'm in business in the United States of America and I'd like to get back there. Now, let's figure out how we can arrange for this visa."

"I've explained it to you, Mr. Rush. There are rules and laws. I don't make them but I follow them."

"Who's the senior man here?"

"He's not in this afternoon. I'm afraid there's really nothing he can do for you. We've explored—"

"Make me an appointment with the ambassador."

"The ambassador?" Mr. Hardy looked incredulous. "The United States ambassador to the Netherlands?"

"That's right."

"Mr. Rush, the ambassador doesn't handle routine visa applications."

"There is nothing routine about this visa."

Regina moved in her chair to make the little boy more comfortable. They had had lunch and come to the consulate and he had fallen asleep on her lap. She had followed Morty from one office to another, listening to higher and higher officials explain with appropriate courtesy and sympathy that no visa could be issued. This was the first time Morty had raised his voice, and she could sense that he shared her own deepening apprehension.

"Mr. Rush," the blond man said in a carefully controlled voice, his glance dropping briefly on Regina, "I will telephone the embassy for you. If you give me your hotel number, I will get in touch with you when the call has gone through. In the meantime, I suggest you explore the possibility of Dutch residence."

She had never seen him so angry. They rode in a taxi to the hotel while he fumed.

"Willy," he said. "What're his politics?"

"I've never heard him say, but I wouldn't guess Democratic."

"We'll try him anyway. I don't know what else there is."

It took two hours for the call to get through to New York, and she could tell from listening to Morty's end that Uncle Willy was not optimistic.

"I know he'll do his damnedest," Morty said, hanging up, "but it doesn't sound good. He'll call if anything turns up. I think I'll just take a trip down to the embassy tomorrow and see what I can do on my own."

"Wait till Hardy calls."

"Hardy's a lackey. Hardy isn't calling anybody."

Morty left for The Hague on an early train Wednesday morning and Regina spent the day getting to know Ernest. She had begun calling him by the American name as soon as he was theirs. Today there was no one to translate for them, and they talked to each other in two languages, walking the streets of a city where a third was spoken. She returned to the hotel in early afternoon to find a message that Mr. Hardy had called to say he was unable to make any further appointments for Mr. Rush. Pushing the paper into her pocket, she took Ernest upstairs and put him to bed for his nap.

Morty returned at four.

"Hopeless," he said, dropping his coat on a chair. "There isn't any ambassador. He's a figment of everyone's imagination. Anything from Willy?"

"No. Hardy called to say he had nothing."

"Think. Who do we know? Who gave big money to Roosevelt?"

"Morty, the people who voted for Roosevelt didn't have big money."

"The Goldblatts." He stopped at the foot of the bed. "Try the Goldblatts."

"They're French. How can the French—?"

"Try. They'll know someone. They know people all over the Continent."

"We don't want someone on the Continent. We want an American with power and influence. We need someone who can pull strings."

He looked worn out. "Will you just try?"

She picked up the receiver, a feeling of utter hopelessness draining the last of her energy. She heard a voice in her ear and she said, "I want to call Paris," and then she lay down to rest and wait for the call.

The phone rang and she jumped. Half-asleep, she spoke to the operator. Somewhere in the distance she heard the words "père" and "fils." The father had left the office, the operator explained; could she speak to the son? Disappointed, she said yes.

"Régine?" the familiar voice sounded in her ear.

"Maurice, I'm so glad to talk to you. Listen, we have a problem."

She explained in detail, her French failing her once or twice. Maurice listened patiently, making appropriate sounds. "And we don't know what to do," she finished. "We thought perhaps you might know someone who could help."

"Yes, of course. You must be very distressed. Of course we know someone who can help. Just a moment and I will find the number. Yes, here it is. Do you have a pencil?"

She reached for the one in Morty's inside pocket and began writing on a piece of hotel stationery.

"Who is he, Maurice?" she asked, jotting the information down almost illegibly.

"Oh, a very prominent man in Holland, in the banking business, you know? He is Jewish of course, but he has friends in the highest places. Now, let me see. It is too late to call at his office. Wait until six-thirty and call the number for his home. You can speak in English. Someone there will understand. You must be sure to give regards from Papa and Mama, especially from Mama. They were great friends once, you understand? They are, I think, third cousins, and he was devastated when she married Papa." Maurice laughed. "Lucky for us that she did, wasn't it? And be sure to remind him of the time you met."

"But I haven't met him, Maurice."

"But you have, Régine. I remember exactly. You and Morty sat at his table at Suzanne's wedding."

They were invited to dinner for the following evening. Ernest would sleep in one of their bedrooms during dinner. Mr. Rijneveld would send a car to their hotel at seven.

Poor little thing, she thought, sitting in the car on the way. A different bed every night, a parade of strangers.

The dinner was haute cuisine, course after course of wonderfully prepared dishes, the creation of a French cook. The Rijnevelds were cordial and cultured, happy to entertain friends of the Goldblatts and eager to help. Between courses Mr. Rijneveld left the table and made a telephone call from another room. Regina could hear him laughing from time to time, and when he returned he addressed them with confidence.

"I am having lunch with an old friend tomorrow," he said. "He and I will discuss your problem."

"Is he attached to the American embassy?" Regina asked.

"Oh, no. He is Dutch and I am Dutch. He is in government and I am in banking. That means we speak the same language."

"I see."

"Ah, but I can tell that you don't see. In banking we need the government, and in government they need the bankers, and everywhere men are in debt to one another. Tomorrow at lunch I will remind my friend of his debt to me and the next day he will remind someone else of a debt to him."

248

"And in the meantime," his wife said in a clear voice, "we will all pray for a miracle."

The next afternoon Mr. Rijneveld's secretary called and told Regina that since it was Friday, she would be unlikely to hear anything until after the weekend but she should not give up hope. Mr. Rijneveld was optimistic that a solution to the problem would be found.

They spent the weekend trying to think of alternatives. Morty wanted to call Uncle Willy and ask what would happen if they smuggled the boy on board ship, but Regina would not let him ask until they had exhausted their legal resources.

"I can't bring up two children and visit a husband in jail," she told him, only half-facetiously.

He shrugged. "Maybe they'd put you away and let me stay out and make a living. You might get a lot of work done in a cell. It's probably quiet."

"Woman's place is not in a cell."

He grinned at her. "It's on Worth Street."

She smiled, but his easy humor had little effect. If the chain that Mr. Rijneveld had begun did not bring results, the possibilities left were too grim to contemplate.

Monday arrived with no word. They alternated leaving the hotel so that someone remained by the telephone, but no one called. They ate a quiet dinner in the room and then put Ernest to bed. Although he napped soundly each afternoon, his nights were restless and Regina could feel herself being worn down. Only that weekend she had begun to sense the flutter of life within her. She had passed the first crucial milestone of her pregnancy. She had come this far, and once again she felt the call of that life, the need to go further, to go all the way.

She sat at the edge of Ernest's bed and brushed his hair with her fingers. She talked to him and he listened as though he understood every word. Two separate lives, and she needed them both.

Tuesday began another day of waiting. Breakfast in the room. Lunch. A nap for Ernest. A glass of milk and then another. Morty had begun to insist that she drink it. Three o'clock. A dull, cloudy Dutch day. Morty was beginning to formulate new plans. If there was no word by five, he would call the States and try to get through to a senator. He should have done that a long time ago. What were they there for if not to help their constituents?

At four the phone rang. The sound was so unfamiliar that they looked at each other for a moment in amazement before Regina reached for it and said, "Yes?"

There were some clicks and some words spoken in Dutch. Then the clear midwestern voice came through. "Mrs. Rush?"

"Yes?"

"This is George Hardy at the U.S. consulate. We're processing that visa for Ernest now. Would you like to stop by about ten tomorrow so we can tie it all up?"

"Ten? Tie it all up at ten?"

"That's right," Hardy said, as though he were suggesting the commonest of meetings.

"Yes, I'm sure we can be there at ten."

"That's fine. We'll need a couple of passport-type photos. I expect your hotel can tell you the closest place to have that done."

"Yes, thank you, yes. We'll see you at ten." She put down the receiver and looked at Morty. "He said it as though there were nothing special," she said, "as though it were the most ordinary thing in the world. 'Can you stop by about ten tomorrow morning to tie it all up?' "

They waited while the small square photos dried, and took them still damp. Hardy had the papers ready and he hurried through the final details as though he had a deadline to make.

"I suppose you'll be sailing soon," he said conversationally as they waited for a secretary to return the finished document.

"First ship that leaves Rotterdam," Morty said.

"Well, good luck to you."

The door opened and a smiling middle-aged woman handed him a folder.

"I guess that's it." He gave Morty an official-looking document.

"Thank you," Regina said, sensing that Morty had decided to renounce courtesy this morning. She took Ernest's hand, and they started for the door.

"Mr. Rush," Hardy called after them, and then, in a lower voice asked, "who the hell do you know? Queen Wilhelmina?"

"Her confessor," Morty said, and closed the door behind them.

They sailed into New York harbor at dawn, watching the sun rise behind the two-year-old Empire State Building, the grandest homecoming of their lives. Standing at the railing, Regina could see her mother beside Poppi, who was waving vigorously. Morty maneuvered them rapidly through customs and led the way to the reception area, where Momma and Poppi had been joined by Richard and Jeanne-Marie. Momma was wiping her eyes and Poppi was arguing with her about something, but the moment they reached Richard, he scooped up his newest cousin and held him high for a moment.

"Hello, Ernie old boy," he said, bringing him down to shoulder height. "Welcome to the family."

250

PART V
SPRING
1933

1

The first word of the *Vogue* article was, "Hatless . . ." It annoyed Morty and made Mother cluck ("How could you have had lunch with a *Vogue* editor without a hat, Regina?"), but Karl Handelman had a good laugh and eventually Morty rather enjoyed it himself, especially since the phones at RR began ringing as soon as the June issue was out. For the first time in four years buyers asked to come to the office to see the designs.

Wafting on the sweet scent of *Vogue,* motherhood, and motherhood-to-be, Regina began a new set of designs. She integrated the daring of her Paris years with what the buyers said they wanted, tempered her work with all the semesters of instruction, and imparted it with her new happiness.

They bought Ernie paints and a scaled-down easel, and mother and son worked together in the crowded upstairs room. Afternoons a woman came when Ernie slept, staying to care for him and prepare dinner. Mother, who had been quietly noncommittal about the adoption, found she could not live without seeing her new grandson twice a week, and Poppi made no bones about adoring him. Even Pop Rush's spirits seemed to rise when Ernie visited.

In August, shortly after Richard and Jeanne-Marie had left, word came that Jerold and Edith were expecting their first child in February. Regina would give birth late in September, and Morty pressed her to move to a larger place, but she refused.

"It's not for the baby," he said, understanding her reluctance. "We're crowded now. Ernie needs his own room and you need a studio. Eventually we'll need a nurse. I don't know where we'll put her. It'll be damned crowded."

"I hope so. I hope I have to step over people. Then I think I'll be able to move."

He laid his palm on her taut rounded belly. "Then we'll just have to step over people," he said. In the other room, Ernie cried out. "I'll go," Morty said. He kissed her belly. "Go to sleep."

She listened for a few minutes to the sound of his voice, speaking patiently, and then she switched off the lamp, turned over, and closed her eyes.

She counted the days of September like coins dropping in a bank. Each

253

one that passed increased her assets. Since August she had stayed home, taking everyone's advice, resting. She watched the clock, refusing to count the day as past until she went to sleep at night. Labor Day came and went and there were twenty-three days to go. She held the banister and walked slowly up the stairs on the tenth of September and there were seventeen days to go. On the morning of the twelfth she looked in the bathroom mirror with dismay. The glass was old and produced a wavy reflection, but it was more than the glass that disturbed her. Her face was full but it looked weary.

"I wish you would stop worrying." He was standing at the open door of the long white bathroom. As she came to the door, he put his arms around her. "You're all right now. You're beautiful. Did I ever promise you anything I couldn't deliver?"

She gave him an almost laugh. *"I'm* delivering," she said, and they went down to breakfast.

Around noon on the thirteenth she felt the first pain. Ernie was at the kitchen table eating a sandwich and drinking a glass of milk. She sat down and touched his arm, and he looked at her with large questioning eyes.

"Is it good?" she asked.

"Uh-huh. But the milk is bad."

"It's not bad. There's just no sugar."

"I like the sugar."

"I know you do, but you're four and a half now. Sugar is just for babies."

"Oh." He looked disappointed.

"I made chocolate pudding, remember?" He had licked pot and spoon. "That has sugar in it."

"Could I have it now?" Half the sandwich was only half-eaten.

"Yes, you can have it now." She took it out of the refrigerator. "I have to go upstairs," she said, putting it on the table. "You can manage that without me, can't you?"

She went upstairs and called the doctor, her composure disintegrating as she waited for him to come to the phone.

"Mrs. Rush?"

She brushed away tears. "It's coming and it's early," she said, "again."

"It's not early," the doctor said.

"Today is only—"

"Today is the thirteenth. That's exactly two weeks until your due date. Don't you remember that I told you two weeks either way was on time?"

"You're sure?" She sounded exactly the way she felt, frightened and almost panicky.

"Absolutely certain," the confident voice said. "I stopped worrying about you weeks ago."

"All right." Her own voice wavered and she wiped her cheeks again.

"I want you to get yourself together, call your husband, take care of your little boy . . ."

She smiled in spite of herself, listening to his mundane instructions, tempted to say that she ran a company that did business in six healthy figures, but when she hung up, she felt better. She called RR and listened with gratitude as a voice she knew and trusted answered with her name.

254

"Karl," she said, "thanks for eating at your desk today. Please could you find Morty for me? I need him."

She went through the stages of waking, hearing a voice. Someone was talking about her, Morty, his voice quite close. Something like: She's all right. And she thought: I know I'm all right. She opened her eyes and he leaned over and touched her shoulder. His tie was off, his shirt unbuttoned, and he needed a shave.

"She's fine,"he said, "seven pounds on the button."

"She . . ."

"Yes. Screamed like a little shrew when she was born. I was outside the door of the delivery room."

"I knew it would be a girl. I used to dream . . . Did you call Momma?"

"At two this morning."

"Morty!" She laughed and tried to pull herself up, but her head was still swimming.

"Stay," he said, patting her shoulder. "Poppi answered and—"

"Poppi!"

"On the first ring. He harangued me about how he can't sleep nights anymore, and besides, he knew I'd be calling."

"Did Momma cry?"

"Copiously. Poppi had to take the phone away from her."

"I really did it, didn't I?"

He leaned over and kissed her. "Like a pro."

"Morty . . ." She tried again to sit, her head a little clearer now, feeling the pain of the stitches as she raised herself. "Why couldn't we sell children's designs to companies that make sheets? You know, puppies and pussy cats and that sort of thing, or maybe"—she rested against the pillow as he adjusted it—"tiny pastel flowers. I bet if you asked Karl—"

He shook his head. "Good-quality sheets are white. They'll always be white."

"But they don't have to be. If someone really tried aggressively—"

"I've ruined you," he said in mock despair.

She leaned back and closed her eyes. "God," she said, "I love being ruined."

Flowers arrived by the bushel, Edith and Jerold, Uncle Nate and all his progeny, Aunt Martha and Uncle Jack, Shayna and Morris. Even Lillian, who had sent nothing when they brought Ernie home, sent flowers from herself and her children. The following afternoon a cable arrived from Richard and Jeanne-Marie, indicating that someone had cabled them the day before, and Regina was quite sure that Morty had not.

They named her Margot after Morty's mother and took her home to a surprised and wary Ernie, an overcrowded house, and a nurse who had thought she would share a private wing of a great mansion with her new charge.

Three weeks later there was a phone call.

"Regina!" Mother's voice cried hysterically. "You have to come here. It's my brother. Hurry."

"Which brother, Momma? What happened?"

"Jackie. Oh, God, it's Jackie."

"I'll be there right away."

She sat on a rocker with her baby in the crook of her arm, nursing placidly, almost asleep. The baby had become round and almost content. In a few minutes Mrs. Ellis, the holy terror, would put her in her crib and she would be satisfied till afternoon. But Ernie would be disappointed. Regina had promised him a walk to go shopping this morning, and now he would have to stay home with the nurse, whom he hated and feared, until his own Mrs. Salter arrived.

He sat on the edge of the bed—against Mrs. Ellis's wishes—watching his sister fall peacefully asleep. He leaned over and touched her cheek, checking behind him first, lest the awful tyrant be present in his parents' bedroom. Regina explained that she must go to see Grandma and they would have to put off their walk until later. She wished sometimes he would complain more, voice his disappointment the way she saw other children do, but he accepted setbacks as though there were no alternative, as though he were already grown and had learned not to fuss.

Aunt Eva opened the door, Aunt Eva, who was always there when the family needed her, caring and capable, the sound of Momma crying somewhere inside.

"Regina," she said, "thank goodness you've come. Your mother told you?"

"Only that something happened to Uncle Jack."

"He died, dear, a heart attack." Aunt Eva held her arm until she was certain Regina was quite steady. "During the night is what we heard. Are you all right now?"

"Yes."

"Go and see to your mother, then. She's in the kitchen. I'm worried about Poppi." And she was off to the living room, where Poppi sat slumped in his chair at the window.

It took a long time to calm her mother down. She kept repeating how young Jackie was, only fifty-seven, how could it happen to someone so young? So terrible, the oldest brother and what he had done for them all and how would they ever live it down? Finally she drank some sweetened tea and allowed herself to be led to her bed. When Regina left the room, Aunt Eva motioned her into the living room.

"I've got Poppi into bed," she said. "I wish that doctor would get here. He needs something to calm him. Willy's gone to look after Martha." Aunt Eva took a breath and sat down. "Oh, dear, Edith will be so upset, and she's in her fifth month, poor child. You got Alice quieted down, didn't you?"

"For a while, I suppose. I don't even know what she was saying. She sounded confused."

Aunt Eva looked at her as though making a difficult decision. "I may as well tell you," she said. "You're bound to find out sooner or later. Jack didn't die at home."

"How awful. Was he at work?"

"No. He'd left work. He was visiting someone."

256

Regina met her aunt's eyes. "I see."

"Do you?"

"Yes, I do."

"How do you children come to know things the rest of us don't know?"

"It was an accident."

"I hope you don't blame your Uncle Jack."

"I never did. I'm glad you don't."

Aunt Eva smiled. She looked drawn and tired, her dark hair graying here and there, but she was still the beautiful woman Uncle Willy had married when he was too young to suit his father. "We keep learning nice things about one another, don't we?" she said, and stood almost immediately to let the doctor in.

The funeral was at ten-thirty the next morning, and Morty drove them uptown in the Packard. They parked a block away and walked back slowly. An ancient car stopped in front of the funeral parlor and Aunt Bertha got out with Arthur and Millie. Izzy would have remained behind, minding the farm and his son.

"Let's not go in yet," Regina said, and they stood half a block away and watched.

"Looking for someone?"

"Sort of."

"Try across the street, just to the left of the entrance to that apartment house."

"Yes." A woman in a dark suit and hat stood in the shadow of the building. "It's the same one. Ten years, and it's the same woman."

A taxi stopped a few feet away and Jerold got out and walked to them. They shook hands and Morty said, "My wife is uncovering family secrets."

Jerold looked at her, and a black limousine passed them at the curb as they stood there.

"That's your mother," Morty said, starting away. "I'll see you inside."

"Across the street," Regina said as though they were alone, as though no one else had ever been there.

His glance moved away and back. "Shall I speak to her?"

"Let me."

They crossed the street together and Jerold waited while she approached the woman.

"Hello."

The woman jumped and looked at Regina with red frightened eyes. "What do you want?"

"I'm Jack's niece. I wondered if there was anything I could do for you."

The woman shook her head. "How do you know?" Her voice was choked, as though she had cried more than she was able.

"I saw you once, a long time ago. He was a good man, my uncle."

The woman nodded, reached into her black leather bag and pulled out a handkerchief.

"You must have made him very happy. He needed someone to make him happy these last few years. Would you like to come to the service?"

The woman shook her head. She was crying now. "I just want . . . to know . . . where they're going to bury him."

257

"I'll write it down for you." She took a pen and paper from her bag and printed the name of the cemetery.

"Thank you."

Regina touched her arm. "Good-bye."

She crossed the street with Jerold. "It must have been nineteen-twenty-three," he said.

"Yes."

"Too long a time for a little fling."

"Much too long."

"It's good to see you."

"How's Edith?"

"Doing well. I made her stay home today. She's in her fifth month, you know."

"Yes." They walked inside the door, and she felt almost overcome by the black murmuring haze of the interior.

"You all right?"

"Yes. I'm glad we spoke to her."

She found her mother and Morty and they sat. It was nearly ten-thirty and her breasts were full. It was the first time she had missed a nursing.

The service was not long, and she heard little of it. From where she sat she could see the immediate family in the front row, two tight-lipped, dry-eyed women with almost identical faces, two pretty little girls dressed for a somber party, and Henry. It was nearly three years since she had seen Henry, not since the night he had brought Margaret to their house for dinner during the Christmas of 1930.

Beside her Momma wept and in the row ahead Uncle Nate held his face in his hands. Poppi moaned in his seat next to Uncle Willy, but in the front row the women and girls of Uncle Jack's family stared straight ahead at the wooden casket. Only Henry, his glasses removed, cried for his father.

On Friday, when Regina wrote her weekly check to Lillian, she raised the amount by five dollars.

2

In February Edith gave birth to a son, and this time it was Aunt Eva who telephoned the news.

"We're just delighted," she said. "He looks exactly like Jerold. They're naming him Arnold French and they're going to call him Frenchy."

"Congratulations. You must all be very happy."

"Happy and fortunate," Aunt Eva said. "We've all had quite a wonderful year. Now, if only Richard would come home."

But Richard would not come home. Richard wrote that he was happier in France than he had ever been. The mood had changed in Paris since the start of the thirties, and for his part, it had improved. Jeanne-Marie had found them a fine apartment with an extra bedroom—the ceilings were high and you should see the moldings—and he was letting all his American friends know that there was a place for them.

Near the end of February Regina found a studio. Morty had suggested she look farther uptown, and she decided on a large room in an office building in the West Thirties. By early March she had a telephone installed, curtains on the windows made from one of her own favorite patterns, and a hot plate and coffeepot, gifts from Morty, on a table near her easel. It was the start of the next step of the dream, a design studio.

The dream drew nearer to fulfillment and the business prospered. Two years later, early in May 1936 they sent Karl and Lucy Handelman to Europe aboard the *Normandie*. It had been Regina who had decided they could not go themselves, and Morty who suggested the alternative. But seeing them off in a mist of confetti and champagne, she felt a resurgence of the wanderlust that had carried her abroad over a decade earlier, that feeling that had never quite grown benign.

It was the most beautiful ship Regina had ever seen, every adornment whispering of elegance and grandeur. They walked through the indoor pool with its mosaic-tiled walls, looked into the theater where movies would be shown, glanced at the magnificent dining hall, and sat finally at a small round table in a corner of the grand salon near a glass panel decorated with enameled sailing ships. The blues and violets of the room's fabrics were lighted softly by tiered lamps of crystal, like so many fountains.

"We'll go," Morty promised as they made their way to the gangplank. "The kids won't be kids forever." He looked at his watch and then at her. "Tired?"

She nodded.

"One wave and we'll go home. Tomorrow's a workday."

He drove east in the Forties and then turned north. Like her studio, their home was now uptown, just upstairs of Poppi and Momma, the wonderful gingerbread house empty and more perfect than when they had first entered it. Even the kitchen window did not stick anymore. The man who had promised to fix it had been as good as his word. But they were a family of four now, and the time had come to move uptown.

He dropped her off early at Worth Street and went back up to Canal. She had arranged to come into the Worth Street office each morning while Karl was away. She set things in order, talked to the new salesman they had hired to keep up with the expanding business, and looked over the early mail. The phone rang and she answered it casually, still reading a bill from a supplier.

"Regina"—it was Morty—"Pop didn't show up this morning."

She put the paper down and felt herself become alert. "What do you mean?"

"He's always in by eight-thirty. I've never seen him late. He's not at the mill and there's no answer at the house." He sounded different, uncertain. "I think I ought to go out there."

Her hand began trembling. "Pick me up," she said with as much authority as she could summon. "I'll be downstairs."

She rang her father-in-law once again before she left the office, but there was no answer. He was seventy-six, nearly seventy-seven, but his health was good. He shared none of Poppi's moods, only a continuous disillusion with the state of business and the cool relationship between his sons.

The car came down the crowded street, slowed, and she hopped in, the motor picking up as she closed the door. Morty drove east toward the Brooklyn Bridge and she sat near him feeling frightened, watching him drive carelessly.

The trip went on endlessly and they drove in unaccustomed silence, the car bouncing from pavement to trolley tracks, veering around corners with tires screaming. He pulled to the curb finally, turned off the motor, got out of the car, and sprinted toward the house. She let herself out and followed, hurrying, reaching the door as he stepped inside. She heard him call, "Pop?" as he disappeared ahead of her into the deep, dark house that Pop had lived in almost forever. "Pop?" somewhere ahead of her, and no answer. She could barely swallow. A sweet old man who loved his grandchildren and could not understand his sons. Why had he lived here so long in darkness and only semicomfort? He had made a great deal of money once and spent little of it. Morty opened the bedroom door with a bang, and she paused, seeing light ahead of her.

"Pop," and then, a moment later, "Don't come in."

She started to cry, forgetting her resolve to be strong, to be a comfort. Ahead of her, in the bedroom, a pair of shiny silver candlesticks stood on

260

a dresser flanking a mirror that hung on the wall, Morty's inheritance from his mother.

"He must've gone in his sleep." He was suddenly in the doorway.

"Come and sit down."

"I'd better call my brother."

"I'll call."

"I'd rather keep moving."

He went to the kitchen and called the mill while she waited just outside the door. She heard him tell his brother, "I'm over at Pop's place," and heard his voice break as he spoke the news. She pulled a chair away from the dining table and sat. It was old and wobbly, but then, she was wobbly, and she was not yet thirty-two.

"I shouldn't've let him live here." He had become pale, and he held one hand whitely on the door frame, as though to steady himself.

"This was his home." She stood and put her arm around him. "He wouldn't have been happy anywhere else."

They walked to the living room and sat on the sofa.

"It's a hell of a way to die."

"It's the best way. He went to sleep. He always said he'd never been sick a day in his life."

Morty nodded, but he seemed to be far away. After a few minutes he raised himself heavily and went to the telephone and started to make all the necessary calls.

He sat up most of the night in a chair in the bedroom, and when she woke at four she knew she would not sleep again herself. It was May, and in a month they would be married ten years. In two months it would be a decade since Poppa died. Maude had died in May, but she did not know the date. She loved May—it was when he had come back to her—and she felt a sadness, almost a resentment, that this lovely month should be doubly spoiled for him.

"Can I get you something?"

"No." He looked toward the bed, his profile just visible in the small light from the shaded window. "Sorry I woke you."

"You didn't." She sat.

"Go back to sleep."

"I can't."

He rocked slightly in the chair. It was the chair she had nursed Margot in. "You can come and sit with me." It was a question, faintly plaintive. She pushed the cover aside. "Bring a blanket. It's getting cold."

She dragged the blanket across the floor so that it followed her like the train on a wedding dress. He took her on his lap, bundling the blanket around her shoulders. He was wearing a silk bathrobe that she had bought him for some birthday long past.

"I could make you tea, Morty."

"No." He had his arms around her. "Pop liked your tea, didn't he? Pop liked you. Remember when we told him we were going into business, he said he'd lend you the money?"

"I remember."

"When I told him I was going to marry you, he thought you were still twelve years old. Then, when he met you he said . . . " His voice drifted off and his arms tightened slightly around her. "I can't remember what my mother looked like anymore."

She reached up and kissed his cheek. It was scratchy with beard. "It doesn't matter."

He rocked the chair gently and she thought of Margot, nursing and falling asleep.

"Ernie got up a little while ago," he said. "Mrs. Salter went." He paused. "I didn't get myself up in time."

"I love you, Morty."

"I know," he said, surprising her. "I wasn't sure ten years ago. I thought . . . a lot of things, but I changed my mind."

"When did you change your mind?"

"When we . . . when we went into business together. No, before that. I think when you got out of the car in front of the temple."

"I loved you in Paris."

"No." He rocked. "You loved Paris. Pop loved Paris. I remember when he visited me. I remember . . ."

She closed her eyes. When she opened them, it was light and he was fast asleep.

Standing up, she ached. Her back ached, her shoulders, her legs.

"I want to drive to Brooklyn," he said, untying the robe and slipping it off. "I want to make sure the windows are all closed. I'll be back before lunch."

"Don't go alone."

He hesitated for a moment. "All right."

The funeral was scheduled for two. They left the apartment before nine and he drove without hurry, reaching the house in three-quarters of an hour. They went inside and began checking windows. Shades that had been open the previous morning were now drawn.

"Stuart must've been here," Morty said, raising a shade in the living room. "Looks like a damn tomb."

"They're all locked in here."

"Try the kitchen. I'll go back to Pop's room."

She checked the kitchen carefully and went back to the bedroom. The bed was bare. She had taken the sheets herself and put them with her own laundry. A handmade coverlet lay over an old wooden rack. She spread it across the bed to cover the emptiness, then stood up. Morty had just secured the last window.

He took a deep breath. "I guess we can go," he said.

"Something's wrong."

"What do you mean?"

"I don't know. Something isn't quite right." She looked around. She didn't really know the room. "Something . . ." She saw herself in the mirror, looked away and then back again. "The candlesticks, Morty. They were right there yesterday morning."

He turned toward the dresser, and in the mirror she saw his face change to ice.

"That bastard," he said, so low it was barely audible.

"Maybe someone—"

"No one else. The windows were all locked. He and I are the only ones who have the key."

She went to the dresser and opened the top drawer, then the second, then the third. They were filled with clothes. There were no candlesticks.

"Let's get out of here," Morty said.

She pushed the last drawer closed and looked around the room. "Maybe you should call him, let him know we—"

He said something vile and walked out of the room. "You coming?" he called from a distance, and she took her handbag off the dresser and followed him out.

Lillian came to the funeral. She sat next to Regina's mother, looking thinner and older than she had at her own father's funeral. There were more people than Morty had expected. Men from the garment industry and old women from Pop's neighborhood all paid their respects. People Regina had never seen hugged her husband and shed tears. When it was over the family went to Stuart's house, and it was late in the evening before they finally got home.

The lawyer called on Monday morning, a man with an old voice speaking in accented English that sounded much like Pop's. Regina passed the phone to Morty and left the room. Ernie, having been told the news yesterday, had not slept well last night. She decided to keep him home from school so that he could benefit from Mrs. Salter's unending patience and her own desire to have him close.

"He said to come around on Thursday morning," Morty said, walking into Ernie's room. "We'll be able to look the will over and he can get things going so we can put the house up for sale. I gather it's fairly straightforward, pretty much fifty-fifty, a couple of items mentioned specifically."

She looked at him without speaking.

"We'll see on Thursday," he said.

He said he would call her from Canal Street, and he left early. She walked Ernie to school and took the subway downtown to RR. The morning passed uneventfully and at noon she called Rush. Morty had not been in. She got a sandwich, came back to her desk, and waited. He did not call.

She had an appointment at two with a new client and she arranged her portfolio before he arrived. He had some ideas for the spring of 1937 and she could tell he was eager to do business. He was younger than most of the men she dealt with, the son of an immigrant moving into his father's business, a young man with new ideas, a man who had weathered the worst of the depression. She thought she would like working with this generation.

At four she answered the phone.

"Want a ride home?"

"Morty! I've been looking for you all day."

"Why don't you close up shop? I'll pick you up in ten minutes."

He sounded odd, as though he were telling her, not asking or offering, and she had a presentiment of something awful.

"Fine," she said. "I'll be downstairs."

He arrived just as she stepped out of the building, and she got in the car quickly to make way for a delivery truck. Kissing him, she smelled alcohol.

"What's happened?" she asked.

"Well, Pop really did it. Funny you don't find out about these things until it's too late." He turned north on Hudson Street. "Want a drink?"

"You've been drinking this afternoon."

"I didn't ask for a commentary. I asked if you—"

"Yes, all right. I'll have a drink."

He stopped at the White Horse Tavern and they went in, sitting at a table in a dark corner.

"I thought the lawyer said it was pretty much fifty-fifty," she said.

"I suppose to old Herman it looked like pretty much fifty-fifty. The fact is, it's almost fifty-fifty but not quite. And that leaves brother Stuart with a small but significant advantage. He's got controlling interest in Rush Woolens."

She felt her heart sink. The waiter placed two brandies before them and disappeared.

"You'll work it out with him, Morty. The two of you will sit down together and—"

"Work *what* out with him? Work something out with a man who comes into a dead man's house at night and steals what he wants for himself?" He spoke with more anger than she had heard in ten years of marriage.

"Did . . . did the will say anything about the candlesticks?"

He reached into his jacket, drew out a folded document, and slapped it on the table. "It's there in black and white. There were four special bequests, the candlesticks for me, something for you, Pop's old watch for Stuart, even something for the sea witch."

She smiled in spite of herself at the description of his sister-in-law. "Did you say anything?"

"I said they weren't in the house."

"And?"

"Stuart seemed surprised. I don't think he knew we'd been there again. He said he hadn't seen them for years, and the witch said she thought Pop had sold them a long time ago."

"You didn't accuse them."

"I didn't accuse anyone of anything."

She took a sip of the brandy. He had told her about the candlesticks one of the first times she had met him in Paris, and the thought of them, of his mother designating them for him, had warmed her. Now they were gone, stolen, and he would not fight for them.

"I hate them," she said. "I never want to see them again. I don't think I could sit at the same table with them."

Her anger appeared to mellow his own. He covered her wrist with his hand. "It's the mill I care about," he said in a low voice. "Do you know what Pop's done to me by giving Stuart the controlling interest? Do you know what he's done to the business?"

She could imagine. "Morty, we'll make it on our own."

"Stuart doesn't know beans about marketing," he said, as though she had not spoken. "He's the best machine man in the world—I'll give him that—

but he can't fill Pop's shoes. He doesn't know what the hell goes on on Canal Street."

"Morty, let's go away for a couple of weeks. Let's go to the country. Let's just try to think things out quietly."

"Karl's away."

"Oh." She had forgotten. Now in the tenth year of their marriage, they had everything they had wanted, everything they had worked for—children, a business they had created with their own wits, a beautiful apartment that suited their needs—and in return, they had surrendered their freedom. "We'll figure something out," she said, taking another drink of the brandy.

"How could Pop do it?" Morty asked.

She shook her head. There were things one could simply not understand.

The lawyer called and talked to Morty about the candlesticks. For the first time, Regina felt a sense of admiration for the old man. He had observed the conflict in his office and was troubled by it.

"The will is quite recent," Morty told her when he was off the phone. "It didn't take much for him to see they were lying. I told him to forget it."

She wished he would not forget it. Angry that she had defended Stuart all these years, that she had tried to include him in their business venture, that she had pressed Morty over and over to reestablish their relationship, she longed now for a confrontation. He had proved himself to be a common thief, and she knew she would never forgive him.

She returned home the following afternoon to hear the telephone ringing. Mrs. Salter covered the mouthpiece and whispered, "She's been calling all day. No name, no message."

"Hello?" Regina said, dropping her bag on the kitchen table and pulling out a chair.

"This is Hannah," a voice said. Hannah was her sister-in-law, the sea witch.

"Yes, Hannah." A prickle of alertness ran across her back.

"I want you to tell that lawyer to leave us alone about the candlesticks."

"I didn't ask him to call and I don't intend to ask him not to. Morty told him to forget it. I expect he wanted to save his brother some embarrassment."

"Embarrassment," Hannah shrilled. "There aren't any candlesticks to be embarrassed about. I told Pop to sell them years ago. He got very forgetful at the end. He didn't know what he had and what he didn't have anymore."

"Really."

"Don't speak to me that way," her sister-in-law said, raising her voice.

"Hannah, you and I both know where the candlesticks are. I think Herman knows too."

"No one knows anything, do you hear me? They were junk, absolute junk. Pick something else out of all that stuff in Brooklyn and leave us alone. Do you think Pop would have given his candlesticks to someone he couldn't even trust with his business?"

"Hannah," Regina said with extreme calm, "don't ever call me again for the rest of your life." She hung up the phone and looked around, trembling slightly. Margot was standing in the doorway, watching her with large, curious eyes. As she saw her mother's face, she broke into a smile. Regina reached over and pulled her onto her lap and kissed her profusely. "Hello, baby. Where's your brother?"

"Visiting Mark."

"That's nice. Were you good today?"

"Mrs. Salt said no."

"She said 'no' to you?"

"No, no, no."

Regina laughed. "You must have tried her patience."

"I tried." Margot's eyes were very wide.

"Poor Mrs. Salter." She stood up, shifting her daughter's weight to her shoulder. "Let's go down and see Grandma before Daddy comes home. I think Mrs. Salter deserves a rest."

Regina called to reserve the house upstate and was greeted with a firm "no" for the first time. They had two children now, didn't they? Hadn't they thought to mention it, or had it slipped their minds?

"But we've had them there before without any problems," Regina said. "We've all been very careful."

But the answer had been given and the house was now a memory.

It complicated the summer. There were other houses available but they seemed undesirable by comparison and children were not particularly welcome anywhere she called. Also, it was late to be looking for July. And Morty seemed to have lost all interest in going away. She decided to send the children to New Jersey with her mother, but then Morty would not visit them.

Karl came back with gifts, good wishes from the Goldblatts, and memories of experiences he had never dreamed of having—that wonderful ship, those marvelous places. Morty filled him in on the events of May, and Karl shared his gloom.

Gloom was the word for it. Pop's decision weighed upon Morty like an irremediable financial reversal. He seemed unable to put it aside. Meanwhile, Stuart made small insidious changes at Rush Woolens. Starting September 1, Regina Rush Fabrics would no longer be able to hire the bookkeeping services at Rush. Fine, Morty said, and went out and hired a part-time bookkeeper who was only too glad to have the work. Since Stuart announced the decision in July, RR stopped using the Rush service at the close of that week. By September RR had achieved a perceptible saving in the new arrangement, but Morty was not cheered.

On the first of August Stuart quietly dismissed the Wolfe law firm. Morty didn't find out about it for almost three weeks, and then only by accident. He told Regina about it after dinner.

"He's moving backward," he said. "In another year he'll have destroyed everything Pop spent a lifetime building up."

"Then you'll sell everything at auction and be well out of it."

"Dammit, it's half mine. How can he be so pigheaded? Why is he so resentful?"

"There are no answers, Morty. You know that."

266

"Stuart got where he is—or where he was before the crash—because of my father and after that because of me."

"Maybe he finally figured that out and decided to prove he could do it by himself. It doesn't pay to destroy him. You have a half interest in the profits."

He looked at her for a moment. "I'm not out to destroy," he said. "I have an idea—for us. If it pans out, we'll have more money than you or I ever dreamed of."

She looked at him expectantly. When he said nothing, she said, "You can't stop there. Tell me."

He smiled and his face lighted up the way it had before the spring and summer had shrouded his life. "I need to do some work with numbers first. I have to be sure. And I may want to do a little experimenting in Paterson. I want to dye some samples." He pushed his chair back from the table. "It's good to be alone," he said. "It's not that I don't like sticky kisses."

"I know."

"When are you bringing them home?"

"Sunday. I wanted to go Saturday, but it bothers Izzy when a member of the family drives up on Saturday."

Morty shook his head. "What a family. Does he still walk all that way to shul?"

"Every week. He says he loves it."

In November, after weeks of rumors and speculation, invitations arrived for Henry's wedding. Shrugging, Morty said, yes, he would go, and Regina sent an acceptance.

The night before the wedding, Henry telephoned. "I have a favor to ask," he said quietly. "It's about my sister."

"Is something wrong?"

"I wonder if you would make sure she goes to the wedding."

"I don't understand."

"Since Phil left her, she hasn't wanted to appear anywhere publicly."

"Oh."

"She didn't go to Jerold's wedding, you know."

"I didn't know."

"You were abroad then, weren't you? Well, we didn't expect it, and Mother was very disappointed. I'll have my hands full tomorrow, and I thought, if you could call for her . . ."

"Of course we will."

"You'll like Sylvia very much, Regina." There was something apologetic about the way he said it.

"I'm sure I will, Henry. Don't worry about a thing."

It increased Morty's distaste for the whole event. They would be six in the car, Lillian and her two daughters besides the three of them—Ernie having been invited—adding to his discomfort. Nothing seemed right anymore, and this newly imposed arrangement made things even less right than usual.

The scene in Lillian's bedroom was disarray and fear. Lillian sat on the edge of her bed as stiff as a pillar of salt and almost the same pallid hue. Leaning against a closet door was Rosalie, her older daughter, now thirteen, her young pale face a mirror of her mother's and lined with anxiousness. Regina had an unpleasant feeling of déjà vu, the generations repeating themselves. She had heard—or more likely overheard—tales of Lillian's hysterical fear at her mother's illness and occasional collapse. Now here was Lillian's daughter watching with wide eyes as her mother refused to participate in a family event that touched them all.

"No one wants me there," Lillian said, looking at no one.

"We all want you there. I'm here to take you."

"Take the girls. They're all dressed. They have new dresses and I've combed their hair."

"Where's your dress, Lillian?"

"I haven't any."

"Rosalie, find me your mother's dress. Come," she said gently, coaxing, "look in the closet. Is it that one? Let's spread it on the bed, carefully now."

"I can't sit at that table and have them all laugh."

"No one will laugh. Adele will be snide and Edith will be charming and Izzy will be funny and Morty will go and talk to Uncle Willy to get away from it all. Rosalie . . ." She turned to the child who had resumed her stance in front of the closet door. "Get yourself ready and take Celia downstairs. Morty's waiting in the car. Tell him we'll be there in five minutes."

The girl gave her mother a last long look and departed.

Lillian stood and took her robe off. She was so thin that clothes that should have draped artfully merely hung, seeming to drag her down from the shoulders.

"You know, when I married him I thought he looked like . . ."—she paused—"like Uncle Mortimer."

"I know," Regina said softly. "I thought he did too."

"Why does it happen that all I ever end up with is the imitation and you get the real thing?"

3

On the last day of December, fifteen years after the gala engagement party for her daughter, Aunt Martha left her apartment and moved in with Lillian. Poppi said it was the right thing to do; mothers and daughters belonged together, but Momma was not so sure.

"Too many women under one roof," she said. "Too many women with too many problems."

But Lillian was happy. When it came right down to it, there was no one she would rather live with than her mother.

During the first week of January, Morty took Regina out for dinner.

"I'm buying a cotton mill," he said after he had ordered drinks.

"Now?" she asked. It was 1937 and people were out of work, mills shut down.

"As soon as I find the right one. Listen to me," he went on, preventing her incipient interruption. "This is my idea. I'm going to make denim, the kind of stuff they use in work clothes, and I'm going to make money because I'm going to sell it for two or three cents less a yard than anyone else in the country, without cutting into my profit."

She stared across the small table at him, sensing his excitement. "Tell me."

"It's so simple it scares me. I don't have to use clean white cotton with no imperfections. Denim is always dyed dark blue. Brown cotton takes the dye just as well as clean, it's just as strong, and it costs a hell of a lot less a pound." He reached into his inside pocket, pulled out two swatches of cloth, and handed them to her. "Tell me which is which."

She felt them without looking at them, then laid them side by side on the white tablecloth and inspected them. She folded them, stretched them, scratched them with her fingernail, and it came to her that he had always been right. He had known that her designs would sell, had known exactly the quality and price range to aim for. He had picked the right time to buy the printing and dyeing plant. Only the silk mill had been a mistake, and ev-

269

eryone was entitled to one. It had been a present to his wife, he said, and presents did not have to yield profits.

"You're going to make it, Morty," she said.

"Let's get a bottle of champagne."

The following Monday he took a train south. He had been in touch with several mill owners, and now there were a few he wanted to see for himself.

Why, she asked him, was he going south when New England was so close and the South like a foreign country?

"The South is the future," Morty said. "The South surpassed the North in spindleage at least ten years ago. New England is running on old equipment now. All the money that was invested in the twenties went south. They have the newest plants, the newest machinery. The South is the place to buy."

She went to the station with him to see him off and continued on foot to her studio, a brisk walk in the January cold. She missed him before she felt his absence, before the dinner for three, before the bed for one. The evenings were bleak without Morty to talk to.

The first night she wrote to Suzanne. "It is four years now since Hitler came to power, and all my optimism has evaporated. I would like to see you, Étienne, and the children come to the States and begin a new life. Every day I see immigrants from Germany in New York and I can only believe that they have made the right decision. The orphanage in Frankfurt that had only a handful of children in 1933 is now overflowing, and I spend much of my time trying to find parents for them. If war comes, I fear no one on the Continent will be safe."

On Thursday postcards arrived for the children from South Carolina and in the evening Morty called and said he would not be able to complete his tour by the next day. He would spend the weekend and return Tuesday or Wednesday.

He came back on Wednesday, filled with enthusiasm for cotton mills and for the South. The weather was unbelievable. He had left his coat in the hotel on all but one day. The people were gracious and friendly—a little slow, of course; that's why it had taken so long.

"The weather can wait," she interrupted. "Tell me about the mills."

"I've found the one I want. Look." He pulled papers out of his briefcase and opened them on the dining-room table. They were large and crackling, plans of a plant and surrounding buildings. "Two hundred looms. I figure at capacity we could do five million yards a month."

She breathed a sound of appreciation and leaned over the plans.

"Over here," he said, pulling a sheet out from under, "are a group of houses they rent to the workers."

"Are they part of it?"

"All part of it."

"They produce income?"

"A few dollars a month each. When we get going, we'll fix them up. Here's what the looms look like." He pulled out another sheet. "This is the building from the outside." And another. "The building alone is worth a quarter of a million."

"What does the whole thing come to?"

"I think I can get it for a million and a half."

"That'll break the cookie jar."

"I know. I'm lining up some appointments with banks. I saw someone down there yesterday, but I won't hear from him for a while." He pulled a chair out and sat down. "It's a good price. It's worth two easily. How are you?"

"Fine." She sat facing him, resting an elbow on the table. "The fall designs are just about finished. Karl brought in a big one last week." She grinned at him. "Come on, you don't care about these little tidbits. You've got bigger things to think about."

"You're wrong. I care about every crumb. It's all part of one big empire we're putting together. A long time ago I thought it had started with Pop, but I was wrong. We started it, in 1929, and we'll put the icing on it one of these years."

"Will you have trouble borrowing?"

He nodded. "I have almost nothing to put up myself. Just what Pop left me, and that's peanuts when you're talking about a million and a half."

"There are things we could get rid of, Morty."

"No." He said it sternly. "We need everything we've got. We'll make money on the silk. Give it time."

She got up and kissed his cheek. "Whatever you say."

"Did your husband reach you?" Mrs. Salter asked.

She rubbed her shoes on the mat and unbuttoned her coat. "No. Did he call?"

"He's going to be late. He said not to wait dinner for him."

It was a week since his return, and he had been busy catching up and talking to banks about a loan. A letter from Suzanne was on the kitchen table, and as soon as she had sent Mrs. Salter home and seen the children, she sat down with it. It began in the breezy girlish style that still characterized much of Suzanne's writing, but after a page, the tone changed and Regina could feel her own spirits descending as she read.

They were indeed concerned about Germany and the madman who led the country. Friends of theirs had recently decided to give up a family business and go to Chicago, where some distant relatives lived. It was sad to think they were leaving. In times like these, one never knew how long it would be before they would meet again. From time to time they talked about their own future in France. Papá talked about retiring, but then, just as often, said he would never retire. No long ago Étienne had inquired about his own prospects in the United States, and really, the answers were most demoralizing. He would not be permitted to practice medicine until he passed the American examinations, which were, of course, given in English. Étienne had not been a student for many years—they were married nearly ten years now, as Régine surely recalled—and the prospect of learning in another language, not to mention being looked down upon by the members of his own profession, was simply more than he could endure. As for Maurice, to leave France would mean to leave the law entirely. Law was far less universal than medicine, and at the moment, medicine seemed narrow enough. So they would continue to be optimistic that Hitler could not last forever and that the insanity across the border would remain confined.

Morty came home at ten, tired and somewhat out of sorts, so she set the letter aside for another day.

Later that week he got a long-distance phone call indicating that a loan for a portion of what he needed would probably come through. Regina taught Margot to cross her fingers for Daddy's mill, and the little girl strutted around for days showing off her hands with intertwined little fingers. That or something else must have worked, because in the last week in January Morty received word that the bank in South Carolina would lend him a million dollars.

"That was the easy part," he said when he reported the news. "It's the rest that's going to be tough."

"Maybe you should take in a partner."

"Like whom? Karl doesn't have a cent. I've been looking around for a buyer for my shares in Rush, but I don't get any bites. No one wants to be a minor partner, especially with Stuart running the place. I've talked to our factor about a loan, but he couldn't give me enough to make it worth writing up the papers. By the way, I'll be late again tonight."

"After dinner?"

"Later than that. Nine or ten."

"Oh, Morty."

"Sorry. It's business."

His gloom descended like clouds black with snow. He called the following week that he would be late, and two days later called again. In the second week of February he started talking to bankers who had turned him down a month before.

"I have a million dollars in my pocket and they won't come across. If I fail, they'll own a damned good piece of property—and I won't fail."

There was nothing she could say. Every day ended a little more bleakly than the last.

He worked late one night the following week and at ten-thirty she suddenly found herself closing the book she was reading and sitting back against the pillows. Phil Schindler. As though it had just happened, she could see him rushing into the Worth Street office, grabbing the phone, and making apologies to Lillian.

Something had happened in the South, and Morty had come back changed. Each day he confided less than he had the day before. Each day he was more depressed. The elation of the approved loan had lasted less than a day. It had not brought him the second loan, and without it, there would be no mill. He had nothing to say and she was unable to offer any cheer. It was suddenly brilliantly apparent that he was finding cheer somewhere else.

The revelation made her heart beat fast and strongly. *This doesn't happen to me.* And suddenly she was thinking of Jerold. They would go somewhere and talk. It would be calm and very quiet. Life with Jerold had a quality of serenity. It was free of crises. It was peaceful.

The door to the apartment opened and closed, then the closet. Water ran in the kitchen. She swallowed so that she would be able to speak.

272

"How's everything, babe?" He bent over the bed and kissed her.

"All right."

"I need a good night's sleep."

"It's late. You should have come home earlier."

"I couldn't."

Why? But she couldn't ask it. To ask was to sound suspicious, and suspicion was a sign of betrayal.

He started undressing. "I don't think I'm going to pull this one off."

"Don't say that, Morty." She felt sorry for him, deeply, deeply sorry. If this terrible thing had happened, if he was seeing someone else, it was because of this, because Pop had given Stuart control of the mill, because he needed to do something and he wasn't ready financially and it was destroying him.

"I'll give it a few more days and then I'm going back down south. Maybe I can get the price down or talk the bank into a bigger loan."

"Don't let it do this to you." She had never felt quite so full of conflicting emotions. She was hurt, angry, and sad. She was almost desperate to know who he was spending his evenings with. She felt a compassion for Lillian that made her previous compassion seem as minimal as a perfunctory "I'm sorry" uttered for reasons of courtesy.

"*Do* this to me?" he echoed, looking at her as though she understood nothing of what he was enduring. "Are you aware that I've had my forty-fourth birthday? Men don't make their fortunes when they're seventy."

"But you're on your way. You said yourself a couple of weeks ago—"

"Regina, that's small potatoes. I have an idea that's worth millions."

She had never heard him use the word before, not seriously, not applied to his life. "It'll be worth the same next year."

"But I won't. I'll be that guy who couldn't get a loan because he had nothing in the bank. I'll be somebody's junior partner. Dammit, I'm not going to be someone's junior partner for the rest of my life."

"You won't be." But that was the key. He was spending his evenings with someone to whom he was senior, someone with whom he had no business relationship, someone who could offer him cheer without a background of children who made too much noise and bank loans that never came through.

"And I'll tell you something else. I'm not going to have people like that creep Hardy in Amsterdam push me around."

"Morty, that's years ago."

"Sure it's years ago. That's when I should have made my move. If you're not established by the time you're forty-five, you're finished. And I'm about to be finished." He reached for the shirt he had dropped on a chair and started to put it on. "I'm going out for a walk."

"What?"

"I can't sleep."

"You've been out half the night."

"I have to think. I can't think here."

"Morty, it's almost midnight." She said it softly, wistfully.

"Don't wait up for me."

*   *   *

273

They had a birthday party for Ernie over the weekend, and then, on Monday, Morty called that he would be late again. It was cold with the harshness of February, and as she undressed, she saw snowflakes drifting before the window. She had spent the day thinking of calling Jerold. There was nothing wrong with calling him. They were the best of friends. She needed comfort, and who could comfort her better than her dearest friend?

The phone rang at eleven and she reached for it anxiously. An operator asked if this was her number, and then Morty came on.

"Regina, can you hear me?"

"Yes. Where are you?"

"Look, I've gotten stuck in Poughkeepsie."

"Poughkeepsie?"

"I had to see a client, and it started to snow. I'm not going to be able to make it home tonight."

There were no clients in Poughkeepsie. "Morty, where are you?"

"In a hotel. It's called"—there was a sound of muttering and voices nearby—"I don't know what it's called. It's out of the nineteenth century. It took me half an hour to get through to New York. I'll leave first thing in the morning or as soon as they get the roads cleaned."

"All right."

"Look, I'm sorry."

"Yes, I'm sure you are."

When she hung up, she cried.

He walked in at eleven in the morning, showered, and changed his clothes.

"I'm going down south again tomorrow," he said, knotting his tie.

"Fine."

"You're angry about last night."

"I have to go now, Morty. I'll see you for dinner." She picked up her bag. "If you're coming home for dinner."

"I'll be home."

She thought he looked rather sad, but changed her mind as she left the apartment. He looked guilty.

He took the morning train on Wednesday, promising to be home Friday night or, at the latest, on Saturday. She dropped him off at the station in a taxi and continued down to her studio. It was quiet and beautiful and all hers and she loved it. She had framed some of her favorite designs and hung them on one wall. She made coffee and sat at her desk, sipping, thinking about Morty, her mind sliding painlessly to Jerold, to sweet, quiet times, the smell of vegetables and hay, the swimming hole with its icy water, Walter Weinberg shivering in a towel . . .

Walter.

As though the longing for Jerold had directed her to that image, Walter Weinberg, Walter, whose family was in banking. The telephone sat on her desk like a silent challenge. I could call and ask a favor, but what a favor: use your influence with Walter. Too big a favor, really, to ask of anyone except, perhaps, on behalf of your husband. But how much longer would he be her husband? She opened her deepest desk drawer and pulled a tissue out of a box. Do you continue to love someone after he has deceived you? They had been partners once. What had happened to dissolve the partnership? In what way had she failed? Had she failed?

She wept into the soft paper handkerchief. Dammit, dammit, I want him to have this.

She dried her eyes and drank a second cup of coffee. Then she dialed the number.

"Regina!"

"Jody, I need to ask you a favor."

"Why don't we talk about it over lunch?"

"No, just on the phone. It won't take—"

"I insist."

She had promised herself. She sat looking at her fingernails, trying to think of the right way to put it.

"I'll show you pictures of my babies and you show me pictures of yours," her cousin said.

"Yes, all right." How very much she wanted to see him.

"Tomorrow, one o'clock?"

"Yes, that'll be fine."

He gave her the address and they hung up.

There was always something so secure and reliable about him. From a distance one would know he was a lawyer. He wore dark colors and black shoes, his shirt starched and white. You sensed in the first moment in his presence that he would help you.

He kissed her when she entered the restaurant, and they went immediately to a table.

Leaning toward her mischievously, he said, "Hatless."

She colored and laughed and said, "I didn't know you read *Vogue*."

"I couldn't help it. Edith read it aloud to me. She was in absolute awe of you."

"She shouldn't have been. She's wonderful. I couldn't help liking her."

He studied her for a moment. "How bad are things?"

She reached in her bag for a handkerchief and shook her head. "I don't know," she said, her voice choked.

"Do you want to talk about it?"

"No. I came because you're an island of peace, whatever else is going on."

"I wish I were. I always think of you that way. We're in the midst of a Reign of Terror just now. Babies come too quickly when you don't think about it, and I didn't think. Frenchy's going to be a genius and Davey's going to send us to institutions, but aside from that we're fine—if they ever get over the grippe. One cough in the middle of the night, and Edith's up for hours."

"Sounds like our place."

"Right now I'm trying to convince my father-in-law that I will buy a house when I am ready, thank you, and he will not buy it for me."

275

"It's generous of him to offer."

"Up to a point. Anyway, it's a pleasure to have a quiet lunch with someone who's over three, and doesn't think she owns me, and knows most of my fondest secrets."

"I want you to do something for me, Jody."

"That's why I'm here."

She told him as much as Morty would have told, and a little extra about Pop and Stuart. He made admiring comments when she explained Morty's idea and nodded when she came to the loans.

"I think Walter's the man to talk to," he said when she had finished.

"Would you?"

"This afternoon, tomorrow morning at the latest. I'm sure he'll do something for you."

"Don't promise, Jody. Just ask him. We're talking about half a million dollars."

"Are you still angry with him for not marrying Shayna?" He had a teasing look on his face.

"It's too long ago to be angry."

"You're right. Time dissolves anger faster than the sweeter emotions." He touched her hand. "Stay well. I'll call you tomorrow."

She took a business card out of her bag and wrote a number on it. "I'll be at my studio tomorrow instead of Worth Street."

He looked at the card. "How do you know where to go in the morning?"

"Sometimes I don't. Sometimes I just walk outside and let my feet take me."

"Don't ever change, dear."

He called the next day at midmorning. Walter would be more than happy to see Morty, and here was his number at home if Morty wanted to call over the weekend.

Morty returned Saturday afternoon.

"It's no use," he said, dropping his suitcase on the foyer floor. "I'm pulling out of the whole deal. It's over."

"Come and sit down." He hadn't kissed her, and the not kissing hurt. "I talked to my cousin yesterday—Jerold. He has a friend in Boston who wants to talk to you."

"What kind of friend?"

"A banker."

His eyebrows rose slightly. "How did you come to ask Jerold?"

"I met Walter years ago. He used to visit at the farm."

"Something go on between you?"

"No. He's the one who didn't marry Shayna."

"Ah."

"I have his number at home."

His eyebrows rose a second time. "Is he like Jerold or is he someone I can talk to?"

She swallowed painfully. "He's nothing like Jerold. I've never known how they could be friends. You might even like him."

He walked into the living room and sat down heavily. "It's too late to start in with someone new. I'm up to here with bankers."

"Morty, you're behaving—"

"I know how I'm behaving. If you'd spent the last month the way—"

"I know how you've spent the last month. I know how I've spent the last month."

He looked at her with eyes full of fatigue. "Look, I've put everything I have into this. I don't have much left over."

She went to the kitchen and got her key. "I'm going downstairs,"she said. "Margot's visiting my mother. I'll be up in a little while. Walter's number is next to the phone."

She came up twenty minutes later. Margot called, "Daddy?" as they entered the apartment, but Morty did not respond. As they approached the kitchen, Regina could hear his voice, low and serious, the way he spoke to people he didn't know well. She said, "Margot!" but she was too late. Reaching the kitchen, she saw Morty bent over to give her a hug. Released, Margot climbed on a kitchen chair and sat watching him. He winked once at her, and Regina moved away.

"No problem there," she heard him say in a more conversational voice. "I've got an appointment Monday anyway, and Tuesday's likely ... Fine. Let's make it Wednesday, then.... Just in time for lunch.... Uh, since twenty-seven. They've done all our legal work. Jerold can tell you anything you want . . . Right. Good talking to you, Walter.... Yes. Twelve-thirty. See you then."

He left the kitchen with Margot up on one arm. "I may have to send your cousin a bouquet of roses," he said.

Monday was the first of March.

"I'll be a little late tonight," he told her, a trifle apologetically.

She stifled every reply and said nothing.

"Not later than eight," he promised. "How's your day tomorrow?"

"Nothing special. I'll be at the studio."

He returned before eight and read to Ernie before he went to sleep. "Weinberg called," he said, closing Ernie's door.

"Will he give it to you?"

"He sounds optimistic. I asked for an extension on the guarantee for the first loan. I'm going to Boston Wednesday, unless I hear from him tomorrow."

"I'll cross my fingers."

"You're a nice kid."

He stayed up late, working with papers in the living room while she went to sleep. She wanted to ask him where he had gone, what he had been doing all those nights, but she was unable to formulate the question. She heard the shower run and was still awake when he lay down beside her, but she could tell he was being careful not to wake her, and she said nothing. In the morning, she went to her studio.

The phone rang at ten-thirty. She wiped her hands on her smock and answered it. It was Morty.

"Can you take off?" he asked.

277

She glanced at the clock. "Sure."

"I want to take a ride and talk to you."

Something cold passed from her throat down into her digestive system. "All right."

"I'll pick you up in half an hour."

She hung up and took the smock off, moving very slowly. It was four years since Phil Schindler had not walked through the door of the Worth Street office, four years since they had brought Ernie home, four years since she had felt the quickening inside her that had been her second child. She washed her hands and brushed her hair, watching herself in the mirror with the curiosity of a stranger, remembering for the first time in many years the afternoon she had seen the curls drop and realized she was beautiful. She felt sick with anticipation, sick at the thought of what he was going to say. She put a silk scarf on and then her coat, closed the door behind her and locked it with a key. The car approached from the direction of Fifth Avenue, the old Packard, a last relic of the departed twenties, and she thought how much she loved him and how glad she was that she had spoken to Jerold.

They drove for such a long time that she could not imagine where or why they were going. He said almost nothing. She asked once, early in the trip, if he had heard from Walter, and he said no. They left the city, and still he drove, the motor singing in high gear. They passed a sign welcoming them to Connecticut, but she did not feel welcome. She wanted to tell him to stop and say what he wanted and let her go back to her children, but she could not. She looked at her watch and remembered that he had given it to her, bought it in Switzerland in 1927 after Suzanne's wedding, when Europe was still peaceful.

He pulled off the road in a clearing near some winter-bare trees and turned the motor off. "Shall we?" he asked.

She looked at him and then opened the door before he had even closed his. It would happen now, on alien ground.

They walked in the clear, skirting the trees. The earth was hard and the air cold. Far away at the top of a hill smoke wafted from the chimney of a little white house.

"Well, what do you think?" he said, and, startled, she stopped walking. "About what?"

"About this," he said with a trace of exasperation.

She looked at him, then around at the trees, a sense of confusion almost dizzying her.

"Is it beautiful? Is it just what we've always wanted? Is it the right place to build your château?"

She pointed a gloved finger at the ground. "You mean this property?"

"Of course I mean this property."

"Is that what you've been doing all these nights?"

"What the hell do you *think* I've been doing?"

"I don't know." She turned away, facing the woods. Like Grandmama's shade tree, these were tall and heavy, capable of casting great shadows. They were friendly trees; birds nested in them.

"What's the matter with you?"

"You said you were seeing a client in Poughkeepsie."

"We don't have any clients in Poughkeepsie."

"Then why did you say it?"

"I figured you'd know I was cooking something up. I thought you liked surprises."

"I do."

"Well, you don't act as though you do. What's happened to you lately? I remember the day I gave you the coat, when the ring almost rolled into the fireplace."

She pulled her glove off and wiped her eyes with the back of her hand. Margot could not have done a messier job of it.

"I started to tell you once or twice, but you've been so distant."

She turned back to look at him.

"I wish you wouldn't do that," he said. He put his arm around her and she couldn't remember the last time he had done that. "Can you walk? It's a fantastic place. I've been to four states, I've seen property that's bigger than this, closer to home than this, a better price than this, but nothing as good as this one. See down there? There's a waterfall that empties into a little lake, and that spills out into a creek. We could dam it up and get some good swimming. Can you imagine a waterfall? I bet I could get Ernie interested in electricity. We might even try to generate our own. It's still a little primitive out here. There are two springs with drinking water, plenty of open space for gardens. I wouldn't cut a single tree. They've probably been here since George Washington."

"It's wonderful, Morty."

"I knew you'd like it."

"I won't ask how you're going to pay for it."

"I've got Pop's money. The land's not much, but I'd like to build something that's really outstanding. Uh . . ."—he paused—"we might not be able to manage it this year."

"No."

"You all right?"

"I'm fine. I'm in awe. I don't know how you could think of this when you had all that other stuff on your mind."

"Hell, we needed a place since we lost the other. I figured if the mill fell through, at least we'd have somewhere to spend our summers. I don't like to send the kids away for so long, and it's time we built. You can take care of that, can't you? I mean, when we get an architect."

"I'll try."

They had turned into the woods, and she could hear the sound of rushing water.

"Regina . . ." They stopped and he pushed his hand across her hair, brushing her ear. "If this goes through with Weinberg, we're still partners, aren't we?"

She shook her head. "This is all yours, Morty. It was your idea and your hard work. I had nothing to do with it."

"You probably landed half a million dollars. That's worth a damned big interest."

"No. It was really Jerold who did that."

"I need someone I can trust, someone who's smart enough to learn every-

279

thing from top to bottom, someone who's young enough to keep things going when I get senile."

"Don't, Morty."

"Dammit, you agreed to marry me with less persuasion."

She smiled at him. "Maybe it was a better offer."

He kissed her lightly and looked at his watch. "Come on. We'd better get back to the city. I want to find out if Weinberg called. You know, I'll have to get up early tomorrow. I think there's a train to Boston about six o'clock."

"I'll go down to the station with you."

"Will you?" His arm across her shoulders held her cozily. "You're still a nice kid, aren't you? Only, next time I get into bed, I want a warmer welcome than last night."

"Next time you get into bed, it better not be an hour after I've gone to sleep."

"Touché. I guess I've been less than perfect." He said it offhandedly, as though it were hardly worth an apology. The car came into view a distance ahead. "We'll need a new car, you know. And you need a new coat. What do you think the kids would like when we make our first million?"

She stopped and laughed.

"What's so funny?"

"I just had an image of a million dollars' worth of ice cream, all in scoops and piled up like a pyramid."

"Come on," he said. "You can sit in the car and watch it melt."

He called from Boston the next afternoon that he had the money, usual rates, six percent, put some champagne on ice, we have a big celebration coming up. By the first of the next month he had resigned his half-time job at Rush Woolens, the papers had all been signed, and they had gone into production. Hesitantly, he said he needed Karl to sell denim and she gave him up, knowing Morty was right, knowing too she could not deny Karl the biggest opportunity of his life.

In the end, the denim sold itself. Using the cheaper raw cotton, they were able to undercut every mill in the country and they sold to the largest manufacturers of work clothes, producing a large commission for Karl and the promise of a profit before the end of 1937.

The phone at RR rang in April and someone with a heavy German accent and a very slight knowledge of English announced himself to Regina as Jakob Dorf. She got a number for Morty to call back that evening and when he got off the phone he told her the man was the owner of the little *Weinstube* in Frankfurt where they had had lunch in 1933 when they were visiting the orphanage.

"They just landed two days ago," Morty said, "and he needs work. I offered him a job running the mill cafeteria."

Regina laughed. "You're going to get southern mill workers to eat German food?"

"Look, they'll give a little and he'll give a little. I'm a little sick of grits myself. If I never see another grit, I won't miss it." He looked at his watch. "He's staying at a place downtown that sounds pretty bad. Let me run down and put them up at a decent hotel till I can arrange for them to go to South

Carolina." He bent and kissed her and she watched him tear off, hat in hand.

He had become the man he had been ten years ago, moving with limitless energy, full of ideas, timetables, goals. He had recounted his departure from Rush Woolens with relish. Stuart was smart enough to know he was losing his best salesman, and his surprise and displeasure at the compounded news had been apparent.

In a mood of optimism Morty suggested that Regina open a design studio with herself as stylist, and agreeing that the time was right, she visited the design schools, looking at portfolios and interviewing students who would graduate in June. Eventually she selected two, a young man and a young woman who accepted her offer eagerly. She leased additional space in the building where she had her own studio and prepared for the opening on September 1.

Morty returned from his visit with the German family in a mixed mood.

"I'm worried about the Goldblatts," he said. "From what Dorf tells me, Germany could blow up any minute. If that happens, I don't think any Jew in Europe is safe."

"Write to Étienne. Maybe if it comes from you it'll carry more weight."

"All right. I'll draft a letter tomorrow."

He hardly knew Étienne, but he wrote as though they were brothers. She read the draft with its occasional words crossed out, substitutions, careful corrections. He had spent hours on it and it was written well and persuasively. When she mailed the final copy, she felt sure it would have the desired effect.

A few days later, on a Saturday afternoon while she was visiting her mother, Uncle Nate called. There was still no telephone on the farm and when Momma said, "Nate! What is it?," Regina left Poppi to listen at the kitchen door.

"Oh, no," Momma said. "How could such a thing . . . ?" Momma stood with her mouth slightly open, shaking her head. "Oh, Nate." She was in tears.

"What is it, Momma?"

"Yes," Momma said into the phone. "Yes. Regina will call. Yes, of course we'll be there." She hung up and pulled a chair closer. "Oh, Regina," she said, sitting down and pulling her apron up to her face, "it's Izzy. He was hit by a car this morning while he was going to shul."

"No." Cold prickles down her arms.

"They never even stopped. Oh, poor Izzy, poor Izzy. He's dead, Regina, and they never even stopped to help him."

Millie sat on a wooden crate in the living room of the house adjacent to Uncle Nate's, looking dazed, her curly hair unkempt around her face, little Harold standing beside her, his sweet face the image of his father's. Looking at him, Regina could see Izzy's happy smile in the days of the bakery under the El. She kissed Millie and tried to say something, but she was unable. She had never felt so sorry for anyone, never seen anyone more alone. Millie had never spoken an unkind word in her life, and when she had brought her husband into the family, he had been derided. Now the fields outside were planted in even rows with cold-weather vegetables, peas and cabbage and lettuce and radishes, and Izzy had done most of it. She sat beside Millie and held her hand, offered her tea and fruit, but as Aunt Bertha had said, all Millie did was shake her head slowly and stare.

"He was a good boy," Poppi said, entering the room unaided. "A good, friendly, hardworking boy. To me he was like a grandson."

Millie lifted her face and looked at her grandfather. Beside her, her son said, "Me too, Poppi," and Millie smiled.

Outside it was dark and clear and starry. Morty stood a distance from the houses, facing Grandmama's wonderful mansion, his back to the road. He had shoved his hands into his pockets, pushing his coat aside.

"Hasn't changed much," he said as she approached.

"There's electricity now, and they got city water a few years ago."

"Twenty years."

"Yes."

He looked drawn, the ebullience of the past month suddenly faded. "Could we sleep somewhere else?" he asked, still facing the old house. "Doesn't Alice have a house over the hill?"

"It doesn't have plumbing and Momma says the roof is shaky. She hasn't stayed there since Poppa died."

"Maybe a hotel," he said, his eyes still fixed.

He had married in the living room of that house and she had given herself to Jerold in the great bedroom upstairs, and those seemed reasons enough why they should not sleep there.

"I'll ask Uncle Nate for the key to Uncle Willy's house. I'm sure Aunt Eva won't mind." She put her hand on his arm. "Come, dear. It's been a long day."

She had never imagined profits in six figures. She had never dreamed of earning half a million dollars in a year. She went south and drew up plans to improve the workers' homes on the mill property. Meanwhile, their own house in the country rose from its foundations over the summer of 1938.

Everywhere there was talk of war, fear of war, signs of war, the Grynszpan affair at the end of thirty-eight and the night of agony that followed for the Jews of Germany and Austria. Gradually war had become inescapable. Suddenly it was clear that no one would manage to escape.

At the beginning of thirty-nine Morty came home one day with a mischievous smile and a glint in his eye.

"I've got a big sale pending," he said, "for Rush Woolens."

"I didn't know you sold for them anymore."

"I don't, but this was too juicy to resist. England's looking for woolens now that they're preparing for war. I can sell them half of Rush's output for the next year. That'll put our heads safely above water for the first time in ten years."

"How does Stuart feel?"

282

"Haven't talked to him yet. I'm going to ask for a commission, since I'm not on the payroll. I don't think he'll want to pay what I'm asking."

"Can he afford it?"

"Sure. It's just more than he'd like to cough up. If he says no, I'll make a phone call and sell the deal to someone else for less. The days when I give my brother presents are over."

Stuart was aghast. Morty sat back and waited. One day later Stuart called back. Was the deal still available? Yes, Morty told him, but not for long. He was going to offer it to a competitor the following morning. Stuart raged. Sitting at an adjacent desk at RR, Regina could hear her brother-in-law's voice. She didn't care who got the contract; she wanted Pop's candlesticks, and Morty had never mentioned them again.

In the evening, Stuart called at home. Morty had a brief conversation and got off the phone looking triumphant.

"We've paid for the château," he said.

She slipped her arm around him. "It's already paid for."

"How do you like that?" he said teasingly. "It must've slipped my mind."

Morty booked them on the *Normandie* for the thirtieth of August. The Goldblatts had refused to listen to reason, and as a last resort they had decided to sail to France to convince their friends to leave the Continent. It had been the hottest summer anyone could remember, and every day a new record for attendance was set at the World's Fair, but the summer was drawing to a close now and the bedroom was littered with steamer trunks and valises in various stages of being packed. A newspaper with blaring headlines lay on the bed, and glancing at them for still another time, Regina stood from her kneeling position on the rug and turned the paper over to obliterate the bad news. Today was Monday. There was going to be a war, and they were leaving for Europe on Wednesday.

Tearfully Momma had pleaded with Morty to cancel their plans. Loyally he had promised they would make the right decision, and Regina had been grateful that he was still willing to make the trip, even if only to pacify her.

The *Normandie* arrived from Le Havre on Monday filled to capacity, having taken a diversionary zigzag course across the Atlantic and sending no radio messages. The passengers thought war had broken out. Regina refused to discuss the matter, but she sat over the paper reading, looking at the faces of the children being sent from their homes in England and France. It was France who would fight. Three million French soldiers now stood ready to march on Germany if Germany marched on Poland. And what of the Jews? There were millions of Jews in Poland, still thousands in Germany and France. Richard, Jeanne-Marie, and their young son George were still in Holland, working and writing, trying to evacuate the Jewish population from the Continent.

The government assured the French Line that the *Normandie* would be cleared in time to sail on Wednesday, but there was a problem with the *Bremen*, which had also just arrived. There were rumors it was being searched for guns.

283

On Tuesday the French Line telephoned to confirm that the Rushes were sailing. Morty said yes and hung up.

"Are you sure you want to go?" he asked.

She turned away from him and started out of the room, but he put a hand on her shoulder.

"We don't have to go," he said. "A lot of people have canceled already."

She broke into tears, tears a long time coming. "What'll become of them, Morty? You've written them, I've written them, Richard has spoken to them. What's left except to go there?"

He sat on the bed and took her on his lap. "They're grown people, Regina. Maurice knows what's going on in Europe."

"Why doesn't he see, then? It isn't Poland and France that madman is after. It's the Jews. He wants to wipe them off the face of the earth."

He said nothing for a minute. A trunk, still open, stood near the closet, and suitcases were everywhere. "Look," he said quietly, "I only asked because the French Line asked. You know I'm ready to go. If war breaks out, they'll turn back and we'll still have our week at sea on the *Normandie.* All right?"

She shivered in his arms. "Thanks, Morty."

Like a messenger of death, the call came in the dark of the night. Morty answered and spoke in the low, even voice he had used when he first called Walter Weinberg. "I see," he said, and then, again, "I see." In the eerie quiet of the night she could hear the voice in his ear but could not decipher a syllable. "We'll have to think about it," he said, and then, "Thank you." He put the phone down and moved back toward her.

"They've canceled the sailing," he said.

She touched him with her hand, warm beneath the light end-of-summer blanket. "Is it war?"

"No. They've only got about two hundred people willing to make the crossing, and they carry about ten times that. It won't pay for them to send the ship."

"I see." She felt very calm. It was settled for her. She had tried and failed, and now she would unpack the trunk and all the suitcases and go back to work.

"They offered to put us on the *Aquitania,*" Morty said. "I told them we'd have to think about it."

She thought. All last week Americans had sailed for England and the Continent, smiling bravely for the news photographers, telling reporters they had been "assured" everything would be all right. She knew now nothing would be all right.

"We'd better stay home," she said. "We'll make the trip when things get better. I'm sure the *Normandie* will be there long after Hitler is gone."

They cabled Suzanne in the morning and began to unpack. Morty got tickets for Thursday night to see Tallulah Bankhead in *The Little Foxes*—three dollars and thirty cents each for orchestra seats—a consolation prize, he explained, and she wore her birthday present, a rope of pearls with an emerald clasp. They had turned a million-dollar profit earlier in the year and could afford all the things they could do without and none of those they really wanted—the safety of their friends. At least the theater was blessedly air-conditioned. On the way to the theater, Morty made a wide circle of Manhattan and drove along the West Side, where the *Normandie* still lay at berth at Pier 88.

Friday morning she slept late, woke, heard giggling and hushing, heard the radio and Morty's voice, decided to get up. Yawning, she walked to the kitchen.

"Mommy!" Ernie said, and she put an arm around him, the thin little shoulders, the beautiful face smiling up at her.

She entered the kitchen and Morty reached out and turned off the radio.

"I think I overslept," she said. "Where's Margot?"

"Regina . . . " Morty said and there was something awful in his eyes.

"What's wrong?"

"Honey . . ." He pulled a chair away from the table.

"What is it, Morty?"

"That bastard's invaded Poland."

She sank into the chair.

"I tried to call Paris, but Britain's cut off all the lines to London and everything's routed through London."

She nodded and pulled Ernie onto her lap, although he was too big now for that sort of thing, ten and a half, and more than half those years spent here. She held him close, protecting herself.

"I guess we just have to wait and see what happens," she said.

"There isn't anything else we can do, Regina."

A month later he handed her a manila envelope marked "Rush Mills." "It's a present," he said, "like nothing you've ever seen."

Inside were three pairs of stockings. She took them out, handling them carefully. They were not silk, but they were fine and sheer and flesh-colored.

"It's called nylon," Morty said. "I think it's the beginning of a revolution."

4

She sat beside Poppi in the living room he had ruled for nearly fifteen years and explained quietly that the United States was now at war. He had followed the events of the last two years, but his memory flirted with him, sometimes sharp as his tongue, sometimes soft and unreliable as his body had become.

"I'm ninety-one," he said.

"I know, Poppi. And you're fine and healthy. I don't want you to worry about this. No one in the family will go. We're all too old and our children are all too young."

"What children?"

"Your great-grandchildren."

"My great-grandchildren." He looked past her. "You remember Romano?"

"Romano." She had heard the name but could not place it.

"He used to give me a shave, but he got old. He retired."

"The barber. Of course I remember." She touched a nick on his face. "That's why you look all chewed up. Who's shaving you now, Momma?"

"Yeah, sometimes your momma, sometimes the old bag."

"Don't talk that way about Mrs. Holzer. She's devoted to you. We'll find someone else to come and give you a shave." She laughed. "Poor Momma."

"Poor me."

"Yes, Poppi. Poor you too."

"Regina . . ." He leaned forward. "You remember my little Maude?"

"Yes, Poppi." She covered his hand with hers. "I remember her very well. We all do."

"You remember that fella she married?"

She looked at the faded gray eyes that saw only a small portion of what they wanted to. "Yes," she said. "I remember."

"What do you think happened to him?" He looked very earnest.

She shook her head. "He went away, Poppi. He wanted to forget."

"Yeah." He leaned back and inhaled deeply. "I used to want to live a hundred years."

"You'll make it," she said, relieved at the change of topic. He fluttered at times from one to another, leaving most of them hanging, floating.

"I don't want to no more. Too many wars and nobody visits me. I wish Momma was here."

"We all miss her." She stood and looked at her watch. "I'll get you another barber, Poppi."

She took the elevator down to the street floor and went out into the cool afternoon. She turned west and walked briskly. It was two years since they had moved, since the day Morty had called to say he'd done it "for the last time" and if she didn't like it, they wouldn't take it but could she meet him on Park Avenue in half an hour?

The apartment was a duplex with uncountable enormous rooms. The kitchen alone was at least equal in size to the living room of the gingerbread house where Richard lived when he was in New York and to which he had returned—thank God, Aunt Eva always said—in the spring of 1940, in the last moments of almost-peace. Regina had never formed any special attachment to the apartment in between, except that she knew Momma would miss the proximity, although the move took them only a few blocks west and a few south, an easy walk, but Morty prodded her to phone their driver and go the easy way. She had not yet availed herself of the convenience.

No one except Morty could have committed himself to such an expensive residence so soon after putting half a million dollars down on a second cotton mill, but Morty, as usual, had done the right thing.

Usual, but not always. She smiled as she approached Park. The war with Japan and Germany would do more than destroy the places they had both loved in Europe; it meant an end to silk. In a way, she was glad there was something to smile about. They had poked their way through the depression, trying to stay at least even, and now, at their moment of imminent triumph, as they began to anticipate huge profits, it was all down the drain in embargo and war.

It was a quarter to three on Monday, the ninth of February. She got off a large elevator designed more for carrying racks of garments than individual people, and walked out into the street, her portfolio under her arm. She wasn't far from Macy's and she had promised a buyer there to drop in one day this week, and perhaps this would be the day to do it. A few minutes earlier, as she had left the third-floor office, she had heard sirens. Now she turned left toward Eighth Avenue and saw smoke rising over the buildings of the West Side and moving east.

"What's happening?" she asked a man passing in the street.

"Must be a fire somewhere," he said, scarcely slowing. "Ask that guy up near the corner. He's got one of them portables."

The man with the portable stood beside a newsstand, talking to a small group.

"It's the *Normandie,*" a member of the group said excitedly as she approached. "Going up in smoke."

"No."

She edged her way past them and crossed Eighth, forgetting Macy's, then zigzagged west and north toward the Hudson, crossing Forty-second Street finally, her fingers freezing in the bitter cold, watching black smoke darken the western sky. She walked until the throngs of onlookers held her back, but she could see the river covered with chunks of white ice, Pier 88, and the smokestacks of the great ship, listing slightly. There were people everywhere, noise and sirens, ambulances and fire engines, policemen pushing the crowd back. A black car stopped up ahead and the familiar chubby figure of Mayor La Guardia got out to view the awful scene, the end of a great ship.

"You okay, lady?"

She nodded, realizing that tears were streaming down her face. She moved so that the man would not see her.

"Saw my brother off on it in thirty-seven," a man in elegant clothes said nearby.

"I sailed her," a woman's voice wailed. "It was like four days in heaven."

Regina moved away from them, warmed by the proximity of the crowd. It was her ship on fire there in the harbor, her promise, her Paris, her France, the twenties of the century and the twenties of her youth, and watching, she knew that Europe itself was going up in flames, that, win or lose, this was the end.

Twelve hours later, while she slept, the great ship, burdened with tons of water, keeled over, never to sail again. It was the death of the *Normandie*.

Ten days later she missed her period.

She assumed it was late, pushed off course by the start of the war, the burning of the *Normandie*. But when she sat and thought about it, when a week had passed, she knew it was none of those things. In her whole life she had tried to prevent a pregnancy only during 1929. Her reproductive system was fickle and unpredictable, and suddenly, unexplainably, it had reawakened.

She stepped out of the shower and dried herself, patted bath powder on her skin from the large puff in the round crystal box from their last trip to France, and opened the door. Across the bedroom, the door to Morty's bathroom was still closed, although there was no sound of running water. She had laughed the day he had taken her through the apartment when she had seen the separate bathrooms on either side of the master bedroom. Now that she was used to them, she enjoyed having them. After showering, she and Morty talked across the bedroom.

She brushed her hair and heard his door open.

"I'm getting gray," he said.

"No you're not." She switched the light off and stepped into the bedroom.

"Well, distinguished, then."

"You've always been distinguished." She walked to the open door to his bathroom. "I have something to tell you that'll make you feel young."

He folded a hand towel, hung it on a rack, and stepped into the bedroom. "Talk."

"I think I'm pregnant."

He touched her shoulder, looking more surprised, more apprehensive, than she had expected. "When?" he asked.

"End of October probably."

"I'll be fifty."

"Yes." She smiled. "I wouldn't be able to make you a party."

"I wouldn't need one." He looked uncertain, as if an important business transaction had suddenly slipped away from him. "You're sure you can go through with it?"

"Of course I'm sure."

"That's very nice." His face relaxed. He moved his hand across her back. "It's better than nice. It's really terrific."

A week later she came home to find him sitting in the living room with the paper.

"You're early," she said, unbuttoning her coat.

"I've got something for you." He took her coat and kissed her.

"Oh, Morty. It's wartime. What could you have found?"

"You know I'm a sucker for a pregnant woman. Especially you. It's in your study."

It was large and rectangular and it leaned against her antique desk, covered in brown paper. She knew it was a painting by the feel of the frame, and she pulled the paper away with nervous excitement, catching her breath as she saw the colors, knowing what it was before the paper was half gone.

"You said once—"

"I know what I said." Her voice hoarse. She stepped back and reached out a hand, touching the front of his jacket. She swallowed and shook her head. It was a Monet, autumn. She could see herself, twenty years old in the little apartment with the view of the Sacré Coeur. And when I get rich, I'm going to buy myself a Monet and just sit and look at it all day.

"Will you?" he said. "Will you give some of it up and come home in the afternoon and look at your Monet and rest?"

"Well"—she had very little voice left—"maybe for a while in the afternoons."

They could not decide on a name. Morty didn't want to use Pop's name, and when Regina suggested Albert or some female equivalent for Poppa, he said no, he didn't care for those either. Finally, in the middle of October, when she was over every hurdle she could think of, he said, "Dammit, let's make it Adam or Eve and be done with it," and that settled the question.

Adam Rush was born the day before Morty's fiftieth birthday, a full-term seven-pound-two-ounce noisy infant and, awake for the first time, she heard the cry, "It's a boy!"

So many flowers arrived they had to be sent home after the first day. It was a sign of how far they had come since Margot's birth. People she had never heard of sent congratulations from southern addresses. Even Walter Weinberg sent a bouquet from Boston. But it was Morty's giant mums, the yellow roses from Edith and Jerold, and the colorful spray from Mother and Poppi that she kept on a table near her bed.

Morty had more than mums for her. "I didn't want to wait till you came home," he said, entering the room with something large and unwieldy. He removed the paper covering. "It's from the *Normandie*."

"How did you get it?" She sat to see it better. It was a lamp and it would light her study.

"Bought it at auction and hid it in my office."

"Poor ship."

He plugged the lamp in and turned it on. "Margot wants you home."

"And Ernie?"

"He does too, but he won't say it."

"It's beautiful, Morty."

"Look great in your study."

"Yes." She held his hand and looked at the lamp. "Yes, it will. I can't wait to get home."

"Where's Alice?"

"She's gone shopping for a spring coat, Poppi." It was the second time he had asked and the second time she had told him.

"She's not here?"

"No, dear, she's not here."

"Where's that baby?"

"Just over there on the floor." She pointed. "See?"

"Oh, there. What's his name, that baby?"

"Adam."

"Adam, yeah. Alice told me. Listen, I got something for you. Help me get up." He stood and took his walking stick.

"Where are we going?"

"In my room."

"Don't step on my baby."

"Nah, I don't step on babies."

The walk to the bedroom tired him and he sat on the edge of the bed, breathing hard. "In the drawer," he said, pointing his stick at the night table.

Regina pulled the drawer open.

"The key," her grandfather said. "You see that key?"

"Yes." She took it out, a very ordinary-looking old key with a white paper tag on it with "Regina" written in his obvious hand.

"It's for you, that key."

"What's it for, Poppi?"

"For you when I'm gone."

"Poppi . . ."

"You ask Momma. She knows. She knows everything."

She put the key away wondering whom he meant, her mother or Grandmama. Sometimes the past visited him and he was not always aware that it was merely a visit.

Adam had a first birthday and took his first hesitant step a few days later. He looked like Morty, but there was something else in his face, a touch of Regina, an echo of Grandmama. He was the joy that let his parents forget the war for a little while each day. He drooled on the fine Persian carpet and Morty said so what, he's just a baby. He cried in the middle of the night and Morty got up before Regina heard the cry, as years ago he had heard Ernie and gone to him. Sometimes Morty took the little boy into the kitchen and had a midnight snack and conversation with him while Regina tried to reason that he was encouraging bad habits that would be difficult to reform. "Hell," Morty said, "no one talks to me in the middle of the night anymore except this little guy. I think that's worth encouraging." So she let it pass, wondering at his energy.

It was Jeanne-Marie who telephoned on the morning of June 6. Up early as usual, she had turned her radio on and heard the news.

"I am going to church to pray," she said lightly. "I wanted to tell you in case you hear of a building collapse. I haven't been to church since I was twelve." She spoke with an irony that seemed to diminish the seriousness of the message, but Regina heard the words and felt her cousin's anguish.

"Have you heard from Richard lately?"

"Saturday, but it was written days before that. I suppose today will be his big story."

"Come and have dinner with us tonight, Jeanne-Marie. Bring George. We'll eat early and get you home before it gets very dark."

There was a brief silence. Then Jeanne-Marie said, "Yes, thank you. We will come. You can show me all the designs for fall and we won't talk for one minute about my husband who is crazy."

"I promise. Not for one minute."

In the fall Richard returned for a brief rest and he and Regina sat and talked quietly about Paris.

"They hadn't been there for some time," he said. "I could tell from the condition of the house."

"You're keeping something from me. I've never seen you so evasive."

"It was just depressing. With all the shouting and the parade and Charley himself walking down the Champs Elysées, seeing Paris was a blow."

"What did the house look like, Richard?"

He looked pained and avoided her eyes. "The damned krauts had been living there. It looked as though they'd gone through the place with a bull-dozer. Nothing's left, nothing of value."

"I see."

"I wish I hadn't. Look, maybe they were able to stash their things away somewhere before the Germans came."

"Yes, maybe they did. I wonder where they went."

"They'll turn up."

"Yes. Richard, is it all true, what we've been hearing? About the Jews?"

"It's true."

"People can't have done what we heard about."

"People did."

She stood and walked to the window, seeing Paris twenty years before through the glass.

"Thanks for looking after the family," Richard said.

"Go home, Richard. I can't talk anymore."

The letter came finally, Suzanne's handwriting on tissue-thin paper. It lay on the letter tray on the small table in the foyer and she found it as she came home from the studio in the afternoon, Adam smiling at her from the door-way to the living room. She took the letter, picked him up, and went into her study, where everything was French and warm and inviting.

"Sit with me, Adam. I have to read my letter," she said, sitting on the little

291

sofa beside the window and pulling him up beside her, feeling his warmth against her skin as a chill settled inside her.

"Ma chère Régine."

Such a long time. The language no longer sliding quite so fluently.

"I am alive, and the children, mine and my brother's, are all well. There is no other good news except that the fighting has ended."

She read, sinking, about how Papá had had a heart attack in the first days after the Boches had swarmed like rats over the country, how Étienne had been unable to get him into a hospital, how he had died at home a few days later, how she saw now that Papá had been the lucky one in the family; he had not lived to see what would happen to the rest of them. The children, all of them, had been saved, thank God, by an organization that had placed them with Catholic families who did not know they were Jewish, and they had suffered only as much as the Christian French had, which was enough for anyone to suffer.

It had not been enough for the Jews.

They had taken Étienne away while he was at his office seeing patients. She had never seen him again but he had warned her; he had made arrangements with a Christian doctor who was a friend and she had gone to them and they had hidden her, sharing precious food, listening to forbidden news on a radio they powered with their own secret generator. Then, in the last days before the liberation, the Germans had taken the doctor away, along with other Parisian doctors, and shot him. Just like that, Suzanne wrote. Just to clean up Paris before they ran.

There was a knock at the door and Regina looked up. Françoise would open the door, come in, and turn down her bed. She waited, the letter wavering in her hand, blown by the breaths she exhaled too fast and with too much force. The door opened and a black woman stood there.

"Mrs. Rush? I didn't hear you come in. You want your coffee now?"

"Coffee?" She cleared her throat. "No. No, thank you." She could not remember the black woman's name and her mind was struggling to produce the right language. "Adam . . ." She kissed his cheek. "Go and get your cookies."

He jumped down and bounded away on legs still chubby with baby fat. He would grow tall and lean one day like his father, but for now he was still comfortably soft and smooth. The door closed and she bent over the letter.

Suzanne had been too late to save Mamá. Mamá had believed that an old woman would be safe, but the Germans wanted the house. Mamá had not been old, Suzanne wrote, only sixty-four when they had taken her away, and no one had been safe. Maurice and his wife would never come back. Marc would have been thirty-five this year.

She sat with the letter beside her where Adam had been sitting. Once on a New Year's morning a young and beautiful and happy Suzanne had slipped into her bed to tell her she had fallen in love. Once on the Left Bank Regina had sat with the young, beautiful students who had known that the last war was over, that the worst of life was behind then. Once Paris had been a place to grow and think and love. Now it was a place to light candles.

She went to the phone on her desk and called the garage. "This is Mrs. Rush," she said hoarsely. "I want my car. Now, please."

She hung up and folded the letter into the envelope, got her bag, and went downstairs. The car was just pulling to the curb and the doorman opened the door for her.

"I want to go to Queens," she said to the driver. She pulled an address book out of her bag and found the page. "Here's the address." She leaned over and showed him the entry.

"Yes, ma'am," he said, putting the car in gear.

She took the letter out again and read it as they drove, glancing out the window from time to time. She had scarcely ever been to Queens in her entire life, except for a trip now and then to the airport and once when Rosalie Schindler had married. The driver stopped once to ask directions, and then they were there, a pretty stone house in a quiet, charming community of well-cared-for homes with old trees and trimmed shrubs. The car stopped and she looked at the house, feeling a return of the old anger, the blending and churning of the old with the new.

"Drive a few houses down and park," she said.

"Yes, ma'am." He drove to the corner, stopped the car, and opened his door.

"Take the key, Tony. I'd like you to come with me, please."

They walked back together and Regina pushed the button and heard the four-tone chime sound inside. The door opened and Hannah, her sister-in-law the sea witch, stood in the doorway.

"Regina!" Graying, her face shiny with cold cream, Hannah clutched her housedress.

"Give me the candlesticks."

"What?"

"Give me the candlesticks," Regina repeated. "You've had them nine years. Now it's our turn."

Hannah looked from Regina to Tony and back to Regina with frightened eyes. Her forehead wrinkled. "Just a moment," she said with a voice that shook slightly.

She hurried away on softly shuffling slippers, returning a few minutes later with the candlesticks pressed against her breast. One in each hand, she offered them to Tony. "I can explain why they're here," she said.

"Thank you, Hannah." Regina turned away, Tony following closely. They reached the car and she took the candlesticks from him and slid into the backseat. Turning once, she saw her sister-in-law standing in the doorway, watching.

Tony started the motor. "I think she thought I was a cop, Mrs. Rush."

"She's a woman with a bad conscience, Tony. I asked you to come with me because I didn't have the courage to do it alone. She ought to be grateful to me. Now she'll be able to sleep at night."

It was dinnertime when they reached home and the doorman told her they were looking for her. She had slipped out without leaving word, and the rush-hour traffic had detained them.

Morty walked into the foyer as she opened the door. "Where've you been?" he asked, looking concerned. Then he saw what she had in her hands and his face changed.

"These are yours," she said, handing them to him. "From now on this family will light candles." She pulled Suzanne's letter out of her bag and thrust it at him. Then she went into her study and closed the door.

There was still fighting in the Pacific, and none of the cousins had come home yet, but for her the war had ended.

PART VI
1947

It was the end of April when the call came, just after breakfast, the wavering voice of the woman who cared for Poppi.

"I'm afraid Mr. Wolfe is ill, Mrs. Rush." In the background Momma was crying hysterically. "I couldn't wake him. The doctor's on his way. I'm so sorry."

"Thank you. I'll be right there." She hung up and sat a moment to steady herself. "Please call the car for me, Lilly-May." She hurried up the stairs. "Get ready for school," she called, finishing her dressing rapidly, running back down the hall to the stairs. "Hurry up, Adam. Don't be late for school."

The car took her swiftly to the old building and she used the stairs instead of waiting for the elevator. The doctor had his stethoscope around his neck as he emerged from the master bedroom.

"I'm afraid he's gone," he said, and Mother wailed. "Are you a member of the family?" he asked Regina.

"I'm Mrs. Friedmann's daughter."

"Ah. Ninety-six, wasn't he?"

"Yes. He was born in eighteen-fifty."

"Nearly ninety-seven."

The doorbell rang and she said, "Excuse me," and opened the door. A man stood there as though he were expected. "Yes?"

"I'm the barber."

"The barber." She stared at him. "Oh, yes, of course. Come in." She had begun to feel slightly faint. "I'm afraid . . ." She knew suddenly she would not be able to say it. Ninety-six years old and never sick a day in his life. They should be having a celebration and she was about to break down. "I'm afraid my grandfather . . ." She turned away, leaned against the wall, and began to cry. Behind her the doctor explained quietly while she dried her eyes. The door closed and she returned to the circle. "I'm all right now," she said calmly. "If you'll just tell me what needs to be done." And moving deliberately, the way Grandmama would have, she took charge.

The *Times* printed an obituary, using a photograph from the late twenties, "Father of attorney William Wolfe, grandfather of the noted writer Richard Wolfe and his brother, attorney Jerold Wolfe; grandfather also of textile de-

297

signer Regina Rush and of Dr. Henry Wolfe." There was a short summary of Poppi's life, capturing the daring quality of his younger years, mentioning the house in New Jersey he had built by himself late in the last century. "Mr. Wolfe is survived by two sons and a daughter, eight grandchildren, thirteen great-grandchildren, and one great-great-grandchild. Funeral services will be private."

"Where did they get all that information from, Momma?" Regina asked after the funeral.

"Didn't I tell you? They sent someone out to talk to Poppa once a long time ago, maybe ten years. Poppa had such a good time that day. He talked and talked. He felt so important."

"He was, Momma."

"Yes. I don't know what I'll do without him."

"You've spent your whole life taking care of people, Momma. Maybe you'll just enjoy yourself now, take a trip, visit Europe."

"I couldn't do that. Taking care of people is the only thing I know how to do. I don't know what to do with myself now."

"We'll find something. Now, you just catch up on your rest." She reached in her bag and drew out the key with the tag. "Poppi gave this to me during the war. Do you know what it fits?"

Her mother looked at it and shook her head. "Nothing in our apartment, Regina. The only lock we have is on the front door. It must be at the farm. Ask Uncle Willy. He knows where everything is."

Poppi's will left the land to Uncle Nate and the things in the apartment to Mother. Mother had Aunt Eva come over and pick what she wanted from Grandmama's jewelry. Aunt Eva selected a piece for Edith and a piece for Jeanne-Marie. Then Mother set aside something for Millie and after that there was very little left. Aunt Martha called to find out what "the provisions" of Poppi's will had been, since no one seemed to have had the kindness to call and tell her. Mother said she didn't know and Martha had better call Willy, and that was the last Mother heard of Aunt Martha for a long time.

Regina asked Willy about the key.

"I expect my father had a drawer or a cabinet with some special things, Regina. Jerold is going out to the farm to look over the house on Monday. I'll ask him to pick you up and you can go out together."

It was not what she had expected and not what she wanted, but Monday morning at nine o'clock she went downstairs and found Jerold waiting. It was the first Monday in May and fine weather.

"I thought I'd take the bridge," Jerold said when they had started. They crossed Manhattan and drove north on the Henry Hudson. "My father says you have a mysterious key."

"It's too small for a door key." She held it in her palm.

"Nate'll probably know." He left the highway and took a series of turns onto the bridge. The Hudson was shining. "You must be married twenty years."

"Twenty-one next month."

He took a hand off the wheel and touched her hair. "You kept it short, didn't you?"

"It was right for me."

"We've been very lucky."

"I've never really told you—I should have—I think Edith is wonderful. She's so pretty and so warm. In another life I think I would have liked to be her friend. She's very right for you, Jody."

"Well, after you married the family legend, I had something of a challenge. We've been very happy."

"I know. I'm glad. I think the only time in my life I ever felt inadequate was when I met Edith. She was everything I had wanted to be and wasn't. All of a sudden I missed that degree I didn't have."

"You and I knew why you didn't have it."

"Even so."

"You left college because I couldn't . . . or wouldn't. I've never done anything as selfless for anyone."

"Yes you have. You did it for me." They had come to the end of the ugly section of the road and were now in the country. "Anyway, it's a long time ago. I just wish," she said very lightly, "that I could sit next to you and feel the way I feel when I sit next to Richard."

She watched his shoulders move. Without looking away from the road, he laid his hand on hers and as quickly took it away.

"That makes two of us," he said.

Uncle Nate said it looked like a padlock key and as far as he knew there was nothing in the big house padlocked. Regina went from room to room, but her uncle was right. Upstairs a linen cupboard was locked, but the key was in the lock. Jerold got a flashlight and they went down to the cellar together, but there was nothing locked down there either.

"Well, I don't know," Uncle Nate said. "Can't be in your old house, Regina. No one's been in there for years and the roof's caving in at one end. I wouldn't try going in. Your ma took most of her things out a long time ago."

"He was very lucid when he gave it to me," Regina said. "There must be something this key fits. What about all the outbuildings?"

"Well, there's the icehouse, the chicken coop, the shed where we kept the old wagon, the stable." He scratched his head and laughed suddenly. "Oh, hell, I know what your key's for. Come along, honey."

It was a frame structure adjoining the chicken coop, and for as long as Regina could remember, she had never been in it. She took Jerold's arm, feeling a twinge of anxiousness.

"The old junk house," Nate said as they reached it. "So that's what Poppa left you. The staple rusted off years ago. We found the lock on the ground one morning. Hinges are probably so full of rust they'll bust when we pull the door open. Wait here and I'll get Harold to help."

"I'll help, Nate," Jerold said quietly, unbuttoning his jacket.

"Spoil your clothes, Jerold."

But Jerold had taken off his jacket and handed it to Regina. At forty-five he was still a slim man, his face only lightly lined, enhancing its fine good looks. He unbuttoned his cuffs and turned them up rapidly. The two men took hold of the edge of the wooden door and pulled. There were creaks of old wood and the sound of metal rasping. Sweat appeared on Uncle Nate's neck and one of Jerold's hands smudged with blood, but the huge door moved outward. Standing back, Regina could not see into the dark interior. She stepped forward as the men relaxed.

"There it is," Nate said, walking inside and tapping something metallic with his finger. "Forgot it was here, this shed's been closed so damn long. You kids remember my sister Maude? What a beauty."

Regina followed him, with Jerold beside her. "Oh, no," she said as her eyes made sense of the dim light. Inside the shed was the Pierce-Arrow.

Nate wanted to talk to Jerold privately, so Regina walked by herself, off beyond the houses in the direction that should have taken her to the swimming hole. She missed it somehow and ended up in the woods where they used to walk at night nearly thirty years ago, when love was something they thought no one but them understood, when being together was the greatest pleasure and the biggest problem of their lives. She would have to sell the Pierce-Arrow or give it away. Poppi had meant well. He had saved the best for her.

"Regina!" His voice rang through the trees.

"Over here," she called back.

He had his jacket back on and his hands were clean, the triangle of exposed shirt still brightly white. He had not aged. He would never age. Today he could have been a college student newly home on vacation, not yet changed into the overalls he would need to start his summer work.

"He forgot who Morty was," she said. "He asked me a few years ago if I knew what had happened to the fellow Maude married."

He put his arm around her. "I can take care of the car if you like."

"We've never told the children. They don't even know Morty was married before."

"Maybe it's not their business, Regina. Maybe this is part of your life, yours and Morty's, and not part of theirs."

"It's just that I remember the secrets that were kept from us and how we found out about them and how I felt about the people who kept them from us. I promised myself I would be open and honest with my children."

"You're honest."

"Yes."

"It's easier to forgive them when you're past forty than when you're less than twenty." They started walking. "And come to think of it, what difference do you suppose it would have made if we'd known? Did we love each other because someone gave us permission? Did it happen because they told us not to? Wasn't it something else, something aside from that, beyond it?" He stopped to get his bearings. "Somewhere around here," he said, "there is a deposit of latex."

Her cheeks warmed and she said "Jody!" chidingly.

"You still blush."

"Only for you."

"I'm surprised there isn't a swamp where I buried those damn things. My God, we had energy."

"It was more than energy."

"Yes." They had reached the clearing around the pond. "If Frenchy ever did what I did, I'd kill him."

"No you wouldn't." She stroked the side of his face and back into his hair. His hair was still thick, without a streak of gray. "Send Frenchy to me. I'll protect him."

"Nate wants to sell a piece of the land," Jerold said.

"Sell this land?"

"It's his now, and things have dropped off since the end of the war. Nate's seventy, you know. Arthur's in trouble down in Florida, gambling trouble. Nate wants to bail him out."

"Will anyone buy?" she asked.

"There's a lot of developing going on. This is pretty far from the city, but he might get a bite from a speculator."

"Find out what he wants and let me know. I'll send you a check."

He turned so that he faced her, resting his wrists lightly on her shoulders. "You're the one person who's never disappointed me," he said.

She felt her eyes fill. They were only a few feet from the swimming hole. She had torn her clothes off that day, gone nude into the cold water as the storm approached. It had been her cousin who had come after her, who had saved her, this man who stood inches from her now. Her leaving college had been a small thing, really, when you came to think about it. "I can't bear to think of this land being broken up," she said, her voice wavering. "They'd take away the woods and the swimming hole ... I'm not ready for that, Jody. I'd like them to be able to retire on this land, if that's what they want."

He kissed her and she accepted the kiss as though they were lovers, as though none of it had ever happened, the twenty years, the marriages, the children, the careers. They had been so careful for so long, a single brief meeting in the thirties when Morty needed the money, and otherwise only the weddings, the table that they shared when the cousins married. They lived only two blocks apart, Jerold in a fine town house just east of Park, but neither had ever visited the other's home. Today was Uncle Willy's fault, a well-meaning family error because the family did not know, because they had kept their secret as the Wolfe family had taught them to keep secrets. She rested against him, her head just on his shoulder, wilted, weakened by the kiss, by echoes of being young mixed with the finely developed sensitivities of mature experience.

"I'll take care of it this week." He cleared his throat. "The sale of the land."

"Yes."

They started walking back toward the fields. Early-spring vegetables were already thriving in even rows.

Aunt Bertha wanted them to stay for lunch, but Jerold said he had an afternoon appointment and she let them go. Nate walked them to the car.

"Good to see you two," he said, rubbing his hands on his overalls so that he could shake hands. "You were always a little sweet on Regina, weren't you, Jerold? Or was that Richard?"

"Both of us. We fought tooth and nail for her, and look what happened."

Nate shook hands with both of them. "Good to see you," he said. "Don't be strangers."

They drove back to the city in almost silence. Turning the corner, Jerold drove slightly past her building and stopped the car.

"You know I want to see you again," he said, looking at the steering wheel.

"I know." She opened the door, got out, and closed it again before the doorman had time to realize that Mrs. Rush had come home.

301

2

"I have a check for the Pierce-Arrow."

"Oh, yes. I'd forgotten." It was September and Ernie had left for college for the first time, leaving the apartment—and Regina—that much emptier.

"We got a good price for it. When they cleaned it up, it was in fine condition."

"Thank you. I'll use it for . . . I'll buy Morty something special." Speaking awkwardly. They had not spoken since that day in May.

"We could have lunch," Jerold said. "I could give you the check over lunch."

Regina looked around the small, cluttered office of Regina Rush Designs. Through the door with the frosted window came the sound of laughter, two of her young designers enjoying a joke. "Jody, dear . . ." The laughter stopped and it was suddenly too quiet. "Is everything all right, Jody?"

"Everything's fine. Walter sends regards. He was down here with his wife for a few days."

"Yes. Well . . ."

"I'll put the check in the mail."

"That would be better, wouldn't it? If you're sure everything's all right?"

"You'll have it tomorrow, dear."

Poppi and his key; Uncle Willy and his awfully good intentions.

She turned south on Lexington, walking carefully over accumulated ice. A bad winter early, and now it was February and Adam was sick. She had telephoned the pharmacy that she would pick the medicine up herself before leaving for work. When he felt less feverish, she would go downtown for half a day and come home with little presents to keep him busy.

"Regina."

She turned. "Jody. Hello." She smiled with genuine pleasure. "How good to see you." She glimpsed him sometimes on Lexington Avenue heading for the subway. Once in a while they even rode partway downtown on the same train, but usually in different cars.

"Going to the train?"

"Not yet. I have to pick up a prescription for Adam. He had a bad night."

"Judy just got over it, but I told Edith to keep her home another day. No use going out in this cold. Come, I'll walk you down." Judy was his only daughter, Uncle Willy's only granddaughter, as pretty as Edith and as special as only one little girl in a family could be.

They walked toward the drugstore.

"How's Morty?"

"Dogging it this week. He flew down to North Carolina on Monday. This is the winter I discovered the truth about why he buys mills in the South instead of New England."

Jerold laughed and took her arm. He opened the door to the pharmacy and they went in. It was small and deliciously overheated.

"Mrs. Rush," she said at the counter while Jerold looked at something down the aisle. She took the small package without paying. Momma thought it was terrible to charge everything, but Morty liked to see monthly bills.

"Does he travel much?" Jerold asked as they stepped out into the cold air.

"Too much. He's developing that big tract we bought down there. Eventually we'll close everything we have in Paterson and move all those operations south. It'll take years, of course. Sometimes I'm not sure where he lives anymore."

"I think you've had a long winter. When the weather moderates, you'll feel a difference."

They had reached the last corner. "How's your winter, dear?"

"Also in need of moderation." He kissed her lips lightly.

"Give my best to the family," she said, turning toward Park.

When she thought about it afterward, she realized it had been late for him to be going to the subway. Usually she saw him only when she left early, and this morning she had not been early. She wondered if he had been waiting to see her.

In sixteen years, which, Morty pointed out early in 1949, meant over eight hundred checks, Lillian had never acknowledged her cousin's munificence. The checks were sent, cashed promptly, and returned by the bank. They were never discussed or even mentioned by either donor or recipient. But for many years, usually on a Sunday evening, Lillian conducted a one-woman round robin, calling her aunts in New York, a cousin or two, and always Regina, as though the family gossip were a kind of payment for the continuing subsidy.

It was the evening of March 20 and Morty was upstairs packing for a morning flight to North Carolina, where the Rush empire was slowly taking shape. From there he would visit mills they owned in nearby states. Regina sat in her study, the *Normandie* lamp alight on the built-in cabinet behind her desk, when the phone rang. She looked up from the letter she was writing to Richard in Rome and answered.

"You sound half-asleep, Regina," the voice chided.

"Lillian, yes, I suppose I am. How are you this evening?"

"*Well.*" There was no doubt from the emphasis that this was to be an excitingly newsy call. "I don't suppose you've heard."

303

Regina glanced regretfully at the half-finished letter on her desk. "No, I don't suppose I have. How's the little grandson?"

"Cute as a button. That's not the news, Regina." She sounded deeply mysterious. "The news is our cousin. The news is Jerold."

She felt a shock wave flow through her, shaking her shoulders. It was over a year since she had seen him that morning on Lexington Avenue, that day she had felt something had been left unsaid. None of Momma's news, none of Richard's letters, had given any indication of something amiss. "What's happened?" she asked abruptly in a low voice.

"Edith's left him." A note of triumph.

"What?" She could not have heard correctly.

"Picked up the children and left him. They're camping out temporarily in an apartment on Park Avenue, friends of theirs who are away. People like that always do find a nice place to stay when they need it, don't they? They never quite know what it's like for the rest of us. With the money her mother left her, she could probably afford to buy the whole building."

"Why would Edith leave him?" Regina asked in a monotone.

"For the same reason any of us would leave our husbands. The longer I live, the more I see my mother has always been right about the Wolfe family. I don't think they've produced a decent man in generations, although you probably don't agree about Richard, you were always so fond of him."

"Lillian."

"He had an *affair,* Regina. Some little tramp he picked up down at the courthouse, I suppose. They're all looking for rich lawyers, and some men don't have the sense—"

"That's not possible," Regina said, interrupting.

"Not *possible.*" Lillian laughed. "Let me tell you, Regina dear, our precious cousin makes my father seem almost like an honorable man. He got her pregnant, if you don't mind."

Her left hand moved convulsively and the pen with which she had been writing the letter flew off the desk. She said, "No," softly, willing it not to be so, willing it not to have happened, not to him, please not to him.

"Well, you can imagine how Edith felt. She's certainly a woman who deserves better than that." It was the first positive thing Lillian had ever said about Edith. "Are you still there?" she asked after a pause.

"Yes, I'm still here."

"Well, you can imagine there's more."

"No." She was almost weeping. "I can't imagine. I can't imagine anything beyond what you've already told me, and I don't believe half of what you've said."

"The tramp gave birth."

She wanted to put the phone down and cry, call Morty and ask him to deal with this crazy woman on the phone who was her cousin. Instead she said, her voice barely more than a whisper, "He let her have the child?"

"You can't really stop them, can you? I suppose if they're out to ruin you, they'll ruin you. Of course, this little girl had a surprise coming. You remember the family secrets?"

"What secrets?" What was this woman talking about? Uncle Jack? Arthur?

304

"That child Grandmama had that she tried to keep hidden from my mother?"

"No." For a moment she thought she would be sick.

"Jerold fathered a monster, Regina."

"No. *No.*"

"For heaven's sake, don't scream. It's been in the family now for generations. Men who can't control themselves deserve—"

"Lillian, *please.*"

"In a way, though, I suppose he's lucky. Giving birth to one of those, she's not likely to make a fuss. Publicly, I mean. One doesn't advertise that sort of thing. Not that one lets on about any child born out of—"

"Listen to me, Lillian," Regina said, gathering herself together for one last effort before collapse, "you keep quiet about this."

"*Regina!*" her cousin said with theatrical surprise.

"You talk to no one, Lillian. Do you understand me? Stay off the telephone."

"For heaven's sake." Lillian sounded offended. "Am I one to blab about family secrets?"

"Not a word, Lillian. Ever. For the rest of your life." She hung up. For as long as I write you checks.

"You're kidding."

She shook her head. She had cried after she hung up, and now she sat on the bed next to his open suitcase. She had not yet told him everything.

"I misjudged him."

"Misjudged him?"

"Jerold. I thought he was . . . I always thought they made a very nice couple."

"They do make a very nice couple."

"Jerold Wolfe," Morty said with quiet amazement. "God damn."

"There's more, Morty. There's something else. There was a child. It was . . ." She could not say it. "It was like Grandmama's." She wiped her eyes.

He said something very softly that she was glad she could not hear.

"It means Margot and Adam . . ." She looked up at him. "It's with us forever now, isn't it?"

"We've survived."

"Maybe we were lucky."

"Regina, pack a suitcase and come south with me tomorrow. I'll phone for a ticket. We'll talk about it away from here."

She shook her head.

"You thought it was buried, didn't you?"

She nodded.

"Don't stay in New York and brood."

She stood and went to the door. "I just want to think. Don't wait up for me."

She sat in her study half the night, looking at the telephone. In some way she had failed him, as the family genealogy had failed them all. They had molded their lives around their genes and now she saw that there was no escaping the destiny of heredity.

305

She could call now and he would answer, but what would she say? Didn't you know I was there if you needed me? But that sounded accusing, and she had no accusation. Would it be enough to say: I love you? Or too much? . . .

At two in the morning Morty woke her where she had fallen asleep at the desk. She went upstairs with him and went to bed, but it was the worst night of her life.

He let her sleep when he left to catch his plane, and she didn't wake until Adam and Margot were getting ready for school. When they had left, she went down to the design studio and spent the rest of the morning and early afternoon sitting at her desk, looking at the telephone. Finally, at three, she went home.

It was four when she picked up the phone in her study and called the number of Jerold's law firm.

"Oh, Mrs. Rush," the secretary said conversationally. "How nice to talk to you. Mr. Wolfe left some time ago. He had a headache, poor thing. Shall I have him call you tomorrow?"

"No. Thank you, it's nothing important."

She hung up and waited as if each step required new thought, another decision. She opened her handbag and looked inside, checking its contents: wallet, keys, handkerchief, lipstick, comb. She clicked it shut and carried it with her to the kitchen.

"Don't wait dinner for me," she said, and a voice answered, "Yes, Mrs. Rush."

She took a lightweight coat from the closet—it was the first day of spring—and buttoned it while she waited in the private foyer outside the apartment door for the elevator. In the street she turned south on Park Avenue and walked, almost aimlessly, for two blocks. Then she took a left and watched the numbers until she came to the one that was written in her address book. It had not been a decision, really. Like so many other things in her life, it had just happened. But she knew as she pressed the bell that nothing in her life would ever be the same again.

The door opened and they looked at each other with the wordless recognition of battle companions. She did not know what to say.

"I should think I'd be the last person in the world you'd want to see right now," her cousin said finally. He was tieless and in his shirtsleeves, the cuffs rolled twice. He looked haggard.

"I think you're the *only* person I want to see."

He regarded her a moment, then held the door open for her. Entering, she felt welcome. It was a house that could be no one's but his, the calm of the Orient. It was a place she could be happy in.

He closed the door and began to roll his sleeves down, as though her arrival had reinstated the missing sense of formality. "What did Cousin Lillian tell you?"

"That you"—she hesitated—"that you had an affair."

"It was nothing as refined as an affair."

She began to open her coat, the buttons one by one, large and round and prominent, ordered specially for her by someone in the industry.

"It was a few encounters that were not quite brief enough and not worthy of being repeated. It was childish stupidity."

"We're all childish sometimes," she said softly.

He watched her for a moment before he spoke, as though taking a measurement. "From a distance," he said in a low voice, "she looked a little like you."

She smiled and flushed and felt relieved. He took the coat and folded it carefully over a chair instead of hanging it, and she was struck by the silence and emptiness of the house, the time it had taken him to answer the door, the fact that he had answered it.

"Where are your people?" she asked.

"Gone with Edith. It's a big apartment, empty till May. She needs them more than I. Why did you come, Regina?"

"I wanted to make sure you would survive."

The answer seemed to startle him. "I'll survive," he said. "I have survived." It was an assurance. She was free to go now. "It's the family . . ."

"The family," she said coolly, "will gather itself together and behave as a family should."

"You know about the child."

"Lillian doesn't spare details."

"Well"—he took a breath—"since you seem determined to stay, we may as well be comfortable."

They walked upstairs to the living room, which was in the back of the house overlooking the carefully tended garden around the stone patio, a piece of bronze statuary partly visible through one window. His hand touched a shoulder blade as he guided her, and feeling the touch, she became tremblingly aware that she had come for more than an assurance of his survival. She had come for her own.

She sat on a small sofa covered in a light-colored fabric sprayed with rosebuds. It was a pleasant room, a combination of both their efforts. It was a room where one could always believe it was spring.

"It died," he said. "Friday." He had taken the chair at right angles to the sofa, sharing the end of the coffee table. "Edith doesn't know it yet. She left on Thursday."

She felt a thrill of excitement and relief. Lillian had been right. The girl would fade from his life. The episode would close for him, although it had just opened for the family.

"I wish you hadn't told Edith anything," she said.

"I didn't."

"Then how . . . ?"

"It came in a letter, just the way it does in bad stories. She wanted to marry me, and when I refused to consider it, she decided to take more drastic measures."

"What a hateful thing to do."

"You sound too angry at the wrong person."

"Not angry enough and not the wrong person. I'm sorry about Edith."

"I think she could have taken either of the things that happened, but both of them, coming so close . . . She couldn't understand why I hadn't told her before we married. I found myself unable to explain. I don't often see myself inarticulate, but I was then. I couldn't talk about it without talking about you, and I couldn't do that. Part of the truth was that I never really believed it."

"I know."

"You did."

"Yes. Something my mother said once. The baby I lost. All those things together." She turned to look at him. "Where is the girl now?"

"In a shelter out of state. I sent her there when she said she wanted to have it. I know an abortion would have made things easier for me, but I couldn't insist. It's not just that they're dangerous and illegal, but I don't really approve of them. It's part of what I used to consider my code of ethics."

"You're too hard on yourself, Jody. We shouldn't have gone to the farm that time. I should have known when I saw you that day last year . . . I did know. I should have said something. If I'd taken the time to—"

"Regina." Jerold sat forward in his chair. "What I have done is my responsibility, and that's the end of it." He sat back. "Where's Morty?"

"South." It had become an almost painful monosyllable.

"It bothers you. I suppose that's better than if it didn't."

She glanced at her watch. "Can I put something together for dinner?"

He went to the fireplace and stood facing the objects on the mantle, carvings of pale pink stone. "There's a steak in the refrigerator," he said finally, not looking at her. "It's more than big enough for two. I was going to make it last for two days."

She stood and smiled at him. "It sounds promising."

"I'll go upstairs and change."

"You don't need to."

"I think I'd like to."

The kitchen was downstairs, with a small breakfast room beside it. Setting the table with Edith's lovely china, she could not imagine Edith leaving this house. She could not imagine her leaving Jerold. As hateful as the girl was who had given birth to Jerold's child, it was easier to understand her actions than Edith's.

She called home and giggled with Adam, listened to Margot's breathless description of a new boy in her class, left a message in case Morty called, and went back to preparing dinner. Jerold came down freshly shaved and dressed. His belt was closed one notch tighter than the marked hole. He had lost weight and his family had left him. She was the only one who understood. That was what each of them was to the other, the one who understood.

They ate and, relaxing, talked about everything else, about the design studio, about the class he taught each fall at Columbia, about the law firm. In ten years Frenchy would be ready to join, the first of the third generation. They had a strong partnership and they offered services that Uncle Willy had had to send clients to other lawyers for twenty-five years ago. His voice strengthened as he spoke, and she knew she had been right in coming. He was only wounded, not defeated. How could Edith have left him at the moment that he most needed someone?

It was a round table, but they sat beside one another, not opposite. When she poured coffee he unlocked a door and came back with a bottle of liqueur, remembering that she liked it, remembering because he had introduced it to her once, a quarter-century ago, in the south of France. It went down hot and sweet like those days on the Mediterranean, those last days before the end came.

308

He pulled his watch out of its little slit of a pocket and opened it. "Frenchy says I'm still living in the last century," he said, but he smiled with the look of an indulgent father.

"It's not one of the mortal sins."

"No." He pressed it shut and eased it back. "I know a little something about them, too."

"No more than most of us."

"Will you forgive me everything forever?"

"I hope so."

"It shows a rather uncharacteristic lack of discrimination."

"Does it? I thought it showed something else."

"I was trying not to see anything else."

"Were you?"

It was always so quiet in a house without servants, without family, only two people in a downstairs kitchen, the oven no longer creaking, the whirring of the refrigerator momentarily ceased, traffic sounds diminished to almost nothing. The darkness had come silently and the light overhead burned without a sound.

"Let me take you home, Regina."

She shook her head without looking at him, her heart suddenly racing.

"Say it," her cousin said. "Out loud. I want to hear you say it, Regina."

She looked at him. "No," hoarsely, for the silent scribe who sat invisibly in the empty chair beside her, taking his notes for the final accounting. "Don't take me home."

"Regina."

Their chairs sideways against the table since coffee, they faced each other. He leaned forward and she moved to meet him, reaching out her arms, which he grasped just above the wrist, their lips touching hesitantly, as though they might burn on contact. He brought her onto his lap, and held her, kissing her face and her neck as she drew her legs up beneath her, becoming a tight, compact ball in his arms, a soul waiting to be born.

"You should go home," he whispered, breathless, holding her so that the choice was no longer hers. "You shouldn't have come. You shouldn't have stayed." He kissed her lips, and it was the way it always was. "You knew how much I wanted you."

Once she had thought she knew what it was to want him.

He helped her to her feet and stood with a small space between them. "I can't do to you what I've done to Edith," he said.

"You did nothing to Edith. What you did, you did to yourself."

"If you stay now, you'll never go back."

"I haven't even asked myself if I want to."

He offered a hand and she took it and he led her up the stairs as once in the summer of another year he had led her up those other stairs to the room with the moonlight and shadows. Up flights of carpeted stairs, passing in a blur glass shelves built in the curve of the wall, filled with small precious objects waiting to be admired, but not now, not this night, not this trip up. And finally into a bedroom, where he put on one lamp and she saw that his face was flushed with the color of health, the color of happiness. Before she could begin to take her clothes off, he put his hands on her, touching her as though she were precious and valuable, as though he were a blind person renewing an old acquaintanceship. She undressed and he said, "I thought I would never see you again like this," and she lay on the bed and reached for him to shorten by a second or two the time until they touched. And afterward, when the great, aching love had been renewed, it was her cousin who cried.

She opened her eyes and looked around the room. Jerold sat on a love seat, a book open in his hands, a lamp shining a narrow light on the page. He was wearing a silk robe with a small print, the shawl collar of a solid dark color. The bed she lay on was a scaled-down version of her own, although the smaller dimensions did not affect her comfort. She and Jerold were so much more nearly the same size or at least within the same range. On the long dresser were pictures of the family: Frenchy like an eerily accurate incarnation of his father, Davey like a little devil, a mixture of his parents, Judith like her beautiful mother. She looked back at him and felt immensely happy.

Jerold turned a page and looked up, saw her awake, and smiled. He marked his place with a card and closed the book. "Seventeen pages and five minutes of very concentrated thought longer than I slept."

"Conclusions?"

"None. Are you still happy?"

"Yes." She shivered. "Oh, yes."

He took an expansive breath. "I feel renewed."

She pushed the pillow behind her and sat. "Do you think . . . ?" He was watching her, and it made her skin glow. "Tell me what you think."

"I want you to tell me how it would have been different—different for you—if we had married."

"Ah." She pulled his pillow over and made herself comfortable, leaning back, the cover just above her waist, leaving her breasts exposed. She took it out and dusted it off, a sacred relic, and told him about it, the other life, the image she had had of herself at sixteen, eighteen, twenty, when one formed images, the image she came back to from time to time, wondering, yearning, the image she had created when life lay blissfully and tantalizingly before her. She had never imagined herself in business. She had wanted to read and study and finish college; she wanted to see more theater, attend more concerts. There were always lectures she had to miss because there were deadlines, so many tickets given away over so many years. She had thought once she might write, just critical essays, she explained apologetically, and one day, if there was time, she would collect Richard's letters and publish them, letters from my cousin. You could see the germs of later ideas in many of them, sense feelings he restrained when he wrote for publication—France in the thirties, the war in Spain, the war in Europe. She sank back on the pillows, having strained forward with the excitement of telling him. She had never talked about the other life to anyone, not to Morty, not to Shayna. She felt slightly ashamed when she thought about it because she thought about it with such loving nostalgia, with such regret.

"It makes such a difference for a woman," Jerold said, "whom she marries."

"I'm not unhappy, Jody. It's just a different life."

"Whom she marries and whom she leaves," he said contemplatively.

"Edith hasn't left you, dear."

"No?" He looked at the pictures on the dresser.

"She's only gone away to think."

"Is that what you've done?"

"It's what I told them I've done."

"When do you expect Morty back?" he asked.

"End of the week. Friday. Saturday if he's kept over."

"Friday or Saturday. Does he go straight home when he lands?"

"Only if it's late in the day. If it's early, he goes to Worth Street."

He looked at the clock on the night table, sat on the edge of the bed, and kissed the skin exposed beneath her neck. "It's only nine-thirty," he said. "Why don't you call and tell them you won't be home, and then maybe we can talk. Maybe we can talk about the future."

The alarm rang at an early, reasonable hour and she awoke beside her cousin, full of the lushness of early love, spring in the temperate zone.

"Call me," he said when he left for work, because she could not answer his phone. "Edith's key is on the kitchen table."

She had left without a key.

"Don't cook anything, darling. I'll bring something home."

She went home and packed a suitcase and went back to Jerold's house. She walked through the rooms, thinking of it as a place to live. In his study she pulled law journals randomly from a shelf and found the articles he had published, the controversies he had taken part in, in careful, precise language. Across the room from his desk, where his eyes would fall when he looked up, hung the silk embroidery Morty had given him twenty years earlier, beautifully framed.

From time to time the phone rang, but she ignored it, feeling free to let it go unanswered, feeling the start of the other life where phones would ring less often and less persistently. She called him and they said nothing sensical to each other for five minutes and she hung up, sharing his feeling of renewal.

She would write for catalogs and go back to school. She would read. She would immerse herself in old pleasures. She had said to him last night, "I need to have Adam, Jody," and he had answered, "I know. I know what you need. I want you to have everything you need. We'll get you Adam."

The doorbell rang, startling her out of her reverie. It was two o'clock. The caller could hardly be Edith. She opened the door and said, "Richard!" and to her surprise, before he kissed her, before he even said hello, he said, "I thought you might be here."

"How?" she asked. They sat up in the living room with coffee. "How did you know I would be here?"

"I guessed." He looked at her with frank eyes. "One of those summers in the early twenties. One of those nice, warm summers." He lifted his cup with two hands, as though he were a truck driver at a roadhouse, and drank. "And then there was that awful business with Jerold and the hotel." He put the cup down and looked at her. "You didn't know I knew that either, did you?"

"No." Softly. "You keep a good secret, Richard."

"And now I want to know all the rest of it. My mother drags me back from Rome for a family crisis and then won't tell me what the hell is going on. My father's not speaking to anyone. My sister-in-law doesn't answer the phone. Tell me what it is, Regina. My brother doesn't go around knocking up women he isn't married to. And what else is there that Mother won't let on?"

"It's the thing that kept Jerold and me from marrying. Grandmama had two children that were badly retarded. One of them didn't live a year. The child that . . . that was born last week was like that one. It was just . . . it was hopeless. It died on Friday."

"Why the hell don't I know that?" Richard said with obvious anger.

"Because the family thought if they kept it a secret, it would go away."

"But you knew it wouldn't go away. Dammit, I have a family. I have a son who's going to grow up and . . . You could have told me. My brother could have told me."

"We couldn't talk about it, Richard."

He stood up. "I'm going downtown. I'll catch Jerold at the office."

She walked downstairs with him. "Come back and have dinner with us. Jerold's bringing something home."

"Regina . . ." He turned to face her while she found his coat. "You're not thinking of . . . you and Jerold aren't planning . . . ?"

"Just thinking," she said evenly.

"You're crazy, Cousin. Morty and Edith. You've got six children between you."

She took the coat off the hanger and folded it over her arm.

"You can't do it," he said.

"Richard . . ." She rubbed the coat idly. "Who was she? The beautiful girl in the midnight-blue Marmon?"

She watched his face change. "That's over twenty years," he said. "She was . . ." He had suddenly lost his composure. "I couldn't even tell you her name. It's too . . . too prominent. She was pregnant with my child that day."

"Oh, Richard." Sorry now that she had asked.

"We were on our way to ask for permission to marry. It was a fool's errand, of course. There wasn't a chance in hell they'd let their daughter marry a Jewish kid who would never amount to anything, even if he was Willy Wolfe's son. They put it in such a way that I knew I could never see her again." He was far away now. "We didn't even get a kiss good-bye. They sent her . . . I think she went to Switzerland to have her problem taken care of."

"I'm sorry."

He shook his head, returning from his reverie, and took the coat, putting it on and looking, suddenly, older than when he had arrived.

"Did you ever . . . did you ever run into her, Richard?"

"Twice," he said, as though he could recall the times exactly. "When I came back from Spain after McGuire died and then during the war. Parties, fund-raisings, things like that." He put his hands in his pockets and looked forlornly around. "Shit, Regina, how could you bring that up? How could you . . . ?" He looked at her, and something seemed to light in his eyes. He opened the door and left without another word.

312

They returned laughing and telling stories, carrying bags filled with containers of food that needed only to be heated. She had set the dining-room table for three, using the dining-room china and crystal. Jerold took Richard downstairs to select wines and they came up with several bottles, arguing playfully about how much they could consume. Richard had become very nostalgic since the afternoon, and while they ate he began to recount the adventures of his childhood, teachers he and Jerold recalled from their years at Stuyvesant, events that left the brothers laughing. She laughed with them, responding to the brotherly warmth, remembering how much she had wanted a brother or sister when she was young. This was how she had always imagined it would be, sitting around a table with food and wine and laughter.

"And the time we went to the speakeasy," Richard exploded. "My God, Regina, do you remember that?" He turned to his brother. "I couldn't've been more than sixteen or seventeen and Regina looked about twelve, her hair was still long then," without taking a breath. "I never told you that one, did I, Jerold?"

"No." Jerold looked so happy, so peacefully content. He reached out his hand under the corner of the table and she took it, accepting the promise of its gentle pressure. "Regina did," he said, draining his glass. "I was very angry." He didn't look angry or sound angry; he looked blissfully unconcerned. "I wanted the first of everything in Regina's life to be with me."

Richard lifted the bottle of wine—it was the second red of the evening—and reached across the table to fill Regina's glass. She saw Jerold shake his head almost imperceptibly, and Richard withdrew his arm and poured for his brother instead.

"I don't want Regina falling asleep," Jerold said, and she knew that he was waiting, as she was, for the moment they would go upstairs together, to the lusty quiet of the bedroom. "You were never in Paris at the same time, were you?" he asked.

"I went later," Richard said somberly. After the girl in the Marmon. After it was all over. They had gone for the same reason.

"Well, we were there together. The whole month of August 1925." Jerold laughed. "Regina wanted me to smuggle a copy of *Ulysses* into the States."

"Hell, Regina, I could have gotten you a copy. Anything you'd want. We had a little business going there for a while."

"It came to me another way," she said.

"It came to all of us," Jerold said. "Like so many things, we waited and it came to us."

Richard yawned. "My brother, the mouthpiece."

They laughed and Richard went on about Paris, all of them joining in, the early beautiful memories and the later ugly ones. A clock chimed ten and Richard pushed his chair away from the table. "Come on, Cousin," he said tipsily, "dinner's over. Let me take you home."

She started to say something, but Jerold answered first, very easily. "I'll take Regina home, Richard."

Richard stood now and looked from one to the other. "The two of you," he said, "you're a couple of dreamers."

"Come, Richard," Jerold said, putting an arm protectively around his brother, "let me see you to the door."

She cleared the dishes while they were gone, hearing the murmur of their voices, a final laugh, the close of the front door. Jerold came back and put his arms around her.

"Are we?" he asked.

"What?"

"A couple of dreamers."

"I hope so, Jody."

"So do I. So do I. You don't know how much I hope so."

After dinner Wednesday the doorbell rang. They exchanged a look and Regina said, "I'll go upstairs."

She was wearing a full skirt that the New Look had made popular and a long-sleeved white blouse with a high neck, her bare feet pushed into new sandals. They had made love before dinner and the meat in the oven had been deliciously overdone so that they had laughed and said it was easier to tear it apart than to cut it. In the effort to do one or the other, Jerold had splashed the shirt he was wearing casually open at the neck and he had agreed she had been right to insist that he not dress formally for dinner.

The visitor was Edith. Retreating to a place where she could not be seen, Regina listened to the painful conversation. Edith's voice was strained from the first syllable, and from time to time she wept.

"Look at you," she said, half-accusingly, half-sorrowfully as they ascended the stairs to the living room. "How you dress for dinner. Your clothes aren't even clean."

"Sit down, Edith, and we can talk. My clothes are just fine."

"And something's burned in the oven, hasn't it?"

"Nothing's burned. Everything's quite normal."

There was the sound of something being moved, the lady of the house pushing a small object back to its accustomed place. "The whole room is haphazard," Edith said sadly.

There was no response.

"I want to know . . ."—a pause—"what that woman is going to do with the child."

"The child is dead."

"Dead!"

"It died on Friday."

"You never told me."

"I haven't seen you since Thursday, dear."

"But . . ." Another silence. "The children miss you so much."

"It's lonely for me too."

"How could you not have told me, Jerold?" She had begun to cry. "We tried to be so honest with each other when we met. How could you keep such a thing from me?"

"It was a family story," he said calmly. "I never really believed it."

"But it's true now. Our children will have to know."

"Our children will live with it as I've lived with it."

There was an inaudible response, and Regina, sitting on the top step,

314

leaned against the wall for support, sharing the pain with the woman a floor below.

"I don't know if I can ever come back to you," Edith said, and Regina knew she was waiting to be asked. It was why she had come here tonight. It was her opening offer. There was no reply. "How could you throw away all those dreams, Jerold?" Edith said in a low voice. "There was so much in our future, and you could have had it all. How can you ever hope for a judgeship if this comes out?"

"I can be quite content without a judgeship."

"*You* can be content. *You.*"

"Let me get you something to drink."

There were tearful sounds, but no one moved. "I suppose," she said finally, "if the child is dead, the woman won't bother you anymore. Perhaps there's still a chance."

"Perhaps."

"Jerold . . ." Edith drew her breath in tearfully. "Jerold, was it my fault? Was it something I did? Was it something I failed in? I know I'm sometimes—"

"Edith," he said gently, "I told you last week. It had nothing to do with you. I'm sorry for it. I'm sorriest that the consequences spread so far and touched so many."

"How can I ever know," Edith asked pitifully, "that it won't happen again?"

"I know," her husband said.

"I wonder if that's enough." And then, in a lower voice, "I loved you so much, Jerold."

A moment later Edith appeared at the head of the stairs a flight below. Regina went into Jerold's study and looked out the window down to the street. The black limousine waited outside the house. As the couple emerged, the driver moved quickly to open the rear door. She could not see Edith's face. Her head was hatted and she was dressed as though to attend the theater, the seams of her stockings straight and dark beneath the fashionably long coat. Beside her, Jerold stood in the stained shirt that his wife abhorred and Regina loved. She had encircled him with her arms when he put it on, feeling the quick of his body close to her palms. Now she could feel his wife's pain.

The door closed and the car moved away. Jerold watched it only a second. Then he came inside and she heard the pad of his feet as he climbed the stairs to the living room. She waited in the study, not certain she was invited. Finally she went down the stairs, stopping when they were visible to each other. He sat in the chair he had taken on Monday afternoon when she herself had come uninvited. His eyes were closed or cast down; from where she stood she was not sure, and his body slouched. She waited, not speaking, and after a minute he looked up and saw her.

"Regina," he said, as though her presence were a surprise, as though he had forgotten everything but his wife's visit. "Regina," with pleasure now, all that pleasure. "Please stay with me," and she ran down the last few stairs to join him.

* * *

315

The alarm sounded and he reached out to silence it, turning back to her as she woke. Scarcely a minute later, the phone rang. She could hear Edith's voice, and then another, and she could tell from the way he spoke, it was Judy, his beautiful ten-year-old daughter. "I miss you too," he told her, and then he hung up, sighing.

"Jody . . ."

"Come with me."

She put a robe on and followed him down a flight of stairs to a group of glass shelves. He took an ivory carving from the lowest shelf, leaving behind a small clean circle in the light covering of dust, proof of the absence of the maid and the lady of the house, who would not have tolerated such a dissolution of order.

"I was going to give it to you on an important birthday, but they're all too far away and I want you to have it now. It's a happy Buddha. You rub his stomach and he brings you happiness."

He was fat and smiling, and looking at him, she smiled back. "Thank you." She rubbed the round ivory stomach.

"Now, go back to bed while I shave, and rub his stomach and stay happy. When I come home tonight, we'll talk about what to do when Morty gets back."

When he left, she went out to meet Adam on his way to school, but she must have been late or else they sent him off early, because he never came and she returned to the house deflated. She needed Adam. Adam, the Monet, and the *Normandie* lamp. But mostly, she needed Adam.

She sat at the glass door in the dining room, a book on her lap, looking out at the garden through the wrought iron that decorated and protected the glass. It was still too cool to open the door, but she thought how lovely it would be to move in and out, to sit in the hidden garden at sunset. Edith Wolfe was said to give beautiful parties in the spring. Surely she had the perfect setting.

She called Jerold and went back to her book, holding her smooth ivory gift in one hand, her promise of happiness. It was past eleven-thirty and she would have to think about lunch soon. Tomorrow it would all be out in the open and the thought of it took away her slight appetite. The phone rang, this time very persistently, but she did not answer it. She turned the Buddha over to inspect the carving and saw a small label marked with letters and numbers. A careful, well-organized man.

The doorbell rang, and she jumped, realizing how nervous she was, the accumulation of last night, this morning, and whatever tomorrow would bring. Holding the Buddha, she went to the door.

"Morty!" Like a ghost, like a stranger from a distant past. "How did you know?"

He came in and shut the door. He was wearing a raincoat which he had not bothered to button and he looked as though he had been up all night. "I called my lawyer to ask him how to report my wife missing and he gave me an address. It didn't click until I got here." He looked at her from his great height. "I've come to take you home."

"I know."

316

"It's why you went to Paris, isn't it?"

She nodded, holding the Buddha tightly in her left hand.

"I always thought it was Richard."

"It was never Richard." Her voice so low she could hardly hear it herself.

"I never quite realized it was this way."

"It was this way." She felt raw, open, peeled. There were no secrets anymore.

"I misjudged him," Morty said. "I've never misjudged anyone so badly." As though that were the crux of the problem, a man who knows men, failing when it mattered most.

"It wasn't your fault. You never knew him." Wondering where he was, how he could have sent Morty without being here himself. "I have to sit down."

He looked quickly at his watch and followed her into the dining room. She sat gratefully in a chair against the chair rail, but he stood and looked toward the garden, taking in the room and all its furnishings.

"This place gives me the creeps," he said.

"Don't, Morty."

He looked at her piercingly, as though, after all these years, he had just learned something about her feelings.

"We did the same thing, didn't we? Ran away to Paris."

She nodded.

"For the same reason. In the end it must have been harder on you than it was on me. I see that now. Living around the corner from him. Being pushed together by people who had no idea what a mess they were making. I was one of them."

She brushed tears away. She would not be able to handle it herself. She needed her advocate, and he was not here. "Nothing happened for twenty-three years. This was the first time."

"I know that. I know you very well, Regina. Better than anyone else. Better than Jerold does. That's part of it, isn't it?" His shoulders sagged suddenly. "I was up all night thinking about it, thinking about Maude, thinking about what you saved me from, a life of self-pity."

"You saved yourself."

"Well . . ." He pulled a chair away from the table, set it down opposite hers, and sat so that he faced her. They were close, their knees almost touching, and she did not want to be touched. "I want to tell you something." He looked older than she had ever seen him. He was fifty-six but his face had aged a decade since Sunday. "The baby that Maude gave birth to was a twisted mess."

Her eyes opened and she said, "Oh no," with the echoed pity of thirty years. "No one ever told me."

"No one ever knew, only the doctor and I."

"How could you—after all that—how could you marry into this family again?"

"How could I not?"

She closed her eyes and put her head in her hand. It was like labor, the struggle to give birth, the painful stages that succeeded one another in the effort.

317

"Regina . . ."

She opened her eyes.

"I understand what happened here, but that's over now. Everyone's going to get over this. I'm sure Jerold will. Edith'll change her mind in a few days. It'll be tough, but we'll all come through it. You're part of a family, Regina, not this one that you were born into, but ours, the one you made, the one we made together. That's the only one that has any meaning now."

She thought: Adam.

"Adam said he talked to you on the phone."

She nodded.

"All five of us, Regina. I've never known anyone in my life for whom family was more important than it is for you."

The family. She could hear them giggling in the night on the way to market, arguing and teasing at the weddings, the brothers laughing at the table over dinner in this room, Adam kissing her in the morning before he went to school. She stood up unsteadily and he rose at the same instant.

"I'll get my suitcase," she said weakly.

"Let me."

"No. Please don't go upstairs."

She climbed slowly, holding on to the banister. When she came to the shelf with the missing piece, she stopped and wiped the moisture from the sweating Buddha on her skirt, then replaced it on the clean circle. Edith would never know it had been moved.

In the bedroom she packed her things carelessly and smoothed the bed so that he would sleep comfortably. Tears dropped on the spread, and she hoped they would not stain. She could not wait to find out.

He took the suitcase from her halfway down the last flight and held her arm to steady her.

"I wasn't invited here," she said, stepping carefully. "I came on my own."

"It doesn't matter."

"It does to me. He had no part in it. He was just here when I rang the doorbell."

At the bottom of the stairs he put the suitcase down. "I want to give you something," he said. He reached inside his jacket—he had never taken off the raincoat—and drew out an old discolored envelope. "I got home late last night and I gave it a lot of thought, you and me, where we've come from and where we're going, this family of ours with its damned secrets. I need someone to take care of this for me, and I can't think of anyone besides you who could do it properly." He gave her the envelope. "Besides, I don't want you to find it in a drawer after you've buried me."

She opened it with parched fingers and pulled out a handful of photographs: Maude as a bride, Maude and Poppi sitting in the Pierce-Arrow, Maude and a friend in dresses almost down to their ankles, Maude pregnant, Maude and Mortimer on a beach. She looked up at him and she could see what it had cost him, see it in his eyes and the sallowness of his skin.

"I can't take them," she said.

"Yes. I think you can."

Holding the envelope, she went to the closet and got her coat. He helped her put it on and she stood before the front door, closing the large buttons as

318

slowly and deliberately as she had opened them on Monday afternoon.

"Just a moment," she said, and went to the kitchen to leave Edith's key in the same place she had found it. Had it all happened in two and a half days? Or was it their lifetime that had been enacted there in the beautiful house with the jade and ivory carvings, the bronze, the glass, the silk; love that spilled like red and white wine into crystal glasses and stained the cloth forever?

"I'm ready."

He opened the door and closed it firmly behind them, lifted the suitcase in his right hand and held her arm too tightly with his left, so tightly she could feel the hurt, the pulsing. The car was waiting down the block toward Park, and as they started toward it, a car careened down the street from Lexington and stopped with a jolt in front of them. It was a large yellow taxi, and as she turned to look, the back door opened and her cousin Jerold got out.

When he's early, he goes to Worth Street. . . .

She saw it for what it was, a miscalculation. He had thought when the call came that they were starting out from the same place. She could hear in an eerie echo the phone ringing and ringing just before Morty arrived. He had meant to tell her. When a careful man miscalculates . . .

They looked at each other across the squares of concrete that were the streets of New York, and she knew he would assess what had happened in a moment, Morty holding the suitcase, Morty holding her arm so hard it would be bruised in the morning.

Her cousin whom she loved.

And then, suddenly, Morty let go of her arm and moved a step away. The unexpected action made her arm nearly lift, and with it, the rest of her. She stood looking at Jerold, experiencing after forty-four years of life a moment of complete and undesired freedom. If I could only tell you, she thought.

The two of you, you're a couple of dreamers.

We *are* dreamers, Jody. It would have been such a good life. We could have done it, twenty-five years ago. Maybe that day on the Riviera when I turned twenty-one.

But we didn't.

She stood between them, two men she loved, had loved, would always love. Hatted and wearing a dark coat, her cousin took a step toward her and stopped, as though he had decided something, all the music of her youth in that man beside the taxi, the last chance for the other life.

We are not people who display our emotions on city streets.

The envelope with the pictures of Maude dampened in her hand where earlier the Buddha had promised happiness. Turning to her husband, she went home to her family.